It Doesn't Have To Be That Way

A Novel By
Mary Rowen

IT DOESN'T HAVE TO BE THAT WAY
Copyright © 2020 by Mary Rowen

All rights reserved. No part of this book may be used or reproduced in any manner whatsoever, without written permission, except in the case of brief quotations embedded in articles and reviews. For more information, please contact publisher at Publisher@EvolvedPub.com.

FIRST EDITION SOFTCOVER
ISBN: 1622535847
ISBN-13: 978-1-62253-584-2

Editor: Jessica West
Cover Artist: Kabir Shah
Interior Designer: Lane Diamond

EVOLVED PUBLISHING™

www.EvolvedPub.com
Evolved Publishing LLC
Butler, Wisconsin, USA

It Doesn't Have To Be That Way is a work of fiction. All names, characters, places, and incidents are the product of the author's imagination, or are used fictitiously. Any resemblance to actual events or persons, living or dead, is entirely coincidental.

Printed in Book Antiqua font.

BOOKS BY MARY ROWEN

1. *Leaving the Beach*
2. *Living by Ear*
3. *It Doesn't Have To Be That Way*

What Others Are Saying About "It Doesn't Have To Be That Way"

SHORTLISTED: 2017 Faulkner-Wisdom Competition

"This book is not to be missed. But before you start, it might be a good idea to put on your Jim Croce album—the chapter titles are his songs. This book is simply… well… fabulous!"
~ *Readers' Favorite Book Reviews, Jon Michael Miller*

"…Women's fiction at its best… highly recommended for readers who like their characters realistic, warm, and thoroughly engrossing."
~ *Midwest Book Review, D. Donovan, Senior Reviewer*

"The author's colorful characters, vivid imagery, and bonds formed feel reminiscent of a Cameron Crowe work or modern-day John Hughes saga, with the perfect dose of eccentricity, love, musicality, and humanity."
~ *Jacqueline Cioffa, Author of "The Shape of Us" and "The Red Bench"*

DEDICATION

For Joanne & Jerry,
with love and gratitude for their support and encouragement.

Also, without Jerry, Fred Flaherty wouldn't exist.

Chapter 1
One Less Set of Footsteps

Molly Dolan
September 7, 2012
Arlington, MA

Joe called the shots for us and I didn't mind. I mean, why piss him off? Sure, he wasn't always easy to deal with, but neither was I. And sacrifice is critical to all good relationships. Right?

So I tried really hard to be ready when he came to pick me up at six on Friday nights. Getting home from work on the bus at rush hour could be hairy, and it usually meant skipping happy hour with my officemates too. But I loved having a boyfriend. Before Joe, I'd fooled around with lots of guys, but never one who felt like husband material. And, to be honest, none who treated me like wife material, either.

My friends had little use for Joe, but I didn't let that bother me. The way I saw it, the minute they glimpsed his sweet side, they'd change their minds about him.

"The dude *gets off* on controlling you," said Diana at work one Monday. "Don't you think it's creepy how he isolates you every weekend? Would it be *that* hard for him to join us for a drink at El Chico once in a while?"

"Oh, he totally would," I insisted. "But Friday's our movie night. It's our *thing*. And all the goods films at the Kendall start around seven."

Diana groaned. "Oh my god. You sound like you're ninety years old or something. So set in your ways."

"Whaddya mean?"

"I mean, last I heard, movie theaters were open on Saturdays too. Even Sundays, if you can believe that."

I hated when she got all sarcastic. "Well, yeah, but Joe and I get takeout on Saturday nights and watch TV. And on Sundays, he usually goes home after lunch."

Diana blinked. "Yeah. I can't even... Molly, I wish you could hear yourself."

But the thing was, I heard myself quite clearly. What Diana didn't know was that I'd gotten shitfaced in *way* too many bars before meeting Joe. I learned the hard way that one-night stands with random dudes lead to tons of anxiety and depression. Playing "married" with Joe was so much better. Maybe a little boring, but it'd be totally worth it when Joe and I got married for real. We hadn't discussed the future yet, but I was sure we would. Soon.

Jeannette, my upstairs neighbor, didn't like Joe either. She considered him selfish and immature, especially when he honked his horn in the driveway to make me hurry up. Jeannette was a novelist who worked from home. The horn drove her nuts.

"Hey Joe, would it kill ya to have a little respect for the neighbors?" she yelled out the window one Friday night as I scurried across the lawn toward his car. Luckily, he didn't hear her.

Two days later, I knocked on Jeannette's door to apologize.

"C'mon in," she called.

I found her in the kitchen rinsing her head in the sink. The whole place smelled like ammonia and peroxide, and her previously gray hair was now dark red and dripping.

"Wow," I said. "Nice change, Nett."

"Wait'll it dries," she said. "Did your rude boyfriend go home?"

"Yeah, but he's not rude, Nett. Really. It's just that the first frame of a film's *super* important to him. If he misses it, he can't enjoy the rest of the movie because then he can't compare it to the last frame. It's a filmmaker thing. You know?"

Jeannette's dark eyes widened as she wrapped a towel around her head. "I thought Joe worked for a software company. Since when does he make movies?"

"He doesn't. Movies are just his hobby."

"No kiddin'," said Jeannette. "I woulda guessed his hobby was jerkin' you around." Before I could respond, her tone softened. "I'm sorry, Molly. That came out wrong. I just wish he treated you better."

"Whatever," I said. "Joe's a hard guy to understand."

Jeannette opened her mouth, then closed it again and sighed. "As long as *you* understand him," she said after a pause.

I nodded and smiled bravely, but something in my throat caught. Honestly, I understood a lot less about Joe than I cared to admit. But I did want to stay with him forever. I mean, I'd already invested a lot of time in the guy.

Then came the Friday that changed everything.

First, Joe called me at work right after lunch, saying he'd be at my apartment at five—rather than six—because he wanted to come inside and discuss something. His words sounded slow and slurry.

My guts shrank. "Joe, what's wrong?"

"Nothin'."

"But...you sound strange. Like... you've been day-drinking or something."

"Oh. Yeah. We released a new product today and we're havin' a lil' work party. But I gotta jump now. Catch y'in a bit."

So much for getting any work done after that. I'd been updating some pages on our company website, but totally lost focus after Joe's call. I emailed Brad, my boss, saying I needed to attend to a personal issue, then headed for the bus stop with my mind scuttling all over the place.

Every time Joe's group releases a new product, he gets a fat bonus check. And now he wants to talk. And we have *been together four years. Well, two officially, but hooking up for almost four, so that counts. So maybe he finally wants to move in together? Or even get married? Oh god. If he gives me a ring today it'll look shitty on my hand 'cause I need a manicure so bad...*

But those were my nerves talking. Manicure or no manicure, I felt ready for the next level. I mean, I didn't love Joe in any kind of crazy, passionate, Hollywood way, but I loved him *enough*. And that was fine, right? I mean, my parents loved each other enough, and they'd raised two good kids. Besides, passionate, Hollywood love only existed in movies and books, and it hurt, too. I wanted to wake up every day knowing my guy was there for me. Joe. Good old Joe.

Should I open the Chardonnay in the fridge? Or wait, because he might bring Champagne?

I decided to wait, even though my stomach felt like it held an army of fighting worms, and the worms were winning. *Calm down! This is a good thing.* But for some reason, as I waited for his car to pull into the driveway, my stress level kept rising. My mom likes to say, "A watched pot never boils," and I think that truth also applies to people who sit by the window, waiting for guests to arrive.

At 5:15, my doorbell rang, and I ran out of the bathroom to greet him. Joe didn't appear to have any Champagne with him, but he *was* sporting new jeans and a black, button-down shirt I'd never seen before. And what was up with the flashy white sportscar in the driveway? Had he gotten a *huge* bonus?

"Joe! Where's the Honda?"

He took a shallow breath that smelled like beer upon release. "Um, hi? Can I come in?"

"Yeah, but...."

He made no attempt to kiss me; he just barged through the doorway and plopped on the couch with a strange smile on his face. "Whassup?" he said, removing his favorite Red Sox cap. His hair hadn't been cut in a while, so he looked sort of grungy and cool with the hat on. But when he took it off, he reminded me a bit of a sad circus clown.

"You're freaking me out," I said, concern creeping in around the edges of my voice.

He nodded and grunted. "Sorry I'm late. Party got crazy."

"Uh huh." I glanced out the window again, and this time I noticed a head in the passenger seat of the white car. "Oh god, Joe! Who's out there?"

The expression on his face turned from fidgety to full-on nervous. "Yeah. That's... what I wanna talk about."

"Okay?"

The vibe coming off him was super weird. Super. "So, Molly?" he said with a slight grimace.

I stared at him and nodded. "Yeah?"

"So, you know how you and I been seein' each other a while?"

"Yeah..."

"So, I've been thinking that... well... maybe things are gettin' a little stagnant. Know what I mean?"

I couldn't stand it another second. "Joe, d'you want to move in here? 'Cause you can."

He frowned and pressed his lips together. "Uh. Not exactly."

"Well, what then? Joe, please spit it out. Say it. Okay?"

"Okay. So there's this woman at my job, an' I really like her. Not as much as you, of course. She's a different kinda cool. But I've been thinking maybe you and me should... branch out a little, you know? Explore other options?"

Wait. Wait. "Joe, I—"

"Hey, now don't take this wrong, Mol. You and me, we got something good goin' on. Real good. It's just that, you know, we're both young, and you know how it is."

My eyes blurred. "No. I don't."

He stood up and tried to hug me, but I wriggled away. Not only did he smell like beer, he stank like some kind of gross cologne too.

"I'm just sayin' maybe we shouldn't be exclusive right now. Like I said, we could branch out a little."

I felt like puking. "Joe, on the phone, you said nothing was wrong."

"It's not."

"Yeah, well, I thought you wanted—" Tears filled my throat and I couldn't speak, so I just stood there and let him wrap his arms around me.

"Don't cry, Mol. It'll be fine."

The phone in his pocket vibrated.

He pulled it out, checked it, then looked out the window.

Suddenly, I could barely breathe. *The woman in the car.* "That's her?"

His mouth twitched, but he held my gaze. "Yeah. But don't hate on 'er. She's my product manager, Krystle. You'll like 'er."

My heart dove into my stomach, and I shoved him away. "Get outta here, Joe. Now. And don't come back. Ever."

A wave of pain rolled across his face. "Aw Mol, I don't wanna hurt you. It's just that Krys and I've been hangin' out a little lately, and she's open-minded, you know? We talked today, and she's fine with me dating the both o' you. That's why I brought her by. I was thinking you guys could meet. She's totally up for it."

I wanted to kick him. "Are you fucking *kidding*? You expect me to be okay with you *screwing* someone else? After you and I've been together *four* years?"

"Two," he said, totally straight-faced. "An' we can work this out. I know it. I'm not breakin' up with you, Mol. I still care about you. A lot."

I couldn't look at him another second. Snatching his baseball cap off the couch, I smacked him on the arm with it, then hit him again, harder. "Well *I'm* breaking up with *you*. Now get outta here! Before I call the cops!" I knew I wasn't being rational, and I didn't care.

"The cops?" said Joe. His phone vibrated again.

"Joe, I'm not fucking around. Get out!" I opened the door and threw his cap as far as I could. It landed on the walkway.

"All right," he said, stepping outside. "If that's how you want it." Then he walked down the steps, picked up the hat, and trotted toward the car without a word.

"Fuck you!" I yelled after him. It felt good.

But after closing the door, I made the mistake of looking out the window again. The woman—who actually resembled me a little, with her long brown hair—was now out of the car and talking to Joe on the sidewalk. She wore a short, stretchy, white dress, and her breasts were bigger than mine.

Joe rubbed her back and kissed her forehead, then climbed into the driver's seat while the woman walked around and got in on the passenger side. Then the car sped away, and I collapsed in sobs on the floor.

Chapter 2
The Man That Is Me

Fred Flaherty
September 7, 2012
Arlington, MA 6:30 PM

The one-eyed black cat kneaded the flannel shirt strewn on the couch next to a Jim Croce album. A few hours earlier, Fred had wrapped the cat in the shirt for the long drive home from Maine to Massachusetts, and the little creature had slept most of the way, probably comforted by Davey's scent on the soft fabric. But now he was "making bread" with his paws, and Fred was pissed at himself.

"Jingoes! I must be losing it. Why didn't I buy a litter box?" He closed his eyes and envisioned his brother's sad little apartment in the Maine woods with the kitchen that always smelled like burnt broccoli. But he couldn't recall seeing a litter box anywhere in the place.

Davey musta let the cat go outside. But I can't do that here, not with all the traffic and coyotes. Missing cat flyers were taped and tacked to trees and telephone poles all over Arlington, and the local newspaper featured stories about coyote sightings almost every week.

Fred had never paid much attention to the cat in the past. Once, he'd asked his brother what'd happened to its other eye, but Davey didn't know. He said the furry critter had just shown up on his doorstep that way. And now that Davey was gone, the least Fred could do was care for the animal. Temporarily, at least.

So after dealing with the cops, the funeral director, and the four-hour drive, he'd stopped by the big pet supply store at Fresh Pond and picked up cat food, plastic bowls, and a couple of cat toys, too. He'd even asked the guy at the checkout if those comfy looking cat beds were worth the money. The guy said no, not really. Cats'll sleep anyplace warm. But a litter box? Why hadn't the guy suggested a litter box?

If I had an automatic transmission, I'd head right back down there now. But his leg ached like hell, and driving even a few more miles would be torture. He needed to rest it.

The kettle whistled, and he shuffled over to the stove to make tea. Through the kitchen window, he saw a new, white Mustang and two young people outside his neighbor Molly's house: a girl he didn't recognize and Molly's bum of a boyfriend. Just thinking about that jerk made him mad; he used the car horn like a doorbell, never combed his hair, and took Molly out on dates wearing clothes that looked like pajamas. *Jackass. You'd think a smart girl like Molly'd know better than to waste her time on him. But what do I know about love? No one's ever mistaken me for Dear Abby.*

Holding the mug of hot tea in both hands, he started down the cellar stairs, favoring his left leg with its lousy injury.

"Osteoarthritis," the doctor said at his last checkup. "That Jeep accident destroyed a good amount of cartilage in your knee, so as you get older, your bones rub right up against each other." He pressed his knuckles together to illustrate. "There's no cushion left. You can thank Uncle Sam for that."

"Arthur-itis?" Fred got a kick out of saying *arthritis* that way. When he was a kid, he'd thought they named the disease after a guy named Arthur. "You calling me old now, doc? One foot in the grave?"

"Naw. Not you, Fred. If I weren't looking at your chart right now, I'd never know you were seventy-two. You got good genes. Just take it easy on that knee."

But those good genes weren't working for him that night. Kitty darted ahead and raced down the basement stairs, and Fred closed the door behind him. If the cat had to make a mess, the basement was the place to do it.

Damn it! I asked that pet store guy the most basic *questions about cats,* he thought as he sat down in front of his Kenwood TS-2000 ham radio. *I made it* clear *I was an amateur. So why didn't he advise me to get a cat box? Guy coulda made an easy sale.* People were so hard to understand sometimes. *I musta said something to make him think the cat went outside. That's the only rational explanation. But damn it!*

He switched on the old radio and watched its amber light flicker and brighten. He'd actually bought a newer, more expensive rig a year or so earlier, but returned it within a week. The reviews he'd read about the new equipment had been alluring, but in the end, he realized he preferred the trusty Kenwood. It worked great on multiple frequencies, and although some hams complained about the noise of the internal fan, he found its low, steady hum almost comforting. Picking up the microphone, he pressed the talk button. "Hello CQ, hello CQ. This is W1RAP in Arlington, Massachusetts, and I'm looking for advice on a new feline."

For a moment or so, nothing but static came back at him, but Fred waited patiently. Taking a sip of tea, he remembered the old bathroom towels out in the garage. *I wonder if a cat might go on those. Ha! Barb's precious towels.*

He'd tossed all of Barb's fancy towels in the trash when she moved out in '87, but his Yankee thriftiness had eventually gotten the better of him and he'd retrieved them before the garbage truck showed up. After all, towels make good dust rags, and you never know when you might need something to clean up a spill or wipe your hands on after an oil change. Or, in this case, rig up a temporary cat toilet.

"Hello, CQ. Hello CQ," he said again into the microphone. "This is W1RAP, and I'm seeking some speedy animal advice."

It was almost seven o'clock and he hadn't started dinner yet. Normally he ate around five and got on the air by 5:30 or so, but the last thing he'd expected to be doing tonight was dealing with a cat. Or Davey's death, of course, but he was trying not to think about that. Getting emotional on the air would be so embarrassing.

Besides, truth be told, he actually felt a good deal of relief. He hated admitting it, even to himself, but his brother—his only remaining family member—had been a real burden in recent years. Not that Fred had stopped visiting the poor bugger. But even though he'd continued his drives up to Maine once a week for the past four or five years, Davey had lost the ability to hold any type of meaningful conversation. And he hadn't smiled in ages.

"How's it going today, Davey?" Fred would ask upon arrival. "You eatin' enough? Mrs. Dougall get to the store for you on Friday?"

Then, regardless of whether or not Davey responded, Fred would open his brother's refrigerator and check for fresh milk, vegetables of some sort—often a bag of peeled baby carrots—sandwich bread, deli meat, butter, and orange juice. Then he'd look for pizza in the freezer, and maybe some ice cream. "Yeah? Any good shows on the tube this week?"

At that point, Davey would usually shrug or mutter something unintelligible.

"Nah, I don't watch it much these days either," Fred would continue. "Although I do still like *60 Minutes*. That's a good one. You ever watch it anymore, Davey? They still run it on Sunday nights, just like in the old days."

But Davey would just grunt or stare. Pretty much the only thing that could still awaken any emotion in the guy was listening to Jim Croce, who'd been a favorite of both brothers since the early 1970's. Otherwise, as far as Fred could tell, the medication had killed every remaining element of Davey's spirit: the good stuff *and* the bad. Which—all things considered—wasn't the worst compromise. Davey's bad side had caused a lot of people a lot of pain.

But on the drive home from Maine that day, Fred had been focusing on better times, like when his baby brother was the star of the Arlington High track team. Such a gentle kid, the kind of kid girls went crazy for. But then the bastards sent him off to Vietnam, and Davey wasn't cut out for that sort of thing. Poor bugger never shed a drop of blood over there, but boy, oh boy, did his head ever get screwed up.

The radio let out a sharp squeal. Then a voice came over fairly clearly, despite some background static. "W1RAP, W1RAP, this is K1QEC. How you doin' tonight, Freddy?"

Fred teared up at the sound of Billy's voice, and he took a minute to cough and clear his throat before picking up the microphone again. "K1QEC, K1QEC. Hello, Billy, old man! How's life in sunny Florida?"

Billy's microphone clicked. "Well, I wouldn't call it sunny today. Good day for ducks, as the XYL says. Whatta rainstorm we're havin'. What's it like up your way?" As he spoke, the static on Billy's end kept building and receding, like the sound of ocean waves.

Fred had to stop and think before answering. He hadn't paid much attention to the weather that day. "Uh, lots of clouds. But speaking of storms, I think I just heard that storm on Jupiter in your last transmission there." He'd been a ham long enough to know that storms on the giant planet could interfere with short-wave radio signals on Earth. "You hear any of that, Billy?"

Billy didn't respond immediately, and Fred bit his lip. Bill's wife Sally had one of those bad types of leukemia—the family had actually called in a priest a few years back to give her Last Rites—but then the doctor had tried some experimental treatment, and Sally had bounced back. That's when she and Billy had made the move down to Florida, and who could blame them? Winter in New England was no place for sick people. And although Billy hadn't mentioned Sally's illness in a while, Fred was pretty sure things weren't great. His friend had grown more subdued in recent months, and he'd been on the air a lot less frequently.

And Fred really missed him. Back when Billy lived in Arlington, the two men would meet at Dunkin Donuts on Friday mornings and shoot the breeze about all kinds of things, including Sally's sickness. But hams don't tend to talk about personal stuff on the air, and somehow, the act of picking up the phone and calling Billy felt strange. Or maybe Fred just didn't want to hear all those painful details.

"Yup," said Billy, after a minute or so. "Good thing we're not on Jupiter, huh?"

Kitty slunk across the floor and settled next to Fred's slippered feet.

"You gotta go, Kitty?" The cat stared up at him with his one yellow eye. "All right, pal, I'm working on it. Hang in there."

"So Bill," he said into the microphone, "whatta you know about cats? Any idea if they'll, uh, relieve themselves on fancy towels?"

Billy chuckled. "Uh, did I copy that correctly? 'Cause I think I just heard you say *cats*. Or maybe I got sand in my ears."

Fred smiled. "No, that's a Roger, Billy. Believe it or not, I've inherited a cat. And I need a litter box pronto, if you know what I mean."

"Oh man," said Billy, and Fred heard a woman's high-pitched giggle in the background. "You got the XYL in stiches over there on the couch."

That made Fred feel a little better. He'd always liked making Sally laugh.

"I wish to god I could help you out, Freddy, but honestly, I got no idea. Maybe it'll pee on a newspaper? Like a puppy?"

"Beats me. But I guess I'll find out."

Billy chuckled again. "So now for the real question. What're *you* doing with a *cat*?"

"Oh," said Fred, pausing for a second, "he belonged to my brother. But, uh, Davey has...signed off, so to speak. I'd rather not talk about that on the air, though." He managed to keep his voice from breaking until he released the microphone button. Then he wept. Hard. It was the first time all day he'd let his guard down. He found some old tissues in his sweater pocket, and when he started regaining control, he blew his nose and wiped his eyes.

Luckily, Billy got the message. Fred had told him a bit about Davey's problems over the years, and Billy was a bright guy. "Oh wow, Freddy. That's a tough break. I'm sorry to hear that."

Fred cleared his throat and waited a few more seconds before picking up the mike again. "Thanks. But that's life, as the song goes. Now this cat, on the other hand," he forced himself to sound chipper, "I could really use some help with this cat."

A microphone clicked over the receiver, and another voice—younger and more feminine—broke in. "Hiya, W1RAP. This is K1CJJ in Wisconsin. The handle here's Lisa. D'ya copy?"

Fred picked up the pen on his desk and wrote the woman's call sign and the name *Lisa* in a notebook he kept solely for the purpose of keeping track of the hams he spoke with each day. Then, at the end of each week—usually on Saturday night—he'd log any new ones into the leather journal he'd maintained since returning from the service in 1960. He was proud of those journal entries—all nine hundred or so—because they represented hams from all over the world: people he'd had *real* conversations with. Never would he have made that many "friends" on any of those crazy things like Facebook, nor would he have learned so much. Based on what he'd read, Facebook involved passing around silly jokes, pictures of food, and idiotic political and religious propaganda. Whereas hams—at least the ones on radio frequencies he preferred—rarely discussed politics or religion. They stuck to technical talk and plain old friendly conversation. And unlike people on the Internet, most hams actually enjoyed getting together in person. His local repeater society held pancake breakfasts once a month, and at least one formal dinner each year. He hadn't been to any of those events in a while—a long while—but in his younger days, they'd constituted a huge part of his social life.

And hams were *smart* too, at least when it came to technical stuff. The hobby required a certain level of intelligence, and most of the hams he knew built and modified their own equipment to suit their individual needs. They also liked experimenting with new ways of making their rigs more efficient, and many would befriend the owners of local electronics shops. Then they'd spend weekend mornings hanging around those places, drinking coffee and discussing things like tweaking antennas and testing new gadgets. Unlike computers that came in boxes ready to plug in and turn on, ham radios were as unique and quirky as the people who operated them.

"K1CJJ, this is W1RAP, and I copy you just fine. You don't happen to have any suggestions for an emergency litter box, do you?"

But before Lisa could answer, Billy cut in again. "Hey, sorry to fall off like that Fred. Had to deal with a family matter. Lisa, this is K1QEC in Florida, and let me just say, I hope you can give old Freddy a hand with his cat issues. I had a dog when I was a kid, but he did his business outside."

Lisa laughed gently. "Aw, I'll bet Freddy's not so old."

IT DOESN'T HAVE TO BE THAT WAY

"Whatever you say," said Billy with a chuckle. "Maybe I should just call him vintage. That sounds better, right? Like wine?"

Fred frowned. He didn't mind the "vintage" joke, but Lisa calling him *Freddy* felt strange. Only his closest friends did that. But Lisa was just following Billy's lead. She had no way of knowing that most people called him by his last name, Flaherty.

"Okay, well I've got four indoor cats, Freddy, so I feel your pain," she continued. "Here's the deal. You're gonna have to get to a pet store tomorrow and buy a simple plastic litter box and a bag of kitty litter. I like the stuff made from pine trees, but that's a personal preference. The truth is, any litter's fine if your cat'll use it. But to get through the night tonight, just take an old shoebox—a big one if you've got it, like the kind boots come in—and line it with a trash bag. Then tear up some old newspapers and toss 'em in there. The more the better. I've had to do it myself a few times. My big guy busts up the litter box every now and then."

Fred nodded and squeezed the microphone button again. "Thank you kindly, Lisa. Although I'm kicking myself right now. You know, I worked as a technician all my life, so I probably shoulda figured that one out, huh? It's not exactly brain surgery."

"Oh no you don't, Fred." Lisa sounded almost snippy. "It's taken over ten years for me to figure out how to make my cats happy. I think learning brain surgery mighta been easier, and you'd probably agree if you met my cats. And I'll bet there're plenty of brain surgeons out there—plenty—who wouldn't know how to build an effective litter box on the fly." She snorted before releasing the microphone button.

Gosh, I can be stupid sometimes, Fred thought. "Oh, Lisa, I'm sorry. I didn't mean to insult you there. I know cats can be finicky. I remember those commercials with that big orange one there, that Morris. Please don't take offense. My brain's not running on all four cylinders today."

But Lisa came back, friendly as ever. "Oh, no worries, Freddy. I'm just joshing. So what kinda technical work did you do?"

He smiled in spite of himself. *I wonder what she looks like.* It'd been years since he'd dated anyone. Not that he hadn't tried after splitting with Barb, but it'd been too complicated. Most of his dates didn't ask many questions about Barb—they seemed to understand that ex-wives are off-limit—but they'd been *far* too curious about the rest of his family, and he *hated* talking about them. Both his parents had died in a crappy nursing home, and Davey, his only sibling, was going off the deep end. But for some reason, the ladies always wanted more info about Dave.

Fred had heard some of the stories and rumors about his brother around town, but he had no interest in adding to that gossip heap.

"What's wrong with him?" one blonde had asked repeatedly. "Doesn't he get lonely up in Maine all by himself?" Another—a cute brunette with a good sense of humor—had continually suggested that she and Fred go visit Davey. Fred told her three times that his brother was shy around guests, and the fourth time she made the suggestion, he gave up and stopped calling her.

Then there was the kid thing, which was even harder to discuss, especially on dates. "I like the *idea* of a girlfriend," he told Billy once, "but I always pick the wrong ones."

There was something about this Lisa, though. Maybe it was her soothing voice. In any case, he felt restless. *Hey, come on, Freddy. Get a grip on yourself. Poor Davey won't even be cremated 'til tomorrow.* Then he felt sad all over again. *Would a little whiskey help?* Nah, then he'd just wake up with a headache. When he couldn't sleep, a Tylenol usually did the trick.

He opened his mouth to tell Lisa he'd worked for the phone company until his retirement seven years earlier, but right then, Billy's voice crackled over the receiver again. "Hey, I missed some o' that last transmission, but I swear I heard Lisa say somethin' about a big guy bustin' things up. You need any help with that fella, Lisa, you gimme a call. Ya hear me?" Billy—that old dog—couldn't resist an opportunity to flirt, but ladies never minded.

Lisa chuckled. "Oh, you're sweet, Billy, but I can handle my kitties just fine. The big one's a crazy old Maine coon cat—almost twenty-five pounds, if you can believe it—but he's a sweetie, a real gentle giant. He and I watch the *Late Show* together every night, and I honestly don't know what I'd do without him." She stopped talking for a second, then started up again. "Oh, and one last thing, Fred. If you don't have any newspapers on hand, you could try dirt instead. In fact, some kitties like dirt even better'n paper. It's a personality thing. You might need to experiment a bit."

Gosh, she sounds like my kinda girl. Smart, honest, practical. Plus, she watches late-night TV with her cat, so maybe she's looking to meet a nice guy. "Well thank you again, Lisa. I'm gonna sign off now and start hunting for a shoe box. Too bad you're so far away. If you lived closer, I'd take you out for coffee."

"Aw, that's sweet," said Lisa. "You know, Boston's got a special place in my heart. My husband and I went up there twice. He was a history buff, so he just ate it up. Ate it right up. Paul Revere... Lexington and Concord... couldn't get enough. But, you know, he's a silent key now... so I don't travel much these days." She paused. "Anyway, good luck with that new feline. This is K1CJJ signing off. 73 to everyone."

Fred's eyes filled up again. A silent key was a ham who'd died, and the change in Lisa's tone implied that her husband's death still caused her significant pain. *I should tell her I'm coming to Wisconsin soon. I could buy a ticket and... oh hell, what am I doing? If I don't go to bed soon, I'm gonna get myself in real trouble.*

"All right, K1CJJ," he said, "73s to you, and thanks again for your help. Same to you, Billy. I'll catch up with you tomorrow. This is W1RAP, signing off."

He lay the microphone down and rolled the chair back from his desk. His hands shook a little, but that was normal for him. They'd been doing that for a while, especially when he got excited or upset. His doctor said not to worry, so he didn't. But he didn't like aging either.

On the radio, Billy said "73" too — ham radio slang for best regards — and made a corny joke about a "litter box *catastrophe.*"

Signing off at the end of the night almost always left Fred with a hollow feeling in his gut. He'd sit there for a few seconds, listening to the emptiness of the house before heading upstairs and putting a Jim Croce record on the turntable. "Bad, Bad, Leroy Brown" usually got his fingers snapping, and "I've Got a Name," still gave him hope. Especially that line near the end about being a fool, but wanting to share his dream with someone else. Even "Operator," the saddest of all Croce songs, helped him feel better, because if a guy like Jim could cry, then damn it, he could too.

But that night, he knew listening to Croce would rip him to shreds. The only thing he'd taken from Davey's place — aside from the cat and the flannel shirt — had been his brother's Croce albums. Of course, he already owned copies of them all, but couldn't stand the thought of leaving Davey's behind for the trash truck. Mrs. Dougall, the neighbor who did Davey's grocery shopping, had offered to clean out the place for five hundred bucks — after the cops went through it one last time — and Fred had gladly written her a check. He had no interest in any of Davey's other crap.

One of these days, though, I'll play his records. It'll be nice to listen to the scratches Davey put in them over the years. But he wasn't ready for that yet. He still found it hard to believe that his poor brother would still be lying dead in bed if Mrs. Dougall hadn't stopped by that morning to see what he needed at the store just a n hour or so after he'd passed.

I wonder when I'll go? After all, it's only a matter of time for everyone, and plenty of people go at my age. Poor Mom was only sixty—just like Davey—and dad was sixty-five. Hell, at seventy-two, I'm ancient for a Flaherty. I just hope I don't end up being one of those people who rots away and no one knows they're gone 'til someone smells them.

He wiped his eyes and sat up straighter. "Aw, pull yourself together, Fred," he said out loud. "Billy wouldn't let you rot. He'd know somethin' was wrong if you didn't sign on for a couple of days and he'd send someone over to check on you."

Shaking his head, he blinked a few times and pushed himself out of the chair. "All right, Kitty. Let's go find you a shoe box." But the animal no longer seemed to be in the cellar. The door at the top of the stairs was still closed, but he couldn't find the cat. Then he glimpsed the window in the far corner of the basement.

Oh no. Just that morning—right before he'd gotten the call about Davey—he'd been moving a box of *QST* magazines and had broken the glass. He'd done his best to block up the window with the box before heading up to Maine, but....

"Jingoes!" The little bugger had escaped.

Chapter 3
Careful Man

Molly
September 7, 2012
Arlington, MA 7:00 PM

My head ached from so much crying, and it was all Joe's fault.

Or was it? I mean, Joe was an ass, but how had I allowed him to delude me so long? All those times he'd said he was too busy to see me during the week, too busy even to answer my calls and texts. And I'd been dumb enough to think he was working his butt off, saving money for our future life together. Meanwhile, he'd been thinking about "branching out" and "not being exclusive." And Krystle, with her hot little body and fancy white car!

What was wrong with me? Everyone—and I mean everyone—had warned me not to wrap myself so tightly around Joe. They'd called out his multiple flaws, but I'd refused to acknowledge them. Once again, I'd surrendered my heart to the wrong dude. But why did I keep doing that? Why couldn't I tell the difference between a good, solid guy and someone who just wanted to screw around?

I needed air. Fresh air.

Sitting on the cold concrete steps stung my thighs, but I stayed there anyway. I'd stopped considering myself Catholic back in high school, but the Catholic belief in sacrifice as a means to salvation stuck with me. And that evening, I craved some sort of salvation.

I thought back to the Friday evening in June, when Joe had arrived at my house with a bouquet of daisies and I'd burst into tears. Maybe I'd cried because he'd never brought flowers before, and flowers meant he cared about me. A lot. Right? So when he mentioned—as I trimmed the stems and arranged the daisies in a vase—that he'd be busy with work people all weekend and *completely* unable to hang out, call, or even text me, I'd wiped my tears and said I understood.

Oh god, I was stupid.

A chilly breeze blew through my hair, but I wasn't ready to go inside yet. A neighbor somewhere nearby was cutting their grass, and I breathed in the sexy, earthy smell and closed my sore eyes.

Wilson Road—with its faded yellow line down the middle—served as a diagonal cut-through between two of Arlington's main thoroughfares. People used Wilson to avoid the traffic light at the intersection, so it was almost always busy, and everyone drove too fast. The locals worried about accidents, but the cops didn't pay much attention since no children lived on Wilson. In fact, I was probably its youngest resident. Everyone else was either an elderly homeowner or a single renter. When people think of Arlington, they think of a family-friendly Boston suburb, but Wilson Road was an exception. Which suited me just fine. After all, I've been an exception in one way or another for most of my life.

Across the street, Mrs. Costa's friend pulled up in a silver Camry. I didn't know the friend's name, but she visited Mrs. Costa pretty often. I watched as she fluffed her white hair and applied lipstick in the rearview mirror. Then she blotted her mouth with a tissue, popped the trunk, and pushed the car door open with her foot. *Who's gonna eat dinner with me when I get old?* I wondered. *And will I ever even be a widow like Mrs. Costa? Or will I spend my whole life single?*

The woman hauled her body out of the Camry and slowly made her way around to the trunk, from which she retrieved a white casserole container. Then, balancing that on her hip, she slammed the trunk shut. I considered going over to help, but felt too shitty. Plus, if Mrs. Costa saw my swollen eyes, she'd ask a million questions. Mrs. Costa lived for drama, and possessed an uncanny ability to spot it too. In her younger days, she'd worked at Town Hall—apparently an endless font of juicy gossip—but now that she was retired, she'd been forced to narrow her focus to our neighborhood and friends in town. Jeannette upstairs had warned me on several occasions that, "We all have a right to ignore Mrs. Costa. 'Cause anything you say to her can—and probably will—be used against you. Somewhere."

But when her friend with the casserole dish stumbled on the walkway—almost dropping the meal she'd prepared—guilt overrode my crappy mood. "Ma'am, can I give you a hand?" I called, barely recognizing my own scratchy voice.

The woman looked startled, but smiled when she saw me. "Oh no, dear," she called across the street. "This is my daily exercise."

"Okay," I said, shivering. At least I'd tried. And if she didn't want my assistance, I'd just stay put and keep an eye on her until she was safely in Mrs. Costa's house. Then I'd slip back inside mine.

I'm a good person, I told myself, but I wasn't so sure. I mean, rather than asking the poor lady if she needed help, I could've gotten off my ass and insisted on carrying the food. And why hadn't I contacted a women's shelter yet? For months—years, actually—I'd promised myself I'd go volunteer at one, because I really wanted to help people who couldn't help themselves. People like Kate. But all I'd ever done was Google local shelters and vow to do something.

Now, to be fair, I didn't have tons of free time, and I didn't own a car either. When I'd finished college, I'd looked at my starting salary and realized I could either buy a car and live with roommates, or live alone and take public transportation. I'd chosen the latter, even though my daily commute involved switching between two buses each way. That was partly because I liked having time to myself, and partly because driving made me nervous. But taking the bus was no picnic either, and I had to get up extra early to be at work on time. When I'd finally make it home at night, I'd often have just enough energy to pour a glass of wine and heat up some frozen noodles or ravioli. I'd watch a little TV, maybe drink another glass of wine, and crash by ten-thirty. And up until that Friday night, I'd spent most weekends with Joe. Joe, the cheating loser scumbag.

The sun sank lower on the horizon, and a truly cold breeze blew across the lawn. My mind drifted to the bottle of Chardonnay lying in my fridge, just waiting to have its cork liberated, as my work friend Diana would say.

Everyone in the FSI office liked Diana, even though she usually drank way too much after work. But she never drove drunk, didn't take herself too seriously, and she'd single-handedly launched the FSI social scene. Back before she'd been hired as the company receptionist, most people had knocked off early and headed home at the end of the workweek. But then Diana, a committed partier, started rallying everyone to go over to El Chico—the Mexican restaurant in our office park—"Just for a quick pop," on Friday evenings. I hadn't expected the idea to take off, but wow did it ever, and El Chico quickly became a vital part of FSI culture. A part I rarely participated in—because of Joe and our Friday night movie ritual—but Diana never failed to invite me to join the crowd. Sometimes, she'd even call me later in the night, in case my plans had changed.

On the opposite side of Wilson Road, Mrs. Costa arrived at the door and welcomed her friend into the house with a half-hug around the casserole container. *Finally!* Time to crack open that Chardonnay! But just as I started to stand, a skinny black cat darted across the street, barely avoiding the tires of a speeding BMW. It skittered beneath a shrub on the far side of my yard, and just before it disappeared, I saw that it had only one eye.

Poor thing. I recognized most of the outdoor cats in the neighborhood, but not that one. It didn't look very tough or street-smart either, which sucked, because I'd read a few stories in the town newspaper about coyotes in the area. But what could I do? Call the animal control officer and tell her a cat ran under a bush?

Then I spotted a man coming down the steps of the house beside Mrs. Costa's and my spirits sank even deeper. *Oh crap. Not Mr. Flaherty. Not tonight.* But it was too late: he'd already spotted me. Damn! I pulled out my smartphone, held it in front of my face, and began tapping its static black screen. That didn't deter him, though. Fred Flaherty was headed straight for me, and the look in his eyes told me he was on a mission.

Shit. Mr. Flaherty could talk forever when he was in the right mood, and I didn't want to talk to anyone.

"Hey Molly?" he called.

Shit, shit, shit. When he didn't have an agenda, Mr. Flaherty—or just plain Flaherty, as most people called him—kept to himself. He'd spend hours in his yard raking leaves, shoveling snow, or adjusting the giant antenna behind his house. Other times, he'd walk out the door, get in his silver pickup truck, and head out without looking across the street or acknowledging anyone who might be around. Then he'd usually return an hour or two later with groceries or a bag from the hardware store. But sometimes he'd leave very early in the morning and stay gone all day. And occasionally, I'd spot him returning in the evening, looking wiped out. Flaherty had a limp too, and when he got home after one of those long days, he'd barely be able to walk when he climbed out of the truck.

I was aware of some kind of bad blood between Flaherty and the "townie" neighbors, but didn't know the details. All I knew was that he'd grown up in Arlington, but none of the old-timey Arlington folks waved when they walked or drove past his house. And he acted like he didn't notice. One time, Mrs. Costa came over to ask if Flaherty had ever said or done anything "weird" to me, and I assured her he hadn't.

And although I got the sense she would've enjoyed adding me to her gossip circle, I wasn't interested. I respected Flaherty, and based on my observations, the guy cared a lot about the community, even though everyone ignored him.

Like the evening—about a year earlier—when he'd come hobbling across Wilson Road, complaining about the cracks in his sidewalk, which he claimed got worse each winter. He said it was *only a matter of time* (one of his favorite phrases) before some unsuspecting person—probably a senior citizen—fell and broke their hip. "It's terrible, Molly. You know, I've asked the DPW *three times now* to come look at these darn cracks, and they promise they will, then do nothing. Why do we pay all these taxes when they won't even fix the sidewalks?"

At the time, I'd been getting home after a rough day at work, and although I felt bad for Flaherty, I wasn't in the mood to discuss his "darn cracks."

"Oh, I'm sure they'll send someone out soon," I said. "But you know, Mr. Flaherty, I gotta run. My ice cream's melting." I was carrying a bag of groceries from the local market, but hadn't actually bought ice cream.

"Ah. Have you tried those insulated freezer bags? I like them 'cause they keep everything cold on the way home from the store." Classic Flaherty.

"No," I said, "but I should. Thanks for the tip. Good night, now, Mr. Flaherty."

Another time, he'd been all worked up about an insect called the Asian Longhorn Beetle, which tunneled into trees and destroyed them by eating out their insides. According to him, the ALB had already killed hundreds of trees in other Massachusetts towns, and it was *only a matter of time* before it arrived in Arlington.

Again, I respected the guy, and didn't want bugs gobbling up the town's trees any more than I wanted some poor elderly person getting injured on his sidewalk, but what could I do? "Hmm," I said. "I hope they figure out a way to kill those nasty beetles before they get here. But hey, I gotta go. I've got something in the oven. It's been nice talking to you."

Then, before he could respond, I waved goodbye and darted into my apartment, leaving poor Flaherty standing alone on my front lawn. As far as I could tell, the only thing he and I had in common was the pavement between us on Wilson Road.

But on that dreaded night—the night of Joe and Krystle—Flaherty had found his way back onto my side of the street.

"You didn't happen see a cat go by, did you?" he asked, his limp so bad I winced. "Little black fella missing an eye?"

I looked across and saw Mrs. Costa on her porch. A stranger passing by would probably assume she was simply out there enjoying the evening air, but I knew better. After all, she had a dinner guest inside. But Mrs. Costa couldn't help herself. She'd spotted Flaherty coming my way and needed to spy.

"Yeah. I did see a cat," I answered. "Just a second ago, actually. He ran under that bush over there."

I wondered why he cared. Flaherty didn't strike me as much of an animal lover. In fact, he was always shooing critters out of his yard. But I was starting to feel weepy about Joe again, so I didn't ask any questions.

"Oh, great. Thanks, Molly. Which bush did you say?"

"The yellowish one," I said, pointing at the shrub, then tapping my blank phone screen. "Sorry, but I'm in a rush. My boyfriend and I are trying to make plans for tonight."

"Oh, sure, Molly. Do what you gotta do."

"Thanks." A tear leaked out the corner of my right eye and I dabbed at it with my finger.

"Hey Molly, you okay?" He sounded genuinely concerned.

I was surprised he'd even noticed the tear. "Oh yeah. I'm fine. Just allergies." I had no intention of telling him my boyfriend problems, which were none of his business. Besides, he was clearly no relationship expert. The only woman—the only *person*—I'd ever heard say anything positive about him was Jeannette, my upstairs neighbor. One time, over a glass of wine, Jeannette had actually confessed that she considered him *hot*. Then again, Jeannette was a little nuts. In a good way, but still.

Because *hot?* Oh god. Mr. Flaherty, with his longish, wild gray hair? He always smelled vaguely of WD-40 and wore the same clothes almost every day: faded Levis and a maroon, long-sleeved t-shirt that said *Morse Code Preservation Society* on the front. Now, to be fair, he had a nice, firm chin, and his face was always a bit tanned, probably because he spent so much time outdoors. And his body was lean and rangy. But hot? No way. Maybe he'd been okay looking at some point in his life, but those days were long gone.

Mrs. Costa continued her surveillance from the porch, and I wondered why she had so much interest in a man she refused to acknowledge in any way. Had something truly terrible happened in their past, or did she suspect Flaherty of something shady? Because come to think of it, he *had* mentioned once that he'd done some kind of top secret military work when he was younger. But watching him as he crouched beside the shrub, I felt only sympathy for the dude.

"Whose cat is it?" I asked, approaching him slowly. My chilly body screamed for me to get inside immediately, but my heart couldn't do that quite yet.

"Well, he *was* my brother's," said Flaherty matter-of-factly. "But my brother, well, he passed away this morning." His voice remained calm, but I got the sense he was having a hard time keeping it together.

"Oh no! I'm sorry, Mr. Flaherty."

"Uh...." Flaherty shook his head and waved dismissively. "Yeah, thanks. It's a tough thing, but it was... a long time coming. I think he's better off now. He... yeah. We're all better off."

I wasn't sure how to respond. "Oh. Was he... old? Or... very sick?"

Flaherty's face half-smiled, half-grimaced. "Well, I can't say he was old 'cause he was twelve years younger'n me. But yeah, he was sick. I'd rather not talk about him now though, if you don't mind. Davey was a complicated guy."

"Sure. Yeah. I get it." I'd never lost a brother, but knew the feeling of not wanting to discuss the loss of someone close.

"Oh, look!" said Flaherty a few seconds later. This time, his tone was almost too bright. "There he is, right under that branch."

I squinted into the bush and spotted the cat's yellow eye glowing up at us.

"Here, little kitty." My neighbor's normally gruff voice sounded surprisingly tender.

"Wow, he's cute," I said.

"Hmm." The man held out his hand and called again to the animal. I considered asking why it had only one eye, but didn't want to invite any more sadness into the conversation. "So... are you gonna keep him?"

Flaherty raised his heavy brows. "Why? You want him, Molly?"

He seemed serious, and I couldn't help thinking how nice it'd be to have a kitty around the house, especially after all the shit with Joe. "Oh, I'd love him, but my landlord doesn't allow pets."

"Nah, I'm just kidding," said Flaherty with a chuckle. "I'm gonna hang onto the little fella for a while. He seems pretty low maintenance, as they say." Then he reached into the pocket of his jeans and pulled out a piece of meat. "Chicken," he said, breaking off a little and dropping it on the ground with a wink. "Let's give him a minute. I bet he comes out for that."

I hadn't eaten meat since high school, when Kate had opened my eyes to the horrific things humans do to animals, so seeing the chunk of chicken come straight out of his pocket grossed me out a little. But I didn't say anything. I just looked down at my phone and tapped the screen again.

"Telephone troubles?" asked Flaherty.

"Sort of," I said, shaking the phone. "My boyfriend doesn't seem to be getting my texts." Just mentioning Joe made my chin start quivering again. Yeah, I was ready to open that bottle of wine.

My neighbor cocked his head to one side. "Hmm. I'm pretty sure all the local cell networks are up and running today. I know a guy who monitors that stuff religiously, and he lets our group know when there's a problem anywhere."

"Huh."

He raised his eyebrows. "Hey Molly, I think I can handle the cat from here. Why don't you go inside and call your boyfriend on the landline?"

"Okay. I will in a minute."

But Flaherty's tone took on an air of concern. "I assume you do have one, right Molly?"

"Um, yeah," I said, slightly irritated. Why would he ask that question? "You've seen Joe around, right? He's tall and thin with curly brown hair?"

The poor guy looked really startled. "Oh no, Molly. I don't mean your boyfriend. I meant a *landline*. I read an article in *Time* the other day about young people getting rid of their home phones so they can save money."

"Oh... yeah," I said, feeling like an idiot. "Yeah, a lot of my friends just have cellphones. It's way cheaper." In fact, I'd been thinking of going that route myself. Especially since the owner of FSI was selling the company, and I'd probably be unemployed soon.

Flaherty sighed, crossed his arms, and rocked on the balls of his feet. "Well, I don't know anything about your financial situation, but if you can afford to hang onto your landline, I'd strongly advise it. Cellphones are great until the towers go down. Then you're in trouble. People around here don't think about earthquakes and hurricanes until it's too late. And a young girl like you, living alone? I'll bet your parents are glad you have a hard-wired phone. If you were my daughter, I'd make sure you did."

I actually smiled. No one had called me a young girl in years. Some bartenders didn't even card me anymore. "Mr. Flaherty, I'm twenty-five years old."

"Oh yeah? Well, you're still a kid to an old guy like me."

I opened my mouth to tell him he wasn't old—even though I certainly considered him to be—but he went right on talking. "And you know, I worry about you over here, Molly. This street. There's so much foot traffic. I see people walking down to the bank and the drugstore at all hours of the night. And I hate to say it, but I don't think that lady upstairs there...," he glanced up at the second floor of my house and rolled his eyes, "... I don't get the sense *she'd* come running down to help if she heard any trouble."

"Jeannette?" I asked, smiling again and wondering how he'd react if he knew she thought he was *hot*.

"Yeah. That one. She seems, I don't know. Flighty."

I suppressed a chuckle. "Mr. Flaherty, Jeannette's awesome. She's just... different. And she'd be there if I needed her. I know she would."

Flaherty shrugged. "I sure hope so. But back to the landline. Hang onto it if you can. Even if you have to work a couple extra hours a month to pay for it."

I started to tell him I was paid on salary, but stopped myself. "Okay. I'll do my best."

His attention had shifted again. "And wouldya lookit that. Here comes Kitty now." The cat's little body was so low to the ground it almost slithered, but the piece of chicken was definitely its goal.

"Does he have a name?" I whispered.

"No idea," said Flaherty. "I just call him Kitty. He doesn't seem to mind."

"Poor baby's hungry."

The cat pounced on the meat and tore at it with his sharp little teeth.

Another thought popped into my head. "Hey, you know, Mr. Flaherty, if we ever had a disaster around here, I'm guessing you'd have your CB radio all fired up, right? So even if the cellphones went down, I could run over to your house and—"

The man's upper body flinched as if he'd been shot. "Excuse me? What'd you just say?"

I froze. Was this the weirdness Mrs. Costa had alluded to? Or had I somehow overstepped? "Or, um, you know... I could just yell to you from across the street, or—"

"No, Molly, what'd you call my *radio*?" His voice still sounded serious, but it'd acquired a slight jokey edge, and his eyes twinkled unmistakably in the evening light.

His *radio*? "Mr. Flaherty, I didn't call your radio *anything*. I was just saying that in an emergency—if you wanted to—you could help me get in touch with my family. With your CB."

"Aha!" he said, his eyes softening even more. "See? You *did* call it something. You called my *ham* radio a CB. And that's a crime in my circle of friends."

Huh? "Um, I'm sorry? But, like, I didn't know there was a difference. You've got that big antenna and, you know...."

Flaherty smiled a sad smile. "Don't worry, Molly. It's a common error. I'll forgive you this time. Okay?"

"Okay. But I really don't understand."

"Hey, like I said, forget it. It's just an old ham thing. We don't like being mistaken for CBers. Maybe someday you'll come over for a cup o' tea and I'll explain." Then, without warning, he bent over and grabbed the cat. Instinctively, I took his arm while he steadied himself, but he straightened up and took a step away from me. "I'm fine," he said.

"Okay," I replied, getting a strong whiff of WD-40. "Just making sure." I'd never touched Flaherty before, and the strength of his arm surprised me. Then, because I felt awkward, I said, "Hey, you know, people have seen coyotes around here, so you might wanna be careful about letting Kitty out again."

"Roger," said Flaherty, long smile lines stretching back from his eyes. "So I've heard. Little bugger got out through a broken cellar window, but I already taped it up. Tomorrow, I'll go down to the hardware store and get a new pane o' glass." He scratched the cat's head, and it purred. "All right, then, thanks for your help, Molly. Have a good night."

"You too," I said as he turned and limped back toward the sidewalk. He waited for a few cars to pass, then made his way across Wilson Road, holding the cat like a newborn baby.

"Molly!"

I couldn't freakin' believe it. Mrs. Costa stood on her front lawn now, while the Camry remained in its spot on the road. How could she leave her guest inside alone for so long?

"Everything okay?" I called.

A motorcycle whizzed by as Flaherty's porch light went out. "Fine," said Mrs. Costa, pointing to her neighbor's house. "Is he bugging you?"

I couldn't believe it. Didn't she have anything else to think about? "No. He just got a new cat."

A minivan crossed between us. "What?"

I knew she wanted me to go over and chat, but I was done. And her poor friend was probably starving. "A cat," I repeated in a louder voice. "A new cat."

Mrs. Costa shook her head. "Crazy," she said, touching her temple with her index finger.

But I held up my phone like a call was coming in and said, "Gotta run! Good night."

Defeated, the woman headed back inside.

Chapter 4
What People Do

Molly
September 7, 2012
Arlington, MA 8:00 PM

    The Chardonnay tasted like metal. At first, I thought it was just my bad mood. But after a few sips, I actually retched. Maybe that explained why I'd found the bottle in the bargain bin at the local package store. Damn. I'd be stupid to drink any more of the spoiled wine, but I didn't have any other alcohol in the house.

    The TV offered little help. I clicked through all the channels — needless to say, my standards that night were pretty low — but I still couldn't find anything to watch. I wanted something to take my mind off myself for a couple of hours, but since I wasn't familiar with the Friday sitcom lineup, none of the shows grabbed my attention. Nor did any of the available movies, and I didn't have the energy to try and figure out the point of some new reality show. And Bill O'Reilly? Yeah, no.

    I switched over to a college basketball game and thought about Joe again. What an ass. A complete asshole! My stomachache worsened, and I grew increasingly pissed. Four years of my life, I'd given him. Age twenty-one to twenty-five. By far the longest I'd ever been with any guy, and now it felt like wasted time. How many other opportunities had I missed because of him, and would I ever catch up? I didn't even have any good male prospects on the horizon since most guys I knew worked at FSI, and they all considered me taken.

    And why was I watching basketball? I hated TV sports. The next channel up the dial featured a Mexican talk show, and although I spoke no Spanish, I gave it a fair shot. But it was no use. A long, lonely night lay ahead of me, and the sooner I accepted that truth, the better.

    I got up, dumped the wine down the drain, and was debating whether to crash on the couch or go straight to bed when the home phone startled me, breaking the silence with a sharp bleat. My parents' number flashing on the caller ID screen shouldn't have been a surprise; my mom called every Friday night. But I was usually out with Joe when she did. She'd leave a message, and I'd call her back Sunday. On several occasions, I'd advised her just to wait until Sunday to call, but she'd always say something like *oh, it never hurts to try.*

Ugh. I mean, I was glad she cared, but we both knew she was checking up on me. Because if I was home on Friday night, then perhaps I was depressed. Once, I actually said, "Ma, I promise I'll never do anything desperate and stupid again, okay? I made a mistake *once*. In high school. *One* mistake. Why can't you forget that and move on?"

"Oh, honey," she'd replied, "if you ever have kids, maybe you'll understand. Besides, I like hearing your voice on the machine."

I hated that too: the subtle reminder that I didn't visit home often enough. But she and Dad lived in New Hampshire now, and getting all the way up there on the train took real planning. Plus, my parents were going through something weird. Dad was spending more and more time at his golf club and less and less with Mom, so her unspoken sadness filled a large amount of empty space in the house.

I let the call go to voicemail. *Hi honey, it's Mom. I'm sure you're out having fun, but I thought I'd take a chance anyway. Nothing much happening here. Dad's out, and I'm reading a really good mystery. Just... give us a call when you can. I love you, Molly. Good night.*

I envisioned her there in the living room with her reading lamp and cup of lukewarm tea: an unwilling victim of Dad's midlife crisis—or whatever it was—but taking it like a martyr. Restrained. Saintlike. A tear ran down my cheek, but I wasn't sure if it was for Mom or myself.

The Gotye song, "Somebody That I Used to Know" started playing on my cellphone, and I ran out of the bathroom to grab it. I'd liked the song enough to make it my ringtone, but that night, the words took on new meaning.

The caller's name came up as *A. Stevers*. As in Andy Stevers, the quiet, handsome, newish software engineer at FSI. But why would Andy call *me* on a Friday night? He and I got along fine at work—part of my marketing job involved writing whitepapers for our products, and Andy was one of the few engineers who responded in a timely fashion when I asked technical questions—but our relationship was strictly professional.

About half of the unmarried FSI employees had crushes on Andy. Probably some of the married ones too. But I did my best not to think about him that way. After all, until a few hours earlier, I'd been in a serious relationship with Joe. And Andy wouldn't waste his time on someone like me. Sure, I was smart, attractive, and reasonably cool, but Andy was on a whole different level.

He ate lunch with the elite engineers—most of whom were super nerdy and seemed to think sales, marketing, and customer support were all one big department—so he was probably brilliant. But unlike the other techies whose appearances ran the gamut from "regular" to "quirky" to "odd," Andy could've modeled for a perfume commercial or something. He had clear luminous skin, deep red lips, and wide-set brown eyes that brooded like James Dean's when he concentrated hard. And he must've known he bore a resemblance to the late movie star, because he usually combed his dirty blond hair back off his face, making his cut cheekbones look even more chiseled. But although he was nice and polite to everyone at work, he didn't flirt. In fact, no one knew if he was interested in men, women, both, or neither. Which only added to his natural allure.

"Hello?" I said. Even in my distressed state, I couldn't resist a call from Andy Stevers. But at first, only loud music and chatter came over the line. Had he butt-dialed me from a bar?

"Molly!" shouted a slurry voice I recognized as Diana's. Someone near the phone yelled something about the Pats while in the background, Taylor Swift sang about never *ever* getting back together with one of her many boyfriends.

"Diana? You okay?"

"Yeah! Whaddya doin'?"

No way was I telling her about Joe when she was drunk like that. "Um, I'm just... home. Joe's working late. But why'd you come up on my phone as *Andy Stevers*?"

Diana's voice dropped a few decibels. "I borrowed his cell. Mine's dead. But listen, Mol." Her voice got even softer. "You *gotta* get down here *now*! *Everyone* from marketing's here, plus most of sales, and some engineering too. Like *Andy*. He's never come out with us before. This is turning into the FSI event of the *year*."

I started to say I was too tired, but Diana interrupted. "Tired shmired. Trust me, you won't regret this. I'm ordering you a beer as we speak, so hurry up."

It was eight-thirty, and what else was I going to do? As exhausted as I felt, I knew I'd be awake for hours, and I really did want a drink. Or two, or three. "Um, I *guess* I can. I mean, Andy Stevers? Wow." Maybe Diana was right about it being the company event of the year. Especially since FSI wouldn't be around much longer. But most employees didn't know that. I was one of the few who knew that Brad, the owner, was actively looking for someone to buy it.

"Yup," said Diana. "But don't *you* be getting any ideas about Andy, lady. If that guy leaves here with *anyone*, it's gonna be me. You've got a boyfriend."

I sighed and felt the ache in my gut again. "You know, I've gotta take two buses to get over there. How late will you guys be out?"

"Late, Mol. Late. Okay?"

CHAPTER 5
BIG WHEEL

Molly
September 7, 2012
Everett, MA 9:45 PM

    Not everyone at work liked me. For starters, many of my peers were younger than me *and* better educated. I had a BA in English while most of them held marketing degrees, and a few had—or were working on—MBAs. And yet, I reported directly to Brad, the founder and CEO. I worked with the marketing team and wrote copy for almost all the company's campaigns—but Brad handled my annual reviews, and neither the marketing manager nor the director of the department could claim me as "their" employee. On the other hand, I was nobody's boss, which I also loved. My official title was "Senior Marketing Writer," and it was basically my dream job.

    Brad and I went all the way back to 2006, when I'd first interned at FSI—then a tiny, fledgling software startup—as a college sophomore. And since I was one of only three employees from that time period still working there, Brad treated me almost like family. The newer people didn't understand, though. And how could they? By the time most of them arrived at FSI, it'd become one of the fastest-growing businesses in Massachusetts. *The Boston Globe* loved featuring us in their business section, and we'd even gotten a few mentions in the *Wall Street Journal*.

    Not that I'd expected to fall into a career at FSI when I went on my first interview there; I'd simply been a college kid looking to land a paid internship. I did all kinds of crazy stuff for the company back then: whatever they needed on any given day. Sometimes I'd make coffee and vacuum the place, while other times, Brad would ask me to answer his phone so potential customers would think he had an assistant. Then there was the day he sent me out shopping with Sue, his wife, to buy office furniture and supplies. And when FSI's first product was about to launch, he asked me to design a little e-brochure and send it to all his professional contacts. He and I just hit it off, and Sue loved me too. So when I was getting ready to graduate college, Brad offered me a full-time marketing position.

It didn't seem weird at all when he took me out to lunch in early 2012, saying he wanted to talk business. But when we arrived at the restaurant and he asked for the most private table available, my gut sank. I knew something major was up.

"Listen, Molly," he began, "I haven't shared this with many people, but FSI's been kicking butt, and life's short. My own kids'll be in college in a few years, and I'd like to spend some quality time with the family — do some traveling, that sorta thing — before everyone scatters."

"So are you... taking time off?"

"You're on the right track," he said, opening his turkey sandwich and removing the tomato from it. Brad hated tomatoes. "Actually — between you and me and this wall here — I'm putting the company on the market."

"You mean—"

"Yeah. I feel guilty as hell, but I'm cutting loose. I've already missed a lot of important family stuff for work, and Sue and I aren't getting any younger."

But FSI was such a thriving, rocking company. "I don't... I mean, what'll happen to—"

"You? And everyone else? Well, first of all, we need to find a buyer. And depending on who that is — most likely a much larger company — some folks'll probably have the option of sticking around a while. But usually when there's an acquisition, sales and marketing are... you know." He clicked his tongue and made a gesture with his hand like he was showing someone the door. "Sent packing. But look on the bright side, Molly. Consider this an opportunity for you to do something different. Something amazing. You know I'll write you a glowing recommendation. But I suggest you get your resume in order."

My resume? "Brad, I don't have a resume. You hired me right out of school, remember?"

He raised his eyebrows. "Well, that's okay. You've got time. But listen. There's something else. Back when I brought you on, I had no clue where FSI was going. I had big dreams, a great wife, and that was about it. We got a little VC money, so those folks own a percentage of the company, and when Mark came on as VP of Sales, I gave him a chunk of equity. But I retained a majority share, and now Sue and I want you and the others who were here from the get-go to have a little piece of the pie. So we talked to our lawyer, and... well, I hope you'll be happy with your bonus, Molly. You deserve it."

I was speechless. I mean, I'd planned to stay at FSI at least until I got married. "Um, thank you, Brad. You and Sue are so cool." Then I burst into tears.

"Hey now, none o' that. This is your chance to show the world what Molly Dolan can do."

But Brad didn't know me as well as he thought he did. He didn't realize how much bad stuff I'd already experienced, and how scary looking for a new job seemed to me.

"Good luck finding a buyer," I muttered, blowing my nose into a napkin. But in my heart, I hoped FSI would remain in Brad's hands for a long, long time.

When I finally made it to El Chico—right around ten p.m.—I spotted most of my marketing coworkers sitting in the back, occupying a large booth and a few nearby tables. Leslie Ann, a manager with platinum-streaked hair, was holding court in a booth littered with cocktail glasses, many of them empty. As I approached, she said something that triggered bursts of laughter, but all I caught was the word *tomatoes*.

No one had noticed me yet. "Oh, everyone knows why he gives her tomatoes," said a sarcastic guy named Jason. "I just wonder what *else* she gets."

Tomatoes? Brad occasionally left tomatoes on my desk because they grew like crazy in his garden, and Sue was the only one in his family who liked them.

"Hi guys!" I said, sliding into the booth. "What's up?"

The group crashed into silence. "Hi Molly," said Leslie Ann. "Wh... ats up with *you*?"

"Not too much," I said, feeling slightly uncomfortable. I knew some people were jealous of my relationship with Brad, but surely they didn't think we had something sexual going on. That'd be gross.

"Molly Mc*Golly*! Where you been, girl?" said Jason, as if he and I were besties. *Oh god, had they been talking about me?*

"Just chillin' at home." *And maybe I should've stayed there?*

"Cool," said Jason. "We were just chatting about that website, *Rotten Tomatoes*, you know, where they rate movies? I'm *so* sick of it. It's like every time I love a new film, the critics *totally* trash it. I'm thinking of changing careers and becoming a movie critic. Whaddya think?"

"Go for it," said Leslie Ann. "You'd kick ass. But look! Molly needs a margarita. Where's that waitress?"

Another awkward silence might've ensued if Diana hadn't bolted up behind me right then and handed me a beer. "There you are, Mol. I thought you'd never get here. What took you so long?"

I thanked her and gulped some beer. "Bus got stuck in traffic. I got the next round, okay?"

"Sure," said Diana, looking voluptuous with her wavy red hair all loose around her shoulders. "Order me a Sam Adams if you can get the waitress's attention. Oh wait. Hang on a minute. I just thought of somethin' I gotta tell Andy." A second later, she was gone. Through the crowd, I glimpsed Andy sitting at the bar, chatting with another engineer.

"Poor Diana," said Jason. "She's hellbent on landing Rebel Without a Cause tonight, but she hasn't got a snowball's chance."

"Yeah," said Leslie Ann. "But it's cute watching her try so hard."

"Hey, who knows?" I said. "I think Andy and Diana would be adorable together." But as I swilled my beer, I couldn't help wondering what it'd be like to kiss him. The guy looked so regal and proper until he smiled. Then his dimples kicked in, and all of a sudden, he resembled a garage band drummer, or a surfer, or... something. His teeth were straight and white with tiny gaps between them, and for some reason, those gaps made him even sexier. Maybe an orthodontist would disagree, but FSI didn't employ any orthodontists.

Take it easy, Molly! I screamed silently. *You're losing your mind. Just drink your beer and go home. You're super vulnerable right now, and vulnerable people do dumb things.*

Leslie Ann dipped a chip into a bowl of guacamole on the table, and I couldn't help noticing how quiet everyone was being. "So I'm surprised to see you here, Molly," she said. "Aren't you usually out with your boyfriend on Fridays?"

"Yeah," I said, sucking down more beer, "but we might be breaking up. It's a long story. I'll tell you another time."

"Oh honey, tell us *now*," said Jason. "You know we're always here for you."

I looked up and down the table. Could I trust them? Normally, I didn't share much personal information with my coworkers, but maybe doing that'd help them understand me better. "So," I began, "I think he's been cheating. He showed up at my house tonight with another woman in the car. A younger one. It felt really fucked up."

"No way!" said Leslie Ann. "That's, like, insane. How long've you guys been together?"

"About four years," I said.

"Wait," said Jason. "So you're saying he wanted a *three-way*?"

"No! No, no, no! He just said he wanted to, you know, see other people or whatever. But can we stop talking about this now? It's literally hurting my stomach."

"Who's having a three-way?" asked Shane, a married guy from the sales department, wandering over from one of the other tables with a couple of shots in his hand. Shane Armstrong was about forty, but he still wore baggy chinos and untucked flannel shirts like a college kid. And although he cleaned up well for customer meetings, his face was always sunburned. The story was that he and his wife spent all their free time doing outdoorsy stuff like sailing and skiing. I'd met his wife—she stopped by the office once in a while—but she wasn't friendly to me. She reminded me of a bitchy girl from my college dorm.

Shane, on the other hand, acted sweet and down-to-earth at FSI, but Diana said he'd do almost anything to close a deal. According to her, most engineers despised him because he had a habit of lying to potential customers about our software's capabilities. Then he'd lean on the engineers to tweak the software so he could make the sale.

He made me nervous too. His eyes often lingered on me a little too long when he walked past my cube or when we saw each other in the hallway. I'd turn away so he wouldn't notice me blushing, but I think he knew. I had no interest in getting involved with a married guy, but did find him disturbingly attractive.

"Molly's boyfriend wanted one tonight," said Jason. "He brought a little hottie over to her house."

"No, it wasn't like that!" I insisted. "He's just a cheating bastard."

Jason turned to Shane. "You ever have a three-way, Shane-o?"

Shane squished up his large, handsome face. "Uh, not recently, but let's leave it right there." He sat down beside me. "So you gonna do it, Molly?"

My cheeks burned as I polished off the beer. "No. And don't listen to Jason. He's totally lying. I'm just... ugh. I'm just having a boyfriend issue. End of story." I hadn't eaten dinner, and the alcohol was going straight to my head.

"Anyone need another round?" asked the waitress, her forehead beaded with sweat.

People began ordering drinks, but I could feel Shane staring at the side of my face. Against my better judgment, I asked the waitress for a Sam Adams, and asked her to bring one to Diana over at the bar, too.

"All right, everyone," said Leslie Ann when the waitress left, "can you guys keep a secret? 'Cause you will *not* believe what I saw yesterday." Then she launched into a story about two employees from customer service kissing in the cafeteria. I couldn't have cared less, but Leslie Ann spoke in such a dramatic way that everyone gave her their full attention.

Or maybe I should say everyone except Shane, who'd pressed his leg hard against mine. "Wanna do a tequila shot?" he asked, indicating the two little glasses in front of him.

My pulse raced. "Thanks, but I hate tequila."

He nodded, downed one of the shots, winced, and tucked a strand of shaggy brown hair behind his ear. "So what's the deal with your boyfriend?"

"I don't know. He's just a jerk," I answered with a shrug. "But I'll figure it out. I'll get over him, you know?"

Over at the bar, Andy Stevers chatted with a guy from QA named Ashish while Diana stood behind them, looking forlorn. She'd obviously had a couple too many drinks already, and I was glad she lived in the new apartment complex down the road, an easy walk from El Chico. But based on the way Andy was acting, I felt pretty certain he wouldn't be taking that walk with her later on. Were it not for the beer in front of him, he could've been sitting in the FSI cafeteria, or in an engineering meeting in our conference room.

"How long were you guys together?" asked Shane as the waitress returned with the drinks. The zipper on the front of my sweater had slipped down a bit—revealing more cleavage than I normally would—and Shane's eyes hung there, shameless.

"Four years," I said, my breath shallow.

"Wow," he said. "That sucks. So you gonna give this guy another chance?" He moved his face closer to mine, and I had a wild urge to kiss him right there in front of everyone.

Instead, I sipped some of my fresh beer. "Prob'ly not. I mean, things between us've been messed up for a while. You know?"

Shane nodded and threw his arm around me like we were old drinking buddies. No one else appeared to notice, but my whole body heated up.

"I hear ya, Molly," he said, his words slurry, his breath smelling like warm tequila. "I been with a few losers too."

"Mmm," I said with a sigh. "Hey, so I should probably get going. I'm pretty tired."

"Aw, c'mon. Whatshu gonna do at home? At least finish your beer. Sure you don't wanna do a shot?"

"Yeah, no."

"Okay, then." He picked up the second glass and downed the liquor. "Damn, that shiz strong."

I laughed. "You should take it easy. You're not driving, are you?"

"Yeah, but don' worry. I'll be okay in a while. You wanna take a walk outside? I could use some air."

I considered that. His arm felt good around me, and he was so much bigger than Joe. Stronger. More confident. But married. *Yeah, married.* "Nah. Thanks. I'm gonna hit the bathroom, say goodnight to Di, and head out." I gulped a little more beer and grabbed my purse. "Nice talkin' to you, Shane." My head spun as he let me out of the booth, but I walked away as gracefully as possible. Damn, he was sexy, but I'd done the right thing.

When I reached the bar, though, I saw no sign of Diana. Andy turned away from Ashish and addressed me. "Hey, Molly. I didn't see you come in."

"Oh, hi Andy. Yeah, I'm actually on my way out now, but... you don't know where Di went, do you?"

He frowned and took a sip from a glass of water. A half-full beer still sat in front of him on the bar. "No, but I'm sure she's around. Hey, you got a minute? I wanna run somethin' by you. Ashish and I have an idea for a whitepaper we were thinking you might wanna write."

"Um... sure?"

The last thing I wanted to do was talk shop, but I couldn't say no to Andy. A blue fleece jacket hung over his barstool, and the little diamond logo on its breast pocket looked familiar, although I didn't know why. "Hey, what's that mean?" I asked, pointing to the logo.

He smiled his garage-band-drummer smile. "It's a local repeater society. One of my nerdy hobbies."

"Huh," I said, assuming it had something to do with software.

"You need something to drink, Molly?" asked Ashish.

"Oh, no, thanks," I replied. "But I am gonna use the bathroom. I'll be right back, okay?" *What a weird night.*

And then it got weirder. Because when I exited the bathroom, Shane was waiting for me in the dark little hallway, a chunk of hair hanging rakishly over one eye.

"Molly, Molly, Molly," he whispered, resting his large hands on my hips. His words sounded even more slurred than before, and he looked at me like I was some kind of supermodel. "You're so pretty, Molly. Like... a beautiful girl."

"Thank you?" I said, my legs turning to rubber. "But I've gotta—"

"Ssssh," he whispered, pressing his fingers gently over my mouth. His voice sounded heavy and wet. "See, I need a sales assistant. I know you're marketing, but I'm a good trainer." With his other hand, he grabbed my ass and squeezed, and I couldn't help gasping. "I want you, Molly."

I wasn't sure if he meant as an assistant or for sex—and I felt buzzed, needy, and confused—but I struggled to keep things on a professional level. "Aw, thanks, Shane," I said, talking faster than I could think. "And I'd love to work for you, but FSI's getting sold, so... I mean... I mean, what am I *saying*? I mean, I'm getting *old*, and I might move away, or... who knows? This's been a really long night. But thanks for the offer. Really. Thanks so much."

Oh god, I really *was* losing it.

"Huh?" said Shane, suddenly appearing slightly less drunk. "What'd you say about FSI?"

Shit. "Nothin'. I said *I'm* getting older, you know? An' I don't wanna switch jobs. You know?"

He looked confused. "Oh. I coulda sworn you said Brad was sellin' it."

Then he threw his arms around me and started kissing my face. His five-o'clock-shadow scratched my chin, and his neck smelled like some kind of guy's deodorant soap, but I pulled him closer and dissolved into his warmth. His marriage—*a piece of paper, a stupid legal document*—blew through my brain and got caught in the pile of debris at the back of my head, along with all the other stuff I didn't wanna think about.

"C'mon," he said, giving me a little push toward the emergency exit that everyone knew wasn't actually alarmed. "My car's right out back. Privacy."

"No. Dude. I can't."

"Oh please, Molly. Please. Just a lil' more. Just kissin'. I promise. You're so fuckin' beautiful."

The El Chico hallway was a dangerous place to be making out with a married coworker, and kissing Shane felt good. Maybe a little too good. "Okay," I panted. "But just kissing. *Only* kissing."

"Promise. Let's go."

Holding hands, we slipped outside. The night air felt clear and cool, and a reckless sensation overcame me. Screw the rules! Joe didn't care, and he'd broken my heart. I could be a little bit bad too. No one needed to know.

But right then, I spotted a male figure on the other side of the parking lot. "Hey! You guys okay?" he called. His voice was familiar, but in my heated state, I didn't place it right away.

"We're fine," said Shane.

The man walked toward us anyway. "You sure?"

"Nosy prick," muttered Shane.

"Yeah!" I called. "No worries!"

The guy stopped and pulled something that looked like a cellphone out of his pocket as Shane opened the door of his black SUV.

"Dude!" shouted Shane. "Go 'way. We good."

"Who *is* that?" I whispered, as Shane helped me into the back seat. But even as the words left my mouth, I realized it was Andy Stevers. *The whitepaper.* I'd promised to go back and talk to him and Ashish.

"Some software douche," answered Shane, climbing in with me, closing the door, and pulling me close. His tone softened. "Holy shit, Molly. You got pretty eyes."

Joe hadn't called me pretty in over a year. "Thanks. But Shane, your wife—"

"She'll ne'er find out." He started kissing me again, tenderly at first, then with more force. I felt guilty, but since we'd been kissing in the hallway, that harm had already been done. Right? I wanted to run my hands up and down his body, but hung onto his shoulders instead.

A minute later, though, he touched my stomach, underneath my sweater. "Hey, what're you doing? We agreed... " But I could feel my resolve fading. And above the waist was probably okay. So I slipped my hands under his shirt. Warm skin. I breathed him in and relaxed.

"This okay?" he asked. "Can I touch here?"

"Just a little," I said. He'd started circling my nipple with his finger, and his heart was beating so fast. Everything inside me ached for him, and I desperately wanted to feel him, naked against my body.

"I gotta take off your pants," he said, pressing his tongue deep into my mouth.

That's when the buzzer in my brain went off. I think it had something to do with the way he said *pants.* It sounded crass and dirty, causing the spell he'd cast over me to shatter like a cheap Christmas ornament. Glancing down, I saw that he'd already opened his fly, and before I could react, he was easing me back onto the seat.

"Hey, wait. This isn't okay." I would *not* have sex with Shane in the El Chico parking lot. No way.

He touched my crotch and my head reeled. "It's fine," he said.

But it wasn't. It was all wrong. "No. Stop."

His face turned dark red and his eyes took on a strange glow. "It's okay, Molly. Calm down."

"No, goddamn it," I said, shoving him away. "Cut the shit. You're married. I'm outta here. Now."

"C'mon, Molly. Don't fuck with me."

I started getting really pissed. At him, at myself, at Joe. I felt sweaty and gross too. Luckily, my bus stop was only a block away. Adjusting my sweater, I grabbed my purse and threw open the car door. "Don't worry. I won't."

Shane seemed shocked, as if no woman had ever rejected him before, and my wine-colored lipstick smeared on his face and neck made him look like an angry clown. "Fuck you, Molly," he muttered.

"Yeah, whatever." But as I stepped down onto the pavement—slamming the door behind me—I saw Jason, Leslie Ann, and a woman with a blonde ponytail coming toward me. Fast. Jason called out my name, and that's when I realized the blonde was Shane's wife, Vanessa. *Oh my god.*

"What's going on?" asked Vanessa, walking even faster.

"Where's Shane?" said Jason.

I smoothed my hair and wiped my mouth. "He's, um, in the car. He's pretty drunk."

"Yeah," said Jason. "That's why I called Vanessa. Dude's in no condition to drive. But... what're you doin' out here, Molly?"

The top of my head burned. "Uh, I was on my way to the bus stop when I ran into him." Turning to Vanessa, I said, "I'm really glad you're here to drive him home."

"Uh huh." Vanessa pushed past me and flung open the SUV's door. I was standing right behind her, so I saw everything.

Shane lay sprawled on the back seat with his eyes closed and his pants still unzipped. "Ha! I knew you'd be back," he said in a nasty tone.

"Shane! You fucker!" screamed Vanessa. "You can't lie this time. There's lipstick all over you."

He sat up slowly. "Oh, fuck." Then he saw me, and his drunken eyes became cruel little slits. "Molly, you betta tell 'er what happened or I will. Ya hear me?"

"The truth?" I said.

"Whaddya think?" Then, before I could say a word, he addressed his wife. "She jumped me, babe. I'm not kiddin'. Fuckin' jumped me. It was all her. Now *you* tell 'er, Molly," he said, turning to me. "I wanna hear it from *you*."

Jason and Leslie Ann stood behind us, taking it all in. "Shane," I said, trying to remain calm, "that's bullshit. We're both guilty."

Vanessa started crying, and for the first time, I noticed the pregnancy bump under her tight pink t-shirt.

"Don't listen to 'er, baby. She's trashed," said Shane. "You know I'd never cheat at a time like this."

Vanessa's crying intensified. "I don't know what to believe!" she wailed. "I wanna trust you, Shane, but—"

"You *gotta* trust me," he said. "I'm your husband, and I love you, Van. She's a... I don't wanna say the word, but you know what I mean. Ask anyone. She's not like us, Van."

I was stunned by his acting ability, especially while drunk. No wonder he closed so many sales deals. All I wanted was to get in the shower and wash his slime off me. Then, with any luck, no one would ever mention this night again. "Go fuck yourself, Shane. I gotta catch a bus."

"See?" said Shane. "She's a coward too."

I wanted to scream that he was the coward, but my throat was tight with tears, so I just started walking.

"Wait, Molly," said Leslie Ann. "I'll drive you home."

But I ignored her and kept going. I could see my bus waiting at the stop.

Chapter 6
Lover's Cross

Molly
October, 2008
Spencer-Simon College
Newton, MA 11:00 PM

I sat on the steps outside the student union building, finishing off a Marlboro Light. Indoors, the annual Halloween mixer rocked and pulsated, but I didn't want to be there. I'd only bought a ticket to deter Becca, my roommate, from hosting a dinner party at our place that night. I may have disliked mixers, but I really loathed hosting parties. Sometimes I got claustrophobic — even panicky — when more than a few guests visited our small off-campus apartment. Especially if they stayed late. So I'd convinced Becca to attend the mixer with me instead.

But all that boozy twerking and grinding to Coldplay, Flo Rida and T-Pain was *so* not my scene. If I could just hold out for one more hour, I'd be able to justify telling Becca I was heading home to crash. And if I could spend the majority of that hour outdoors, all the better. It was a beautiful night, and unseasonably warm for late October. Perfect for smoking cigarettes.

College had turned me into a weekend smoker, which was *sort of* a good thing, because I drank less when I smoked. But I'd also been coughing a lot more than usual. Life was so complicated.

Anyway, the nice weather had enticed lots of students out from wherever they would've been on a less gorgeous night, and many of the ones I spotted were clearly under the influence of intoxicating substances. One in particular caught my eye: a senior classmate named Ethan Fricke. Ethan looked *really* messed up. At one point, he actually walked straight into a guy who was texting on the lawn. "Yo, dude!" said the guy who'd been bumped, but Ethan continued on, clueless and unapologetic.

I felt bad for him, and it didn't hurt that he was super cute. Some girls I knew had nicknamed him *chubby Zac Efron* because he resembled a bulkier version of the gorgeous actor. "Hey, Ethan, you okay?" I called, standing up slowly and approaching him. I wasn't sure he knew my name, but figured he'd probably recognize me from around campus.

"What are *you*?" he asked, his breath reeking of pot. "You got red shoes."

"Yeah, I'm Dorothy from *The Wizard of Oz*." I clicked the heels of my makeshift costume and saw that he was wearing a New York Jets jersey. "And you're a baseball player, right?"

"No. Jets play football."

"Oh, sorry. I don't know sports."

He assessed me with his hazel eyes and took a few steps toward me. "Can I kiss you?" he asked.

I'd kissed plenty of drunk and stoned guys in college, but couldn't recall anyone asking so politely. "Um, sure?" I said, tilting my head to one side.

Tentatively, Ethan took both my hands and kissed my lips in a soft-but-not-wimpy way. A little thrill shot through me, and I kissed him back. Then we looked at each other and smiled. I'm not sure I'd ever experienced a sweeter moment.

"What's your name?" he asked.

"Molly."

"Hi Molly. Can we kiss again?"

The next kiss was more passionate, but still polite. I felt a little like we were playing spin the bottle at a party.

A couple of guys walked by, and one called out the requisite, "Get a room!" My thoughts exactly.

"So," I said, stopping for breath. "Do you... wanna go to my apartment?"

Confusion clouded Ethan's face again. "Uh, no. I can't. I... yeah. But I'll see you around, okay?"

"Um, sure?" Of course I was surprised and a little hurt, but I'd learned the hard way that the fastest way to freak a guy out was to act smitten right off the bat.

"Okay," Ethan repeated. Then he took off, half jogging across campus.

Oh well. It was only October. I'd have plenty more chances with him before graduation.

IT DOESN'T HAVE TO BE THAT WAY

And I did. Suddenly, Ethan was everywhere. Maybe he'd always been around and I just hadn't noticed, but after Halloween, I spotted him at all kinds of school events, off-campus bars, and house parties.

He and I wouldn't start talking right away, though. We'd usually steal glances at each other from across the room for a while, and I'd wonder if perhaps he'd lost interest in me. But after a few drinks, we'd inevitably wind up near the keg together, or sitting on the same couch, or stepping outside for a breath of fresh air at the same time. Then, we'd make more intense eye contact, and shortly thereafter, we'd find ourselves groping each other like animals.

In bad weather, we'd slip off into a dark corner, an empty bedroom, or even a closet. But if it was nice outside, we'd just duck behind some trees or a building. Twice, we attempted drunken intercourse—and possibly even succeeded—but most of our activity involved clumsy kissing, touching, rubbing, a good deal of heavy breathing, and very little conversation. All of which I enjoyed, except for the very end. Because at some point before crashing someplace together, Ethan would always announce that he needed to leave.

Now if I'd been more confident, I would've just asked him why. Like me, he lived in an off-campus apartment, and every week—as I attended classes and worked at my FSI internship—I'd fantasize about waking up in his arms on a Saturday or Sunday morning. But our weekend hookups, regardless of how sweaty or sexual, always ended in separation. Even worse, Ethan didn't provide excuses I could investigate. In other words, he wouldn't say he needed to study for a big history exam the following week, or claim that his parents were coming to take him to breakfast in the morning. He'd just say he needed to go. Then he would.

"Maybe he has, like IBS, or something," suggested my roommate Becca one Sunday morning as I made coffee. "Or maybe he wets the bed. Some grownups do, you know."

I hit the *brew* switch, and Googled *adult bedwetting*. "Enuresis is more common in men than women," I read out loud. "According to research, one in every hundred adult males wets the bed."

"See! Told you," said Becca.

I went on reading to myself about medications that can help with the condition, and alarms that can wake a person before they have an accident. "Sounds manageable," I said.

Becca got up and checked the coffee. "I guess. Of course, he might just have an ugly schlong and doesn't want you to see it in daylight."

I knew she was trying to make me laugh, but I wasn't in a jokey mood. "No. I've seen it in pretty good lighting. It's nice."

"Well then, I'm going with the medical thing. But you should probably confront the dude. You've screwed him, after all. It's not like he's some kinda stranger."

But Ethan *felt* like a stranger to me, in many ways. We were learning how to touch each other and make each other feel *really* good. His thoughts, though, remained a mystery.

The shrink I saw for several months after my high school 'incident' had advised me to take it slow with men in college.

"Don't rush into intimate relationships," she said when I confessed how badly I longed for a nice boyfriend. "High school has been challenging for you, and you'd be smart to focus on making new *friends* before you embark on college dating."

Ha! Sure, I nodded and agreed, but I was on a mission. High school hadn't been a challenge; it'd been a disaster. I'd never even kissed a boy, and I needed to fix that. Fast.

Freshman year in college, then, I abandoned all control and entertained a steady parade of males, all quite willing to fool around with me while intoxicated. By December, I'd actually lost count of how many sweaty dudes had disentangled themselves from my damp bed sheets on weekend mornings, pulling on pants and promising to call soon.

"Cool," I'd reply nonchalantly. I'd usually roll over and pretend to go back to sleep. Because everyone knows guys avoid clingy girls like they're diseased. Especially girls who act clingy from the beginning.

But once the guy was out the door, I'd lie awake with my eyes open, hoping he'd turn around and come back. I'd think about the way he'd kissed, the way he'd smelled, the way he'd held me. Wouldn't he like me as a steady girlfriend? I mean, we'd had fun together, right? And if we became a couple, he could have me whenever he wanted. Three girls on my dorm floor were already in committed relationships with boys they'd met that year; boys they'd hooked up with once or twice before getting serious. When would my turn happen?

That's when I'd restart the clock in my head: the clock that kept track of each hour and day that passed after an awkward Saturday or Sunday morning goodbye. But inevitably, Friday would roll around with no word from the dude. So I'd head back out fishing again. On occasion, I'd do a double—the slang term Becca and I used for hooking up with same guy two weeks in a row—but for some reason, twice seemed to be my limit. After two, the dude's interest in me waned. Fast. At best, then, I was a two-night stand.

But Ethan was different. Not only did he keep returning week after week, he made no empty promises. He never said he'd call or text; he just *showed up*. So many guys lied with their mouths, but not Ethan. The way I saw it, he used his body to tell the truth.

In fact, I was fantasizing about Ethan's body one Friday afternoon in April as I darted into the school cafeteria with an airtight plan for the next twelve hours: scarf down a tuna sandwich, run to my internship, knock off early, hurry home, shower, and head out for the evening with Becca. Graduation loomed just five weeks away—in other words, Ethan and I needed to get serious soon—and several big parties were happening around campus that night.

The air radiated with the pregnant, muddy smell of spring, and hope surged through my veins. I'd bought a sexy new pink sundress that really accentuated my legs and breasts, and even Becca agreed that Ethan wouldn't be able to ignore me in it. As I gazed around the cafeteria looking for a seat, I imagined him unzipping the dress in my bedroom. Radiohead would be playing on the stereo, I'd kill the lights, and he'd slip the straps off my shoulders. Then the two of us would collapse on the bed like movie stars, and all those months of waiting would pay off.

We'd already made a huge breakthrough the previous Saturday night behind the school library. I'd given Ethan a hand job while he rubbed my crotch, and we'd had *almost* simultaneous orgasms. And right before he left, he'd said, "I wish I could sleep with you, Molly."

So the stage was set. We were both ready.

"Hi Molly," Lucinda called from a table behind the salad bar, startling me back to reality.

"Hey Luce." Lucinda and I had never been close, but we'd lived in the same dorm freshman year. I'd always felt a bit sorry for her because she hardly ever partied on weekends; instead, she'd hang out in the hallway on Friday and Saturday nights, knitting and chatting with the other girls as we came and went.

"How've you been?" asked Lucinda.

The last thing I wanted to do was make small talk. But Lucinda looked lonely, and I had to sit someplace.

"I'm okay. Just rushing around. I gotta be downtown in less than an hour. Can I join you for a minute?"

"Sure," said Lucinda. "What's downtown?"

I sat and took a big bite of my sandwich. "Internship," I said, chewing and gulping some Diet Coke. "The boss offered me a job after graduation. I'm psyched."

"That's awesome."

"Definitely," I said, taking another bite. Lucinda's oversized handmade sweater looked like something my mom would wear. "So what're you up to? Any idea what you'll do when we get outta here?"

A mischievous smile spread across the girl's face. "Sorta," she said, leaning across the table toward me. "But don't tell anyone 'cause I don't have a job yet. But yesterday, my boyfriend asked me to move to New York with him. New York *City*. Believe it or not, he got a job on the *stock exchange*. I keep pinching myself in case I'm dreaming." Then, to illustrate I guess, she pinched her cheek hard.

"Wow. That's so cool." I tried not to sound patronizing, but couldn't imagine Lucinda having fun, even in New York.

"I know. I haven't told my parents yet, though."

I chewed and glanced at the clock on the wall. "Hmm. Do they like your boyfriend?"

"Oh yeah," said Lucinda. "Everyone likes him. You've met him, I think. Ethan Fricke? Finance major? Kinda cute and really quiet?"

I coughed up a clot of tuna. "Ethan?"

"Uh huh. We live together this year, but I'm still a little shocked. I mean, moving to New York's a big deal."

My throat felt paralyzed, like I couldn't swallow. I sat there staring at Lucinda's round face, utterly stunned. Could *two* Ethan Frickes exist? At the same small school?

"You okay, Mol? Are you choking?"

Choking, no, but maybe having a stroke. Because I couldn't move. Lucinda and Ethan? *Impossible*. But even as I denied it, a blurry memory of the two of them going to a semiformal together freshman year drifted through my brain. Some girls had set them up, but only because they'd wanted Lucinda to have a date for the dance. It wasn't supposed to turn into anything! My arms started trembling.

"Molly?" Lucinda looked terrified. "Do you need help?"

I was gonna puke. "Something... wrong way," I said, standing and covering my mouth with a napkin as my stomach retched. The bathroom was over by the doorway, and I wasn't sure I'd make it.

"Lemme help you," said Lucinda, grabbing my arm.

"No!" I said, shoving her away and bolting.

"Feel better, Mol," she called after me. "I'll take care of your tray."

All weekend long, I stayed in my room, sick and unable to eat or study. Becca tried to console me, but nothing helped.

By the following Tuesday, I was back in class, but my college partying days had officially ended. When I returned the pink sundress to the mall store, I actually cried when the cashier asked if I wanted to exchange it for something else.

"No," I said, sobbing. "I've got enough clothes."

The poor cashier, who was only about a year older than me, frowned and handed me my money without another word, and I spent a chunk of it on a jug of wine at the package store on the way home.

The only thing that cheered me up—because the wine only made me sadder—was Becca assuring me she hadn't seen Ethan anywhere since my ill-fated lunch with Lucinda. Maybe he'd spotted us eating together in the cafeteria, or maybe she'd told him about our weird conversation. But whatever the reason, he was lying low too.

I considered hunting down his apartment and confronting him, but what good would that do? Not to mention that poor Lucinda didn't deserve to witness such a thing. She'd sounded so excited about moving to New York with Ethan, and who knows? Maybe he'd start being faithful to her now.

In any case, Ethan Fricke was no longer my business. My business was accepting the fact that yet another one of my dreams was dead.

Chapter 7
Hey Tomorrow

Molly
September 8, 2012
Arlington, MA

As soon as I opened my eyes to the morning, I knew I'd had a rough night. My brain quivered in that unique way it does when attempting to shake off an overload of bad stuff, and my stomach prickled with a blend of hunger and disgust. My left knee ached too. But why?

For one precious minute, my mind drew a blank. I did the math and determined it was Saturday, but Joe wasn't in bed beside me. Because... oh. Yeah. Then it all started flooding back, and those cold floodwaters showed no mercy. I saw the woman in the sporty white car and me shouting at Joe, and then... wait. Wait. Had I almost fucked Shane Armstrong? Yes. And... his wife appeared in the parking lot, and...

I sprang out of bed and ran to the bathroom, making it just in time to puke in the toilet. Most of what came out was nasty yellow fluid, but I dry heaved for what felt like fifteen minutes, snot streaming from my nose and tears rolling down my face.

Eventually, though, my body relaxed, and I washed my face with warm water and crawled back into bed. Surely something good had happened in the midst of all that awfulness. I mean, Diana had been at El Chico, and Andy Stevers too. Andy, who'd wanted my thoughts on a whitepaper. What a clusterfuck. How would I ever face people at work on Monday? I closed my eyes and tried to go back to sleep. As if.

The coffeemaker was leaking again, and this time, I couldn't blame Joe. *Seriously?* It'd leaked the previous Saturday too, but Joe sucked at making coffee, so I'd assumed he'd screwed something up. But when brown water and gunk started oozing out of the machine the morning after the Shane Armstrong travesty, I realized my problems were bigger than Joe.

"What the actual fuck!" I yelled, temporarily forgetting about Jeanette sleeping upstairs. Jeannette—who wrote her erotic novels under the *nom de plume* Ginette de Montreux—was pretty chill, but she could get bitchy when someone disturbed her sleep. She tended to work late into the night, then sleep until noon or later.

A minute later, someone knocked on my door. My first thought was Jeannette, but why would she go through the trouble of leaving her apartment and knocking when she could just stomp on the floor like she usually did when she wanted my attention?

Was it Joe? Oh lord, I didn't wanna see him. Not yet anyway. I looked like shit and stank of vomit. Plus, I hated him. I tiptoed across the room and peeked out the window, but saw no car in the driveway or on the street out front. Weird. Joe hated the bus. Could it be a religious canvasser or something? At 8:30 on a Saturday morning?

Knock, knock, knock.

"Hang on!" I shouted, whispering, "fuck you," under my breath. I caught a glimpse of myself in the mirror on the wall. *Matted hair. Dark circles. Ugh.*

Knock, knock, knock.

"Coming!" *What the hell?*

But as I gripped the doorknob, I froze. *What if it was Shane Armstrong? Or Shane and his wife?* My legs stiffened and my heart pounded, but I forced myself to look through the peephole.

Oh my god! Mr. Flaherty stood on the steps, looking uncomfortable. My sigh of relief was so loud he probably heard it through the door. Not that I wanted to see him either, but he was better than any of the other alternatives. Had his cat escaped again?

"Molly!" he said when I opened the door. "Are you all right?"

"Yeah?" I answered, puzzled by the concern on his face. "Are *you*?"

He half-winced. "Pretty good. Kitty's settling into his new home. But you took quite a toss on my sidewalk last night. I wanted to help, but you were gone by the time I made it to the door."

My knee. Suddenly, I remembered falling on the way home from the bus stop. I'd actually caught my toe on one of those sidewalk cracks Flaherty had tried to get the town to fix.

"Oh yeah," I said, rubbing my sore leg. "Yeah, I'm fine. A little bruised, but no blood. Thanks for checking on me, though." Any other time, I would've at least *asked* if he wanted to come in, but not that day. I felt pukey again and dizzy too. Plus, I didn't even have coffee to offer the guy.

"Well, that's good to hear. But I knew it was only a matter of time before someone got hurt out there. And next time, it could be worse. You didn't bump your head, did you?"

I smiled the best smile I could manage for my poor, concerned neighbor. "No, just the leg. But it's fine. Really. Thanks again for coming by, Mr. Flaherty. The town really needs to fix that sidewalk, huh?"

He shook his head and muttered *damn town workers* under his breath before sighing and addressing me again. "I'll tell you what, Molly. How 'bout *you* give the DPW a call Monday morning. That might help. I'm sure they're sick of hearing from me, but maybe if they got a call from a young person they'd pay attention. Especially since you got hurt. They should worry about getting sued."

I already knew I wouldn't call, but I really needed to lie down. "Um, okay. I'll try. You know, I work on Mondays, but I'll definitely try."

"Aw, that's great, Molly. I appreciate it. Nothing to it but to do it."

"Right." I was just about to close the door, when Flaherty took a deep breath and focused his hazel eyes on mine. "Molly," he said, dropping his voice, "I hate to ask, but did you have too much to drink last night?"

Something like an electric current shot through me. I mean, my personal life was none of his business. He'd crossed a line. "Um... no, actually. And I've gotta go. I'm working on something for my job."

"Oh, hey. Don't be mad, Molly. I just... well, I shouldn't say this, but I've been around the block a few times and I've seen girls get into a lotta trouble with booze. And I'd hate for anything bad to happen to you."

I wasn't sure what to say. Part of me wanted to call him out for being sexist; I mean, alcohol can get *girls* in trouble? What the fuck? *Shane* was the one who'd been trashed. *He* needed to worry about alcohol, not me. But I couldn't help feeling flattered too. At least Flaherty cared. "I'm not mad, Mr. Flaherty. But I really gotta go. Okay?"

"Yeah. Take good care, Molly," he said. Then he turned and limped away.

I closed the door behind him, my head spinning. "Crazy-ass dude," I said out loud. The coffee disaster in the kitchen would get cleaned up later. I was going back to bed.

Chapter 8
A Long Time Ago

Molly
2001
North Andover, MA

My parents first learned of Kate's existence one evening at Sunday dinner in October, 2001. A month earlier, our country had been viciously attacked, and most Americans—whether we knew it or not—remained in shock. We'd never imagined having to process such an extreme amount of horror and pain. Yes, airports had reopened and most of us were going through the motions of working and studying, but our heads and hearts were locked in grief mode.

And the threats kept coming. Every day, we awoke to fresh stories of terrorism and anthrax in the mail. Several innocent, totally unsuspecting people had already died after opening suspicious packages, and no one had any clue as to who the next victim might be. Nobody felt safe.

Perhaps that's why patriotism blossomed almost overnight in North Andover. In past years, flag owners in town—maybe ten percent of the population—tended to break out Old Glory on July 4th, Veteran's Day, and Memorial Day. But during fall of 2001, homes *not* displaying at least one flag constituted the minority. Red, white, and blue banners hung in windows of homes, office buildings, and restaurants. People draped them over barn doors, mounted them on pickup trucks, displayed them on t-shirts, and pinned them to lapels in record numbers.

Meanwhile, most locals who normally decorated for Halloween chose to skip the fake gravestones and plastic skeletons. Which totally made sense, but as a high school freshman, I found the glut of flags more disturbing than ghoulish stuff. Of course, people flew them as reminders of America's bravery and power, but all they did for me was keep the fear of another attack at the forefront of my brain.

Not to mention that I was also dealing with *personal* stress totally unrelated to 9/11. Because that year, I'd enrolled in our town's public education system after attending grades K-8 in Catholic school. All summer, I'd stressed out about the change, even though my parents, friends, and a handful of neighbors spent hours reassuring me I'd adapt easily to life at North Andover High. Then, after only a few days there, 9/11 happened and everyone's attention shifted to bigger things. Which I understood. But it sure didn't help me feel more welcome in public school.

Meanwhile, Mom obsessed over terrorist stuff for weeks. She didn't stop going to her job as a paralegal, but spent most of her free time on the Internet, investigating theories on the likelihood of Al Qaeda targeting Boston next. And apparently, lots of folks online harbored similar concerns, because every night at dinner, Mom would share her terrifying new fears with us.

And speaking of dinner, Mom took a post-9/11 vacation from cooking as well, claiming she had no energy for it. But Dad and I couldn't cook much more than pancakes and scrambled eggs—and my brother Tim was away at college—so the family had been on an almost exclusive diet of takeout food.

My dad balanced the lack of homemade food by drinking more alcohol. I don't know if the liquor made the fast food taste better, or if Dad just couldn't handle Mom's anxiety. In any case, he'd have a Jack and Coke as soon as he got home from work, another with his pizza, (or Chinese food, or chicken wings), and at least one more after dinner.

For me, it felt like all our family problems had been placed under a magnifying glass. Mom had always been somewhat fragile, and Dad had a habit of over-imbibing. But that fall, Mom seemed ready to snap at any second, and Dad was tipsy—if not drunk—every single night. Is it any wonder, then, that I was drawn to Kate, who seemed remarkably brave and stable?

In October, Mom's boss convinced her to see a therapist, and some of her paranoia subsided.

"I hope everything tastes okay," she said one evening in November, her face flushing as we sat down to the first real dinner she'd cooked in months. She'd set the table with candles and our best china. "Molly, I left the roast medium rare for you."

"Thanks, Mom," I said with as much enthusiasm as I could muster. "That's really nice of you. But... I'm not eating meat anymore. I'm a vegetarian now."

IT DOESN'T HAVE TO BE THAT WAY

The color in her cheeks faded. "A vegetarian? Why, honey?"

I'd been dreading that question since I got my first whiff of the roast cooking earlier. "Um, I haven't eaten meat for the last few weeks. My friend Kate at school's a veg too, and she's been teaching me a lot. Like *a lot*. Like, it's so terrible how animals are murdered for food. I don't wanna be involved in that anymore."

Dad fixed his glassy eyes on me. He'd had two Jack and Cokes already, and had opened a bottle of red wine for dinner. "Stop talking crazy, Molly. No one's murdering anything around here, and your poor mother's been working on this meal for hours."

"I know," I said, doing my best to communicate my shared concern for Mom. "And I'm psyched about the potatoes and carrots. But, you know, someone *did* kill the cow. And... I don't wanna eat her."

"Her?" repeated Dad. "Molly, what the hell? Your mother didn't kill a cow. Now cut this out and have your dinner."

"I know *Mom* didn't kill her, Dad. It's not her fault. Or yours. I just don't wanna eat the cow. Okay?"

Dad's eyes widened. "No. *Not* okay! We're not puttin' up with this. You'll eat the goddamn beef or you'll spend the night in your room."

What? "Dad, I'm hungry and I'm not a baby!"

"Don't be so hard on her, Ken," said Mom. "It's just one meal." But she sounded anxious and hurt. "Molly, honey, who *is* this Kate?"

I took a sip of water. "She's a new friend at school, and she has a book that shows how animals are slaughtered. It's called *Dead Meat*. And then there's this band called the Smiths—well, they actually broke up a while ago—but their lead singer—a guy named Morrissey— loves animals *a lot*, and I've been listening to their records a lot, and... yeah. So I don't wanna eat any more meat."

"*What?*" said Dad.

Mom took a deep breath and shook her head. "All right, then," she said. "Don't eat the roast. But protein's important for growing girls. Let me heat up a can of beans."

I only liked beans if they were cooked in something like soup or chili. The thought of a can of beans alone sounded disgusting. But my dad was getting really pissed.

"Why don't I go make a peanut butter sandwich?" I suggested.

"Oh for god's sake!" said Dad. "Cut this crap out *now* and eat the food your mother prepared."

Just the sight of the chunk of beef in the middle of the table made me wanna barf. "Dad, I can't—"

"Yes you can."

"Ken, don't make her," said Mom, reaching for the bottle of wine and pouring some into her glass. Mom hardly ever drank alcohol.

"She's acting crazy," he insisted. "She'll eat this food and she'll like it."

Oh no I wouldn't. "Dad, listen to this thing Morrissey said, okay? He said, 'How come people get all upset when an animal eats a human, but no one pays any attention when people eat animals?'"

"Ahhhhh!" yelled Dad, throwing up his hands in frustration. "What kinda moron is this guy? Anyone with half a brain knows animals were put on Earth for people to eat."

But I'd gone way too far down the Morrissey road to even consider rationale like that. "That's freakin' creepy!" I said, jerking my chair back and jumping to my feet. "I'm goin' to my room 'cause I *wanna*, not 'cause you sent me."

"Now look what you've done, Ken," said Mom as I bolted up the stairs.

"Don't blame me!" Dad shouted. "Blame her wacky new friend!"

Chapter 9
The Hard Way Every Time

Molly
September 8, 2012
Arlington, MA

By ten a.m., I'd cleaned up the coffee mess and showered too. I looked acceptable, but couldn't bear the thought of going out, even though Starbucks was just a few blocks away. The fuzz in my brain had dissipated, leaving it free and clear to obsess over the Shane Armstrong situation from the previous night. What would my coworkers think of me? I filled the kettle to make tea, hoping to find a movie on *Lifetime* or the *Hallmark Channel* to escape into for a couple of hours.

But peace wasn't in the cards for me that morning, because right before the kettle whistled, Mom called the home phone. I didn't pick up and she didn't leave a message. *Please,* I thought, turning off the burner. *Please leave me alone.*

A second later, though, my cellphone went off. Guilt chewed at my stomach as Gotye sang about his addiction to certain types of sadness. "Somebody That I Used to Know" had officially become my least favorite song.

Of course, I didn't want Mom worrying about me; I just didn't feel like talking to *anyone,* so I hoped she'd find something else to do for a while. But if she called a third time, I'd have no choice. Three Mom calls in a row meant panic was setting in, and a police car in my driveway might be next. It drove me crazy that she couldn't forget my one big mistake from high school, especially since I'd made so many intelligent decisions in recent years. And on those times when I *did* screw up—like I had with Shane—I didn't tell her. So why did she *still* always think the worst?

The landline bleated again and I grabbed it on the first ring. "Hi Mom. Sorry I missed you before. I was in the bathroom."

"Oh, honey! I'm so glad you picked up. I was just starting to get concerned."

Starting? "Mom, I'm fine."

"I know. I just... so how *are* you, honey?"

"Like I said, fine. Just really tired. I went out with friends from work last night and we stayed out late. I'm taking it easy today." As I spoke, I plopped onto the couch and pulled a throw blanket over my legs.

"Oh. I thought maybe you went out with Joe."

"No. Joe's working all weekend on some big project."

"I see. But you're sure you're okay, honey? Your voice sounds sad."

I sighed silently and took a deep breath. "Mom, why do you keep asking that?" I knew I wasn't helping my case by sounding irritable, but I couldn't help it. What would it take for her to trust me?

"Okay. Okay. It's just that you... oh, I don't know. When're you coming home to visit, honey? It's been quite a while, you know."

The last time I'd gone to New Hampshire had been July 4th weekend, and it'd been a shitshow. I'd brought Joe along, and when my sister-in-law—she and my brother lived a block away from my parents—caught us smoking weed in her backyard, she'd had a hissy fit. Not only did she banish Joe from her property forever, but also claimed that my little nephews were scarred for life.

"Yeah, I'll come visit soon, I promise. But don't forget, you're always welcome down here too." That sounded nice, but was actually a mean thing to say. Mom didn't drive on highways anymore, and she'd never been comfortable on trains. Plus, she was my mom and she was lonely. I needed to make more of an effort.

"I know, honey. It's just that, well, I didn't wanna mention this, but I've gotta touch of sciatica right now. Nothing serious, but the doctor said it needs rest to go away. So I'm tryna stay off my feet as much as possible."

"Sciatica, Mom?" I wasn't exactly sure what that was, but Brad complained about it sometimes. He said it was painful. "Why didn't you tell me?"

That's another mean thing I'd do to Mom. If I found out she'd withheld any personal medical information from me, I'd make her feel guilty. But when she did tell me about a health concern, I'd make light of the situation and change the subject. I hated acknowledging that my parents were getting older. Deep down, I longed to have better relationships with them, but actually talking to them was hard.

"Oh it's nothing, honey. Nothing at all. I shouldn't've mentioned it. But...," she stopped to take a breath, "I do have one favor to ask."

"Cookies, right?" I guessed, because cookies were easy. A bakery in Arlington Heights made macaroons to die for, so I usually brought a box when I visited my parents.

"Oh. Yes, those're always nice, but... well, I was hoping you could come alone. Without Joe, I mean. We all like Joe very much, but it'd be nice to have a visit with just you."

I bit my lip and sighed silently. I mean, Mom and Dad had *never* liked Joe, and I understood why. He sulked through family dinners and other times when the Dolans got together, and whispered things directly to me even with everyone else within earshot. He also wasn't known for saying thank you. A rude guest, quite frankly. But my parents wouldn't dream of saying that directly to me.

"Sure, Mom. No problem. It's just that I might not get up there for a couple weeks, okay? Work's really busy now, and there's a lotta... stuff going on. But it'll be soon, I promise." I closed my eyes and hoped she'd accept that.

Mom said nothing for a second, then let out a long, heavy sigh. "Okay, honey. We just *miss* you. The house is too quiet these days."

The guilt that'd been pooling in my stomach seeped into my chest like sewage.

"I know Mom. And I miss you. But I gotta go. I gotta take another call."

She seemed surprised. "Oh, all right, honey. Don't let me keep you. Talk to you soon. I love you."

"Love you too, Mom. Bye." I hit the *off* button and fell back on the couch, drained and ready to really cry. Why did I have so much trouble being honest with her? A normal daughter would've told her mom about Joe's bad behavior — perhaps skipping a few details — but I felt unable to say anything at all. It made me sad because Mom and I had been really close when I went to Catholic school. But when high school hit, things fell apart fast.

Chapter 10
Photographs and Memories

Molly
2001-2003
North Andover, MA

Kate defined cool. No one could argue that, even though she wasn't 'popular' at our suburban high school. Smart and confident, her wide face and bright eyes radiated her passion for life and adventure. Most kids probably felt intimidated by Kate, but rather than admit that, they just kept their distance and rolled their eyes.

During her three years in North Andover, Kate didn't join any sports, clubs, or activities. And although she earned excellent grades, teachers didn't reward her with the respect and praise they gave other bright kids. In fact, they actually seemed to discourage her from participating in class sometimes. Kate said she didn't give a shit, but it bummed me out a lot. I mean, aren't teachers supposed to enjoy lively discussions?

Sure, Kate's opinions could be controversial and inflammatory, but still. She kept things interesting. She believed classic literature was being taught in sexist, outdated ways, and spoke out about it every time she got the chance. When our freshman English class read *Great Expectations* and the teacher called Estella a shallow person who took advantage of Miss Havisham's wealth, Kate flew to the girl's defense.

"Do you have any idea how limited a poor woman's options were in Victorian times? I mean, what would you have done if you were Estella? Pass up an opportunity like that? And it's unfair to call her shallow when Miss Havisham raised her to be incapable of love. If you think about it, Estella's the ultimate survivor."

When we read *Macbeth*, Kate argued that Shakespeare had "disgracefully" allowed one of his strongest, fiercest women—Lady Macbeth—to "inexplicably degenerate into an unstable, sleepwalking character." And she did her best to convince the class that Scout in *To*

Kill a Mockingbird was destined to grow up "a powerful, kickass lesbian."

That was another thing about Kate: she made a big deal out of advocating for gay rights and loved telling people how she'd marched in a couple of Boston Pride parades. But in 1997, most North Andover teachers and students preferred not to talk about gay rights at all, especially in class. And if any of them considered "powerful kickass lesbian" to be a flattering term, they weren't going to admit it publicly. Therefore, Kate—who'd moved to town from Cambridge, Massachusetts just in time to start ninth grade—quickly became known as an oddball.

That didn't bother her either. In fact, I think Kate enjoyed distancing herself from the locals as much as possible. She never missed an opportunity to refer to the Merrimack Valley as "the Masscrack," and didn't bother lowering her voice either. Sometimes, she actually spoke louder as her words grew nastier.

Like the time in the cafeteria when she went off on a rant about the word *minga*, which, for some reason, is a popular curse word in the Merrimack Valley.

"Do you realize that most people here don't even know what *minga* means?" said Kate.

I sure as hell didn't know. "Really?"

"Yeah. But I did some research, and I'm pretty sure it means *penis*." She dipped a baby carrot into a container of hummus and popped it in her mouth. "*Penis*. Can you believe that?"

I drank some water and shrugged. "Okay. Wanna cookie?" Talking about penises *anywhere* made me nervous, but I *really* didn't wanna discuss them in the lunchroom.

"No, really," said Kate, not picking up on—or caring about—my discomfort. Some kids at the next table glanced over in our direction, and I blushed. "So when people say stuff like, '*Minga*, hurry up!' and '*Minga*, you're stupid!' they're really saying 'Penis, hurry up,' and 'Penis, you're stupid.' I don't get it."

"Me neither." The kids at the next table were definitely listening. I could tell by their sudden silence and smirking faces. "Hey, so I was thinking maybe we could go to the movies on Saturday. My mom said she can drive."

Kate sighed. "*Migna*—I mean *penis*—I can't. I'm going to that show in Cambridge, remember?"

"Oh yeah. I forgot." Which wasn't actually true, but I'd been hoping she'd skip the show and hang out with me instead. Kate still went back to Cambridge almost every weekend to see indie bands at clubs like TT the Bear's and the Middle East. Leaving me stranded in the Masscrack with nothing to do.

    I'd had a great group of friends during my eight years at St. Bernadette's, and took it for granted I'd always be popular. But North Andover didn't have a Catholic high school, so at the end of eighth grade, all my close pals from St. Bernie's applied—and got into—Catholic high schools in neighboring towns.

    Not me, though. My grades were fine, but my brother Tim had just completed his first year of college, and money had suddenly become much tighter in our household. So my parents met with a financial planner one evening and informed me the next day that I'd be attending the town's "very well regarded" public high school the following year. "That way," said Dad, "we'll have more than enough money to devote to your college education."

    I could've argued. I mean, I'd never heard any concerns about money when they sent Tim to Central Catholic High School in Lawrence for four years. But arguing with Dad—a branch manager at a bank in Methuen—about finances was a lost cause. I went to my room and cried for a few hours, wallowing in the unfairness of it all. Eventually, Mom came up and talked to me. She said that if she and Dad could travel back in time, they'd send Tim to public high school too. But it was too late to change that. They'd learned from their mistake, and wanted to do things right the second time around. Lucky me. So, in September of 2001, as my pals from St. Bernie's headed off to various Catholic schools in the Masscrack, I laced up my sneakers and walked to North Andover High.

    The transition was shaky, and not only because of 9/11. Another major problem was that most NAHS kids seemed to recognize me *just enough* to believe I'd gone to public middle school in town too. After all, we had a good-sized school system, and I'd lived in North Andover all my life. I'd shopped in the local grocery store with Mom, had attended lots of town festivals, played on a couple of youth soccer and softball teams when I was younger, and took dance lessons at a studio on Main Street until I was nine. So, when I traversed the high school corridors, people would make eye contact and nod, but that was it. I guess they assumed I already had friends at the school. But those assumptions were wrong.

For the first week or so, then, I pretty much skipped lunch. I'd stroll into the cafeteria with a vague smile on my face, pretending to look for someone. Of course, I really just hoped anyone at all would invite me to join them. But they all went about their business, and eventually, I'd leave and head to the school library where I'd do homework or read. Then, when I got home at the end of the day, I'd pig out. But that got old fast, and starving through afternoon classes was no fun.

September 11th brought the tragedy nobody could've imagined, and school was closed for a couple of days. And yes, like everyone else, I watched the news in shock and mourned with the country, but I also took some time to reassess my attitude and behavior at NAHS. I'd have to try harder.

So, when school reopened, I gathered my courage and entered the caf as confidently as possible. As you might imagine, the overall mood was downbeat and anxious. But as I waited in the food line, I gazed around the room, and that's when I spotted Kate, sitting alone with a book and a salad. Her jeans were torn in a way that looked natural but funky, and her faded black t-shirt said *Sonic Youth* on the front.

"Hey," I said, walking over to her with a plate of pasta and a milk, "mind if I sit with you?"

Kate held out her hand in a welcoming manner while continuing to read.

Whatever, I thought, pulling out a chair. At least I'd get to eat. And maybe I'd find someone friendlier the next day.

From my safe spot, I assessed the social scene. A large group of super popular girls sat together at one table, a bunch of band kids shared another, and some well-established nerds had pushed several tables together. Strength in numbers after a tragedy. I got it.

But not everyone had so many good friends, hence, many of the tables were occupied by just two or three kids. Perhaps one of them had a spot for me?

My eyes fell on Margot, a petite freshman who'd taken ballet with me in second grade. She and two other girls giggled about something, and I tried unsuccessfully to catch her eye. Still, she was a possibility. I recalled her being nice in second grade, and we were both dressed similarly in plain Gap jeans and boat-neck sweaters.

"What're you smiling about?" asked Kate, startling me back to reality. She closed her book, and I glimpsed the title: *The Basketball Diaries*.

"Oh, nothing. I was just remembering the days when I used to take ballet. I was the clumsiest kid in the class, but my mom thought I had so much potential."

"Ha! That's mothers for you."

"Yeah. Mine's crazy." I didn't necessarily feel that way, but it seemed like an appropriate response.

She shrugged. "Sorry for ignoring you. I'm just really into this book. Have you read any stuff by Jim Carroll?"

I'd never even heard of the guy. "Uh... no. I don't *think* so. What class are you reading it for?"

Kate rolled her eyes. "Yeah right. Like any teacher *here* would have the balls put *this* on their reading list."

"Oh. So you're reading it... for fun?"

"Yeah. You could say that. It's pretty dark, but pure genius."

I wasn't sure what she meant by *dark*, but it sounded intriguing. "Huh. Cool."

She shrugged again. "You can have it when I'm done if you want."

"Thanks. But I'm like, up to my ass in homework. And you know, I'm not really a basketball fan."

Kate's eyes opened wider. "Trust me, sweetie, it's *barely* about basketball."

"Oh." I couldn't help feeling dumb, but it was called *The Basketball Diaries*. And sweetie? That was an old lady word.

But Kate smiled generously. "The title's deceptive. So, what's your favorite book ever? Like... ever."

Kids didn't usually ask questions like that. "I dunno. I liked *The World According to Garp* a lot."

Kate nodded. "Yeah, that's pretty good. Although John Irving did call it a soap opera."

Okay, so now *she* was confused. "No," I said. "I think you're thinking of someone else. 'Cause John Irving actually wrote *The World According to Garp*."

"Well *duh*," said Kate. "Everyone knows that. But he still called it a soap opera."

"No suh!" I couldn't believe an author would say such a thing about his own story.

"Yes suh!" she replied, mocking me gently. "And, you know what? He's right. It's just a really *good* soap opera. I adore Roberta. She's my favorite character."

"Oh, you mean the football player who becomes a—"

"Yeah, the transgender woman. I love her."

The bell rang and I stood up. I'd managed to eat most of my lunch, so that was good. Maybe now my stomach wouldn't grumble all afternoon. "Well, thanks for letting me sit with you."

"Sure. We can sit together tomorrow too, if you want."

I wrinkled my forehead and did my best "thinking hard" act. "Um... I'm supposed to make up a math test during lunch tomorrow, but I'll look for you if I get a chance to eat." In fact, I was planning to try Margot's table the following day. Margot and her pals seemed much more like my type.

"Okay, well I'll be here."

The next day, I scanned the cafeteria from the doorway until I spotted Margot's group. Then, I made a beeline toward her and said hello. One of the friends said hi, but Margot just gave me a half-wave and went on talking. I smiled and walked away.

"No one better to sit with?" said Kate as I approached her lunch table.

"What?" I asked, feigning shock. "Oh no. My math test got postponed. I'm not taking it 'til next week."

"Just kidding," she said. "I'm glad you're back."

As the weeks passed, Kate and I got to know each other better. At first, we only sat together at lunch, but then we started hanging out after school a little too. Sometimes, she'd annoy me because she seemed to know so much about everything. Then again, I learned a lot from her, and it was nice to have a pal.

But on weekends, she'd go "home" to Cambridge. She'd take the bus on Friday afternoons, and wouldn't return to North Andover until Sunday afternoon or evening. Sometimes her dad would drive into the city to get her; other times, one of her older friends would give her a ride.

"I'll take you with me one of these days," Kate promised many, many times. "As soon as I find you a place to sleep." But she stayed at her friend Cara's house, which was tiny and had only one bathroom. So Cara's parents weren't even psyched about Kate staying there, let alone another kid they'd never met.

I always acted like I didn't care one way or another. But in reality, the whole situation sucked. All my friends from St. Bernie's had gone off to their new schools, where they'd found new friends and activities to keep them busy, so they hardly ever had time for me on weekends. I felt abandoned by everyone.

On the other hand, Kate's Cambridge crowd sounded a little scary. She talked a lot about the older guys she'd met in Harvard Square, and showed me the excellent fake ID they'd made her. With it, she could get into all the 21-plus clubs, and sometimes she'd crash on the guys' couches rather than going back to Cara's house after an evening out. Cara would apparently tell her parents that Kate had taken the late bus home to North Andover, and they'd ask no questions. And although Kate claimed she trusted the guys "like big brothers," I had my suspicions. After all, I had a *real* big brother, and would *never* expect Tim to make me a fake ID or take me to a 21-plus nightclub when I was still in high school.

"Would you and Dad let me go to Cambridge with Kate some time?" I asked Mom one Saturday at the beginning of sophomore year. But I wasn't sure if I wanted her to say *yes* or *no*. It was pouring outside, and I'd just finished reading *The Catcher in the Rye*. I missed Kate most on rainy weekends.

Mom looked up from the laundry she'd been folding and frowned. "I guess I'd need more information. Like what would you do and where would you stay?"

I shrugged. "We'd just hang out with her friends and stay with one of them, I guess. Kate knows lots of people."

Mom shook out a damp sweater and hung it over a chair to dry. "I don't know, honey. She seems to have an awful lot of freedom for a fifteen-year-old." Picking up the laundry basket full of towels, she headed toward the bathroom. Then she stopped, turned, and faced me. "Hey, what's up with Teresa these days?"

"Gymnastics stuff," I answered. I hadn't even tried calling Teresa — my best friend from St. Bernie's — in weeks, because she always claimed to be busy.

"Hmm," said Mom. "I didn't think the gymnastics season started this early."

Tears of frustration welled in my eyes. I knew Teresa was blowing me off, but didn't want to admit it. I felt like such a loser; my parents had a better social life than me, and they hardly ever went out.

"Mom, it sorta seems like you don't like Kate." As soon as those words left my mouth, I regretted them. It wasn't fair to take out my friend issues on Mom.

She drew back her head as if she'd been slapped. "Now that's not true, honey. I *do* like Kate. She's a very nice girl. I think she's a little... sophisticated for you. But I don't dislike her. Not at all."

"What's wrong with sophisticated?" I think I was being combative because I liked arguing better than crying.

But Mom—who hated conflict—refused to take the bait. "Honey, please don't use that tone with me. There's nothing *wrong* with sophisticated. I was just giving my opinion. Come on. How 'bout we hit the mall and check out the summer clearance sales?"

I liked the mall and really wanted a new pair of jeans, but I was too worked up. "Sorry. I gotta do homework."

"Okay," said Mom. "I'll go alone, then. And hey, please take your laundry upstairs."

She didn't care. Nobody did. So, I ignored the laundry, stomped off to my room, slammed the door, and cried until I fell asleep on the bed.

Not surprisingly, Kate adored edgy, offbeat films. Since theatres in the Merrimack Valley played mostly mainstream movies, she and I spent countless weekday afternoons in front of her TV, watching videos and DVDs. Kate's favorite director was David Lynch, and we watched *Eraserhead* and *Blue Velvet* about a hundred times each, give or take a few. But one day during our sophomore year, when school was canceled because of snow, we trudged to the local video store and rented *Thelma and Louise*. The movie was more than ten years old at that point, but neither of us had seen it, and Kate had read somewhere that it featured strong female characters.

That sort of thing was right up Kate's alley, but I didn't expect her to fall in love with it. And yet, she did. Not only did she flip out over the film, but she became obsessed with the characters played by Geena Davis and Susan Sarandon. And I mean *obsessed*. By spring, Kate had tossed out most of her torn jeans and Chuck Taylors, and had adopted a whole new wardrobe of high-waisted pants, denim blouses with the sleeves chopped off, headscarves, little cowboy booties, and cat-eye sunglasses. She'd been shopping in thrift stores since middle school, so she knew where to get the good stuff. And lucky for her, her brown hair was naturally curly, so once she caught the *Thelma and Louise* bug, she just stopped blow-drying it and was good to go.

Now, I liked *Thelma and Louise* a lot too, but not the way Kate did. And I certainly didn't have the balls to show up at school dressed like a movie character. But every time we watched the film, I felt a stronger bond with my friend. Especially when she talked about buying—or stealing—a convertible, and heading west together on the highway. My guts would shudder with little spasms of hope, but voicing my true feelings somehow felt too intimate. So I'd just say something like, "Yeah, that'd be cool." Sometimes I'd fantasize about sharing an apartment with her when we grew up, like the people on *Friends*. Maybe with other roommates, or maybe just Kate and me.

One day in June, she and I took the bus to T.J. Maxx. We were hoping to buy some new summer clothes. When we arrived, I needed to use the bathroom.

"Cool," said Kate, popping earbuds into her ears. "I'll go check out the bargain racks." She was wearing a black tank top, denim shorts, tall cowboy boots, and a bandanna around her neck, cowgirl-style. Typical Kate.

I was only gone a few minutes, but when I returned, I was shocked to see Teresa, Samantha, and Brynna—three of my old pals from St. Bernie's—pretending to be perusing athletic wear as they whispered and giggled behind Kate's back.

"Hi guys," I said. "What's up?"

"Molly!" they all screamed and started hugging me. "Oh my god! What're you doing here?"

"Shopping."

Kate turned around, slowly and dramatically. "Do you *know* these people, Mol?"

"Yeah," I said, hoping she hadn't noticed the girls laughing at her. "Kate, this is Teresa, Sam, and Bryn. They went to St. Bernadette's with me. Guys, this is my friend, Kate."

The girls said hello to Kate, but she didn't answer immediately. "Well, I'd say it's nice to meet you ladies," she finally replied, "but that's not really true. I think you know what I mean." Her voice didn't sound quite normal, and it took me a second to realize she was speaking with a slight southern drawl, similar to Susan Sarandon's in *Thelma and Louise*.

"Huh?" said Teresa.

Kate nodded. "Oh, okay. Maybe I just imagined y'all ogling me like I was a masturbating monkey in the zoo or somethin'. Silly me. Hey Mol, I've got tons o' homework tonight. I'm gonna split."

I didn't mind shopping alone, but I wanted to support Kate. Besides, if I stayed at the store, the St. Bernie's girls would trash Kate mercilessly the minute she left. "Yeah, I gotta go too. So... bye guys. See you around."

Kate and I left in silence. But once we were outside, she turned to me. "Do you miss Catholic school?" she asked, losing the Southern accent.

"I don't think so. Not anymore."

"Good. 'Cause those girls are real douchebags."

I thought about that before answering. "Yeah. You know, they used to be nicer, but I guess everyone changes in high school."

All that summer—the summer before junior year—Kate went to Cambridge as often as she could. Then, she'd come back to North Andover where she'd relay story after story about the amazing indie bands she'd seen, particularly ones featuring female singers and musicians. She also became more outspoken as the weeks wore on, apparently caring less and less about offending people with her loudly-voiced opinions. As for her wardrobe, she'd updated it with two pairs of Doc Martens, a few vintage crocheted dresses, and some knee-length ball gowns from the 50s, but she still dressed like a character from *Thelma and Louise* on casual days. Her iPod went everywhere with her, and she generously shared her earbuds with me so I could sample her music *du jour*. But I didn't possess the mental capacity to keep track of it all. The biggies, though, were Sonic Youth, PJ Harvey, L7, and Sleater-Kinney.

And, to tell the truth, I wasn't crazy about any of them. I mean, I liked some of the songs, but none blew me away. And because I *hated* being stared at by other kids in the school cafeteria, I got in the habit of seeking out the most remote lunch tables available when classes resumed in September.

I was extra glad I'd snagged a corner table the day Kate whipped out her earbuds and declared that she'd marry Tori Amos if she ever got the chance.

"Uh, women can't marry women," I said, pressing my finger to my lips.

"Not yet," she said more loudly. "But they will soon. And some people think Massachusetts'll be the first state to allow it."

My guts tensed up. "Yeah, but Kate, you're not gay. And I doubt Tori Amos is either."

"Who knows what anyone is?" she said. "Sexuality's fluid. Besides, marriage is about respect, or at least it should be. Sex is secondary."

I couldn't even imagine an appropriate response to that, so I changed the subject instead. "Hey, have you ever seen the lead singer from the Strokes?"

Kate shrugged. "Yeah?"

"Well, don't you think he's adorable? They were on *Saturday Night Live* this weekend and I think I'm in love with him."

"In *love*?" said Kate. "How do you fall in love with someone after seeing him sing a couple of songs?'"

Damn it, she knew what I meant. "Not *love* love, you know, but the guy's *gorgeous*. I'd *do* him. That's for sure." I didn't normally talk that way, but I'd been smitten by Julian Casablancas's cuteness. Not to mention that Kate's behavior that day was making me really anxious.

She looked straight at me. "So you're saying wanna *fuck* him? The guy from the Strokes? You *lust* after him?"

I glanced around to see if anyone was listening. "Um, yeah? Maybe."

"Okay, then say what you mean. Sex is sex and love is love."

"All right. Calm down. It's just an expression."

Kate smiled. "I know. But don't say you love someone when you don't, okay?"

She was driving me crazy. "Sure. It's a deal. But *you* just said you'd marry Tori Amos. And you've never even met her."

"That's *different*," said Kate, not missing a beat. "'Cause I know what she *stands* for. But you don't know the first thing about this Strokes guy. I mean, what's his message? I've heard that "Last Night" song about a thousand times, and I still don't know what the hell he's talkin' about. And consider this, every member of the Strokes is a guy. With a *dick*. They have no idea how it feels like to be raped. Or pregnant with a kid they don't want. Don't you see, Molly? They don't get it. But Tori Amos does. She's been through shit and she speaks for *us*. And honestly, I think she'd make a good wife."

Kate had a way of taking things to a whole different level, and it could be infuriating. "Okay. Whatever. Just keep your voice down. People'll hear you."

"So fuck 'em. I don't give a shit."

But I *did* give a shit, especially since I'd developed a huge crush on a junior in my Latin class named Mark Rosen. I was pretty sure Mark didn't have a girlfriend, and he seemed to like me a lot too.

So a few days later, when my Latin teacher grouped me with Mark for a translation project, I could barely exhale the breath I'd just drawn.

"Let's see," said Mr. Trombly, handing me a few sheets of paper, then doing the same for Mark. "Three poems by Catullus for you two. And... Julie P. and Richard... you guys get three poems by Virgil. All right?"

He went on like that, pairing up students and poetry, but I'd stopped focusing. I mean, what'd just happened? Did Mr. Trombly know how much I liked Mark? Did he have ESP or something? My body got all hot and melty, even though the classroom was chilly. My forehead actually started sweating. I tried breathing again, but ended up snorting by accident. Luckily, nobody but me seemed to hear.

"Okay," said the teacher, strolling back to the front of the classroom. "Here's how this works. Coordinate with your partner, find a time and place to meet—I'd suggest the library—and translate your poems into English. None of them translate perfectly, but do your best. This'll count for a quarter of your term grade."

The *library*. The town library was a lovely, romantic old building. And now Mark and I were going to meet there. Maybe even at night. What a perfect opportunity for us to kiss, or for him to ask me out, or both. My face felt so red I couldn't look in his direction, so I pretended to be studying the Roman poems. I'd had several high school crushes before Mark, but he was different. I was older now, and felt ready for a real relationship. Plus, Mark was so funny. And smart. And a little goofy, with his wavy blond hair and shy smile. My parents had met each other in high school, so maybe Mark would be my husband someday. Sure, it was a long shot, but still.

I couldn't wait to tell Kate about the Latin project. But the minute I walked through the cafeteria door, she grabbed my arm, her face flushed. "Molly! Denise is having a party next Friday. A huge one. You *have* to come."

"Who?"

"Denise! The amazing girl I told you about? The one I met at TT's? At the Thalia Zedek show?"

I did my best to remember. "You mean that girl you smoked weed with in the bathroom?"

"Yes! She lives in Allston and she said I can bring a friend. It's gonna rock so hard. Please say you'll come. Please."

"But my parents—"

"Fuck 'em. No. Wait." Kate stopped and held up her hands. "Wait. I'm sorry. I didn't mean that. I just meant... lie. Totally lie. My parents wouldn't let me go to this party either, but they'll never know the truth.

I'm just gonna tell 'em I'm staying with Cara, and you can do that too. Don't worry, if your mom calls my house, my mother'll tell her Cara's parents are totally cool. I stay there so much she doesn't even bother to check anymore. It'll be fine."

"Okay? But... where will we *actually* stay?"

Kate shrugged. "Who knows? Maybe with my friend Micky. Or maybe at his brother's. Whatever. We'll figure it out."

"But aren't those guys, like... older?"

"Yeah, a little. But no worries. They're cool. We might be able to crash at Denise's too. It just depends how many people show up for the party. Oh Mol, you'll *love* Denise. I know you will."

I felt lightheaded with excitement. Not only had I been paired with Mark Rosen for the poetry project, but Kate was finally inviting me to Cambridge too. "Okay. Lemme talk to my mom. But guess what just happened in Latin?"

Friday, the day of the party, I woke up to my period and nasty cramps. Huge bummer, for sure, but I remained psyched. My parents had reluctantly agreed to let me go to Cambridge with Kate for one night only. I'd take the bus into the city with her that evening, attend the party, and stay at Cara's house. Then, Dad would pick me up in front of the Harvard Coop—one of the few places in Cambridge he knew how to find without a map—at noon on Saturday. I'd also need to text them every couple of hours during the party so they'd know I was all right.

Kate adored the plan. "It's perfect, Mol! Now we can crash anywhere. All we have to do is get you to the Coop by noon Saturday, and how easy is that?"

I actually felt a little giddy as I made my way down the corridor toward Latin class. Further down the hallway, a group of drama club girls pored over a magazine, and as I got closer, I saw that it was a catalog of prom dresses. I'd always been jealous of those girls, partly because they were such a tight little clique, and partly because I wished I were brave enough to try out for a school play. Every time auditions were held, I considered going, but always eventually chickened out. And Kate? Forget it. Once, I tried to convince her to try out for *A Christmas Carol* with me, but she made a face like I was nuts and said, "Why would anyone waste their time *pretending* to be some fictional character when real life is so *exciting*?" And maybe it *was* exciting for her.

For me, not so much.

Anyway, as I got closer to Latin class, I overheard one of the girls—a beautiful, broad-shouldered senior named Courtney—say, "Rosy wants us to dress up all 70s. Like, he wants to get one of those powder-blue tuxes with the satin stripes on the pants. You know? And I'm like, *no!* It's, like, my last prom, and I wanna look *sexy!* The prom's not a *comedy*."

I froze. Rosy was Mark Rosen's nickname, and he often played minor roles in the school plays.

"Hi?" said Courtney, as I stumbled to a stop in front of the girls. Although she lived a few blocks from my house, Courtney and I were a year apart in school and had never spoken more than a few words to each other.

"Uh, hi. Sorry. I think I forgot something in my locker."

"Well you better go get it," said Courtney. "Bell's about to ring."

The drama girls bid each other hasty goodbyes and scattered, but I stood there frozen, trying to process what I'd just heard. Courtney wouldn't make up a story like that. *She was going to prom with Mark!* Tears began streaming down my face, and impulsively, I turned and headed for the nurse's office. I wasn't the kind of girl who faked sick, so if I told the nurse I had bad cramps, she'd let me lie down for at least one class. And no *way* could I handle Latin with Mark that day. No way in hell.

At lunch, I blurted the whole thing to Kate, and before she could even comment, I asked her the question that was killing me. "D'ya think Courtney asked Mark or he asked her?"

The cafeteria smelled like burnt macaroni, which made me feel even more nauseated. I couldn't stop thinking about Mark's hands on Courtney's large breasts. Courtney, who was planning to wear something *sexy* to the prom. I didn't understand. I mean, didn't Mark have a crush on *me*?

"Who knows?" said Kate. "Who *cares*? It's a stupid prom. Besides, *you're* gonna work with Mark on the Latin project. So *you'll* actually get to *talk* to him."

"Kate!" I whispered. "People *talk* at the prom. And dance and kiss and—"

"It doesn't matter. Listen. It's a bullshit dance. Did you ever meet anyone who married their prom date?"

"Yes! My parents!"

Kate rolled her eyes and actually laughed. "Okay, so they're an exception. Plus, they hate each other now, right?"

"No! They don't! They may not be the happiest couple ever, but they get along fine at least... at least half the time."

"Okay."

"But that's not the point. I mean, I didn't even know Mark and Courtney were *friends*. So how can they go to the prom together? I'm so *mad*, Kate! Do you think she pressured him or something?"

"Who *knows*? It wouldn't surprise me. She's a bitch, right?" Kate paused for a second. "Hey, I have an idea. Let's you and me go. As a couple."

I didn't acknowledge that. "Maybe their mothers are friends or something? Like, maybe they're *pressuring* their kids to go together?"

Kate spoke louder. "No, I mean it, Mol. Seriously. Like... we could dress up like Thelma and Louise, and... yes! Oh my god, Molly! We. Would. Kick. *Ass*."

"Kate! Shut up, okay?" We were sitting right in the middle of the cafeteria, and my head ached. I wanted to cry, scream, and disappear at the same time, but all I could do was stab at my cheesy yellow pasta with a plastic fork.

"Hey, I'm not joking. I really think we should do it."

"Yeah." I pushed my tray aside. "Look, I gotta go to the bathroom. I think I'm gonna puke."

Kate drew her head back and focused her bright blue eyes on me. "C'mon babe. Stay focused. Our bus leaves in five hours."

Oh shit. With all the Mark stuff, I'd temporarily forgotten about the party in Cambridge. Plus, I *hated* it when Kate called me *babe* in public. "Oh, Kate. I honestly don't know if I can go any more."

"You'll be fine. Just take some deep breaths."

Deep breaths weren't gonna help. The only thing that could possibly help would be Mark saying he'd changed his mind and wanted to take *me* to the prom. I rubbed my temples and looked over Kate's shoulder, and almost like magic, there he was. *Mark*. Paying no attention to me, but edging in between a couple of boys at the table behind us.

"Ohmigod, he's right there," I whispered. "Don't turn around, but Mark just sat down with Jake and Reuben."

Kate shrugged. Grabbing my fork, she scooped up some macaroni and tried to feed me like a toddler. "Eat up, little girl. You're gonna need some carbs in your tummy for this party tonight."

I wanted to murder her. "Kate!" I hissed, pushing the fork away. "Cut the shit!"

"Hey, what the hell?"

Why didn't she care about Mark and me? Didn't my feelings matter at all? "Fuck it," I said, "I'm not going to the party, okay? I'm sorry, but I can't do it tonight."

"Oh, come on, girl," she said, assuming her Susan Sarandon accent. "You promised. Besides, I might need your help if things get outta hand. I'm counting on you."

Mark and Jake cracked up laughing about something, and Kate turned to glare at them. "Something funny, guys?" she asked, her accent growing even stronger.

The boys looked startled, then confused. "Nothing *you'd* care about," said Jake with a smirk. I'd never liked Jake.

Black spots started dancing in front of my eyes. "I think I'm gonna faint," I said, standing up slowly but angrily. "I gotta go see the nurse."

Mom picked me up at school half an hour later.

"I'm all right now," I told her, climbing into the car. "I've just got bad cramps and I'm starving."

"But... you look like you've been crying, honey. And the nurse said you were very upset about something."

I sighed. "I had an argument with Kate. Okay? We'll get over it."

A glimmer of hope flashed in Mom's eyes. "But what about your trip to Cambridge?"

"It's not happening today," I said as calmly as I could. "And don't even try to hide it. I know how happy that makes you."

"That's *not* true, honey! Of course I want you to have fun. But your father and I *worry* about you. So many bad things can happen to a girl your age. If you ever have children, you'll understand."

Chapter 11
These Dreams

Molly
September 28, 2012
Arlington, MA

The blue lights on the cruiser making its way down Wilson Road flashed in their strange carnivalesque way, but the siren was off. I left my wine on the kitchen table and darted to the living room for a better view. *Oh lord.* The car stopped right in front of my house.

I held my breath as the officer in the passenger seat climbed out and looked around, his right hand resting casually on his holster. About thirty seconds later, his partner emerged from the vehicle, a phone to his ear.

My heart raced. Cops never showed up for good reasons, did they?

Had Dad crashed the car on the way home from the club? Because he always drank too much there. And Mom hadn't been feeling great when we spoke last week. Her sciatica was still bugging her and she had a cold too. But she'd been cheerful enough, talking about how excited my brother's kids were about Halloween, and how she'd bought a pretty new sweater for the holidays. I'd planned to tell her about my split with Joe, but stopped myself at the last minute. I guess I just wasn't ready for all the questions and other crap that comes with breakup talk.

Meanwhile, the cop on the phone kept talking while the other one paced around. Yeah, I was freaking out.

Ever since the Shane Armstrong disaster, I'd kept a low profile at work. I continued to do my job well, but stuck with email communication whenever possible and avoided face-to-face meetings. I'd also been leaving the office by six p.m. Some nights, I wouldn't even bother saying goodbye to people. I'd just shut off my computer and go.

Because people looked at me differently now, and some averted their eyes when we passed each other. Even Diana was acting weird. She and I still ate lunch together most days, but I caught an occasional glimpse of distrust—or was it disgust—in her eyes. As for Shane, I'd only seen him from a distance. He no longer walked past my cube.

Needless to say, I hadn't returned to El Chico. And, since Joe and I weren't on speaking terms, the past two weekends had been ridiculously quiet. I'd watched a ton of movies, and killed a lot of time on the Internet. I *had* ventured out once—the previous Saturday afternoon—but what a mistake that'd been.

I'd been feeling lonely and sorry for myself. I mean, it was almost eighty degrees outside and the sun was shining, so why was I sitting around being bored? Why not take the bus into Davis Square, do a little thrift-store shopping, then stop somewhere for ice cream or coffee? Maybe even a beer. I was starving for a change of scenery and maybe a bit of fun.

So there I was on the bus, wearing both eyeliner and lipstick, and doing my best to scope out two different cute guys. One sat directly across the aisle, and the other was a few seats in front of me.

The bus pulled into the Square, and I checked my reflection in the window. I looked good. But... no. No, it couldn't be. Across the street, standing in line at the movie theater. *Joe*. Seriously. With the same woman he'd brought to my house a few weeks earlier.

I wanted to be wrong—or hallucinating—but no matter how many times I blinked, the couple wouldn't disappear. And Joe's gangly, paunchy body and weak chin were impossible to mistake. The woman, on the other hand, wore cutoff shorts and a tight tank top that flattered her figure. She had beautiful, thick hair, and smooth, tanned skin.

What the hell was she doing with Joe?

In any case, my sense of adventure had vanished. I got off the bus, walked into the first thrift shop I came across, decided everything in it was too expensive, and caught the next bus home. All I could think about was Joe *branching out*. Why was it so easy for him and so hard for me?

I'd actually been making a lame attempt at branching out that evening when the police showed up on my street. Or maybe it was more like branching *in,* because I'd been clicking around on Facebook, checking to see if guys I'd hooked up with in college were still single. I didn't feel ready to create a profile on Match or eHarmony, so I was starting with familiar faces. But cops?

Oh God, I promise to visit my parents WAY more often if you just let Mom and Dad be okay. Please. I'll be a better daughter. Much better. Really. My stomach ached with fear.

But after another moment or two of desperation prayer, I peeked out the window again and literally groaned with relief. Because the officers were heading up *Flaherty's* steps. I'd been spared!

So, did I grab the phone and call Mom immediately? Hell no. In true, foul-weather-Catholic fashion, my "sincere" promise to God was already skittering toward the dark shadows of my consciousness. Besides, I had to keep an eye on Fred's house. Poor Fred! What did the police want with *him*? I repositioned myself on the couch for a better view.

Mr. Flaherty—dressed in his jeans and long-sleeved Morse Code shirt—answered the door promptly, demonstrating no obvious signs of tension. He shook hands with both officers before escorting them into his home.

My level of concern surprised me. After all, it was just Flaherty, and he and I were hardly friends. But he *had* just lost his brother, and I was pretty sure the cops weren't there to inspect the cracks in his sidewalk.

Then I glanced over at Mrs. Costa's house, and there she was on the porch, pretending to water her flowers. But who did she think she was fooling? The flowers had long been dead, and the watering can appeared to be empty too. Clearly, she was shamelessly waiting for some sort of show to start. And if Fred came out in handcuffs, she'd have the news all over town by noon the next day.

But was I any different or better, hiding out across the street in my living room?

Flaherty and I had last spoken the Saturday morning after my encounter with Shane Armstrong. But despite his warning about women and alcohol, I'd been drinking as much as ever, if not more. And I didn't care. While I waited anxiously for the police to emerge from Flaherty's house, I got up, retrieved my Chardonnay from the kitchen, and refilled the glass.

Mellow out! I chided myself. *He's a sweet old dude who minds his own business.* Right? Although he *had* been pretty calm the night of his brother's death. Could he have been involved somehow? *No! Most people's only brushes with crime come from watching TV and reading books.*

The past can be a bitch, though. And her ugliest memories have a way of sticking around.

So, as I continued to watch and wait, I distracted myself by focusing on the guys from college I'd recently hunted down and attempted to "friend" on Facebook. The first was Pauly McIver, a polite, square-jawed, shy-until-he'd-downed-a-few-drinks type I'd nicknamed "The Marlboro Man" because back in the day, he'd resembled a younger version of the cowboy in the popular cigarette ads. Both times I'd been with Pauly, I'd walked away with a nasty rash from his mustache, but his profile picture showed him to be clean-shaven now and his status was "single."

Todd Cohn was second. Todd also claimed to be single on Facebook, but I didn't necessarily believe that. He had olive-skin, and was very handsome. A soccer player in college, he and I had only fooled around once, on a weekend when his girlfriend was away. But he'd lied and told me they'd broken up. So for all I knew, his Facebook status was a lie too. On the other hand, people do change.

Then there was Kyle Halenewski, the beautiful, artistic man I'd lost my virginity to in May of sophomore year of college. Friending Kyle on Facebook felt weird, but I did it anyway. My one night with him, in 2007, had started innocently enough at a college poetry slam. Some people from my English class—including Kyle, a senior—had performed, and Kyle had *totally* killed with his poem, an intense piece about someone questioning their sexuality. Not surprisingly, he was crowned the overall slam winner.

So I congratulated him, of course, expecting a thank you and maybe a hug. Instead, he invited me back to his apartment. I'd always been attracted to Kyle—he looked like a cross between an emo boy and a preppie—and he'd always been kind to me.

But sex with him felt... well, disappointing. He was gentle, for sure, and everything was consensual, but it all happened way too fast. I could tell he felt bad when he knitted his brow and asked if it'd been okay for me.

"Oh, yeah. Yeah, fine." I was no connoisseur, after all, and I was incredibly tired. I just wanted to fall asleep with him.

Right then, though, we both noticed a blood stain on his beige sheets. I blushed and apologized, but Kyle burst into tears. Confused, I promised to wash them, but he said that wasn't the issue. Sniffling loudly, he muttered something.

"What'd you say?" I asked, my heart pounding.

He sobbed harder. "I... I... that was *unconscionable."*

What? "What d'ya mean, Kyle?" I pulled my sweatshirt over my head because the room was chilly, but he just sat there, naked and crying. I tried not to look at his penis.

"I never woulda touched you if I knew you were a virgin," he finally said. "Never."

"But I *wanted* you to. It's okay."

"No. It's not. You don't understand."

He was right about that last part. "I think I should go," I said, and he nodded. So I did.

I never fully processed that night, and it was a relief when Kyle graduated a month later, because seeing him on campus afterwards made me super uncomfortable. He'd wave and try to smile, but his pain was palpable and it sucked. I guess the only positive result of it all was me being a lot more cautious about casual sex junior year. Then, senior year, I met Ethan Fricke.

Ethan. I couldn't bring myself to type his name into the Facebook search box. Because what if he was married with five kids? Or dead? Maybe it was better to keep him a mystery.

Flaherty's door opened. The cops had been inside almost twenty minutes, and I held my breath as they trotted down the steps and headed for their car. Mr. Flaherty waved goodbye to them, but they didn't seem to notice. They just got into the cruiser and drove away without the blue lights. Mrs. Costa shook her head and scurried back inside her house.

What a nasty person. I mean, didn't she have anything better to do than sit around hoping something bad would happen to her neighbor? Couldn't she use her copious free time volunteering or something? Maybe helping out at a school, or the library? Or taking a shift in a soup kitchen, or a homeless shelter? Or a shelter for battered women....

That did it. I hauled my butt off the couch, opened a new browser window on my laptop, and googled *women's shelter Boston*. It wasn't the first time I'd done such a thing, but I'd never followed through. Sometimes, I'd get caught up in painful memories about Kate; other times I'd talk myself out of it with excuses like *I don't have time* or *I can't make that commitment now*.

But in truth, I *did* have time. Not nearly as much as Mrs. Costa, but still. And I wasn't a kid anymore; I was twenty-five. Sure, it'd be upsetting to be around people with bruises and worse, but I could do *something*. I could make a difference. I could. Of course I could.

The sheer number of women's shelters in the Boston area unnerved me—my simple three-word search resulted in over ten pages of results—but on the other hand, I was glad so much help existed. I clicked the first shelter on the list, then clicked a button that said, *apply to volunteer,* and downloaded the application form. The name and address stuff was easy, but when I got to the "essay" questions about why I wanted to help, what skills I could share, and when I'd be available to come in for an interview, anxiety took over. Besides, I felt a little buzzed from the wine. So I closed the website, promising to get back to it the next day.

Which left me staring at Facebook again. None of the guys I'd sent friend requests to had responded yet. But the empty search box at the top of the page waited patiently for Ethan's name.

Oh what the hell? I typed *Ethan Fricke*, and up he popped. The photo was poorly lit and he was wearing a Yankees baseball cap—*the Yankees?*—but he looked all right. His face had grown fuller—a chubbier Zac Efron, I guess. More importantly, he was single.

So, before I could talk myself out of it, I clicked the *Add Friend* button, and closed the laptop. Done. Then, in an attempt to calm my jittery stomach, I flopped on the living room couch and turned on the TV, where yet another couple searched for happiness on *House Hunters*. Exactly what I needed to help me sleep. As the realtor discussed *en suite* bathrooms and closet space, my brain began to shut down.

Joe had despised *House Hunters*. One Saturday, about a year earlier, he'd come strolling out of my bathroom, wearing only a towel after a long, hot shower. "Assholes," he said, pointing at the television.

I shrugged and went on watching, but Joe wasn't finished. "Look at those people, Mol. Throwin' their lives away."

"Whatever," I answered. I was a little pissed at him for using so much hot water. Now I'd have to wait an hour for the tank to reheat unless I wanted a lukewarm shower.

He headed into my bedroom and returned a few minutes later, dressed in sweats and raking through his snarls with my hairbrush. "You know they're idiots, right? These losers've been scrimpin' and savin' for years to make a down payment on a house, and now they're gonna work like pigs to keep the fucking thing from gettin' foreclosed on. You know what happens now, Mol? After they buy it?"

"What?" I asked. All I wanted was for him to shut up so I could hear the show.

"Nothin'! Their social life's over. They'll be eating ramen noodles for the rest of their *lives*. But they *will* be able to afford screwing, cause that's free. So they'll end up with five or six kids, then have to figure out how to feed *them* too. Sounds fun, huh? Glamorous."

I didn't answer.

"Hey, sorry to break this to you, Mol, but the American dream sucks. You ever notice how they never show these pathetic people after they buy the fucking house?"

The couple on the program was trying to decide between an urban townhouse and a freestanding home in the suburbs, and I liked both. "That's not true, Joe. They do follow-up shows all the time—"

"Yeah. Like a month after the sale, right? I'm talkin' a few *years* later. When they're sleepin' in separate beds, with their teeth an' livers rotting, and their kids bummin' cash off 'em, and—"

"Joe! Shut up! You're full of shit and you know it. Having a family's awesome, when you're ready. You're just in a bad mood."

He shrugged. "I may be hungover, but that doesn't mean I don't understand life. I'll give you this much though, maybe a small percentage of people *do* enjoy bein' married with kids. But the rest are on a slow trip down hell's highway. It's simple science. Evolution, and all that. People weren't meant to be monogamous."

"A slow trip down hell's highway?" I said as the show broke for commercials. "That sounds like a bad AC/DC song."

But Joe didn't laugh. He just picked up the remote control and switched the channel to a football game. I never found out which house the people bought.

Chapter 12
Next Time, This Time

Molly
September 29, 2012
Arlington, MA

Around three in the morning, I awoke on the couch, still slightly buzzed and thinking about Joe. I considered dialing his number, but instead got up, used the bathroom, and checked Facebook to see if anyone had accepted my friend requests.

Two notifications waited for me in the semi-darkness: one new friend and one direct message. Both were from Ethan Fricke.

For a second, I couldn't breathe, but luckily that problem didn't last long, because deciphering Ethan's message required a fair amount of oxygen. It appeared to have been written by someone who was either very drunk or not at all comfortable with the English language. And since Ethan had gotten decent grades in college, I went with the drunk theory.

Hi Molly. Long time no se. Lools like your in boston. me too sometimes. Can yu hae dinner soon?

Wow. At least he was local, part-time anyway. I poured a glass of water, and sat down to compose a reply. By four a.m., I'd settled on:

Hi Ethan. Yes, I'm in Boston, and would love to meet you for dinner. What part of the city are you in?

That seemed okay. Not too desperate, not too casual. Short, cool, and to the point. I hit the "send" button and went to bed.

My new coffee maker had finally arrived, but just as it started brewing, Flaherty's gray head bobbed past my window. I was still in my pajamas but in a better mood than usual because of Ethan. Of course, I was also curious about the reason for the police being at

Flaherty's house the previous day. So I got up and opened the door. "Hi, Mr. Flaherty. Looking for your cat again?"

The man rolled his eyes. "Yeah. Little bugger. I fixed the cellar window, but today, he ran right out the front door."

"Oh no. You want help looking for him?"

Flaherty's face brightened as if I'd offered him the winning Megabucks ticket. "Well if you don't mind, Molly, that'd be great. I think he ran under your porch, and I have trouble getting down on the ground some days. Got a touch of the arthur-itis, you know?"

"Oh sure." I couldn't tell if he was trying to be funny by mispronouncing arthritis, or if he just didn't know how to say the word properly. "No problem." I padded down the steps in my stocking feet, then crouched and peered under the porch. "Yup. He's under there all right. His little yellow eye's glowing."

"Well whatta you know? I think he likes you, Molly. You wanna lure him out with this cheese?" As he'd done the other time, Flaherty reached into his jeans pocket, but instead of sandwich meat, he pulled out a chunk of a cheese stick tied to a piece of twine. It was linty and a little gross, but I took it from him, touching only the twine.

"He loves playing with these things," said Flaherty. "And they're so much cheaper than the cat toys they sell at that pet store in Cambridge. What a rip-off that place is."

"Hmm." I tossed the cheese under the porch, and the cat pounced, then started licking it. I pulled the string toward me, and he followed the cheese out until his head was visible.

"Can you grab him?" asked Flaherty. "I swear he doesn't bite."

"Uh... sure." I knelt down and reached under the cat's body, managing to get a grip on his ribcage. But instead of trying to squirm away as I'd expected, he put up no resistance at all. He just let me scoop him right up, then rubbed his face against my stomach and buried his head under my elbow. "He's a snuggler, huh?" I said, standing and scratching the kitty's neck.

"Oh yeah. Nice little guy. You can hold him for a while if you'd like."

I wasn't sure how to respond to that. The cat did feel cuddly and warm, but admitting that was awkward, so I just smiled and handed him over to Flaherty. "I think he'd rather be with you," I said.

"Aw, thanks."

We both remained silent for a few seconds, then Flaherty looked straight at me. "So didja see the cops over at my place yesterday?"

"Um... yeah. I did. Is everything okay?"

"I guess so. At least for the time being. Hey Molly, you don't wanna come over for a cup o' tea, do you? After you get dressed, I mean?"

That totally caught me off guard, not to mention that the thought of going into his home made me a bit nervous. But I could tell he really wanted to talk.

"Oh thanks, Mr. Flaherty. Sure, I'd love that. Maybe in an hour or two?"

It occurred to me that I should tell him I had plans later on, though, just in case. I'd read that violent people are much less likely to do bad things if they know the potential victim is expected someplace soon. Not that I really believed Flaherty had violent tendencies, but after what'd happened to Kate, I wasn't taking any chances. "I just can't stay too long, 'cause I'm meeting my boyfriend later."

Flaherty's face tensed for a second, and he breathed a short—almost pained—breath before smiling weakly and nodding. "Whatever you can do is great, Molly. I'll be home all day."

Chapter 13
Dreamin' Again

Fred
September 29, 2012

    He carried Kitty home, folded and put away the clean laundry he'd left on the table, and turned on the heat under the kettle. It'd be nice to have a visitor, and he liked Molly.

    A lot more than he liked the cops who'd stopped by the day before. He'd been gracious and polite with them, but they'd treated him like he was some kind of criminal, or at least an accomplice to a crime. Like it was his fault that Davey got screwed up, and he hadn't even tried to help. Which was completely false but talking to cops was tricky. They asked strange questions in strange ways.

    And speaking of strange, why was Molly still hanging around with that bum of a boyfriend? He hadn't seen the guy around in a while, so he'd thought maybe she'd handed him his walking papers.

    If she were my daughter... he thought. But he didn't have a daughter, or a son for that matter. He'd wanted kids, but it hadn't been in the cards. Not that he and Barb didn't give it their best shot. And during her fourth pregnancy—in 1986—they'd finally gotten a lucky break. That time, he'd believed with all his heart he was going to be a father.

    All the other miscarriages had happened early in the game—in the first month or two—so even though they'd been tough, he and Barb had managed to bounce back. But number four was different from the get-go. She'd cut out *all* the booze and started eating healthier the minute the pregnancy test came back positive. And she waited until she hit the four-month mark with no problems before telling people. So everyone was optimistic.

    In the evenings, she'd yak on the phone with her mother about their favorite boy and girl names, and they'd discuss—for hours—paint colors for the baby's room as if the perfect shade of green could end the Cold War or make that terrible disease AIDS stop killing people. But

IT DOESN'T HAVE TO BE THAT WAY

Fred didn't complain, even when he saw the phone bill. It was nice to see Barb smiling so much and browsing through catalogs that sold baby stuff, circling things she liked. One of her girlfriends from work was planning a baby shower, and Barb had bought a pretty yellow maternity dress for the occasion.

But all that only made the loss—at five months—so much harder. Almost overnight, Barb stopped being a glowing mother-to-be, and became an angry, bitter wife.

"It's your *secrets*!" she screamed the day she came home from the hospital. It was March, and even though Fred had turned up the thermostat at least three times, the house felt cold and damp. "Your secrets ate me up on the inside. No wonder my baby girl died."

She wasn't making sense, but her words pounded his already flattened heart like a blunt instrument anyway. Nothing had ever made him as sad as the baby's death. For two days and nights, he hadn't slept or eaten, and his stomach felt like it'd been replaced by motor oil. *His kid. His child.* Those tiny kicks he'd felt in Barb's belly—the life he'd helped create. *How could she blame him?*

And he'd done everything in his power to help things work out. He'd done all the housework so Barb could rest, and made countless trips to the convenience store for ice cream and peanut butter cookies. He'd even begged her to quit her job at the Estee Lauder counter so she could sleep in every morning, but she'd refused to do that. He'd loved and wanted that baby as much as Barb. He was sure of it.

"Angel," he said, sitting on the edge of the bed. "We'll get through this. I promise. You know what they say, 'When the going gets tough, the tough get going.' We'll give it another shot when you're ready."

But Barb just cried harder. "No. I'll never be tough enough. Nobody's tough enough to survive your bullshit."

"Barb, what're you talking about? What bullshit?"

"You know what I mean. That bullshit with your brother. It's killing us all!"

What? "C'mon, Barb, that's not fair. Davey's got nothing to do with this."

"Are you *kidding*? He's a poisonous man and he poisoned our baby. He poisons everything!"

"But..." Fred swallowed hard against the pain in his gut. Of course Davey had problems, but Barb was being irrational. "Listen, Angel, we might have a medical issue."

His wife let out a shriek. "Medical issue, my ass!"

Jingoes, he needed her to calm down. After Barb's third miscarriage, he'd done some research at the library, and had learned a lot about test-tube babies and some new drugs that helped make people more fertile. But Barb hated it when he tried to teach her things, especially "lady stuff." His best shot was to act dumb. "Well, I don't know, Barb. Maybe we could go see one of those specialists. My friend Billy and his wife saw one in Boston and—"

"I'm not seeing a *specialist*!" screamed Barbara. "I'm going to the *cops*. Your brother's ruining our lives and I can't take it anymore. I can't take *any* of it. I wanna divorce. I really do."

It wasn't the first time Barb had used the "d" word, but Fred hadn't taken her seriously in the past. She'd yell it sometimes when she got very upset, and occasionally when he refused to do something for her. Like the Sunday he'd been on his way to help Billy test a new transceiver, and Barb had announced—out of the blue—that she wanted him to take her furniture shopping.

But after the baby's death, she didn't ask him to do things with her anymore. He'd try to make her smile by baking corn muffins or picking up fancy pastries at the bakery on Sunday mornings, but she'd never eat any of it. So while she ignored him, he'd sit next to her at the kitchen table and promise that when the sun warmed up the earth in the spring, everything would feel better.

It didn't, though. As the weather improved, their relationship deteriorated. Shouting and screaming became an everyday thing. Then, one night in late April—and what a terrible night that was—Barb left and moved back into her mother's house in Medford. And by July, despite his protests, their divorce was well underway. The judge ordered him to pay Barb half of what the house was worth—which meant taking out a big loan—and then Barb shocked the crap out of him by heading off to California to start a new life. Since she worked for Estee Lauder, the company even helped her find a job at a makeup counter in some Los Angeles department store.

Fred didn't believe any of it would stick, though. Barb was the only woman he'd ever loved, and they'd been through hell together. It couldn't just end with her moving away. He talked to Billy about it, and Billy told him he and Sally had separated for a few months in the late 70s. "It happens to most couples," said his friend with a shrug. "If you're lucky, you figure out how to patch things up."

But months passed with no word from Barb. A year went by, and another, and another. Fred started to wonder if maybe he wasn't among the lucky ones. Then came the day in 1991, when he read in the paper that Barb's mother had died. So he went to the wake—full of hope and dressed in a brand new suit—only to spot his ex-wife in the receiving line with a new guy and two healthy-looking toddlers.

Twin boys. Meaning that she'd probably seen a fertility doctor after all. In any case, he couldn't face her. He walked straight out of the funeral home without even paying his respects, called Billy from a payphone, and got sloppy drunk in a bar with his buddy.

"At least you know it's over now," said Billy. "You're a free man. No more questions running around your mind."

But one thing still bothered Fred: He couldn't figure out why Barb hadn't gone to the cops about Davey yet. After all, she knew at least one incriminating thing about his brother, and she'd made her hatred for him crystal clear.

Finally, he wrote her a letter. And a couple of weeks later, he got this response:

> *Fred,*
> *Please don't write me again. I have a new life and I don't love you. I never loved you. Our marriage was a mistake. Please stop dredging up the past.*
> *Barbara*

Dredging up the past. The phrase made him think of old cars and dead bodies being pulled from riverbeds. And yet, Barb had used those exact words to describe their marriage. *Boy oh boy, old Billy was right.* He and Barb were done.

He did have a little money, though. A few thousand bucks he'd been saving to spend on Barb if she ever came back. He'd dreamed about taking a little Cape Cod vacation, or even going on one of those all-inclusive cruises he'd read about. What a fool he'd been.

But not anymore. The very next day, he ordered a new multiband antenna for the back yard. A tall one, too—fifty-three feet. So big it needed to be installed in a concrete base. So much for the nice, grassy yard Barb had wanted for cookouts and flowers. It was *his* property now. He could do whatever he wanted on it.

Chapter 14
Operator

Molly
September 29, 2012
Arlington, MA

Flaherty's porch smelled mossy, and the doorbell — probably purchased by his ex-wife or mother — played the same little chime as the doorbell at my family's old house in North Andover. I hadn't thought about that chime in years.

He answered within seconds. "Come on in, Molly. I hope you didn't bake something just for me."

I handed him a foil-covered paper plate. "Oh it's nothing, Mr. Flaherty. Just some brownies I made with a mix. I was baking 'em for my boyfriend and thought you might like a few." I hadn't wanted to show up empty-handed, so I'd thrown the brownies in the oven before showering.

"Well, thank you. That's very thoughtful. And please call me Fred. Mr. Flaherty sounds so formal."

"Okay," I said as he signaled for me to follow him through the doorway. "Fred it is."

"Oh, wait a second." He stopped in his tracks. "I gotta ask you to keep the chocolate away from the cat. I hear it can kill 'em if they eat it."

I smiled. The man's attachment to the little cat was so sweet. "No problem." But my smile faded when I stepped into the living room. It was super clean — the sparkling windows put my dirty ones to shame — but no curtains framed them, and the air was chilly and stale. The wall-to-wall carpet was the color of mustard, and the brown corduroy couch and matching chairs were worn. Everything looked like it'd been there since the 80s. Maybe even the 70s. The non-working fireplace — which had been sealed off and covered with painted wood — only added to the cold, sterile atmosphere.

Then I saw the record player. It was silver and clearly quite old, but I could tell Fred still used it. The plastic lid was open, and several vinyl

IT DOESN'T HAVE TO BE THAT WAY

records and their jackets lay scattered on the floor. As we walked past the stereo, I noticed Jim Croce's album *Life and Times* on the turntable.

"Jim Croce!" I said. Croce had died years before my birth, but my parents loved his music, and my dad used to play his tapes when we went on long car rides. I'd secretly liked the songs too. Most of the other soft rock stuff my parents were into—Seals and Crofts; Crosby, Stills & Nash—had been *too* soft for me, but Jim was cool. Even when he sang ballads, he didn't sound wimpy. I also thought he was handsome in a regular, sincere guy kind of way.

"You know Croce?" asked Fred, turning around.

"Well, not personally or anything."

Fred frowned.

"I mean, I know he's dead," I said. "But I grew up listening to him. My parents were big fans."

"Hmm. Yeah, I guess you'd call me a big fan too. Never did see him in concert, though. Oh well. So what's your favorite Croce song?"

"Oh, I dunno." I felt a little funny opening up to Flaherty about something like that. "I like the one where he's in the phone booth. You know, when he's trying to call his ex-girlfriend?"

"'Operator.' Great song."

When I was ten or eleven, I'd snuck the cassette tape with that song on it up to my bedroom one night and listened to it a whole bunch of times without telling my parents. They wouldn't have minded me borrowing it, but I wasn't comfortable admitting that I liked something of theirs so much. That guy in the phone booth had really affected me, though. He'd seemed so real. "It's sort of cool how he pretends he doesn't care about the lady, but you can tell he does."

Fred's eyes softened. "Yeah. All those times he tells the operator he's just calling so he can let the girl know he's fine, but..." His voice caught and he turned away. "C'mon. Let's go have tea."

"Okay," I said, following him with a knot in my stomach.

Flaherty pulled himself together pretty fast, and the kitchen was much warmer than the living room. It smelled like soup and WD-40, and an empty Campbell's Chicken Noodle can sat in the sink beside a bowl with a little broth in it and a big spoon. Fred set the plate of brownies on the counter. "Sorry it's so messy. I was hungry, so I made an early lunch."

I smiled. "I wouldn't call this messy. You should see my kitchen. The thing I hate most is cleaning the floor. And it gets dirty so fast! I don't know how."

Flaherty lifted the kettle and turned on the gas beneath it. Then he took two tea bags out of a drawer and got two mugs down from a cabinet. "Hmm. For me, the hard part's keeping up with all the dishes. You wouldn't think it'd be a big deal since it's just me and Kitty, but..." He sighed.

I looked around and saw no sign of the cat. "So... where *is* Kitty?" I asked. I really wanted to talk about the police being there the previous day but wasn't sure how to broach that topic.

Flaherty chuckled. "Oh, he's no dummy. He likes stayin' cozy and warm, so he's probably snuggled up on his pillow down in the hamshack."

"Hamshack?" Did Flaherty have some kind of meat smoker in the basement?

The kettle whistled. "Yeah. Ever seen a hamshack, Molly?"

"Uh, no. I don't think so. I, uh... I'm not actually sure what it is."

His eyes twinkled. "No kiddin'?" Opening his clean—but almost empty—refrigerator, he took out a quart of whole milk, then slapped himself on the forehead. "You know what? I don't have any sugar. I never use the stuff."

"No worries. I don't use it in tea either."

He looked relieved. "Phew. But, you know, I should pick some up next time I'm at the store. It's good to have in the house for guests." He went over to the fridge and wrote *sugar* on a piece of notebook paper that was stuck to the door with a magnet from the local bank. His old-fashioned penmanship reminded me of Catholic school and the nun who'd taught me in second grade. "My shoppin' list. I have to write everything down these days." Also on the list were the words *Sanka* and *margarine.*

The only other guests I'd ever seen entering Flaherty's house were the cops, but all I said was, "Me too. I've got a terrible memory." That wasn't actually true, but I wanted to be sympathetic.

"Oh yeah? Wait'll you're my age. It gets worse with time." He poured hot water over the teabags and handed me one of the mugs. "I hope this is okay."

"Thank you," I said, helping myself to milk and taking a closer look at the white mug with a picture of the Empire State Building on it. "You like New York City?"

At first, he didn't seem to get the reference. "New York? Oh, right. The cup." He paused. "I guess I can take it or leave it. I've only been there a couple times. That cup there's a souvenir from my honeymoon."

He laughed humorlessly. "I should probably toss it, but it's a good size. It's hard to find good cups these days. Most of the ones in the stores are either too big or too small. Have you noticed that?"

"Yeah. Definitely." I didn't actually think too much about the size of my coffee mugs, and the part about his honeymoon just made me sad. "Have you ever been to Bed, Bath and Beyond? Or HomeGoods? Those places usually have a good selection."

He looked perplexed. "I don't think so. I gotta admit, I don't shop for kitchen stuff very often. Just food."

"Yeah." I didn't know what else to say. I felt like I should sit down at the table, but Flaherty kept standing there, looking restless. I wished he'd mention the police.

"Hey Molly," he said, his eyes falling on the plate of brownies. "Would you mind if I put those away? They smell delicious, but I don't want the cat to get at 'em. Of course, if you'd like one, help yourself."

"Oh no. I mean yes. Please put them away. I had no idea chocolate was bad for cats. I'm sorry."

"Don't be silly! Bringing 'em was very nice. I'll have one for a treat tonight. I just don't want the little guy gettin' sick."

"I understand."

He rocked on the balls of his feet, which seemed to be a nervous habit. "So you wanna see the hamshack? I know you have plans in a while, but this won't take long."

The thought of going into his basement made me a little edgy, but I didn't have the heart to say no. Slipping the phone out of my pocket, I saw I had good signal, and could only hope the same would be true on the lower level. I'd never called 911 before—and didn't expect to that day either—but you can never be too careful. Right?

"Sure," I said. "But yeah, I can't stay long. It's already 12:30, and my boyfriend's coming over around one."

He glanced at the clock on the wall. "Oh, we got plenty o' time." I thought I sensed disappointment in his voice but couldn't be sure. "I hope you don't mind me going down ahead of you, Molly. The light switch's down there. Everything's a little backwards in this house. I don't know who did the wiring. It was before my time."

I was more than happy to let him go first. "Sure. Whatever works."

"Just watch your step. The stairs are a little steep."

In my cheeriest tone, I said, "Thanks for the warning!" but held the mug of tea in one hand and my phone in the other. Just in case. I couldn't help wondering what Diana would say if she could see me.

Diana thought all old dudes were creepy, but Fred wasn't giving off any creepy vibes.

His stairs were *creaky* though, and very steep, as he'd warned. Once we reached the bottom and my eyes adjusted to the lighting—and my nose to the much stronger smell of WD-40. Two long metal tables ran along the front wall, and above them were rows and rows of shelves. Electronic equipment pretty much covered every *inch* of space on the tables *and* the shelves. There were five or six large, radio-looking things adorned with all kinds of knobs, dials, and buttons, and crammed in around them—and everywhere else—were various speakers, headphones, computer parts, microphones, cords, calculators, and all kinds of other small devices I couldn't identify at all. *What the hell?* I couldn't help gasping.

"What d'ya think?" he asked, sounding like the parent of a kid who'd just performed in a school talent show.

I shrugged and continued to stare. In addition to all the techie stuff, pens and pencils were strewn around everywhere, along with elastic bands, notebooks, bits of wire, and random tools like pliers, screwdrivers, and hammers. Many of the electronic items were labeled with black Dymo stickers—most of which were illegible—but one, on a large boxlike device, said *Battery changed 2/4/09*. Several coffee mugs and spoons were also in the mix, and in front of the largest radio-thingy stood a single swivel chair.

"What *is* it?" I asked, remaining on the bottom step in case I needed to bolt. I checked my phone again for signal and saw two bars. Definitely enough to make a call.

"My ham radio equipment," answered Flaherty. "Or most of it anyway. Quite a collection, huh?"

"Um, *yeah....*" I'd had no idea the hobby involved so much *stuff*. What'd he do with it all?

I turned around to see if there was more, but the other side of the cellar, with its classic 1970s paneling, was relatively empty and organized. A litter box, a gray cat-climbing structure, and a couple of small metal feeding bowls occupied one corner. And curled up, asleep on a large yellow cushion, lay Kitty.

"His favorite spot," said Flaherty. "I had a feeling he'd be down here." He smiled a tender smile. "See that writing on his pillow, Molly?"

I looked more carefully. Embroidered on the cushion were some black dots and dashes, but they didn't look like writing. "Not... really. I just see a... random design?"

IT DOESN'T HAVE TO BE THAT WAY

"A-ha!" said Flaherty, obviously amused. "Except that it's not random at all. It spells the word 'pal' in Morse code. P: *di dah dah dit*, A: *di dah*, L: *di dah di dit*."

"Oh. I... see. That's... interesting. Did you, uh, make that cushion yourself?"

He chuckled softly. "Me? Nah. I can sew a button on a shirt, but that's about it. This was a gift from my friend Billy when he and his wife moved to Florida. His wife, Sally, made it. Very talented lady. She used to make all kinds of great stuff back in the day."

"Hmm. It's nice." Not my style, but clearly a thoughtful gift.

"You know it's funny," continued Flaherty, "I always thought it looked outta place in my living room. Too... big and bright. But Kitty took to it right away, so I brought it down to the hamshack for him. Seems fitting, I think. My little pal, you know?"

I detected a slight sadness in his voice as he spoke those last words, and decided it was a good time to change the subject. "So Fred," calling him Fred felt so strange, but I forced myself because he'd asked me to, "I can tell ham radio's a pretty cool thing, but I don't understand what it... does."

He sighed. "It's not exactly the rage with your generation, huh?"

"Not really."

"Well, in a nutshell, every ham has his own—or her own—antenna, or tower, as we like to call 'em. I'm sure you've seen mine in the back yard?"

"It's a little hard to miss."

He sighed again. "Right. Fifty-three feet. I don't think the neighbors like it, but it's a good one. Anyway, we use our transmitters—our radios—and towers to send signals to other hams. We don't rely on infrastructure like telephone lines or cell networks."

"Huh," I said, in the most enthusiastic voice I could muster, although he was already losing me. I've always found technology confusing. Even at my job—where I wrote marketing material about computer software every day—I relied on the engineers to provide me with proper techie language for the brochures and web pages I created.

"Of course, it gets a lot more involved than that, like when we boost our signal with local repeaters. But in its simplest form, ham radio works antenna to antenna."

"Huh," I said again. I had no idea what a local repeater was and felt certain that asking would only lead to a long and complicated explanation. "So why's it called *ham* radio?"

He shook his head. "Good question. And no one seems to have a good answer. The best explanation I've heard is that *ham* is short for *amateur*. If that makes any sense. See, the official name for ham radio is *amateur radio*."

"Hmm. That's kinda weird," I said, eyeing the equipment again. "And you don't exactly strike me as an amateur, Mr. Fl... Fred."

This time, the sadness in his voice got more pronounced. "Yeah, well, maybe not in the radio world. But when it comes to life... oh boy."

I had absolutely no idea how to respond to that, so I checked my phone screen again. "Yeah, I hear ya. But you know what? I gotta run in a minute. 'Cause my boyfriend, you know. He's on his way over."

"Oh right. You wouldn't wanna keep him waiting."

Did I detect a note of sarcasm there? And would it be too weird to ask Flaherty outright about the police? I really was curious, but the timing didn't feel right. Not yet, at least.

"So here's a question," I said slowly. "Please don't take offense, but what makes all this stuff better than a phone? I mean, phones are so easy. And cheap. Comparatively, anyway."

He said nothing for a few seconds. Then he smiled a tired smile and closed his eyes. When he opened them again, he seemed newly energized. Maybe even a bit younger. "Well, like I was saying, that's the difference between creating your own signal—which travels over the airwaves for free—and using someone else's network—"

"But—"

"No, hear me out. You do realize that every time you pick up a telephone, you're using someone else's network, right? And if that network goes down, you lose your ability to communicate."

"Yeah—"

"Yeah. And those networks can *easily* go down. Or get overwhelmed during an emergency. Remember what happened after 9/11, when all the cell networks got overloaded? But *hams* were able to keep some lines of communication open. They also did a tremendous amount of work during Hurricane Katrina. And in Haiti, after the earthquake."

Without warning, I got a little emotional. "Wow. That's... kind of awesome."

"Yeah it is. And those are only the big ones that make the papers. Most of our work's... smaller stuff, you know? Coastal flooding, heavy snowstorms, that sorta thing. We try to be helpful when we can."

Again, I wasn't sure what to say. "So... *you've* done stuff like that?"

"Oh sure. I didn't make it to Haiti or New Orleans, but local work, sure. The Blizzard of '78—long before you were born—was one of our biggest projects here in Massachusetts. I'll never forget *that* winter."

"My parents have pictures of it," I said, glad to finally be able to contribute to the conversation. "My dad's school was canceled for a week."

"I believe it," said Flaherty. "The whole state was shut down. Most of New England, in fact."

I nodded and sighed. "So how'd you get *started* in all this ham stuff?"

"Oh, I got hooked on electronics and radio stuff as a kid. Anything with wires or batteries. Then, in '58, I enlisted in the Army, and they sent me over to Frankfurt. In Germany. They put me in a special group, intercepting Soviet Code. Top secret stuff." He smiled when he said those last three words and shook his head. "We thought we were savin' the world from the Russians."

I'd never imagined Flaherty doing anything so interesting. "So you were a Cold War spy?"

He let out a little laugh. "Well, you could say that, but believe me, it wasn't like the movies. Mostly we sat around listening to transmissions and signals. Wacky stuff, some of it. Seems like a million years ago. It's a different world now."

I nodded. "Yeah, but it must've been cool being part of all that. I mean, it sounds exciting."

"Well, I guess some of it was. Europe was still rebuilding after the war, so people felt hopeful. And I got to see some of the world. And hell, three years in the service and the worst injury I got was this bum knee. Crazy thing. Jeep I was riding in rolled over one day." He paused, then winced. "But I got the last of the Flaherty luck. My brother Davey was twelve years younger, so when that poor bugger signed up, they sent him straight to Vietnam."

"Oh. That sucks."

He shook his head. "You don't know the half of it, Molly."

We sat silently for a few seconds, and Fred's eyes traveled someplace far away. When they returned, he forced a smile. "Jeez, how'd we get talkin' about all this?"

I shrugged. "Um, ham radios?"

"Oh right! And I wanted to ask you a question, Molly. Whatta you pay a year for that smartphone of yours?"

Phew. The old Fred was back. The Fred with an agenda. He seemed much more at ease.

"I'm not actually sure," I answered. "It's a monthly fee, you know?"

"Right. But how much every month? If you don't mind me asking."

I didn't mind but couldn't help wondering if he was gonna suggest I ditch my phone and get a ham radio or something. "Uh, a little under a hundred, I think. But I might switch to a cheaper service."

"And cut it down to what? Fifty a month?"

"Probably. Which is pretty good, I think. That's with unlimited calling, texting and data."

He raised his heavy eyebrows. "Well it depends what you consider good. That's still six hundred a year. And what happens if you break your screen?"

I shrugged. "Get a new phone? It's not so bad if you have insurance."

"Right, but that insurance isn't cheap. Right?"

In fact, I didn't actually have insurance and had replaced my phone twice on my own dime, but I wasn't about to tell him that. "Yeah, but I *need* a phone, Mr.... Fred. You're always talking about women and safety, and I don't think I'm gonna get into ham radio. You know?" I smiled so as not to come across as sarcastic. "I need a phone in case I get injured or something. Or some creepy guy starts following me down a dark backstreet."

"Um hmm," he said, his voice taking on a fatherly tone. "But I think you're smart enough to avoid backstreets at night. And people *did* survive for thousands of years without smartphones."

"Yeah, but *everyone* has 'em now." I knew that sounded bratty, but I couldn't help it. As he'd pointed out himself, the world was moving forward fast. And I wanted to stay with it.

Fred nodded like a teacher who disagreed with his student but didn't want to patronize the kid. "Maybe. But you *could* get one of those TracFones they sell at Radio Shack for very little money. Then you wouldn't have a monthly contract, and you'd still have a solution in an emergency."

Was he out of his mind? Did he really think I'd be able to live a normal life with a burner phone and no apps? Not even email? "You know, I just don't think that'd work for me. I'm not an indie kind of person like you. I mean, I respect you so much, but I guess I'm pretty mainstream. You know?"

He smiled kindly. "Not exactly. But I like the word *indie*. Most people just think I'm a nut."

"No they don't," I said, although I wasn't so sure. "But speaking of phones," I glanced down at mine, "I gotta go." Bummer that we hadn't discussed the police, but I'd told him Joe was coming over at one o'clock, and it was 12:58.

"Ah, well, thanks for stopping by, Molly. Hey, you wanna give those brownies to your boyfriend? No offense, but I'm a little afraid of Kitty gettin' into 'em. He can be a sneaky guy sometimes."

I didn't want the brownies—I had plenty—but got the sense that Fred would feel guilty if he threw them out, and the poor guy was obviously worried about the cat.

"Oh, sure. I don't wanna make Kitty sick. I wish I'd made banana bread or something."

Fred shook his head. "No. Don't blame yourself, Molly. You did a nice thing and I appreciate it. But that little bugger... he broke into a box of crackers in the pantry one night, and if he ever ate the chocolate...."

I felt an unfamiliar warmth in my heart for Fred as I started up the stairs with him behind me.

"Thanks again, Molly," he said, when we were back in the kitchen. Rocking on the balls of his feet, he retrieved the plate of brownies and handed them to me. "I hope you can come over again for tea soon."

"Sure thing. And thank *you*."

I turned and marched across the street with what I hoped resembled a sense of purpose. But as I unlocked my door and stepped inside, loneliness hit me hard. Damn it, I was in a worse situation than *Fred*. I mean, at least he had Kitty to keep him company.

A strange urge to run back to his house and tell him Joe had canceled last minute came over me, but I flopped on the couch instead. "Get a grip on yourself, Molly," I whispered. Besides, Fred was a boring old dude. I'd be better off finding a good movie on TV and getting lost in someone else's story for a couple of hours.

Chapter 15
Time In A Bottle

Molly
Spring, 2004
North Andover, MA

All friends argue, I'd remind myself, over and over again. *And Kate was being a total jerk that Friday in the lunchroom.*

Those things were true. I'd been *crazy* upset about Mark going to the prom with Courtney, and Kate had acted like it was no big deal. Anyone hearing that part of the story would side with me. I had every right to be pissed and stay home from her friend's party in Cambridge.

But after I'd dragged my butt up to my bedroom, changed into cozy sweats, and crawled underneath the covers, Kate started texting me. Then emailing. And when I ignored both, she called. Multiple times.

"I was a complete shit, Molly," she said over voicemail. "Plain and simple. No excuses. I'm so, so sorry. I'll *never* treat you like that again. I promise. Just give me one more chance. Please? I'll be at the bus stop at five. See you there?"

Unfortunately, I'd sunk way too deep into my private cave of blankets, cramps, and self-pity to even consider her plea. The sky outside was gray, and the air was damp and chilly. Not to mention that Kate hadn't cared about leaving me in North Andover any *other* weekend. What was unique about this time? If she really wanted my company in Boston, she'd have to wait until a Friday when I felt better. And less pissed off.

Mom totally agreed. "I think you're making a smart choice, Molly. I'm sure you and Kate'll be best friends again by Monday, but I'm glad you're staying in tonight, safe and warm."

"Yeah."

She smiled. "Hey, how 'bout I go out and rent a video, and we'll watch it together? That new one with Hugh Grant just came out on tape. *Love Actually*, I think it's called."

IT DOESN'T HAVE TO BE THAT WAY

Kate wasn't in homeroom Monday, though. At first, I didn't think much of it, because her mom would often let her sleep in on Monday mornings and drive her to school a little late. Kate got good grades, and her Boston weekends often left her exhausted. But right before lunch, the principal, Mrs. Mack, called me into her office to ask if I knew where my friend was.

"No," I said. "Maybe you should call her parents?"

"Well, unfortunately, I've spoken with them several times today. Kate was expected home last night, but they haven't been able to reach her."

"Oh!" My stomach tightened. "I mean, she went to a party in Cambridge over the weekend."

Mrs. Mack frowned. "A party? Are you sure? Because her parents are under the impression she was staying at an old friend's home. They didn't mention any party. Molly, I need you to tell me everything you know. Right now."

I stared, unable to speak.

"And no secrets," said the principal, her tone sharpening. "Kate may be in trouble. The police are already involved."

Dread spread through my body like ink in a glass of water. "Um... she... the party was at a girl's house. A girl named Denise."

The principal jotted something down and picked up the phone. "What else?"

"Not... I don't... I don't really... know more."

"Well think hard, please. You seem to have more information than anyone else at the moment. And stay right here. An officer will be in to talk with you soon."

Several hours later, Kate was identified as the teenager who'd been rushed by ambulance to Beth Israel Hospital on Saturday morning after a dog walker discovered her unconscious, bleeding, and wrapped in a towel in a Cambridge alleyway. She'd been beaten, raped, and left to die. But after several days of hospitalization, her prognosis brightened a bit, and the doctors became cautiously optimistic about her chance of survival.

Mom, Dad, and I drove into Boston to visit Kate about a week later, but she didn't even open her eyes while we were there, and her mother—who'd been staying at the hospital 24/7—was incredibly cold to me. I didn't exactly blame her, but it still hurt like hell. She obviously believed I could've prevented—or at least lessened the severity of—the attack if I'd been with Kate. I didn't know what to think. All I knew for sure was that I wanted to hang out with my friend again, and that the evil person or people who'd done those horrible things to her deserved life in jail.

But as the weeks passed, the police investigation raised more questions than answers. And when Kate could finally speak—a bit—she had no recollection of the incident. The police somehow managed to figure out Denise's address in Allston, but when they went to her house, Denise admitted she'd been completely wasted at the party. She recalled Kate being at her home at some point but had no idea when she'd left or with whom. One of the guests said they'd heard Kate talking about some other party, but that was it. And none of the DNA samples taken from Kate's body provided any leads.

As far as her health was concerned, Kate had multiple injuries—both internal and external—and would need plastic surgery on her face as well. But the worst news was that she'd suffered some form of brain damage that was most likely irreversible. When her parents learned that, they asked the hospital to remove my family and me from the approved visitor list.

"They're being ridiculous," said Mom as I sobbed at the dinner table. "I know they're suffering—God knows they're suffering—but none of this is your fault, Molly. Kate made some bad choices and you made some good ones."

Good? "Mom!" I screamed through my tears. "If I'd been with Kate, the two of us would've been together, and she'd probably be safe at home right now. Oh my god, I still can't believe she was lying in that alley alone all night, and—"

"If you'd gone, you'd be in the hospital too," interrupted Dad. "Maybe even dead. You heard what that Cambridge cop said. *You* were the smart one. *You* used your head. It's a shame your friend didn't."

But I couldn't accept that. I just couldn't. And when Kate was discharged from the hospital—over a month later, in a wheelchair—no member of her family would speak to my parents or me, despite all the flowers and cards we sent.

And although I could accept—from a rational standpoint—that I wasn't morally responsible for what'd happened, I also couldn't imagine living the rest of my life without Kate's forgiveness.

IT DOESN'T HAVE TO BE THAT WAY

Thanks to the assistance of the school nurse—who let me eat lunch in her office every day--and the North Andover High guidance department, I made it through the last few months of junior year. I attended as many classes as I could bear, but the teachers pretty much left me alone. They didn't call on me unless I raised my hand, and I hardly ever did. As for the Latin poetry project—the one I was supposed to do with Mark Rosen—Mr. Trombly abruptly canceled the whole thing with no explanation whatsoever. I spent prom night weeping in my room.

Meanwhile, none of the other kids messed with me either. Sometimes I'd walk into a classroom and people would suddenly stop talking, but I didn't care. Most days, I stumbled around feeling like I'd just woken up; my head was perpetually foggy, and the voices around me often seemed distant and muffled. The school social worker called Mom and recommended therapy, but I refused.

The only thing that gave me any hope was thinking about senior year and the possibility that Kate would return.

Then, on my way home from school one June day, I spotted a *For Sale* sign on Kate's lawn. It'd been raining and windy all morning, and the sign was such an assault to my sensibilities that I actually believed it'd blown into Kate's yard from someplace else. Because Kate *couldn't* be moving. She'd only been in North Andover for two years, and her parents took great pride in their gorgeous yard and huge vegetable garden.

But the sign remained until, about a week later, it was replaced by one that read *Sold*. That's when I realized I *needed* to find out what was going on. So I crossed my fingers and tiptoed up the front steps. Kate's mom answered the door, dressed in a bathrobe. Her lips were stained purple and she smelled like wine. "We're goin' t'Arizona," she said, slurring her words but still managing to sound aloof and nasty. "Katie's gotta heal."

"But..." My eyes filled with tears. I felt like I was being strangled. "Can I please talk to her? Just for a minute? She's my best friend and—"

"Friend? Yeah. With friends like you, sweetie..." her voice trailed off, and her chin trembled. "Katie don' even know her own name half the time, let alone yours. Now get outta here. I mean it. Get outta here right now."

I don't think I'd ever felt worse. I'd been emailing, texting, and calling Kate for weeks with no response, but had managed to convince myself there was a good explanation—like maybe her doctors wouldn't let her use electronic devices because she'd had a concussion—and that things would soon change. I simply couldn't face the possibility that Kate no longer cared about me.

But that brief exchange with her mom changed everything. Suddenly, I knew Kate and I would never watch another David Lynch movie together, or sit in the cafeteria talking about Morrissey, Tori Amos, or Carrie Brownstein. I don't remember walking home, but I cried into my pillow for the rest of the afternoon.

Perhaps my only real achievement that summer was getting a driver's license, and honestly, that only made me more anxious. Because even though I'd sort of enjoyed my weekly lessons with the patient driving-school teacher whose car reeked of cigars, I had no desire to actually control a vehicle. Too many horrific things can happen in the amount of time it takes to change the radio station. So, although I *would* occasionally drive to the pharmacy or maybe even the local mall on my own, I usually just walked or took the bus.

I was sleeping like shit too. I'd crawl into bed around midnight most nights and close my eyes, but almost immediately, the name *Mick* would start haunting me. Mick, Kate's "friend" in Boston. When she'd first mentioned the party to me, Kate had said we might stay at his place. But none of Denise's party guests questioned by the police recalled anyone named Mick being there.

Could Kate have said *Vick?* Or *Dick?* Maybe *Rick?* Or even *Mike?* It made me crazy to realize that *my* brain—which might hold the key to identifying the attacker who'd so brutally damaged *Kate's* brain—refused to cooperate. But if I could somehow extricate that information from my dense skull, Kate's mother might give me another chance.

"Honey, you've gotta stop beating yourself up," said Mom one morning as she got ready for work. "You're gonna make yourself sick."

Couldn't she see I was already sick? "I'm *not* beating myself up! I just wanna help. I can't stop wishing I'd gone to that freaking party."

Mom laid her purse on the kitchen table and sat in the chair beside me. "I think that's called beating yourself up," she said softly. "And you know, honey, I agree with your father on this one. If you'd gone to the party, you probably would've been hurt too. Maybe even worse than Kate."

"So what! Then people would feel sorry for me instead of blaming me like they do now. Everywhere I go in town, people stare. They hate me. I'd rather be in physical pain."

Mom closed her eyes for a few seconds and muttered something, maybe a prayer. "Molly," she finally said, "Kate's dealing with much more than just physical pain. From what I've heard through the grapevine, she won't ever be the same again."

"Yeah, I know. And neither will I."

Since I'd never bothered looking for a summer job, I spent the hot month of July in the house, reading and watching TV. Every time I thought about going back to school, I felt sick to my stomach, and occasionally fantasized about running away from home. But I knew that was a bad idea. Then I came up with a good one.

"Hey guys," I asked my parents one night at dinner, "do you think I could be homeschooled? Just for one year?" I'd done a little research and had learned the school system's requirements: Parents needed to sign a bunch of paperwork; then they had to help their kid keep up with the curriculum at home. And in my case, the workload wouldn't be too bad, because I'd already covered most of the core requirements. It might be lonely, but it seemed far better than the alternative.

I expected my parents to freak out, but instead, they looked at each other and shrugged. "Molly," said Dad, "we need to talk about something."

I felt my gut shrink with angst as Mom began twirling her fork really fast in her pasta. My parents had always bickered, but they'd been fighting more than usual that summer, so my first thought was that they were splitting up. "What?" I asked.

"Well, we've been thinking about... moving," said Dad.

Huh? "Moving? Together?"

Dad laughed uncomfortably and Mom actually gasped. "Well, yes," said Dad. "Of course."

I sat there, momentarily speechless. "Really?" I finally said. "Where?"

"Well, with your brother up at UNH, we could save a bundle if we lived in New Hampshire."

Mom jumped in. "But you know," she said, shooting Dad a sharp look, "money's not the most important thing here. This is about *you*, Molly. After all that's happened, we thought you might appreciate a change of scenery."

For the first time since Kate's attack, a tiny pang of joy seized my heart. *Moving!* My parents had lived in North Andover since before Tim was born, and I'd never heard them discuss moving. I looked back and forth between them, trying to get a read on their faces. "Seriously?"

"Yes," said Mom. "We've already looked at a few houses."

It was better than a dream come true, because I hadn't even dreamed it. "Where? I mean... what part of New Hampshire?"

Dad finished chewing the food in his mouth, cleared his throat, and pointed his fork at me. "Probably North Hampton. It's a good time of year to buy houses near the ocean. End of the tourist season, you know?"

The ocean. My eyes filled up and I actually got dizzy. Pushing my chair back from the table, I stood on shaky legs. "I gotta go lie down."

"You okay, Honey?" asked Mom, also standing.

I nodded, and Mom rushed over to hug me.

"You look like you're gonna cry," she said.

"Yeah..." I gasped for breath. "But I'm good. They're happy tears."

Chapter 16
Recently

Molly
September, 2012
Arlington, MA

"Eat those up, would ya, Molly? My friend Helen baked 'em this morning. She's always bringin' me desserts, and the doc wants me to stay off the sugah." Mrs. Costa pushed the plate of Italian cookies closer to me, then rolled her eyes toward Fred's house. "So I saw you over *there* yesterday."

"Yup," I said, determined not to gossip about Fred. Twenty minutes earlier, Mrs. Costa had called, saying she was doing her fall cleaning and had found a kitchen chair in her basement that I might like. Which was a bit odd, but I did need kitchen furniture. So there I was, perched on a fancy love seat in her living room, drinking lemonade and wondering why I'd been dumb enough to fall into her trap.

I mean, the chair was nice enough, but Mrs. Costa clearly had ulterior motives. First of all, she was wearing lipstick, a frilly blouse, and the type of creased slacks she normally wore to church: pretty much the opposite of cleaning attire. And the cookies were icy in the middle, so I suspected they'd been in her freezer for a while, not baked that morning.

"So was his place *filthy?*" she asked.

"No! He actually keeps it really clean. A lot cleaner than mine, for sure."

She raised her penciled eyebrows and sucked her teeth. "Hmm. Well, you know what they say when men are too clean, don't ya? The first sign of insanity."

Anger swelled in my chest, and I chose my words carefully. "But it *wasn't* too clean. It was just right. And he's not insane. I know he's a little different, but he's a cool guy." *So there.*

Mrs. Costa was just getting started, though. "I see," she said, sipping her lemonade through a straw. "Well, let me tell *you* a few things. For your own safety."

The word *safety* triggered me a little. I desperately wanted to believe Fred was nothing more than a lonely, misunderstood man, but Mrs. Costa *had* known him a long time. "He seems pretty safe to me," I said.

The woman sniffed and licked her upper lip like one of those yappy miniature dogs. "Oh dear. And as you know, I *hate* talking trash about the neighbors, but this is important, Molly." She paused and licked her lip again. "Listen. When Fred Flaherty was a little boy, he spent a few years in the Nutty Crest."

"The *what*?"

"You know, the Nutty Crest," Mrs. Costa said matter-of-factly. "That school down there on the Cambridge line? The place for kids with... problems. I don't know the real name of it, but that's what we used to call it." She dropped her voice to a stage whisper. "'Cause everyone who went there was a little *coo-coooo*." She added a singsong tone to that last word and traced big, loopy circles beside her ear with her index finger. "I never trusted him after that."

My stomach started to hurt, and not from the sugary lemonade or the half-frozen cookies. Part of me didn't give a rat's ass about Fred having issues as a child, but then again, the cops *had* been at his house a few days earlier. And Kate had trusted the wrong man....

"Okay. Thanks, Mrs. Costa. But I gotta get going. I've got some work to do at home."

"Oh sure, Molly. Just lemme tell you one more thing."

My stomachache got worse and I couldn't help sighing. "Okay."

Her face assumed a pious expression. "Well, back before we got cable on the TV, the noise from Flaherty's radio thingy would *buzz, buzz, buzz* through our set all the time. Every night. *Buzz, buzz, buzz.* Just like that. Anthony, my late husband, used to say he was spyin' on us and sendin' the information to the government." She rolled her eyes. "Who can say? But that's why we got the cable. I hate payin' that bill, but I don't want that old loon knowin' my personal business."

"Huh," I said, suppressing a laugh. I mean, even if Fred *was* a spy, why would the government care about Mrs. Costa? "I dunno. I think Mr. Flaherty's pretty harmless these days."

"*Harmless*?" she said, leaning across the table and inadvertently sharing her stale breath with me. "Molly, lemme tell you somethin' else. That man's *far* from harmless. He may be good lookin', but don't let that fool you. In high school, he was a *mouse*. Skittering around." She scratched all ten of her fingernails on the coffee table, apparently illustrating the type of skittering Fred had done in his youth.

"And his baby brother David?" she continued. "He was even worse, from what I've heard. Oh, he was normal for a while, but then he got all whacked out too. I don't know if it was drugs or what, but that family's got some loose screws. It's very sad."

She didn't sound sad, though; she just rolled her eyes again. "God bless those poor parents. That's all I can say. They were saints. They didn't deserve those two nutters."

I was starting to hate her. Was there even one ounce of compassion in her heart? "Mrs. Costa, I don't think it's fair to say that about Fred. He's very sweet nowadays."

She licked her upper lip more voraciously. "No. He's a trickster. A good-lookin' trickster. You shouda seen the way he tricked that Barbara. Now *there* was a gorgeous girl. And she married him, for cryin' out loud. Until she smartened up, that is."

I sighed again. "Thanks, Mrs. Costa, but I really do have to run now."

"Awright, Molly. But I think he was hittin' Barb. I know I shouldn't say that, but I think it's true. And I wouldn't wanna see you get hurt."

Hitting? "Mrs. Costa, Fred wouldn't hit anyone."

She shrugged. "Yeah, but Mrs. Jacoby... you don't remember Mrs. Jacoby, do you? I guess she died right before you moved here. But she lived in that brown house on the corner and she heard a lady screamin' over there one night, right before Barb moved out. If you want my opinion, he was beatin' her. It's none o' my business, but that's what I think."

I shivered when she said that. "So... his wife left him?" I leaned back to avoid another onslaught of her breath.

"Oh yes! *Many* years ago. Of course, I don't know the whole story. All I know is she told Mrs. Jacoby her husband was keepin' secrets and she needed to get away."

"But keeping secrets doesn't mean he was *hitting* her," I said. "That could mean almost anything."

Mrs. Costa shrugged. "Believe what you want, Molly. Me? I got opinions. And if I was you, I'd stay the heck away from that house."

I stood up, my stomach on fire. Part of me wished I'd never accepted her invitation. Then again, maybe Fred did have a violent side. "Thanks, Mrs. Costa."

"Any time, Molly. I hope you enjoy the chair."

I did my best to smile. But I hobbled across the street—the legs of the chair assaulting my shins—as fast as I could, then ran to the bathroom and vomited.

Chapter 17
Child Of Midnight

Molly
2004
North Hampton, NH

I loved the house in New Hampshire. It was smaller than the one in North Andover, but everything about it was brighter. And better. I even got a glimpse of the ocean from my bedroom window when it wasn't too foggy. Seagulls screamed overhead, and the salty stickiness of the air made the whole place feel like an island. Weirdly enough, it was only about twenty-five miles from North Andover—close enough that my parents were both able to keep their jobs and commute—but the emotional distance seemed infinite. For a while, anyway.

On the first day of school, kids smiled and greeted me warmly like they meant it. Because they *did* mean it. I was a *real* new girl at Winnacunnet High, and the skin on my arms tingled all morning long. When the bell rang after my last class before lunch, I realized I'd gone four straight hours without thinking about Kate.

But the familiar lunchtime dread returned as I stepped into the cafeteria and bought a grilled cheese sandwich. *Confidence*, I thought. *Act confident and people will accept you.* And it worked! A girl named Amanda from my English class called me over to sit with her and a few other girls.

It felt so normal, almost like a movie about high school. The people at my table were obviously smart, well-respected kids, and we chatted about regular, non-controversial things like teachers, lunch food, and what we'd done over the summer. After all the drama and sadness of the previous year, mundane was amazing. I longed for nothing more.

Then Lynn, a blondish girl with short hair and dull gray eyes, asked, "So why'd you move from North Andover, Molly? My mom's cousin lives there, and it's, like, just a few exits down 495, right?" Her tone sounded competitive—almost accusatory—but I shrugged it off.

Lynn struck me as one of those insecure people who always felt the need to compete.

"Yeah, it's like half an hour away," I said. "But my parents wanted to be near the beach. Plus, there was an issue with my brother's tuition. He goes to UNH."

"Ohhhh. I see," said Lynn as if I'd let her in on some huge secret. "Your folks wanted the in-state rate. Don't they call that carpetbagging?" She smiled and gave me a gentle poke on the arm, but I was shocked. Was she suggesting that my family had done something unethical?

"Um... I don't know. I mean, the main reason we came here was for the beach."

Lynn squinted. "Uh huh."

Luckily, Amanda interrupted that line of conversation by whispering, "Hey look, there's Eddie! He got a cute haircut." And with that, everyone at the table shifted their attention to the boy.

I was pretty sure Amanda had changed the subject on my account, and I was grateful. *But carpetbaggers? My parents? What the hell?* I'd have to ask them about that at dinner.

Someone tapped my shoulder, and looking up, I saw a slight boy with shoulder-length reddish hair standing behind me. "Hey," he said, "you new here?" His pale skin was spattered with acne, but his features were sharp and delicate, almost feminine. He wasn't exactly attractive, but he had something sexy going on. Plus, he was a boy, and at North Andover High, very few boys had spoken to me.

"Yeah. I'm Molly."

"Cool name."

"Thanks," I said. "What's yours?"

"Brian. I'm in your math class so I wanted to say hi."

"Oh, cool. Hi Brian." I was doing my best to act nonchalant, but couldn't help feeling excited. Was it possible that I'd finally start enjoying school again?

The bell rang, and everyone started gathering their stuff. Lynn grabbed her books and popped the last bite of ham sandwich into her mouth. "Brian's your man if you wanna buy weed, Molly," she said, smirking and heading for the door.

Brian shrugged. "Thanks for the intro, Lynn," he called, but she ignored him.

I wasn't sure how to respond, so I just smiled and headed toward the door like everyone else. But when I stopped to let a few people pass, Brian remained beside me.

"Have you lived here long?" I asked.

"All my life. But I'm leaving soon. I'm sick of this puny Atlantic Ocean."

"Puny?" I couldn't help smiling.

"Puny compared to the Pacific. I'm moving to L.A."

I wondered if everyone hated their hometown. "That's cool," I said. "I'd like to go to California someday." We made it out of the cafeteria and into the hallway, and Brian and I both turned left. "Are you a senior?" I asked.

"Yeah. Or I should be. I'm a few credits short, you know?" There was something very innocent about his demeanor, even though he smelled like cigarettes and apparently sold pot.

"That sucks. Will you be able to make 'em up before graduation?"

"No idea, but I'm not gonna sweat it. Like I said, I'm going to L.A. soon. My dad's a film editor, so I can hang with him."

"Oh. Will you graduate?"

"I dunno. I need to talk to my guidance counselor. I don't think it really matters. I wrote a screenplay over the summer, and my dad said it's decent. So I might just fuck school and try selling that."

"Wow. Cool." His plan didn't sound very solid, but what did I know? We were approaching an intersection in the hallway, and an arrow pointing to the left said *Foreign Languages*. "I'm going to Latin," I told him.

"Okay," he said. "Bye for now. See you in math tomorrow."

I watched him saunter away, swinging his arms like he was out for an afternoon stroll. It occurred to me that he wasn't carrying any books. *Nice guy,* I thought. *But not my type.*

The next day, there was no extra seat at Amanda's table. Amanda looked truly upset. "No worries, Molly," she said. "We'll find you a chair."

But although we both scanned the area, there were zero free chairs nearby, and the cafeteria was much busier than it'd been the previous day. And the last thing I wanted to do was make a scene by dragging a chair from the other side of the room. "You know what?" I said. "I'll sit somewhere else today." Lunch was only twenty minutes long, and we'd already wasted five of them.

"There's plenty of room outside," offered Lynn.

Amanda shook her head. "Oh, no. Stay inside, Molly. The bugs on the lawn are *disgusting*."

"Are there *tables* out there?" I asked.

"No," said Amanda. "Just a hill, and it's dirty and gross."

With her fork, Lynn dipped a chunk of pork chop into a plastic container of gravy. "Yeah, but it's nice and sunny."

I was starting to wonder if Lynn had hidden the extra chair or something, but that seemed paranoid. "Okay," I said. "I'll go catch a few rays and see you guys tomorrow."

I walked out the back door as calmly as possible but felt discouraged. It was only my second day of school, and already I was eating alone. *Think positive*, I reminded myself. I gripped my tray and started climbing the grassy hill, which was fairly crowded. Some kids sat and chatted as they ate, while others read books or sunned themselves. One girl was drawing in a sketchpad. From somewhere in the distance, I caught a slight whiff of marijuana smoke.

Okay. This is kinda cool. I found a spot where I could sit without invading anyone's privacy and allowed the sun to warm my face. Lots of kids were eating alone, quite possibly by choice. But just as I bit into my pizza, a male voice called my name. I turned to see Brian ambling down the hill.

"Hey," I said.

He squatted next to me. "Hey, Molly. How's your day going?"

Over the next few weeks, I learned a lot about Brian. For starters, he was failing both math and science, which was a problem because he'd flunked those classes junior year too. Meaning he couldn't graduate in the spring without summer school, and he was *so* not into that. Also, as Lynn had mentioned, he sold marijuana. His business was pretty smalltime, but he did manage to earn enough cash to pay for gas, butts, and car maintenance. So yeah, he and I were very different on the surface. On the other hand, we shared the same basic dream: to fall in love—for real—with the right person. He was gay and closeted, though, so he'd decided he'd need to move to Hollywood to find his happiness.

We got along great. But because I'd learned the hard way that having only one close friend at school's usually a bad idea, I forced myself to mix things up at lunch. About half the time, I'd sit indoors with Amanda, Lynn, and the other girls, and would eat outside with Brian the other half. Being around Brian was almost always more fun, but occasionally, he'd be in a terrible mood and nothing could shake him out of it. On those days, all he'd talk about was booking a flight to L.A. I didn't blame him, either. His mother didn't accept his homosexuality—she believed it was a phase he'd grow out of—and he'd never had a boyfriend. So the poor dude was really frustrated.

Amanda, on the other hand, was always pleasant to me. Behind her back, some kids said she was fake, but I could tell she was the real deal. Some people in this world are just friendly and kind, and Amanda fell into that category. Most of the other girls at the lunch table were nice to me too, with Lynn being the one exception. Whenever she spoke to me, I got the sense she was trying to make me squirm.

Like the day she asked how we were dealing with the rodent problem in my house. I told her we didn't have a rodent problem—because we didn't—but she rolled her eyes and said her mom was friends with the realtor who'd sold my parents the house, and that the basement was full of mice. Which was ridiculous—I mean, I did laundry in the basement all the time and had never seen any sign of a mouse. But Lynn spoke with authority, and I'm sure at least some of the girls at the table thought I was lying.

Another time, she made me feel self-conscious about my shoes for no reason at all. I owned a pair of Doc Martens that I'd bought while shopping with Kate: the classic Mary Jane style with double buckles. I didn't wear them much because they brought back too many memories, but one day I did, and Lynn noticed immediately.

"Hey," she said. "Cool Docs. You got 'em at that second-hand store up in Rye, right?"

"No."

"Are you *sure*?" she asked. "'Cause I saw a pair *exactly* like them there last week. They even had the same scuff on the toe."

"Yeah, I'm sure. I got these a few years ago."

"Hmm," said Lynn. "I don't know. I mean, a lot of people don't like admitting they buy things secondhand. Especially shoes. I've heard you can catch foot fungus from them."

What the fuck? "Lynn," I said, trying to keep my voice level, "I have no problem buying things secondhand. Shoes, whatever. But I got these ones new. Okay?"

"Fine," she said, looking indignant. "No need to get snippy. It's just a weird coincidence. That scuff on the toe is, like, identical."

I stopped wearing the Docs to school after that and ate lunch with Brian for the rest of the week.

Brian—who'd grown up in Hampton—told me Lynn had been incredibly unpopular until freshman year. At that point, she'd apparently made some major changes to her appearance, and greased her way into Amanda's social group with money.

"She used to be a real dork," said Brian. "Then her father sold his company, and they moved into one of those giant houses down on Plaice Cove. She started dressing better, and having all these parties, and all of a sudden, she was popular. Pretty gross if you ask me."

"How do you know all this?" I asked. Brian was driving me home along Ocean Boulevard, and even though it was January and really cold outside, we'd rolled the windows down so we could feel the salt air on our faces.

"I stalk her," he said. Then he laughed. "No, just kidding. I used to hang out with her in elementary school. When she lived in *my* neighborhood. Before they moved up in the world."

"Ha," I said. I liked Brian's neighborhood, but it was definitely a little run-down. "I just wish I knew why she hates me so much."

Brian shook a Marlboro Light out of a pack of butts, stuck it in his mouth, and lit it. "I doubt she hates you."

"Well she doesn't *like* me."

"Ever consider that she's gay and has a thing for Amanda? And she's jealous 'cause Amanda likes you so much."

I laughed. "I guess you never know."

"You said it, girl," said Brian, his eyes smiling. "So, what's old Lynnie giving you shit about these days?"

"Oh, just... everything. It's like no matter what I say or do, she twists it into something weird or derogatory. Or she acts like I'm lying."

"She's a dildo," he said, exhaling smoke.

I borrowed his cigarette and took a drag. I didn't really enjoy smoking, but it was fun bumming hits off Brian.

"You better not pick up my filthy habit, lady," he said. "I don't wanna be responsible for your cancer." On the word "cancer," his voice rose in pitch and trembled a little.

"Brian, you okay?" It wasn't like him to get emotional that way. I'd gotten used to his occasional anger and pessimism, but I'd never seen him weepy.

"Yeah," he said as a tear slid down his cheek. Carefully, he pulled his Honda Civic over to the side of the road and looked out at the waves as they raged their winter battle against the shore. I watched too. I loved living near the ocean.

"You wanna talk?" I asked.

Brian wiped his eyes and found a napkin in the glove box for his nose. "I'm sorry," he said, sobbing. "I just realized how much I'm gonna miss you. I talked to my dad last night, and he wants me to come out to L.A. next week. We booked a flight and everything. JetBlue."

A sick feeling settled in my stomach. Another friend moving far away. How could that be?

"You're sure you don't wanna graduate first? 'Cause I've been thinking maybe we could combine our parties." Kids had already started planning graduation parties, and the trend in Hampton was to double or triple up with friends.

"Nah. I can't deal with that summer school bullshit, so Dad said screw it. I'm gonna go for a GED."

"And your mom's okay with that?"

He shrugged. "She'd rather have me finish up here, but she's tryna date too, and we've got a small house. So I'm harshing on her lifestyle, you know?"

I looked at Brian's delicate face and my mouth quivered. "What'll I do without you? I'm gonna miss you so much."

A few more tears rolled down his face. "Aw, I'll miss you too, Mol. You're a blast to hang with." He tossed his cigarette out the window and gave me a hug. In all the time we'd known each other, we'd never actually hugged, and the strength of his arms surprised me. He smelled like smoke and something medicinal—maybe acne medication—and I allowed myself to bawl into the shoulder of his leather jacket.

"Hey," said Brian, releasing his grip after a minute and sitting back. "Wanna get high?"

I'd only smoked pot twice before—in Kate's garage—and hadn't really liked it. "Nah," I said. "It makes me kinda paranoid."

"Hmm. So... how do you relax?"

"What d'ya mean?"

"You know, like, when you're stressed out? Or when you can't sleep."

I thought about that. "I dunno. I... watch TV. Or read a book. Sometimes it works."

"Oh god. You ever try Valium?"

"*Valium*? No! I wouldn't even know where to get it."

Brian grimaced. "Well, I know where to *get* it. The thing is, you can't take that shit for kicks, 'cause it's freakin' addictive. But it's a lifesaver when you can't sleep."

I thought about all the nights I'd spent flopping around in bed as the clock's fingers crept closer to morning. "It sounds useful."

"It is," said Brian. "It really is. Lemme see what I can do."

After school on Tuesday, I asked Brian if I could go to the airport with him and his mother the next morning, but he said I'd be wasting my time. "You'd miss a whole day of school, plus you'd have to deal with my mom and her shitty pop radio all the way home."

"I could handle that." We were standing in the corridor because I needed to go make up a Latin test. Which meant Brian wouldn't be driving me home that day.

"Yeah... but no. My mom..." he sniffled, "she'll want some time to talk to me on the way there. Alone, you know. We fight a lot, but she's still my mom."

He smiled, but I could tell he was holding back tears. I wondered if we'd ever see each other again.

"I'm gonna visit you this summer," I said even though I knew I probably wouldn't have the money. And even if I did, my parents would probably say no.

"You freakin' better. I'll be hangin' with Johnny Depp by then, so he and I'll take you out. We'll show you a good time."

"Um, if you start hanging with Johnny Depp, text me *right* away and I'll be on the next plane."

"Deal," said Brian. "But you know, I'm gonna be texting you 24/7 anyway. I'm gonna miss you so much." As he spoke, he patted the side pocket of his denim jacket, then dropped his voice to a whisper. "I got you a little present."

I started to shake my head—I mean, I hadn't gotten him anything—but Brian pulled me in for a hug and whispered in my ear. "Shhh. I'm gonna put somethin' in your hand, and you're gonna take it and not say a word, okay? Not even 'thank you.' Just stick it in your purse and act like nothin' happened."

"Okay?" I said, a little scared.

He wrapped his hands around mine and I felt him slip a small plastic baggie into them. "What...?" I started to whisper, then recalled his instructions and dropped it in my purse.

"I love you," he whispered, giving me a stronger hug. "And these are only for insomnia. Nothin' else. Take one and wait. Never two at the same time. Promise?"

"Yeah. Of course. Thanks." I was one breath away from bursting into tears, but Brian clearly wanted me to stay cool. Plenty of kids and teachers were still milling around, even though classes were officially over for the day.

"Now go ace that test," he said. "I'll be in touch soon."

At first, Brian really did text a lot, but the longer he stayed in L.A., the less frequent his messages came. His dad was an assistant editor on some new TV crime series, and Brian was helping out by doing stuff like checking facts and making coffee runs. One day, he mentioned that he was getting quite friendly with a "cute, slightly older intern" named Glen. Then Glen asked him out for dinner one night, and after that, the texts *really* slowed down. Every week or so, he'd send a joke or a picture he'd taken with his phone, but that was about it.

Of course, I was happy for him—Brian deserved romance in his life—but I felt abandoned too. I mean, what are the odds of a person losing *two* best friends, two years in a row? And I'd lost Theresa after eighth grade too. What was wrong with me? I'd read an article in *Cosmo* about women who don't do well in platonic friendships—they fare better with boyfriends and husbands—so maybe I was one of them?

But none of the boys in North Hampton really did it for me either. There were a couple of cute ones, but none as cute as Mark Rosen, and I still had a crush on him even though I hadn't seen him in months. Some nights, I slept well, but when I didn't, I'd pop one of Brian's Valiums. His little plastic bag had originally contained twenty-five pills, and after I'd used six of them, I started worrying about running out. So, I hid the baggie away and decided to save the rest for emergencies.

Then the worst thing imaginable happened.

IT DOESN'T HAVE TO BE THAT WAY

Unlike most seniors, I took the bus to school. With Brian gone, I didn't have access to a car, and honestly, even if I did, I wouldn't have wanted to drive on the icy, snowy roads that winter. Lynn gave Amanda a ride every morning—and Amanda's house wasn't far from mine—but no way in hell would I ever ask Lynn to drive me too. I couldn't stoop to that level, and besides, sitting alone on the bus was *way* better than dealing with her subtle insults.

But one Friday, when the wind chill was below zero, Lynn's silver Prius pulled up beside me at the bus stop. I'd been nursing a cold with a hacking cough, and was thinking about turning around and walking home. Maybe I needed a three-day weekend to rest and recover.

"Wanna ride?" asked Lynn, rolling down her window just far enough to be heard.

Amanda sat in the passenger seat with a concerned look on her pretty face.

"Sure," I said and climbed in, too sick for pride.

"Holy fuck," said Lynn. "You sound like shit, Molly."

I sniffled. "I know. Thanks for the ride."

Amanda turned around, her forehead deeply creased. "Oh sweetie," she said. Then she looked anxiously at Lynn.

Lynn kept her eyes on the road. "We heard about your friend who OD'd. That's really awful."

"Yeah," said Amanda, turning to face me again. "*Really* awful."

What the hell? Were they talking about Brian? That seemed unlikely, because I'd gotten a text from him around three a.m. saying he'd just seen Gwen Stefani in a restaurant. "I'm confused," I said, my stomach tightening.

Amanda looked even more distressed, but Lynn drove on calmly. "The girl who moved to Arizona. Your friend from North Andover?"

Arizona? Despite the cold, my skin heated up. "Kate?" I whispered. How did they know about Kate? I'd never mentioned her.

"Yeah. Kate. Poor thing. I guess she was pretty depressed." Lynn's voice sounded almost robotic.

I started coughing like crazy, but managed to spit out some words. "Lynn, I think you're... mixed up. Kate... got beaten up in Boston... but that was last year."

"No, Molly..." said Amanda, bursting into tears.

"Wha..." I did my best to breathe through my hacking. "What's goin' on?"

"Pull over, Lynn," said Amanda in the firmest voice I'd ever heard her use, and Lynn did as she was told. When the car stopped, Amanda got out, climbed into the back seat with me, and threw her arms around my neck. "Oh Molly, I'm so sorry. Lynn found out... she heard about your friend..."

I stopped coughing, and my head, already filled with snot, began to throb.

"She died," said Lynn. "It was in yesterday's *Globe*." She paused, then reached over the seat and laid a hand on my shoulder. "I always read the obituaries for kids, you know? And when I saw that she used to live in North Andover, I called my cousin down there, and... yeah. I guess the whole town's talking about it. She OD'd on Oxy or something."

I still didn't believe it, or didn't want to anyway. My mom's paralegal job was at a firm on the Andover-North Andover line, so she would've heard if Kate had died. Was I dreaming? But when I looked into Amanda's cloudy eyes again, I knew I wasn't.

I pulled away from her as my stomach lurched. Somehow, I got the car door open and my head outside just in time to puke Cheerios and blueberries all over the icy street.

After Amanda and Lynn got me into the house, I collapsed on the kitchen floor. Amanda offered to stay, but I wanted to be alone. My mind felt like it was scattered all over the room, like a deck of cards that'd been tossed from a very high place. Tears poured down my face, but I didn't have the strength to wipe them away.

Eventually, I hauled myself up the stairs and climbed into bed. I wanted to fall asleep, but visions of Kate as a dead person haunted me. I imagined her parents finding her, and how she'd looked in her casket. I imagined her being buried or cremated. Had she ever forgiven me? Or did she hate me all the way to the end?

Opening my nightstand drawer, I dug around until I found Brian's bag of Valium. Nineteen pills remained. Brian had emphasized the importance of taking only one at a time, but he'd also been talking about normal insomnia, and this was an exceptional situation. So, I took two.

I needed to shut my brain off for a while. I didn't want death, but also didn't want to feel life's pain either. Unfortunately, the images in my head wouldn't stop, so after twenty minutes, I took two more pills.

Closing my eyes, I pulled the comforter up around my ears. My head felt very heavy, but somehow light too. Like it was sinking into the pillow, but also starting to float. *I'm going to sleep now*, I thought. *Finally.*

Right then, though, a ringing sound startled me back to consciousness. *The phone. Whatever.* It stopped, then started up again. *What the hell?* I tried sitting up, but couldn't, and that's when I panicked.

How many pills had I taken? My arms and legs were lead, and my head was a bowling ball. I felt glued to the bed, immobile. Was I in trouble? Had I overdosed? It occurred to me that I had no idea how strong the pills were. Oh god, I'd taken four. And I really didn't want to die. I had to do something. Somehow, I swung my legs off the bed, flopped onto the floor, and crawled to the phone. My first call was to 911. The second was to my mother.

Chapter 18
Hard Time Losin' Man

Fred
Saturday, October 27, 2012
Arlington, MA

He waved across the road to Molly, who was obviously going someplace fancy in those high-heeled boots and that tight sweater. Probably with that boyfriend of hers. Her very snug jeans were tucked into the boots, and she was carrying a pocketbook. He sighed as he dragged his trashcan up the driveway. When would Molly realize she was wasting her time and money trying to impress that bum?

"Hi Fred!" she called, walking right past the two empty trashcans on her curb. Her landlord — a surly guy who'd bought the house and renovated it years ago when property in Arlington was still cheap — didn't live in town, so Molly and that woman upstairs, Jeanette, shared trash duty. Jeanette typically put the barrels out on Friday morning, and Molly brought them in that night. Or, if she forgot — as she just had — she'd collect them at some point on Saturday.

"Hey, the trash truck came a while ago, you know," he said, pointing to the barrels. He hated when people left trashcans out overnight. They made the neighborhood look sloppy, and if the wind picked up, the barrels sometimes blew into the street, which was both dangerous and dumb.

But Molly clearly had other things on her mind. "Thanks," she said, continuing along toward the bus stop. "I'll grab 'em later. Have a good night!"

He scowled and considered taking Molly's barrels in himself, but felt funny about going into her yard when she wasn't home. Not to mention that if Jeanette saw him, she'd probably come down and start chatting him up, and he wasn't in the mood for that. Jeannette could really put him on edge. He didn't deny that she was a looker — she was small and curvy and right around his age too — but she was much too bold for him. In winter, she wore a fake leopard-skin coat and matching hat that made her look like Joan Crawford in some old movie, and sometimes, in summer, she'd actually put on a *two-piece* bathing suit and sunbathe in the front yard! Needless to say, he'd try to stay indoors when she did that—he felt like a peeping Tom out there with a half-naked lady across the street—but if he *had* to do something outside or get in his truck, he could never resist taking a quick glance over at her. For a woman in her late sixties, she was a hot ticket.

Flirty too. And to be honest, when she'd first moved in, he'd enjoyed the flirtation. But one day, a small brown box from Amazon had accidentally been delivered to his door, and he'd opened it before noticing Jeannette's name on the mailing label. Of course, he'd shoved the book back inside the box as fast as he could when he realized the mistake, but not fast enough to avoid seeing the cover, which showed a bare-chested man clutching a half-dressed woman. The title mentioned something about passion and seduction, and across the top, written in swirly pink letters, was Jeannette's writer name, *Ginette de Montreaux*.

After that, being around Jeannette made him feel funny inside. He simply wasn't comfortable with women who could talk—or write—openly about sex. His mother had never uttered the word in his presence, and he couldn't recall Barb saying it either. Certain things just didn't need to be discussed.

He dragged his trashcan into the garage, then went back in the house and turned on the kettle. For most of the day, he'd been down in the hamshack, listening to people in Florida and New Jersey talk about a hurricane named Sandy that'd done some damage in the Bahamas, but had been reduced—at least temporarily—to a tropical storm. Earlier in the week, meteorologists had worried about Sandy becoming a serious threat to the Northeast, but then she'd started weakening.

And not that he'd ever admit it, but he was a little disappointed. Of course, he'd hate to see anyone get hurt or killed, but ever since the day Molly had asked about his ham radio public service work, he'd been feeling guilty about his lack of involvement in recent years. So, he'd decided that if Sandy started surging up the East Coast, he'd volunteer to help out.

Volunteering always made him feel good about himself, and he'd been so blue since Davey's death. It'd be nice to find something to boost his spirits.

Poor Davey. That was the only way he could think about his brother anymore; the word *poor* was part of his name now. Which was crazy because Fred had been the poor brother for so many years. *Painfully shy. The slow boy. The oddball.* Mean kids in elementary school had bullied him so badly that his parents sent him to a special school for a while. But that didn't stop the teasing. He remembered when Davey was born—he'd been in seventh grade and thrilled to have a new brother—but a boy named Kenny had made him cry by saying the baby was already more mature than him.

Which of course wasn't true, but by the time Davey started school, he was clearly a very different child than Fred had been. In fact, just before Fred left for the Army, he'd overheard his neighbor Mrs. Petrella—Joyce Costa's mother—saying that six-year-old Davey would grow up to be president someday. Everyone adored Davey back then.

Fred blamed the bad changes in his brother—a hundred percent—on the war in Vietnam.

"His hair's long," said his mother when she first caught sight of her younger son walking toward them in Logan Airport. Davey had been in Vietnam for over a year and had only written a couple of letters home.

"Yup," said Fred. "And look at that tan." He wanted to keep his mom calm, but everyone knew that soldiers in Vietnam didn't spend much time lying around on the beach. He held his breath, hoping like hell that his brother wasn't hooked on drugs like some of the vets he'd read about in *LIFE* magazine.

But Davey acted *almost* like regular old Davey for the first week or so back in Arlington. He still had that wide Davey smile, and when he flashed it, the ladies still swooned over his sparkly blue eyes. Gretel, the high school sweetheart who'd waited for him while he was overseas, came around almost immediately, and she and Davey fell back in together as if he'd never left. It wasn't until about ten days later that Fred—who was working full time at the phone company by then but also living at home with his parents—noticed Davey getting quiet. Maybe even a little spacey at times. His eyes would lose their focus and he seemed to be seeing something far, far away.

Gretel left the house sobbing one Saturday afternoon, and Davey started hanging around with a bunch of slightly older ladies who wore gobs of makeup and skimpy, short skirts. It was 1972 and miniskirts were the style, but Davey's girls didn't look healthy or cute in them. Most were much too thin, and they all smoked too much. And every time Fred saw his brother, he'd be with a different one. His mom and dad weren't wild about any of the girls, but they didn't say much to Davey. After all, he'd fought in that terrible war so far away, and they were just thankful he'd returned on two feet. So many other boys hadn't.

But Fred *wanted* to talk to his little brother. It just wasn't easy like it used to be. Part of the problem was that the two men had different schedules, but even when they were both home at the same time, Davey had less and less to say. The family house was a modest, three-bedroom Cape, and it'd been crowded and noisy before Davey went to Vietnam. But after his return, he got in the habit of staying out late, then sleeping in his room with the door closed until about four in the afternoon. For clothing, he wore tight jeans and t-shirts, and Fred found lots of empty liquor bottles in the trash. Then, after being home less than two months, Davey left home one day to go shack up with one of his girlfriends in Cambridge. He didn't have a job, so Fred assumed the girl covered the rent.

Of course, their parents were distraught, and kept hoping Davey would get his head straightened out soon. But one Sunday in 1973, Davey called and said he was coming over for family dinner. He didn't talk—or eat—much, but as their mom served dessert, he announced that he was moving to a town called Plymouth, Maine. He said he wanted peace and quiet and had heard about cheap rent and good jobs on the farms up there.

Farming? thought Fred. *Davey'll be a lousy farmer.* But it was the 70s, and everyone was trying crazy things. So, Fred wrote it off as a phase. He expected to see his brother back home the minute the weather got cold.

But winter arrived, and Davey remained in Maine. During the holiday season, he came home for a few boozy days, then went straight back to Plymouth. And the next year, he did the same thing. Soon, that became the norm. Each time he showed up in Arlington, Davey was a little heavier and more ragged, his drinking problem growing progressively worse. No one knew what to do. By the time the 80s rolled around and Fred was in his early forties, *he'd* become the normal Flaherty brother.

"You're my late bloomer," his mother would tell Fred, and it was true. Because in Fred's case, the Army had significantly improved his social skills. Now, he had a good job, drank very little alcohol, and was dating Barb, a beautiful girl he'd met at his buddy Ed's Christmas party.

Him? Fred? With a girlfriend like *Barb?* Nobody would've believed it back in high school. Fred barely believed it himself. Sure, he'd shot the breeze with Barb for a while at the party, but he'd almost keeled over when Ed came up to him at work the next day to say she thought he was cute. Girls like that didn't go in for him. But he'd summoned up his courage and asked her if she wanted to go see *Kramer vs. Kramer*. And she'd said yes.

They got along pretty well too. Barb was almost sixteen years younger than him, and she had some strong opinions, but he didn't mind too much. Yes, she'd occasionally make him feel stupid—especially when she was with her girlfriends—but most of the time she was very sweet. She also supported Ronald Reagan and Fred didn't, but they both liked going to plays and movies, and eating at the Italian restaurants in the North End. Actually, Barb preferred fancier dining, and would sometimes drop hints about trying places like L'Espalier and Maison Robert. But Fred hated wearing dinner jackets and wasting money on food he couldn't even pronounce. And, since he was always the one who picked up the check, they usually ended up in the North End. Then, one night, after they'd been dating almost a year, Barb asked if he was ever going to propose marriage.

He'd almost stopped his Corolla right in the middle of Route 2, but somehow managed to keep driving. "You're... saying you wanna get married?"

Barb's tone turned slightly hostile. "Only if you do. But if not, I'm thinking we should split up. I'm twenty-six, you know. All my friends are married and most already have kids."

Kids. He liked kids but could never quite picture himself a dad. Maybe the father of a teenager, but a baby? They were so little and fragile. On the other hand, Barb certainly seemed like the kind of girl who knew how to take care of babies.

"Gee, that's... that's a lot to think about. You know, I'm still thinking about going back to college."

Barb sighed. "Oh Freddy, let's face it. You're never gonna do that. You make too much money to quit your job."

He didn't know what to say. He did earn a good salary at the phone company, but he'd always kept the idea of college in the back of his mind. It sounded sort of silly, but sometimes he dreamed of becoming a schoolteacher. He believed he'd be really good at teaching electronics to high school kids. On the other hand, Barb was so pretty and clever, and he'd never get a chance at another woman like her. "So... you really wanna get married?"

"I'd like to. Yeah," said Barb. "But only if you can come up with a better proposal than that. And a ring while you're at it."

As soon as they announced their engagement, though, life for Fred and Barb took a few turns for the worse.

For starters, Davey's drinking hit a new low. Around midnight on Christmas Eve in 1982, he showed up on the family doorstep already drunk and thirsty for more booze. Their parents were in bed, so Fred let him in and told him to be quiet, but Davey just turned on the TV and grabbed a bottle of Canadian Club out of the liquor cabinet.

When it became apparent that his brother wasn't up for conversation, Fred hit the hay, but it was a good thing he got up early because in the morning, he discovered Davey passed out on the living room rug, a puddle of vomit beside his head. He cleaned it up as well as he could before their parents awoke, but the carpet stank for months.

Then, in June of '83, Fred had to put his mom in a nursing home. She'd been getting more and more forgetful, and he and his dad were finally forced to admit that she wasn't just "a little senile" anymore. One day, she burned herself badly in the shower because she couldn't remember how to turn off the hot water. Another time, she went outside to bring in the clothes from the line and ended up three blocks away and lost. But although Fred's father agreed that she needed more care than they could provide at home, he couldn't handle the logistics of the move; he just cried every time Fred tried to discuss it with him. So, Fred called Davey for help and advice, but Davey provided neither.

"Just do what you think's best for Ma," he said, sounding drunk. "I trust you, big bro."

It was no great surprise, then, when Davey skipped Fred and Barb's wedding too. Nor did he make it down to Massachusetts when their father had open-heart surgery. Fred found it all upsetting and disheartening, but Davey was an adult who apparently didn't care about his family anymore, so Fred had no choice but to be the dependable son. And when his dad's health deteriorated to the point where he also needed twenty-four-hour care, Fred sat the poor bugger down and had a really hard, tearful talk with him. Then he wiped his eyes and called the nursing home. *When the going gets tough...* he reminded himself.

On St. Patrick's Day, 1984, everything changed again. Fred was putting on his overcoat at work—the guys in his department were heading out for a corned beef and cabbage lunch—when his desk phone rang. Barb had suffered her first miscarriage just a week earlier, and he was in no mood for celebrating, but none of the guys at work knew about that, and he did need to eat. He'd dropped a few pounds since the miscarriage.

"On my way down," he said into the receiver, assuming it was his buddy Ed on the line.

But the voice on the other end was Davey's. "I'm comin' down to see you, brother. Now. I gotta crash with you and Barb for a few days. Okay?"

Fred and Barb were living alone in the house on Wilson Road. The mortgage had been paid off years ago, and Fred made more than enough money to cover the nursing home expenses for his parents. Every once in a while, Barb would complain about Arlington and say she wanted to move to a fancier town like Belmont, but Fred always put his foot down. He and Barb could save a bundle by staying put.

"Hey Davey, I'm sorry, but Barb's... sick. She's... havin' female problems. How 'bout you come see us in a week or two—"

"No. No way. This can't wait. Remember, that's my house too. It's my *right* to sleep there."

Fred couldn't believe it. Davey hadn't even come home for Christmas that year, and he never called his parents in the nursing home, let alone offered a dime for their care. *Rights?* He sighed. "Uh... sure. Just not today, Dave. Like I said, it's not a good time."

But Davey had already hung up. And six hours later, he showed up on the doorstep. His blond hair was so greasy it looked brown, and he was sporting several days' worth of whiskers. But all that paled in comparison to the long, ugly gash on his forehead. The cut was starting to scab over in some places, but it looked very sore and possibly infected. "What the hell, Davey? What happened?"

"Work accident," said Davey, glancing over his meaty shoulder. "Now lemme in, will ya?"

Concern and exhaustion consumed Fred, and he stepped aside as Davey pushed past him. "A *work* accident?"

"Yeah. I work on a farm. Remember?"

"I know, but—"

Davey shook his head. "I'll tell you the story later. Right now, I gotta take a shower."

"Jingoes, Davey." His brother looked slightly better cleaned up. He'd shaved too—probably using Fred's razor or maybe even Barb's—

IT DOESN'T HAVE TO BE THAT WAY

and was dressed in the flannel pajamas Fred had lent him. But his beer gut made him look pregnant—which was sadly ironic, as Barb had just miscarried—and the cut on his head was bleeding again. "Let me grab you some paper towels." Fred spoke softly so as not to disturb Barb, who was resting in the bedroom.

"Thanks, brother," said Davey when Fred returned with the towels. His voice was anything but soft.

"Hey, keep it down a little, huh? I told you Barb's sick."

Davey shrugged.

"So, have you seen a doctor about that cut?"

"Nah. It's fine and I don't wanna talk about it. Got any beer?"

Fred knew his brother didn't need more alcohol, but he headed for the refrigerator just to keep the peace. Barb didn't want Davey sleeping in the house, and Fred was prepared to pay for a hotel room if it came to that. He'd do almost anything to avoid fighting with Barb, and the last thing he needed was Davey yelling at him.

When he returned to the living room, his brother was watching the Bruins game. "Good year for the B's," said Davey, taking the can of Bud Fred handed him and flopping into an armchair. "They could win the Cup this time around."

"Yeah, that's what I hear," said Fred, trying to figure out how to ask his brother to leave. He had no interest in hockey.

Davey took a big gulp of beer. "O'Reilly's an animal. Gotta love the guy."

Fred studied the TV more carefully. All he knew was that Terry O'Reilly was a star on the team. But then he saw something move in the doorway and was startled when two cops in uniform entered the living room. Barb had apparently heard the doorbell and let them in, because she was right behind them, in her long, silvery bathrobe.

"David Flaherty?" asked the older of the two cops, resting a hand on his holster.

Davey turned slowly toward the men. "Yessir."

Barb looked weak and pale, but she had managed to put on some pink lipstick. "Fred, these officers asked about Davey. What's goin' on?"

"Ma'am, we just need to ask your guest a few questions," said the gray-haired cop. "David, where were you last night around eleven?" The other cop—a younger guy with red hair—stared at the cut on Davey's forehead.

"Sleepin'," said Davey.

"Sleeping," said the older officer. "That's not a place."

"Yeah," said the younger cop. "Like *where* were you sleeping? Here? At your brother's house?"

Davey's eyes lit up for the first time since his arrival in Arlington. "Uh-huh. That's right. Freddy and I always hang out the night before St. Paddy's. Family tradition."

The older officer glared at his partner, then turned back to Davey.

Barb's eyes widened as they met Fred's.

"So," said the older cop, taking a step closer to Davey, "what'd you and your brother do to celebrate last night?"

Davey spoke slowly but steadily. "Nothin' special. It's a religious holiday in Ireland, you know. We just sat around, had a couple beers. Like I said, family tradition."

The gray-haired cop took another step toward Davey's chair and raised his voice. "Don't play games with us, David. We're watching you closely. I think you know why."

Davey shrugged and assumed a dopey face. "No. I don't."

"Oh really?" The cop's eyes bulged. "So, you're saying you don't know what happened to Elizabeth Barton last night? In that bar on Harlow Street in Bangor? And by the way, what happened to your head?"

"Who? 'Cause I never heard o' that lady. And my head? Farm accident. Had a little run in with a shovel the other day." He chuckled humorlessly.

"Hmm," said the older cop, his eyes glued to Davey. His partner gazed around the room, probably trying to figure out how to redeem himself after giving Davey an alibi for the previous night.

Turning to Fred and Barb, the older cop asked, "So whadda you two say? Was David here in your house last night? All night? Think about that. And tell the truth."

"Yeah," said Fred without missing a beat. "Yes, he was. Everything he said's true."

He'd never lied to a police officer—or any other authority—in his life, but his brother had served his country and come back all screwed up, and nobody cared. Whatever Davey'd done, well, he'd help him make amends later on. Maybe he'd gotten drunk and stolen cash from a woman's wallet, or maybe he'd cracked up her car. Whatever it was, Fred was sure it could be fixed without involving the law. Davey had enough problems without a criminal record.

"Hmm," said the cop again, looking straight at Barb. "How 'bout you, ma'am? Would you testify under oath that David was here in your home on the night of March 16, 1984?"

IT DOESN'T HAVE TO BE THAT WAY

Barb's face tensed up, and she laid her hands on her stomach as if the fetus were still inside. "Uh-huh," she said softly, her eyes darting back and forth between her husband and his brother.

"You don't sound so sure," said the cop.

"What can I say?" said Barb, shrugging her shoulders. "I am."

Fred tried to keep the frustration out of his eyes, but damn it, why was Barb lying in such a lame way? Was she trying to get them all arrested?

"All right," said the older cop. "We'll be in touch." He continued to look straight at Barb. "But if any of you should change your mind or *suddenly* remember something"—he said *suddenly* in a particularly sarcastic way— "just stop by the station and talk to whoever's on duty. Elizabeth Barton's in the hospital and will be for quite some time. I'm sure she'd appreciate any help she can get. Men who hit women deserve to be punished."

Those last words were a punch in the gut to Fred. *Oh please,* he thought. *Please God, let this be a mistake.* Davey had always been a gentle guy. He wouldn't hit a woman. He couldn't.

Barb showed the police out in dead silence. Then all three Flahertys stood near the window, watching the car's taillights disappear. "Okay, you shithead," she hissed, turning on Davey when the cops were out of sight. "What happened? 'Cause if you beat up a lady, I'm turnin' you in."

Davey walked over to the coffee table, picked up the beer he'd been drinking, and guzzled the last of it. "Honestly, I got no idea. Mistaken identity. Simple as that."

"Bullshit," said Barb. "You already lied about bein' here, and it looks like someone took a hatchet to your face. Tell the truth. Right now."

Fred was shaking a little as he put his arm around his wife. "Honey, how 'bout you go in the other room and let me talk to Davey?" *Davey's not violent. He's never been violent.* Those words kept running through his head, over and over. "It sounds like there's been some kind of misunderstanding."

Barb's eyes blazed, but Fred could feel how frail her body was. The miscarriage had done a real job on her. "Your brother's a sick man," she said, still holding her stomach.

"I'll take care of him," Fred whispered in her ear. "Just go get some sleep."

"You bettah." She pulled away and slunk off toward the bedroom, looking queen-like with the shiny bathrobe rolling and curling behind her.

Fred felt like he was drunk, even though he'd only had a few sips of beer. Glimpsing his reflection in the window, he saw a face that looked more like his father's than his own. *Oh god, I'm getting old.* He was forty-four but felt sixty. "Siddown, Davey," he said, laying a hand on his brother's shoulder and easing him onto the couch beside him. "Please tell the truth. The whole truth. What the hell happened?"

Davey covered his face with his hands for at least a minute, and when he looked up, his eyes were red and watery. "I'm a little fuzzy on the details, Freddy. I mean, you know, I was sittin' there in the bar, gettin' my drink on, mindin' my own business. And she was bein' a bitch, you know? That much, I remember. She was... she was making fun of my... manhood. Said I couldn't get it up. For no reason. No reason at all. She was drunk and stupid, and I got mad."

Oh lord. Am I dreaming? "Dave, tell me you didn't *hit* a lady because she made a dumb comment."

"Hey, she came back at me!" He pointed to his bloody forehead. "With a steak knife. She's the one who oughta get arrested!"

Fred let out the breath he'd been holding. "Davey, I can't believe this."

Davey covered his eyes with his hands again. "Look, I know it sounds bad, but if you were there, you'd understand. It was *humiliating*."

Fred didn't know what to say. Clearly Davey was injured, but if the Arlington police were looking for him, there had to be more to the story. "Don't you remember Dad teaching us never to hit girls?"

Davey stared at the floor.

"Dave, talk to me. Please. What *happened* to you in 'Nam?"

Davey looked up at Fred with his teary eyes but remained silent. Finally, he whispered, "Fred, you gotta help me. You're all I got left."

It was true, and he had to do something. But he couldn't allow his brother to go on hurting people either. Things needed to change. Immediately. Looking Davey straight in the eye, he said, "You gotta see a shrink, man."

Davey gripped the back of his neck with his hand and rolled his head around. "Yeah. Probly." The cut on his forehead was oozing pretty badly again.

"No, I mean it," said Fred. "I'm gonna make *sure* you do."

"Okay. But I need a *regular* doctor first. My stomach's all fucked up."

Fred raised his eyebrows. "You don't have a *doctor* doctor? Davey, weren't you exposed to Agent Orange in Cambodia?"

"Probly," said Davey again. "But the Army checked me out when I got back. Gave me a clean bill of health."

Neither man spoke for a minute, and Fred closed his eyes. Finally, he opened them and said, "Dave, you've been home twelve years. Are you saying your last checkup was twelve years ago?"

Davey smiled for the first time all evening. "Hey, I'll be fine, brother. But boy, I'm glad I have you."

Brother. Fred always felt a pang of compassion when his younger sibling used that word, but he kept his voice steady. "I'll help you this time. But you're gonna hafta help yourself too."

Chapter 19
New York's Not My Home

Molly
Saturday, October 27, 2012
East Boston, MA

Except for a couple of flights out of Logan as a kid—family trips to Orlando and Philadelphia—I'd never been to East Boston before. I'd heard there were some good restaurants and bars in that neighborhood, but it's all the way on the other side of Boston from Arlington—and across the Harbor too—so I'd never explored the place.

But for Ethan Fricke, I'd go almost anywhere. We'd finally talked on the phone, and he'd told me he worked as an airline pilot who often spent the night at a hotel near Logan. In fact, he'd be in town on October 27th and asked if I'd be available to meet him for a beer or two at around 7:30.

"Sure," I said, trying not to sound too excited. "I don't know my way around Eastie, but I'm sure I'll figure it out. Where should I meet you?"

"How 'bout Star's Pub? It's right across from the Orient Heights T station, and they know me in there. Will you be driving or taking the train?"

I didn't want him to know I didn't own a car. "Um, I guess I'll take the T. Then I won't have to worry about parking."

"Good idea. Plus, you can get smashed. Can't get a DUI on the T."

"Right."

But I didn't want to get smashed with Ethan. Especially not after what'd happened with Shane Armstrong. A big part of me did hope to sleep with him, but only if I was fully conscious and gave clear consent. And if I decided not to, I wanted to do that the right way. No ambiguity, no accusations of being a tease.

Besides, Ethan had screwed with my head in college, so he wasn't necessarily trustworthy. For all I knew, he'd lied about being single. Maybe he had a wife or a serious girlfriend. Or three.

In any case, my plan was to stay in control and ask all the questions I hadn't asked in college: questions that could've saved me months—if not years—of grief and misgivings. Ethan Fricke wouldn't play me for a fool again. Still, when I thought about him, my body got lighter and my stomach buzzed as if I'd swallowed a bee.

The trains and buses were smelly and sweaty, but after sitting on various ones for over an hour, I ended up at the Orient Heights T station around eight o'clock. Fashionably late. The only problem was, I saw no pub across the street.

So, I started walking in the most logical direction. The neighborhood was different than I'd expected. In school, I'd learned that the Kennedy family had settled in Orient Heights when they first came to America from Ireland in the 1800s, so I thought it'd be fancier. It didn't seem dangerous or anything, just sort of old and run-down. And every building had a different shape, size, and color. Nothing matched.

As for Star's Pub, a guy on the street pointed it out after I'd walked for a few minutes. The neighborhood bar occupied the first floor of a triple-decker house. A handful of people stood out front, smoking. Inside, it was crowded, kind of dark, and larger than it appeared from the street. Many of the women wore skinny jeans and Ugg boots, and lots of guys wore hoodies. The air smelled vaguely of stale cigarettes and many years of spilled beer.

About fifteen tables were visible from the door, most of them occupied by people sharing pitchers and eating burgers and nachos. A couple of older guys played Keno at gambling machines in the corner, and the long wooden bar on the opposite side of the room was packed. Multiple TVs hung above it, but they were all tuned to different channels showing different sporting events. "Don't You Want Me?" by the Human League played loudly on the jukebox, but no one danced or even seemed to acknowledge the music.

A few customers glanced over as I stood in the doorway, but even though I looked nice—I'd spent quite a while on my makeup and carried a newish Coach bag—they all turned away without smiling. I wondered what Ethan liked so much about the place.

And speaking of Ethan, where was he? My eyes kept scanning the room, but I saw no one resembling him. Had his flight been canceled? The weatherman on the news the night before had been all worked up about some hurricane down south called Sandy. Could that be the problem? I pulled out my phone to see if Ethan had texted or sent a Facebook message, but no. Then again, if he was stuck in the air, he wouldn't be able to use his phone. Right?

A wrinkly-faced woman with white hair got up from her seat, glared at me, and shook her head. I didn't know why, but I felt a sudden urge to leave before Ethan showed up. Maybe the whole meeting thing was a bad idea. But when I looked toward the older woman again, she was minding her own business, moseying off in the direction of the restrooms. I relaxed and remembered my adorable, chubby Zac Efron from college: his dimples, soft brown hair, and gentle kissing style. Over the years, as the real Zac Efron had matured into a beautiful man with chiseled cheekbones and glowing skin, I'd imagined Ethan evolving similarly. And since he was an airline pilot, maybe he'd even arrive in uniform.

That image cheered me up, so I decided to order a beer. He was probably just running late. Clutching my purse tightly, I headed over to the bar where the music wasn't so loud. Every stool was taken, so I stood between two guys—both heavyset dudes with bald heads—and signaled to the busy bartender. The song on the jukebox switched to Taylor Swift's "Never Getting Back Together," and I couldn't help thinking of my dreaded night with Shane Armstrong.

Why? Why had I trusted that asshole? The only positive thing that'd come out of the whole nasty affair was that Andy Stevers had started talking to me more at work. Yes, really. Once or twice a week, he'd stop by my cube to ask the type of questions other engineers asked over email. Things like confirming the date of a meeting or checking to see when I needed updated information for documents I was editing. I sometimes got the sense that he wanted to mention that night at El Chico, but he never did.

A sign on the wall said Pabst drafts were on special for $2.50, so I ordered one. But as I pulled out my wallet to pay the bartender, the guy on the barstool to my right turned around to check me out.

"Molly?" he said.

"Hi!" I answered instinctively. I kept my voice steady for the duration of that one syllable. Then my heart jumped off a cliff and my hands started to tremble. I was looking into Ethan's eyes.

The dude had Ethan's nose too. And lips. But the rest of him? Oh boy. Let's just say that any similarities to Zac Efron ended there. And *chubby* isn't the word most people would use to describe the man.

His stomach extended far out in front of him, and there were rolls of fat on the back of his neck. The bald spot was sad too, but not nearly as sad as his front teeth, which had turned a grayish color and seemed to be eroding around the edges. I knew Ethan was just about my age—after all, we'd been in the same college class—but he looked like an unhealthy man in his forties. What the hell had happened?

"Ethan! Wow! Sorry, I didn't recognize you. At first, I mean. From the back, you know. It's been a while."

He smiled with those gray teeth, extending his hand but remaining seated on the barstool. "Yeah. For sure. So how *are* you, Molly? You look terrific."

I shook his hand with the best smile I could muster, but when I noticed a couple of molars missing on the left side of his mouth, I went silent for a second. "Um... I'm good," I managed. "How 'bout you?"

"Good. Good. Flyin' a lot, you know? Seeing the country, one airport at a time." He scratched his neck nervously. Perhaps he'd assumed I'd be overweight and losing my teeth too.

"Wow. Yeah, that's exciting. I never knew you wanted to be a pilot." I considered mentioning the Stock Exchange but stopped myself. After all, Ethan had never discussed his post-college plans with me. I'd only heard about the Wall Street thing from Lucinda.

He shrugged. "Yeah, crazy story. I almost ended up at Goldman Sachs after graduation, but then... things changed."

Apparently. I wondered what'd happened to Lucinda. "Huh. So... I guess flying's what you enjoy now?"

He shrugged again. "Pretty much. I... my dad died right after school ended—had a heart attack in our driveway—and basically, I fell apart for a while. Like... a while. And Goldman wasn't gonna wait forever, you know?" He chuckled uncomfortably. "Death really sucks."

I felt awful. "Yeah. It does. I'm so sorry."

"Thanks. But, you know, I learned a lot about people. The ones who stick with you when things go bad. And the ones who don't."

"I know what you mean. Fair weather friends, right?" If I had to guess, Lucinda was in that category.

Ethan cocked his head to one side, and for a second, I saw the college boy in him again. "Yeah. That's life for ya." He sighed, then sat up straighter and spoke more cheerfully. "But hey, you don't wanna hear any more of my sob story. What've *you* been up to? And did I hear you order a Pabst?"

The jukebox started playing Joan Jett's "I Love Rock & Roll."

"Yeah," I said. "It's on special tonight."

"It's always on special here! One of the many reasons I love this bar. A stellar brew, and they keep it nice and cold. You need another?"

I smiled. "No, I'm still waiting on the bartender to bring my first one." By that point, I'd totally ruled out sleeping with him, but also felt ashamed of my shallow nature. Because I was pretty sure that if he looked like a movie star, I'd be wondering if his hotel was within walking distance.

Ethan appeared not to notice my inner distress as the bartender deposited a beer in front of me. "Put that on my tab, Tommy," he said. "And bring us two more, okay?"

"Oh no," I said, holding up my hand. "I'm good with this."

"No worries. Just gettin' us some backups. This your first beer of the night?"

"Um, yeah, but—" I was already trying to think of an excuse to leave early.

"So, drink up! First one always goes down easy."

The bartender scurried off toward the taps, and Ethan smiled a wide smile. "So whaddya do these days, Molly?" he asked.

At least he was right about the Pabst being nice and cold. I took a big sip. "I work at a software company. In marketing."

"Nice," he said as the bartender dropped off the "backup" beers. Instinctively, I reached for my purse, but Ethan rested his hand on my arm and smiled sadly. "Tonight's on me," he said, polishing off the beer he'd been drinking. "So, software, huh? That's awesome. You like it?"

I shrugged, taking another sip and feeling the need to tell Ethan I wasn't living out some amazing corporate dream. Maybe it was the way he'd touched my arm—bringing back memories of those nights when I'd let him touch *everything*—or maybe I just felt incredibly sorry for him. "It's an okay job. But the company's actually closing soon. Most people don't know yet, but the owner's a friend, and he told me."

"Huh!" said Ethan. "But *you* just told *me*. I betta sell all my stock in that place before it goes down the toilet."

"Oh, it's not a public company or anything. It's just—"

He patted my arm again. "Relax, kiddo. I'm goofin' on ya. I'd never betray your confidence, even if I did own stock, which I don't. In anything."

It occurred to me that I'd never actually had a *conversation* with Ethan. But now that I was getting to know him a little, he seemed very kind, but also, well, boring. And those teeth. How did they get that way? We'd only been out of college five years. "Ha!" I said with a forced smile. "So, what airline do you work for?"

He chuckled. "One you never heard of. It's really small. Hey, wanna do some shots for old times' sake?"

A fuzzy memory of sitting in the quad with him one night, passing a bottle of sweet liqueur back and forth floated through my mind. "Nah, that's okay."

But once again, he acted like he hadn't heard me. "Two shots of peach schnapps, Tommy!" he called out to the bartender.

"You know, I don't really do shots anymore," I said.

"Really?" he asked, sounding disappointed. Then he rallied. "All right, then. I had a couple when I was waiting for you, but I can handle a couple more. Hey look, there's an open table over there. Wanna grab it?"

I didn't, but also didn't feel like standing at the bar any longer. "Yeah, sure." I picked up my two beers and waited while Ethan downed both shots, then hoisted his body off the barstool.

"Ugh," he groaned, guzzling at least half of his full beer like it was water. "I gotta get some of this weight off."

I pretended not to hear him as we made our way over to the empty table. Gregg Allman's "I'm No Angel," had begun playing on the jukebox, and I wondered how we'd talk when it was so loud in that part of the room. At least it felt good to sit down.

But Ethan remained standing. I noticed that his hands were shaking a little, and his beer was almost gone. "Hey, I'm gonna go grab one more," he said. "You need anything?"

"No. But don't you have to fly in the morning?" He'd mentioned something about that on the phone. "Isn't there, like, some rule about pilots drinking the night before a flight?"

Ethan glanced at the clock on the wall and rolled his eyes. "Yeah, but it's bullshit. I need to unwind or I can't sleep. And then what good am I at the controls? Right?"

I nodded, thinking of all the people who'd be on his plane the next day, oblivious to the fact that their pilot was either very hungover or still drunk. "I'll wait here and hold the table."

I watched him head toward the bar, but the spot where we'd been standing was now occupied by three really tall guys. Ethan tapped each of the dudes on the shoulder, but none of them budged, so he started making his way around to the back of the bar, where it was less crowded.

But wait; I could give him one of my beers. "Ethan!" I called over the music. I didn't want to leave the table alone because two couples had just walked in and were looking around for a place to sit. "Ethan!" I called again, but he didn't hear me.

What the hell am I doing here? I wondered. I couldn't see Ethan at all because he was on the other side of the bar, but I knew for a fact that the evening wouldn't end well. He was already halfway to trashed, and based on our history, he probably expected at least a little action from me.

And... no way. No way in hell.

Clearly, he was alcoholic—and I felt bad about that—but it didn't change the fact that he was putting a whole bunch of innocent passengers at risk. I considered asking the name of his airline again so I could call and report him, but then started wondering if he even *was* a pilot. I mean, don't commercial pilots need to a pass physical exam or something? Was the whole pilot thing bullshit?

I took another sip of beer, shivered, and realized how much I hated Pabst. Right then, someone tapped my shoulder, and I turned to see one of the guys in need of a table. "Excuse me," he said. "Any chance my friends and I can steal a couple of your chairs?"

"Um, sure. A friend's using one..." I glanced over at the bar, but Ethan was still nowhere in sight.

I'm not quite sure what happened next. I guess something finally triggered some reflex inside me. I jumped up. "Hey, you know what? I'm actually leaving anyway."

"Oh, no!" said the guy. "No worries. We just need two chairs. We got a table over there and—"

But I'd already grabbed my purse. "It's okay. Really. I gotta catch a train." I couldn't bear to look in the direction of the bar again, so I held my breath and bolted out the door.

Once on the street, I broke into a run and didn't stop until I reached the Orient Heights T station. I slid my Charlie Card through the sensor, then stood there trembling, trying to catch my breath on the outdoor platform. All I could think was that Ethan might come after me, and what would I say if he did?

Luckily, an inbound train arrived less than a minute later, and I leaped onto it, still panting. When the doors closed, I was so relieved that I flopped into a seat and began sobbing. The only other occupants of the car were two young women in short, clingy dresses and high heels, obviously heading into the city for a night out. They exchanged glances, then eyed me with concern.

"Are you all right?" one of them asked.

"Yeah. I'm fine," I said, attempting to calm down. I'd never been more grateful for sobriety. At least I could think clearly.

The women returned to their conversation about a friend who was apparently meeting them downtown, but they continued to shoot concerned glances in my direction.

I wiped my eyes and gazed around the train. On the opposite side of the subway car was a poster that said—in both English and Spanish—*DOMESTIC ABUSE? NOWHERE TO TURN? CALL US FOR SAFE, CONFIDENTIAL HELP.* Beneath the words was a phone number with a 617 area code, and the name of a women's shelter.

Serious guilt began filling my brain. As my breathing normalized, the reality of ditching Ethan Fricke in a bar felt more horrific by the second. Sure, he'd been a jerk to me in college, but *I'd* gone searching for *him* on Facebook. And *I'd* been excited enough about dating him to pack a toothbrush and extra pair of underwear in my purse. And then I'd blown him off, because he was fat and drunk with rotten teeth.

I imagined him shuffling back to our table with his fresh beer. What thoughts had run through his head when he'd first seen the other people sitting there? Had he looked around for me, assuming I'd found a better table? Or did someone tell him right away what'd happened? And when he'd realized I was actually gone, had he looked for me outside? Had he cried? Was he crying now? I couldn't bring myself to conjure up that image.

Because *why* hadn't I said a proper goodbye to Ethan? *I mean, what the fuck?* At the very least, I could've lied and said I had a migraine. Instead, though, I'd just run. Like I'd been doing all my life. Running from things that upset me, avoiding things I didn't want to face. Meanwhile, those pretty young women across the aisle kept glancing over at me, looking concerned.

I felt sick to my stomach.

Finally, at the subway stop before mine, the women got off the train and I dug in my purse for a pen and scrap of paper. Then I jotted down the phone number from the banner about domestic abuse.

I could do *one* thing right: I could call the shelter the next day and inquire about volunteering there.

Chapter 20
I Am Who I Am

Fred
1984

He decided to find Davey a regular doctor first. After all, his brother looked like he might drop dead any second, and if he died, his mental health wouldn't make much difference. Then, once they got a handle on what was wrong with his body, they could start looking for a good shrink.

So, he made a bunch of calls and got Davey an appointment with an internist close to his home in downtown Plymouth, Maine. But Davey didn't go. He said he forgot. Fred sighed and booked a second appointment, but Davey missed that one too, claiming his truck wouldn't start.

"Jeez, Davey, what're you doing?" Fred asked his brother on the phone. "You know you gotta see a doctor."

"Yeah, but my battery's dead."

So, when he scheduled the third appointment, Fred also took a sick day from work, and left Arlington at the crack of dawn to *chauffeur* Davey to the damn place. Then he sat in the waiting room for what seemed like hours—reading an old copy of *Newsweek*—until the doctor brought Davey back out. Fred had hoped for some kind of news at that point, but the doctor just said they'd get a call when all the test results came back from the lab.

"Damn it all!" he shouted out loud as he drove down Route 95 with the sun already setting. "Barb's gonna be pissed." When he'd left home that morning, he'd promised her a nice dinner later on at a swanky new restaurant in Cambridge, never expecting to be in Maine so late. And he still had a four-hour drive ahead of him.

At least he'd brought along his mobile rig. "Billy," he said into the microphone, when his friend's voice came over the air, "I need a big favor."

"You name it, Freddy. What's up? You sound pooped."

"Yeah, that's about right. But listen. For now, I'm hoping you can give my XYL a buzz on the landline and tell her not to wait on me for dinner. I'm gonna be late. Real late."

"No prob, Freddy, but where the heck are you? Your signal's pretty choppy."

He wasn't in a chatty mood. "Yeah, I just left my brother's place in Maine and traffic looks bad."

"Gotcha. That's a Roger, my friend. I'll give the XYL a jingle now. You just drive safe. W1RAP, this is K1QEC, saying 73s for now."

Even with the weak signal, Fred could hear the sympathy in Billy's voice. Good old Billy. Sure, he could be rough around the edges at times, but he also knew when it was time to say goodnight and 73s.

About a week later, Davey's blood work came back, and the doc wanted to talk to him in person. So once again, Fred made the trip up to Maine and escorted his younger sibling to the office.

As it turned out, many of Dave's organs weren't working so well, particularly his liver. The doctor prescribed pills, of course, but also told Davey he had to quit drinking. If he didn't, he said, the medicine could actually do more harm than good.

"I'll quit today," said Davey. "Thanks for everything, Doc."

But after picking up the drugs at the pharmacy, Fred watched his brother toss the little orange bottles in a drawer and pour himself a whiskey.

"What're you doing?" he asked. "And didn't the doc say to take one of those pills as soon as you got home?"

"Uh huh. But one more day won't matter. I've gotta ease into this thing. I can't just go cold turkey."

As for a psychiatrist, the doctor suggested a few guys in Bangor, but by then, Davey'd decided he no longer needed a shrink.

Fred wasn't putting up with that, though. He knew his brother had to get his head straightened out, so he told Davey that if he wouldn't go to therapy on his own, he'd drive to Plymouth once a week and drag him there.

"Okay," said Davey. "Whatever you want."

So poor Fred—who only got two weeks of vacation a year from the phone company—hauled his butt to Maine three Tuesdays in a row. He didn't see any progress in Davey—and Davey refused to talk about the therapy with him—but he figured it had to be better than nothing. All he wanted was to free his brother—the charming, blue-eyed guy who'd once been captain of the Arlington High track team—from the bloated, drunken, smelly creature who'd taken over his body.

But Barb. Oh boy, she was *not* a happy camper. In her opinion, Fred's time—and more importantly, *her* time—was being wasted for all the wrong reasons. She and Fred had planned to spend two weeks on the Cape that summer, but at the rate Fred's vacation days were getting chewed up, it was doubtful they'd even get away for a long weekend. So, the third time Fred left home to drive up to Plymouth, she threatened to tell the police about Davey not really being at their home the night Elizabeth Barton was beaten.

"That'll put an end to all this, Fred," she said. "They'll throw him right in the slammer, where he belongs."

Then, while Fred was gone, she called the Plymouth police and somehow convinced someone there to tell her that Elizabeth Barton had been knocked to the floor of a bar by "some scumbag," and that a critical nerve in her left eye had been damaged, leaving her almost blind in that eye. She'd been scheduled for surgery, but it was too early to tell if it'd do any good.

"This time, I really am callin' the cops," she announced when Fred returned home that night, bleary-eyed from so much driving.

He was too tired to argue much. "Barb, you don't know if Davey was the scumbag. It coulda been anyone."

"Oh for cryin' out loud, you *know* it was him. And now that poor woman'll never be the same. It's my civic duty to turn Davey in."

"Barb," he said, taking his wife's hand, "do what you gotta do. But I'm asking you to at least *try* seeing Davey's side of this thing. *Try* to remember what he's gone through. That's why I'm bringin' him to the shrink now. I'm doin' my best. I really am. I know this woman's hurt bad, but so's Davey."

Barb ripped her hand away. "Oh my god. What a sick, warped thing to say. *Elizabeth* didn't fuck up your brother. She's an innocent victim. Why should *she* have to suffer?"

Fred's eyes filled with tears. "I don't know, Barb. Look, I know it's not fair. The world's not fair." He sighed. "And you're right about this

Elizabeth. A hundred percent. She shouldn't have to suffer. But if you think about it, Davey's an innocent victim too. *He* was just doing his civic duty when he joined the service. So, who do you blame for what happened to him? The government? The war? God?" He stopped talking to wipe his eyes. "Look, I don't know the answer. I'm just hopin' he can get fixed up. I want everyone to get fixed up."

The fourth time Fred took Davey to the shrink, the shrink called Fred into the office and said Davey had manic depression. According to him, the disorder usually shows up in people between the ages of fifteen and twenty-four, and Davey had returned from Vietnam when he was twenty. So, it made perfect sense.

"Yeah, I don't know, Doc," said Fred in the politest tone he could muster. "The thing is, my brother was *completely* normal before he left for the war. I think he got shell-shocked. Or whatever they call it these days."

The shrink nodded. "I've considered the option of PTSD quite carefully, Mr. Flaherty. But after observing David for several sessions, it's my professional belief that the timing of the war was something of an unfortunate coincidence. In other words, David would've become ill even if he'd stayed home. Manic depression is a disease. It doesn't care where its sufferers live or what they do."

Fred wasn't having that, though. "Doc, before my brother saw active combat, he was the happiest kid you ever met. Had a million friends and girlfriends. Then he comes back to the States, moves up here to Maine, and starts drinkin' like a fish. Think about that. Doesn't that sound like shell-shock to you?"

The doctor closed his eyes. "I hear what you're saying, sir, and yes, there may be some PTSD involved as well. But I went to school for pharmacology, and it's my recommendation to treat David with lithium. We'll start with a low dose and increase it as needed. I'll be checking his blood regularly to make sure his levels are correct and stable."

Fred didn't know what to say.

"Of course, if you'd like a second opinion," said the doctor, "feel free to get one."

"No way, José," said Davey when Fred suggested the second opinion. "I like Doctor Hart. I can talk to the guy. He's cool."

"Well, sure you can talk to him. He's a shrink. Talking's his specialty. But listen to what he's *sayin'*. He wants to put you on *lithium*, which'll make you even sleepier than you are now. Plus, you're not supposed to drink alcohol on it, and I'm pretty sure you've got a drinking problem." He stopped to catch his breath. Davey looked like he might punch Fred, but Fred didn't care. His brother's health was worth a sock in the face. "Can't you see what you're doin', Dave? You're killin' yourself. And I don't wanna let that happen. We need to find someone who can actually *help*. I'm even thinkin' you might wanna look into AA meetings."

"Oh no," said Davey, making a *pssh* sound with his mouth. "None of that higher power bullshit for me. Besides, Doc Hart said it's fine to drink a *little* booze with the lithium. Just not too much."

Fred's head ached. "C'mon, Davey, who're you kiddin'? You don't know the *meaning* of a little booze. At least be honest with yourself."

"I'll cut back."

"Yeah, I don't think it's that easy."

"Fred, I'm goin' with this plan. And you know what else? *You're* off the hook, 'cause I can drive *myself* to Doc Hart's. So there. That'll make old Barb happy, won't it?"

"Wait. Hang on a second, Dave." Fred felt numb. "Listen, I'm glad you're willing to drive, but let's try *one* more shrink. Just one more. Then we can make an educated decision. I've already got a name and number of another guy in Bangor. Please."

But Davey shook his head. "No. Uh-uh. I'm stickin' with Doc Hart and that's final. Now go home to your wife. She's the one you should be worried about."

Fred's hands were tied. His thirty-three-year-old brother seemed headed for an early grave, but he was an adult with the right to refuse Fred's help. Almost every time the two spoke on the phone, Davey slurred his words, and sometimes he said things that didn't make sense. But if Fred even *suggested* that he might be drinking too much, Davey would hang up.

Eventually, an incident occurred on the farm—an incident Davey refused to discuss with Fred—and he got fired. Of course, he was livid at first, but then he applied for disability and got approved. That calmed him down *a lot*. Especially when he started getting paid to sit home all day and drink. At least Uncle Sam was acknowledging his service.

In those days—when he was still married—Fred would visit Davey about once a month on a Saturday or Sunday, but it always depressed the hell out of him. From what he could tell, his brother only left the apartment about once a week to shop for food and booze. Although he did claim to drive into Pittsfield every now and then. There were a couple of good bars there, he said, and some pretty women too.

Chapter 21
Maybe Tomorrow

Molly
Sunday, October 28, 2012

I dreamed about Ethan all night. Or maybe I should say I dreamed about him during the brief periods when I actually slept. But I kept waking up, and when I did, I'd think even sadder, more agonizing thoughts. That bald spot, Ethan's painful story, those rolls of fat on the back of his neck... it's no wonder that when I actually got out of bed around six, a bad taste—both literally and figuratively—hung in my mouth.

Purple mucus mixed with the toothpaste I spat into the sink, remnants of the two glasses of wine I'd sucked down while writing a bullshit-filled Facebook message to Ethan.

> *Let me explain, Ethan. I have a serious boyfriend. I went out with you last night because my boyfriend and I had a big fight. But being in the bar with you made me feel so guilty that I panicked and ran. I know I did a terrible thing, and you deserve so much better than me. I wish I could go back in time and erase what I did. I'm very, very sorry. I hope you can forgive me. – Molly*

Then I hit the *send* button and promptly unfriended him. I couldn't stand the thought of ever dealing with the guy again.

Would Ethan believe my lie? Probably not. But as I washed out my coffee pot, I could only hope. Across the street, Fred appeared to be packing his truck for a road trip. He tossed in a duffle bag and something that looked like a sleeping bag too. Then, much more carefully, he placed several pieces of electronic equipment on the floor of the back seat.

Strange. In all the time I'd lived in Arlington, I'd never known Fred to go anywhere overnight. I had a habit of looking out my window each night before going to bed, and his red pickup truck was always there in his driveway. For some reason, I found that comforting.

That Sunday morning, he'd dressed up a little too. Instead of jeans, he wore khaki pants and the type of navy-blue jacket they sell in the L.L. Bean catalog. I couldn't help smiling. Where the heck was he going? But before I could mull that over anymore, one of the empty trashcans on my curb blew over and started rolling down the sidewalk.

Damn, I'd forgotten to take the barrels in. That hurricane was supposedly regaining strength and heading toward New England. I shoved my feet into flip-flops and darted down the steps, the wind whipping my hair. A jet roared overhead, and once again, I thought of poor Ethan and the unfortunate souls on his flight. Assuming the pilot stuff was even true.

Maybe I need to go back to therapy. Grabbing the rolling trashcan and dragging it up the driveway, I tried consoling myself with the knowledge that at least my night with Ethan had been better than the one with Shane.

Not that the Shane situation had improved at all. The dude didn't get up in my face or anything—we both avoided each other as much as possible—but he was clearly spreading rumors about me at FSI. A stranger watching me interact with people on the job wouldn't notice anything odd, but I felt the difference every day. My coworkers never joked around with me anymore, nor did they share personal stuff the way they once had.

At lunchtime, Diana and I would drive somewhere in her car because I could no longer handle eating in the building cafeteria. Shane only stopped in there for an occasional snack, but just the thought of running into him could send me into panic mode. Walking through the office corridors was bad enough, so I'd been drinking less water and coffee to cut down on trips to the bathroom. The only spot at work I felt truly safe was in my cube.

I should've begun looking for a new job, but my energy level was pitifully low. I guess I was depressed, and I had no one to talk to about it all. I mean, Jeannette upstairs was awesome, and I loved it when she came down to have a glass of wine with me, but she didn't know anyone at FSI so she couldn't really give solid advice. And my parents still didn't know Joe and I had broken up.

Then there was Diana. Sure, she claimed to be a true friend, but I didn't trust her completely. Part of her job as company receptionist was supporting the salespeople like Shane—especially when they were busy or on the road—but sometimes I felt like she could've been a *little* less supportive of *him*.

"Oh Molly, you know I *have* to help him," she explained once. "I have no choice. Besides, when the company does well, we all do well, so why wouldn't I wanna help our top sales guy?"

'Cause he tells everyone at work I'm a slut? I'd think. *And is it really the receptionist's responsibility to arrange a surprise baby shower in the office for the asshole?* But I didn't ask Diana those questions because I didn't want to piss her off. Apparently, she saw no problem in agreeing with me over pizza that Shane was a disgusting prick, then going back to the office and shopping online for pink and blue balloons and decorations.

"Hello, Molly!" Fred called from his driveway. He closed the back gate of his truck with a slam and looked enthusiastic about whatever he was doing.

"Hi, Fred," I yelled over the swirling breeze. "Where you goin'?" Sometimes I still felt weird calling him Fred.

"Feel that wind?" he said as if that answered the question.

"Uh-huh. A hurricane, right?"

"That's right! Sandy! She's headin' up the coast. I'm driving down to Rhode Island in case they need hams for emergency communication." He sounded solemn but a little excited too.

"Really?" I waited until a car passed between us, then jogged across the street so I could hear him better. "So, you're, like, on a rescue crew or something?"

He cleared his throat. "Nah. They haven't deployed any teams yet. No one's sure how bad New England'll get hit. But I booked a room at a hotel on the beach in Westerly. I'll be nearby if they can use me."

"Wow. Cool."

"Yeah. I was tied up during Irene last year, but I'm ready for action this time. We'll see."

I imagined Fred in a tiny tent on the sand, calmly talking to the police or National Guard on his radio while wind and rain stormed around him. "Well, stay safe, okay?"

"Always," he answered, climbing into the truck with a wink. "No one wants to see an old guy get washed out to sea." Then he closed the door and gave me a wave that was more like a military salute.

He reminded me of some old actor, heading off to war in one of those black-and-white movies. The navy-blue jacket made his hair look even more silvery than usual, and his tanned face actually seemed to glow a little as he drove away.

"Go get 'em, Freddy," I whispered, my heart swelling. I wondered what Mrs. Costa would think if she knew her "nutter" of a neighbor was risking his life for the sake of complete strangers. But for once, she didn't seem to be around.

At least I knew what I was going to do when I got back inside. If someone Fred's age could motor off into the wind to rescue hurricane victims, I could do something good for the world too.

It still took me a while to make the call. I used the bathroom, poured some coffee, and ate a bowl of Apple Jacks. I hadn't been hungry earlier but was suddenly famished. Then I wiped down the sticky counter and swept the floor. Finally, when I'd run out of excuses, I dialed the number from the subway banner.

"Refuge Shelter Boston," said the woman on the other end. She sounded stuffy, like she had a cold. "Are you in need of assistance?"

"Me? Oh no. Not at all. I'm just, uh, calling about volunteering. I'd like to... volunteer there."

The woman sniffled. "Great. Do you have any experience working with battered women? Or families in crisis?"

Familiar guilt flooded me. "No, not yet. But I wanna change that."

"Good. Let's start with a few questions, then. First of all, what's your name and are you over twenty-one years of age?"

"Yes. My name's Molly Dolan."

"Thanks, Molly. Now what sort of volunteering are you interested in?"

Was there more than one type? "Um, you know, working in the shelter. Like, maybe playing with kids or helping women find new places to live. That kinda thing?"

"Oh, that'd be great," said the woman. "We'd love to have you on board. But before you can work with our guests, you'll need to fill out our online application, which includes signing up for an orientation session and a few evenings of training. We run sessions here almost every week, as you'll see when you do the application. There's also a background check."

Orientation and training. Darn. Even though I knew why those things were required, they were such a pain. I just wanted to get started. "Okay. Where are you located?"

"We're in Jamaica Plain."

Oh lord. Jamaica Plain — commonly known as J.P. — was about as far from Arlington as any Boston neighborhood could be. Getting there wouldn't be easy, and I'd need to start with the training stuff. Actually,

I wasn't even sure *how* to get to J.P. on public transportation. "I see. That's a little tricky, since I'm in Arlington and I don't have a car. But I'll figure it out—"

"Arlington?" interrupted the woman. "Oh, that's a real hike. But you know, Molly, we do have a thrift shop right over in Somerville if you'd be interested in volunteering there. Somerville's a lot closer to you than Jamaica Plain."

I thought about that for a second. The store would *definitely* be easier to get to than the shelter, and I'd only have to deal with clothes, not suffering humans. But then I thought about Fred driving all the way to Rhode Island to make a direct impact. "Yeah, but I'd rather come to the shelter. If you have room for me, that is."

"Oh," said the woman with a snort and half a chuckle, "we've got room all right. Unfortunately, we've got plenty of guests."

I thanked her, hung up, and let my head fall on the kitchen table. Then, after a few minutes, I gathered my energy, sat up, and went online. I blasted through the no-brainer questions on the shelter's application and did my best to tackle the trickier ones. When it asked why I wanted to volunteer, I wrote, "A close friend's life was cut short by violence." It didn't seem like nearly enough—particularly since the form provided six or seven lines for that answer—but it was better than nothing, and I was determined to finish the thing. When I'd written something after every question, I hit *send*.

Next, I clicked the *Orientation* button. As the woman on the phone had said, the shelter ran sessions quite frequently. But they were all at seven o'clock on weeknights, and I usually worked until at least six-thirty. So, the only way I'd be able to get to Jamaica Plain by seven—especially on public transportation—would be to leave work early. *Very* early, because that was rush hour too. And since the sessions ran until nine, I wouldn't get home until ten at the earliest. Probably closer to eleven. Why was helping people so complicated?

In any case, I couldn't commit to an orientation session until I talked to Brad about the work thing, so I closed the website and clicked over to Facebook where everyone was chatting about Hurricane Sandy. Of course, no one knew what path the storm would take as it made its way toward New England, but the National Hurricane Center was issuing all kinds of weather and flood advisories. I thought about Fred and shivered.

Chapter 22
Hard Times Be Over

Fred
Thursday, November 1, 2012

He couldn't remember the last time he'd felt so good. Cruising back home down Wilson Road—noting the multiple tree limbs down but seeing no other obvious hurricane damage to the neighborhood—he checked his image in the rearview mirror and nodded. Something was different, but what? Did he look healthier? Stronger? Maybe even younger?

Sandy had shown her real wrath to New York and New Jersey, mercifully sparing most of Rhode Island. But hurricanes are always unpredictable, so Fred had set up his radio equipment at the hotel, and quickly connected with a few local hams also standing by to assist. None of them had known each other beforehand, but they'd formed a team and worked together to do what they could.

Two of the guys had linked up with the East Coast Hurricane Radio Network and sent damage reports to the Red Cross while he'd provided storm updates to members of the State Emergency Management Team. In other words, their roles had been minimal, but that wasn't the point. The point was that they'd been *ready* for any and all action *if* the storm had turned and struck Rhode Island harder.

Finally, on Wednesday night—Halloween—when Sandy was officially pronounced over, the little group had gone out for pizza and beer to celebrate, and that'd been great. It always felt good to unwind after working a disaster, and all the guys had had opportunities to test their equipment in real storm conditions. Which was important, because you can't know where your weak spots are—and fix them—unless you give them a trial run once in a while. For example, one of the guys had noticed that his standing wave ratio fluctuated when the rain turned torrential, but Fred—an antenna expert—had given him loads of advice.

That'd been his favorite part of the whole trip. He'd acquired so much knowledge over the years, and sometimes—with all the new technology—he wondered if that knowledge still held value. *I guess some things don't change*, he thought with a little smile as he parked in the driveway. *I've got some good years left in me.*

But instead of hopping right out, he closed his eyes and thought back to the days when he'd been able to do so much more. He recalled the mighty hurricanes "Bob" and "Gloria," and of course the legendary Blizzard of '78. Gosh, it was hard to believe so many years had passed since that devastating snowstorm, and even harder to believe he'd only been in his late 30s back then. *Just a kid, but tough.* He'd been more than happy to work around the clock for several days, helping radio operators at some of the Boston hospitals arrange transportation for doctors and nurses when the roads were nearly impassable. At least seventy people had died in that storm—some had heart attacks, some were asphyxiated, others froze in their cars—but Fred and his buddy Billy were lucky. All the people they'd personally helped had survived.

In fact, Governor Dukakis had sent them both personal thank you letters. And although Fred wasn't the sort of guy who'd frame a letter and hang it on the wall, he did keep it in his top desk drawer. And every once in a while, he'd take it out and re-read it.

But ham radio had been more than just a service project for him in his bachelor days; it'd also been his primary source of friendship and fun. Those monthly pancake breakfasts and semi-annual dinners put on by his local repeater society were the highlights of his social calendar, and he'd looked forward to each one the way little kids look forward to birthday parties. Sure, the married guys would bring wives and families, but Fred and the other bachelors would always find a table near the back of the room and shoot the breeze about radio stuff for hours.

Unfortunately, things changed after he and Barb got married. With her department store makeup and bored attitude, she didn't hit it off with the other ham wives—known as XYLs—who tended to laugh at dirty jokes and even tell them once in a while. Fred kept hoping she'd give those girls more of a chance someday, but as time wore on that seemed less and less likely.

"I'm not comfortable talking to people I have nothing in common with!" she yelled at him one frosty February night as they drove home from a dinner with her car window wide open. "And you reek! I feel like I'm gonna be sick." She was all bent out of shape because he'd left

IT DOESN'T HAVE TO BE THAT WAY

her at the table for half an hour and returned smelling like cigarettes. But he hadn't smoked at all that night, not even a puff. He'd just stepped outside for a breath of air with a few smoking pals and had gotten caught up in a very interesting conversation about the breakup of the Bell System.

"I'm sorry I was out there so long, angel. Everyone was asking me questions about the Ma Bell thing because of my job. You know how hams love talking about communication."

"Oh, for crying out loud. Your wife's stuck at a table listening to a bunch of bleach-blonde Mondale voters, and you're out there yakking about a goddamn monopoly that needed to be broken up? What's there to talk about? You used to work for New England Tel and now you work for AT & T. Big whoop. Your paycheck hasn't changed."

That hurt, but he didn't let it show. "Hey, come on, Barb. You know it's a big deal for me. My new boss is lousy, and some of my department's gonna get laid off soon." He didn't dare tell her he was planning to vote for Mondale too.

Barb shook her head and stared out the open window.

She wasn't being fair. He saw his ham buddies so much less now that he was married. Didn't he deserve a little fun? "You know, babe, you might like the other ladies more if you... well, if you got to know them. They're good people. They really are."

"They're not my type, Fred. That's obvious."

Why? Why was she always so negative about his stuff? His fingers on the steering wheel were freezing, and he couldn't smell any smoke at all. But if he asked her to close her window, they'd end up in a real fight. "All right, Barb. All right. I promise never to do that again."

Barb laughed bitterly. "No, you won't. Because I'll *never* go to another one of those things as long as I live."

"Oh, come on. Give it one more try. I'll stick by you like glue next time. I promise."

But she pointed her index finger toward her mouth, pretended to gag, and said nothing until they pulled into the driveway. Then she told him to take a shower before his stench made her vomit.

After that, he went to the ham dinners and breakfasts alone, but it felt strange because he had to keep making excuses for why his wife wasn't there. Then, after he and Barb divorced, he quit socializing altogether for a while. He'd never felt comfortable talking about his marital problems with anyone other than Billy, so how would he broach the subject of Barb moving out? It was easier to just stay home.

Eventually, he gave the parties another shot, but by that point, most of the old bachelors had either gotten married or moved away, and the new hotshots dominating the scene thought the whole world depended on software. They were decent enough guys, but the stuff they talked about went right over Fred's head a lot of the time, so he cut back to one or two breakfasts a year. Then Billy and Sally moved to Florida, and he pretty much threw in the towel.

But the Hurricane Sandy trip had awakened something dormant in him, evoking memories of what ham radio was like at its best: that unique camaraderie between people. Not to mention that one of the Rhode Island guys had given him links to some exciting new articles on the Internet about bouncing radio signals off communications satellites, and Fred was really looking forward to reading them.

All right, he thought, stepping down into the driveway and noting that his bad knee barely hurt at all. *I should probably get this equipment inside before it rains again.* It felt nice to be home.

Then he looked across the street, and there she was. *Jeannette.* Heading straight in his direction.

Oh gosh. Why? Her skirt was short—way above her knees—and she wore cowboy boots and a cowboy hat too. But there were no horses in Arlington! Besides, if she tried riding a horse with those bare legs, she'd get an awful rash.

He opened the back door of the truck and focused his attention on the radio stuff, but that didn't stop Jeannette.

"Heya, cowboy!" she said slapping him on the shoulder.

He turned and got a better view of those legs—very nicely shaped legs—and his face felt hot. "I'm no cowboy," he replied, fumbling with some wires on the back seat. "You're the one with the hat."

"Oh, I'm just gettin' in the spirit. I heard you were out savin' lives all weekend."

His heart sped up and he kept messing with the wires. They were fine, but he had nothing else to do with his shaky hands. "Pssh. I was just in Rhode Island on storm standby. All told, they got very little damage down there."

"Uh-huh. That's not what I heard."

"From *who*?" His guts squirmed.

Jeannette cocked her head to one side. Her blue eye shadow and red lipstick made her look a little like the old-fashioned doll that used to sit on his mother's bureau. "Well, Molly for one. She told me you were out rescuin' damsels in the wind and rain."

He chuckled and did his best to sound calm. "Damsels, huh? That Molly's got some imagination. I thought *you* were the writer over there."

Jeannette laughed her throaty laugh. "Well, she and I *did* kill a bottle of wine together the other night. But you know? Maybe the girl's got a gift. Maybe I'll bring her to my next romance writers meeting."

Fred knew nothing about Jeannette's romance writer meetings and didn't care to. "Well, I'm glad you're both safe. I'm surprised to see all these tree limbs down. "

"Safe? Oh yeah. But we did lose power for almost twelve hours. Good thing we had that wine." She winked.

"Twelve hours? That's somethin'."

"Yesiree. But we survived. Of course, we would've invited *you* over if you'd been around. I was a little worried about you, mister. I really was."

For the first time in years, Fred didn't feel an immediate need to escape Jeannette. Her sexuality was usually *way* too much for him, but the trip had boosted his confidence. "Jingoes," he said, "I shoulda given Molly a key to my house. I wasn't thinkin' straight the other day. I've got a generator, you know. You girls coulda come over here."

Jeannette laughed again. "Aw, Molly and I are tough birds. But a generator, huh? I guess we shoulda figured that out, seeing as yours was the only house on the street with any lights on." She paused and smiled. "You're smart guy, Freddy."

Oh boy. Maybe not *that* confident. He grabbed the entire pile of wires and tossed them on the ground, hoping to distract Jeannette from his face, which was starting to burn. "If I was smart, I woulda thought about you girls."

Jeanette batted her lashes. "Fred, listen to me. We had *fun*. And we were *fine*. They didn't even lose power down in East Arlington, so we ordered takeout from China Dragon. And you know, I'm glad Molly told me about your adventure, because now I'm thinkin' of putting a guy like you in my next book. I haven't plotted it out yet, but I'm imagining this sexy radio man, travelin' around, savin' women from natural disasters. And of course, there'll be plenty o' romance along the way. Romance makes the world go 'round, right?"

He felt very grateful for the cool breeze that blew across the driveway right then. "Sure, Jeannette. Whatever you say. But I gotta get this stuff in the house now. Nice to see you, though."

"You *too*," said Jeannette, glancing down at the delicate gold watch on her plump wrist. "Ooh, and I've gotta catch my bus. But maybe you could come over someday for a cup o' tea? Molly tells me you like tea, and I've got some really nice ones upstairs. I buy the loose leaves at a little shop in Harvard Square, and lemme tell you, Fred, you haven't tried tea until you've had a cup of this new ginger and cardamom one I've got. They say it's good for the *libido*." She winked again. "Not that I'd know anythin' about that."

He felt his stomach shrink. That was the problem with Jeannette. Eventually, she always managed to cross that line. "Thanks," he said. "But I drink the regular stuff from Lipton's."

Jeannette seemed to sense that she'd upset him. "Okay, Fred. How 'bout this? I'll pick up some Lipton next time I'm at the store."

"Sounds great," he said, bending down to get the wires. "Take care now."

"You too. Take *good* care." She started to walk away, and he breathed a sigh of relief. But when she reached the bottom of the driveway, she turned around and smiled. "But you know, I'm gonna get some of that *libido* stuff too. Just in case you feel like tryin' it."

Chapter 23
It Doesn't Have To Be That Way

Fred
Sunday, November 4, 2012
Arlington, MA

"I hope I didn't wake you," said Molly, handing him something warm wrapped in tinfoil. "It's banana bread. My mom's recipe."

As he usually did on Sunday mornings, he'd been sitting at the kitchen table in his pajamas and robe, eating toast, listening to Croce, and scanning the obits in the *Globe*. Later on, after a shower, he'd probably finish reading the last of those fascinating online articles about ham radio and communications satellites. Then, he'd call his new friend in Rhode Island on the radio to discuss them.

"Oh no, I've been up a while," he said, adjusting the lapel of his bathrobe. "Sunday's just my lazy day." He didn't like being seen in pajamas. "You wanna come in?"

"Um, sure? If that's cool."

He enjoyed Molly's company, of course, but felt a little self-conscious about the way he and the house looked. "Oh yeah. As long as you don't mind a messy house. I haven't had a chance to do the dishes yet."

"Oh, you should see my house. I haven't cleaned in two weeks."

He doubted that but opened the door wider so the girl could step inside. The stereo was turned up pretty loud, so he hurried over to the receiver and adjusted the volume.

Molly stopped in the middle of the living room and frowned. "Wait. I know this is Jim Croce singing, but I don't recognize the song."

"Oh yeah. This wasn't one of his big hits, but it's a nice one. It's called 'It Doesn't Have to Be That Way.'"

"Sorta sounds like a Christmas song," said Molly.

"It is. In a way."

The song told the story of a couple who'd broken up over the holidays, and for a year or two after his divorce, Fred cried every time he heard it. Honestly, it still made him sad. He no longer wanted Barb back, but the song reminded him of Christmases he'd spent with his family—especially when Davey was little and still believed in Santa Claus—and also his three Christmases in Germany, in the Army. He didn't like holidays anymore, but when he was in the right mood, he enjoyed remembering the good ones.

"C'mon, let's go eat some banana bread," he said, leading Molly into the kitchen. The last time she'd visited, he'd gotten emotional in front of her, and he didn't want that happening again.

"Okay. And hey, Jeannette told me about your rescue mission in Rhode Island."

He shook his head and sighed. "Rescue mission? That Jeannette's somethin' else, isn't she? I think she lives in a different world than the rest of us. Have a seat, Molly." He picked up his plate with the toast crumbs on it, moved it to the counter, and turned on the kettle.

Molly sat at the table and laughed nervously. "I guess it's because she's a writer. But actually... Jeannette's one of reasons I came over here today. I wanted to... uh, warn you about something."

"Warn me? That doesn't sound good." He didn't want to appear worried, though, so he chuckled as he unwrapped the banana bread, grabbed a knife from the silverware drawer, and got a couple of clean plates from the cabinet.

"Well, maybe *warn's* the wrong word, but..." Molly was clearly having trouble making eye contact. "Okay, I'll just say it. I think Jeannette's got a crush on you, and she might ask you out. Or something. There. That's it."

"Oh boy." Now *he* couldn't look Molly in the eye, so he focused on cutting two nice slices of bread and putting them on the plates. For the past few days, he'd been thinking about Jeannette's legs a *lot*, and also about that sexy tea she'd mentioned. "I hope I've got butter," he muttered even though he knew he had plenty. Slowly, he opened the fridge and took out the butter dish, then laid it on the table with the other stuff.

Molly started buttering her bread, and he realized he had to say something. "Well... that's very nice, I guess. But I'm not her type." He sat down to butter his bread too, and neither of them spoke for an awkward minute.

Finally, Molly looked up at him. "She's a fun person, Fred. She really is."

Fun, yes. That was the problem. "You know, Molly," he said slowly, "she's probably a little *too much* fun for me. But thanks for letting me know. You're a good kid."

"Sure," she said, taking a bite of her bread. "So, here's a weird question. Do you mind if I ask how old you are?"

He shrugged. "Seventy-two. You takin' a survey or somethin'?"

"No. Just wondering. Actually, Jeannette wanted me to ask you. She wants to put a character like you in some book she's writing."

The kettle whistled. "Jingoes!" he said, getting up to shut it off. "She mentioned that the other day too. Crazy. There's nothin' to *write* about me." He grabbed two mugs and two teabags. "No sugar and a little milk, right?"

"Yup. Hey, Fred, what does *jingoes* mean?"

A change of subject! Excellent. "I have no idea," he said, trying to keep his hands from shaking as he poured the scalding water. "My dad used to say it all the time. I think it was a substitute for *Jesus* or *Jesus Christ*. He didn't like swearing or taking the Lord's name in vain. My parents were what people used to call *lace-curtain Irish*. Always tryin' to be classy, even though they grew up dirt poor." As he spoke, he poured milk into the steaming mugs, carried them to the table, then sat back down and took a bite of the bread. "This is delicious, Molly."

"Thanks. It's a little dry. My mom used to make it better. I mean, she still does, but I haven't had hers in a while. So... would you *consider* going out with Jeannette if she asked you?"

Oh boy. "Look, I dunno. I really don't go out with ladies these days. I'm a homebody."

"Yeah. I get that. It's just that I feel sorta responsible for her being all hot and heavy for you. I told her about your radio thing the night of the storm, and she got so excited. She thinks you're... amazing."

"Hot and heavy?" A crumb of banana bread stuck in his throat. He took a sip of tea, but it was too late. For as far back as he could remember, he'd gotten these tickles in his throat, and all he could do was ride them out. He gasped for air, then started hacking like crazy.

"Where do you keep your water glasses?" asked Molly, jumping up.

Coughing like a bastard, he pointed to the cabinet over the sink. Molly filled an avocado-colored glass with tap water and handed it to him. "Don't talk. Just drink."

After a moment of intense coughing, he managed to say, "I'm fine. Something went... wrong way." He swallowed as much water as he could and breathed carefully, his eyes tearing up as he calmed down. "There. That's better. Thanks, Molly."

"Sure. Of course. I'm gonna grab some water for myself too, if that's all right." Then, without waiting for a response, she did.

Breathing more easily, he wiped his eyes.

Molly sat down with her water. "You look better now. Phew."

"Yeah, I get that tickle every once in a while. My brother used to get it too. It's no big deal." He took another sip of water, and for some reason he remembered his mother bringing the green drinking glasses home one day in the 70s. She'd called the avocado color "very stylish."

Molly looked straight at him. "So, are you doing okay? I mean, you did just lose your brother. That's gotta be a big deal."

No one ever asked him personal stuff like that. "Oh, yeah. I'm fine." He pressed his lips together and breathed out through his nose. "But if it's all the same to you, I'd rather not talk about poor Davey. He... well, he had problems with alcohol and... other stuff too. He was on all kinds of medicine, and he could get violent sometimes too. At least that's what people say. I never saw it. But let's leave it at that. Davey was a complicated guy."

"Hmm."

"And please, whatever you do, *don't* talk about him around the neighborhood. Especially not with that old b... witch next door. Joyce Costa."

Molly frowned. "Don't worry, I won't say a word. But... you know, she thinks—"

"What?"

"Uh, maybe I shouldn't say this, but I'm pretty sure Mrs. Costa thinks there was, like, violence between you and your wife. But from what you're saying, it sounds like maybe it was your brother who had the problem? I don't know. I'm just... I just wish Mrs. Costa would treat you better."

He stood up, walked over to the window, and looked out at the street where he'd spent most of his life. Maybe he didn't have many friends in town, but the house was paid for and he had space for all his radio equipment. He could put up as many antennas as he liked in the back yard too, and no one could do a thing about 'em.

"Molly, I don't care *what* she thinks." He turned and faced the girl. "But I *never* hit Barb. I've never hit anyone, if you want the truth. Not even as a kid. I'm not a fighter. But if that witch wants to believe I'm a bad guy, let 'er. Davey suffered enough in this life. I'll be damned if I'm gonna let her gossip destroy his good name now that he's dead."

Molly frowned in her concerned way. "I understand," she said. But she didn't sound so sure.

He sighed and leaned against the counter for support. Some days, he didn't understand either. "Listen. My brother was a great guy, but the war ruined him. That's the long and short of it. And when things got really bad, he moved to Maine so he wouldn't bother us with his problems anymore. He tried to hide but, like they say, sometimes you can't do that."

Molly stared, blinked a few times, and pushed her plate aside with half a piece of banana bread still on it. "I just don't get why Mrs. Costa watches you so closely."

Something about Molly made Fred believe he could trust her. "Listen, there's a lotta water under the bridge between me and old Joyce. We go all the way back to grammar school, when I was a real oddball. Then, when Davey got back from 'Nam, I tried to protect him. I did everything I could, but that didn't do my marriage any favors. Hindsight's always 20/20, you know? At the time, though, I didn't feel like I had a choice. My poor brother seemed... helpless." His voice broke.

"I'm sorry," said Molly.

"Thanks." He rubbed his eyes again, blotting tears with his fingers. "It was all a long time ago, but it doesn't always feel that way. Especially when... well, you know those cops who were here a couple weeks ago?"

"Yeah?"

"Yeah, well, they were askin' about a case Davey mighta been involved in. A bad one. Someone got killed, Molly. But I don't believe Davey coulda done that. I... just can't."

Molly got really still when she heard the word *killed*. "Oh," she said. "But... they waited until he'd... passed away? To talk to you about it?"

"No." He laughed bitterly. "No, they've been here a few times. And I tell 'em everything I know, every time. Davey didn't give me a lotta information, especially as he got older. Between the drugs and the booze, and the... Molly, have you ever seen someone who's just not *there*? That was Davey, after a while. His eyes looked like little blue marbles buried in fat. He didn't even go out, except to see his shrink every once in a while. A neighbor lady did his grocery shoppin'. She's the one who found him the day he...." He sighed a heavy sigh. "He was like an invalid. Alone all the time."

Molly didn't seem to know what to say. "So... why do the cops think he..."

Surprisingly, Fred felt a small sense of relief after getting some of that bad stuff off his chest. "Oh, they've got their reasons, but I don't buy 'em. For one thing, Davey *did* hit a woman back in the 80s. A terrible thing, of course, but a long way from murder. He wasn't a killer. I just know it."

Molly started chewing her lip, and her eyes got huge. He realized he'd probably said too much, but it was too late stop now.

"Yeah. Yeah. And unfortunately, when Dave hit that woman in the 80s, I protected him. *Big* mistake. Huge. I actually lied to the police, and lemme tell you, I regret that every day, Molly. I thought I was helping, but I was doing the opposite."

"Hmm," said Molly.

"Anyway, that's probably why Joyce thinks I hit Barb. Barb wanted me to turn Davey into the police, and I wouldn't. I couldn't. So Barb did some screaming about it. Loud screaming."

"I... see."

He sighed. "Yeah. But like I said, this other case... this... murder case. It's really tough." He shook his head and wiped his eyes again. "A woman's dead, and her family wants truth. Justice. And I can't blame 'em. I would too. But there's no evidence against Davey. Absolutely none."

Molly looked pale. "Where did it... happen? Or would you rather stop talking now?"

He *never* wanted to talk about it, but he'd gone too far to quit.

"They found her behind a hardware store near Davey's house. In 2002. And yeah, my brother *was* at the store earlier that day. He needed a new toilet plunger, of all things. And the store had one of those video cameras, and Davey was on the tape. Clear as day. He bought his plunger and left. But according to the owner, one of the ladies workin' that day made a comment about my brother's size, and Davey got offended. Which makes sense, because Davey hated people talkin' about his body. Then, a couple hours later, a customer found the lady out back. Strangled. Earlier on, she'd been wearing a scarf, but it was gone. So the cops jumped in a cruiser and went straight to Davey's apartment."

"And... what happened?"

"He was half asleep on the couch with a beer. Watchin' TV. Swore he drove straight home from the store. Hadn't touched a soul. And every time I asked, he said the same thing. I musta asked him twenty times, and his story never changed. They found no blood or fingerprints either. Nothin'. Of course, they arrested him anyway, but eventually, they had to let him go. And they never found that scarf. They searched his house and truck about a thousand times, but it never turned up."

"So why are they so sure it was him?"

"'Cause he was *Davey*. Cops hated him. He wasn't a likeable guy after the war."

Molly sat silently and sipped some more water. "And this was in 2002?"

"Uh huh. But now the family's all worked up again because Davey's dead. They know they can't put him in jail, but they want closure. They've got a new lawyer and lemme tell you, the guy's a pit bull. He's convinced the cops can find that scarf if they start looking again, and maybe there'll be some DNA evidence. And you know, God bless 'em. I hope they find what they're lookin' for. But I wish they'd investigate some other people too. Seems to me they just pinned the thing on Davey from the get-go."

"Yeah. It sounds that way."

"America. Home of the free, right? Innocent until proven guilty?"

Molly nodded but looked a little scared. "Uh-huh."

Suddenly, he realized he'd said *way* too much. "Hey, I'm sorry, Molly, I didn't mean to... get into all this."

"No, I'm glad you did."

"Listen, Davey was no angel, and if he's guilty, he's guilty, but jeez." He paused and took a deep breath. "I know it sounds crazy, but if you'd *known* him. Before the war. He was... Davey was the *sweetest* kid. *Everyone* loved him. Everyone. And he was *my* little brother. You know, when I got home from the service, I taught him Morse code, and he and I used to..." His voice broke as he thought about Davey in his young, innocent days.

Molly looked overwhelmed. "I'm sorry," she said softly.

He composed himself as well as he could. "Thanks. You know, it sounds silly, but Davey and I used to send each other messages in Code. I was an Army veteran, and he was about eleven years old, but that was one thing we had in common. We'd tap messages into each other's palms or sometimes on the dinner table. He was a natural too. Great little coder, that kid."

Molly smiled with moist eyes and drank some water. "It doesn't sound silly, Mr. Flaherty. And Davey was lucky to have *you* for a big brother. My older brother Tim went out of his way to avoid me as much as possible."

"Are you and Tim close in age?"

"Sorta. He's about five years older than me."

"Ah. See, I was *twelve* when Davey was born. Technically, he could've been my son. We never competed at sports or... anything. That made for very little arguing when he was young. He looked up to me and... oh I adored him."

Molly finished her water. Fred got the sense she wanted to say something else but she seemed tongue-tied or something.

"Yeah," she finally said, sniffling and wiping her eyes. "Life is just... it can suck sometimes. But I understand why you protected Davey. Sometimes it's hard to know the right thing to do."

"Thanks. That means a lot, Molly. You're a good egg."

"You are too," she said, standing up. "But I gotta get going now."

"Oh yeah?" he asked, trying to sound cheerful. "Big date with the boyfriend?"

"No. Actually, we broke up."

Finally. "Oh. Sorry to hear that."

"Nah, it's okay. Things weren't... working out. Anyway, I'm glad we got to talk, Mr.... Fred. And I hope things... you know, get sorted out soon."

"Yeah. Me too." Then, just as he was about to open the door for her, he had an idea. "Hey, Molly?"

She turned to him slowly. "Yeah?"

"Um, I was just thinking—if you're not busy—there's a ham radio pancake breakfast next Sunday. You're welcome to join me if you want. Just, you know, for a change of pace. It's usually a nice group of people."

"A *ham radio* breakfast?"

Stupid me! Of course she doesn't wanna go. I must be losing it. "Yeah, maybe not, huh? I was just thinking you might enjoy meeting some hams. I haven't been to one in a long time, but the repeater society does a nice job, and oh... I dunno. I'm planning to attend. The food's usually good, and people bring their wives and kids, so it's not all techie talk. As a matter of fact, there're some lady hams in the group now too. But it's probably not your cup o' tea."

"Um, yeah—"

"Hey, forget I asked, okay? But if you change your mind, I'll be leaving here around nine on Sunday. It's up in Saugus."

"Thanks. I'll think about it. Have a good rest of your day, okay?"

He closed the door, wondering what was wrong with him. In the living room, the record had finished playing. He considered flipping it over but decided to take a shower before doing that and getting started on his online reading. Just in case anyone else dropped in. Molly seeing him in his pajamas was one thing, but if Jeanette rang his doorbell, he wouldn't answer. At least not until he was dressed.

Chapter 24
Spin, Spin, Spin

Molly
November 5, 2012
Everett, MA

The minute I arrived at work Monday, I knew something was very wrong. I was almost an hour late—my bus had gotten a flat tire, so the passengers had to wait for a replacement bus—but being late wasn't usually a problem at FSI. The weird thing was that as I made my way through the office with my bagel and coffee, everyone—even people I knew fairly well—glanced up without waving or saying hi. I'd grown accustomed to people at FSI being distant with me, but not silent. Not everyone.

"What's going on?" I mouthed to Diana at the reception desk. She looked miserable.

"Check your email," she said.

I felt dizzy. I'd stayed up too late the night before, and was already cranky, thanks to lack of sleep and the flat tire. "Did someone die?" I whispered.

Diana shook her head and wrote on a notepad, *Brad sold the company*. Then, once I'd read the words, she crumbled the paper into a ball and tossed it in the trash.

"Oh my god!" I whispered. I'd planned to act surprised when the sale was announced, but had also assumed it wouldn't occur for quite a while. Like, a year. Or more. So hearing the news that day truly shocked me. "What the hell?"

Major layoff, wrote Diana. *In two weeks.*

Again, Brad had warned me about the layoff, but hadn't mentioned it would be so soon. "Holy shit."

"Yeah," she whispered. Then she wrote, *Go to your desk. Now. Brad asked us not to discuss this today.*

I nodded and made my way over to the marketing area, where my coworkers all made brief eye contact with me before immediately burying their heads in work. And once I'd read the email from Brad, I understood why: my sweet boss was clearly gutted over the situation. But the message also promised that most engineers would remain employed at FSI for at least six months—if they wanted to be, of course—and that a few select employees from each department would be invited to stay on throughout the transition period. Perhaps even longer. Which explained why everyone was so "busy."

But I knew I wouldn't be one of the select. The day of our lunch, Brad had said I'd need to leave FSI after the sale, no matter what. He'd said that if anyone from marketing got to stick around, it'd be someone with a family to support.

I collapsed in my chair and opened a document. It was one of the white papers I'd been working on for Andy Stevers's group, and it was essentially complete. All I needed to do was read through it one last time before sending it off for approval, but I couldn't even focus on the first sentence. All around me, keyboards clicked and no one spoke. FSI sounded a little like a factory that day.

Tears formed in my eyes and rolled down my cheeks as I reflected on how screwed I was. Because I'd ignored Brad's advice. I hadn't started a resume or even researched *how* to write such a thing.

I pulled the lid off my coffee cup and took a sip, but the coffee had grown lukewarm. And although I'd been starving half an hour earlier, just looking at the cream cheese-laden bagel made me feel like vomiting. I pushed breakfast aside and rested my head on the desk.

Devan, the guy whose cube backed up to mine, was whispering into his phone, apparently to someone in his product marketing group. "Yeah, I know," he said, "that's why I'm calling an emergency meeting tomorrow morning. I'll invite Brad.... Yeah...yeah, he needs to know how much effort we've put into this thing... I know, we've been working our *asses* off... okay, awesome... I'll email him now."

I groaned silently. What a kiss-ass. I mean, everyone at FSI worked hard, but Brad didn't go to product marketing meetings unless his input was critical. Besides, Devan was a single guy who lived alone, so I was pretty sure he wouldn't be asked to stay anyway.

"Hey, Molly. You okay?" The voice was gentle and kind, but I jumped as if someone had shouted in my ear. I turned around slowly to see Andy Stevers. He was smiling like it was any other day.

"Oh. Yeah, I guess. Considering the circumstances."

"I hear you. But do you have time to talk about that document?"

Wow. I mean, Andy and the other engineers probably wouldn't lose their jobs for a while, but still. His casual nature on such a bleak day was odd.

"Sure. Hang on a second." My screen saver had come up, so I wiggled the mouse to make the paper visible again. "Voila!" I said softly. "See, I was just proofing it. Can I send it to you right after lunch?"

He smiled again, exposing those little gaps between his teeth. "Wow. I guess we're on the same wavelength, huh?"

I didn't know what to say, and luckily, he didn't seem to expect a response.

"Hey Molly," he went on, "I know you're busy, but any chance you're free for lunch? It'd be good to talk about the paper and... maybe some other stuff too." He smelled clean, like laundry detergent or something.

"Lunch?" I'd never eaten with Andy, nor had I ever seen him eat with anyone who wasn't an engineer.

"Only if you feel up to it, of course. And if you have time."

Time? Time was the *only* thing I had. "Sure," I said, my voice trembling a bit. "That sounds great."

"Oh, good. Is one o'clock okay?"

I nodded numbly, my heart fluttering.

"Perfect. I'll meet you here. But let's not eat in the caf. I'd rather have a little privacy, you know? You good with that sub shop down the street?"

"Uh-huh," I squeaked. "Whatever works."

I needed air. Fresh air. My first impulse was to text Diana, but halfway through writing the message, I stopped and deleted it. Knowing I was going to lunch with Andy would only make her jealous, and I had no idea why he wanted to talk to me. Better to treat this as business and nothing more. Although he *had* mentioned privacy. And yes, I really did need air. I got up and snuck out of the office through the back door.

All the way down in the elevator, I obsessed over him. *Andy Stevers. Andy fucking Stevers. Andy fucking Stevers wants to eat lunch with me. Privately.* But when I stepped outside and assessed the quaint brick building that'd become my home-away-from-home, tears filled my eyes again. What a day. I simply couldn't get a handle on it.

My mind drifted back to sophomore year in college, when FSI was housed in an old building near my school. Those memories were so vivid: the first time I met Brad; the thrill of earning his trust and being given real responsibility; those laid-back Friday afternoons when one of the employees would run out to the liquor store for a case of beer which we'd all share as we finished up another successful week on the job. How did those six years pass so quickly? And me? How did such a promising prospect become such a hot mess? And where would I end up now? If Andy hadn't just invited me to lunch, I probably would've started sobbing uncontrollably, but I was suspended in some strange space between deep sorrow and something like hysteria.

And then I saw *him*. Shane Armstrong. Descending from his black Navigator in a business suit, probably returning from a customer meeting. I had nowhere to hide. He'd already spotted me. Perhaps if I darted up the front steps and through the door, I *might* manage to jump on the elevator before he made it there, but maybe not. And sharing an elevator with Shane was my personal definition of a nightmare. So I stood my ground.

"Molly," he said, addressing me directly for the first time since our night in the El Chico parking lot.

"Hey," I said, wishing I had a cigarette, even though I hadn't smoked since college.

"See the email?" he asked, waving his phone.

"Yeah. Sucks, huh?"

He shoved the phone in his pocket and smirked. "Yeah. But you knew about that all along, didn't you? Thanks to your boyfriend, Brad. Lucky you. Sorry I can't chat, but I'm late for a meeting. Some of us still have to work, you know."

My boyfriend, Brad? "Are you freakin' kidding, Shane?" I wasn't sure if I was feeling empowered or getting ready to totally lose it. "You're some kinda sicko if you think Brad and I are anything more than good friends."

He smiled his rehearsed smile, the one that apparently convinced customers to buy thousands of dollars worth of software from him on a regular basis. "Oh, right. I'm the sick one." Sneering, he took a few steps closer and I smelled coffee and tobacco on his breath. "D'you have any idea how much *pain* you've caused me, Molly?"

I hated him and his hideous baby face. "Pain? Shane, you *trashed* my reputation here at FSI. What pain have I inflicted on *you*?"

He laughed humorlessly. "Seriously? How d'ya think it feels gettin' kicked outta your house with a new baby on the way? Terrific, right? My wife hasn't spoken to me in weeks. You know where I was just now? With my divorce lawyer. And now I'm gonna lose my fuckin' job. So yeah. I'd say I'm in pain. Thanks to you. Bitch."

Then, before I could even digest his words, he spat on the ground and stormed into the building.

I paced around outside for about ten minutes, trying to keep it together. Finally, when I felt certain Shane had made it up to FSI on the fourth floor, I took the elevator to the second—in an attempt to avoid running into any coworkers--and hurried down the hall to that floor's bathroom. An older woman was washing her hands when I entered, but I slipped into the handicapped stall, and when the woman left, I allowed my tears to flow freely.

What was wrong with Shane? How could he talk to me like that, and why couldn't he see that he'd caused his own pain by initiating our entire sexual encounter? He'd been the perpetrator, but it was my fault? And why couldn't FSI people see what a prick he was? Even worse, did they honestly believe I was sleeping with Brad?

I hated Shane with every ounce of hatred my hate glands could secrete, but also knew I needed to calm down and breathe. So I emerged from the stall, washed my face, and applied fresh lipstick and mascara. My eyes looked puffy, but since I didn't carry concealer in my purse, I just dabbed at them with cold water. Shane Armstrong may have ruined my reputation at work, but he wasn't going to make me cancel lunch with Andy too.

The sub shop was a typical hole in the wall, but being there with Andy made it feel funky, rather than just old-fashioned. With his brooding good looks and combed-back hair, he reminded me of a model in one of those retro photo shoots. "They've got great meatball subs here," he said.

"Cool," I said. "I used to love meatballs, but I'm a vegetarian now. I think I'm gonna get the salad wrap."

A concerned look spread over his face. "Does it bother you to be around people eating meat? Cause I'm cool with veggies too."

In the four years I'd been with Joe, he'd never once asked if I minded him eating meat, and Andy and I weren't even on a date. "Oh god, no. I'm used to it. It's all good."

The guy at the counter looked back and forth between us. "You two all set?"

"Yup," I said, and we placed our orders then headed to a table to wait. Andy grabbed a water from the refrigerator and I took a can of Diet Coke.

"So," he said, fixing those dark eyes on me, "any thoughts on where you'll be working next?"

I shrugged and cracked open the soda. "No idea. I need to get my resume out there. Actually, I need to *do* a resume. I just wanted to work at FSI forever, you know?"

"I hear you," said Andy. "And I believe you. But you should probably know that Shane Armstrong just told everyone in an engineering meeting that you had prior knowledge of the sale. He's convinced you're having an affair with Brad."

"He said all that in a *meeting*?"

Andy nodded.

I sighed. "Okay, full disclosure. I knew Brad wanted to sell at some point, but not *now*. That email this morning was a total shock. And Brad and I are friends, period. Shane's such a complete asswipe."

Andy nodded again and raised his well-shaped eyebrows. "Yup. He is. I've worked with him long enough to know that. And by the way, I also know you didn't jump him that night at El Chico. I saw you guys in the parking lot, remember?"

I remembered far too well, but hadn't planned on discussing that over lunch. "Yeah. Thanks for trying to help. Unfortunately, I made a really stupid decision." Talking to Andy was easier than I'd expected. He was crazy handsome, but there was something very down-to-earth about him too.

He cleared his throat as the sub shop guy delivered the sandwiches to the table. "Yeah, you definitely didn't make the *best* choice, but Shane was obviously just as into it as you. If not more so. That's why I kept asking if you were all right. I'm sorry if I seemed creepy or sexist, but men do bad things to women sometimes. Especially when they've been drinking."

For a second, he reminded me of Flaherty the morning after that awful night, when he came over to check on me because I'd fallen on his sidewalk. "Yeah, that's true. But you know, Shane spoke to me today for the first time since... then. Apparently, his wife's divorcing him, and he blames me for... everything."

Andy groaned. "Oh please. That guy cheats on his wife every time he travels. There's a female executive at a bank we work with in New

York, and lemme tell you, it's pathetic. He doesn't even attempt to hide it. We took her group out to dinner a few weeks ago when we were down in the city for a meeting, and Shane actually gave me his FSI credit card and told me to forge his signature on the check because he couldn't wait to get the woman back to his hotel. It was gross, dude. I feel bad for his wife and that kid he's got on the way. Imagine having Shane as a dad?"

I couldn't help smiling. "Yeah, I guess I shouldn't complain. I'm just one of the many women he treats like shit, but that poor kid'll have him forever. And yeah... his wife. Life must suck for her."

Andy took a bite of his sandwich, chewed politely, and drank some water. "I'm sure it does. But let's talk about you now. 'Cause Molly, you're great at what you do. And you deserve another great job."

"Thanks. That's nice of you to say." I tried to cool the blush I felt coming on with a sip of cold soda.

He sighed. "So, why are you—and don't take this the wrong way—but why do you let Shane walk all over you? He's hurting you, both personally and professionally. You don't have to put up with that."

I couldn't help feeling defensive. "Well what am I supposed to *do*? Email the whole company to set things straight? 'Cause that doesn't seem very professional either. And what would Brad think if he saw an email from me, saying, *Hey everyone, guess what? I didn't actually attack Shane like a dog in heat.* You know? That'd just make everything worse."

"Agreed. But what about HR? Did you talk to them?"

I'd never seriously considered going to HR because every time the idea crossed my mind, I'd think about Shane's pregnant wife. "Look, I didn't wanna get him fired. I just wanted the whole thing to go away."

"But it hasn't, and *he's* gotten away with blatant sexual harassment. And what've you gotten?"

I shrugged and bit my lip. "I'm fine. Don't worry about me. It could've been so much worse."

The look in Andy's eyes changed to something like disappointment. "Sure. And maybe it *will* be worse for his next victim. 'Cause that guy's got a pattern going, and he doesn't give a shit about anyone except himself. He's dangerous, Molly, and who knows where he'll stop? You hear about guys like him on the news all the time, right? But not until they beat someone senseless. Or kill 'em. Or whatever." As he spoke those last words, his voice trembled a little and his eyes got shiny, like he might cry or something. Then he blinked again, sniffled, and took another bite of his sandwich.

I was totally caught off guard by his passion. I mean, it was cool that he cared, but why did he care *so much*?

"Trust me," I said. "I've known people who've been abused. And I mean seriously. In the worst way possible. It's... horrific."

"Me too," he said with a sigh.

Suddenly, I felt more exhausted than I'd felt in a long time. I'd barely touched my lunch, and it was almost two o'clock. "Hey, I've gotta get back to work. If it's okay with you, I'm gonna bring this sandwich back to FSI and eat it at my desk."

Andy took a deep breath, then reached across the table and laid his hand on mine. "Good idea. And, hey, I didn't mean to freak you out. There's some other stuff I should tell you. Not about Shane, but... other stuff. Not now, though."

He was practically holding my hand. *Andy Stevers was practically holding my hand.*

"Okay," I managed to say.

But he kept looking into my eyes. "So I don't know if you're... in a relationship or something, but I was wondering if you'd wanna have a drink with me sometime."

Was I in a dream? I mean, being asked to lunch with Andy was one thing, but drinks? "Um, yeah. I mean, sure. That'd be... great." Did my voice sound normal? I couldn't tell. My ears felt like they were stuffed with cotton.

He smiled. "Awesome. I'll bring this food over there to get wrapped up."

Normally, I'd deal with my own lunch, but my head was spinning a little, so I just shrugged and allowed Andy to take my sandwich. Then I sat there—numb—until he returned with a paper bag.

But when he put on his blue fleece jacket with the little diamond logo on the breast, I came to my senses just enough to notice the words *ARRL, Amateur Radio* next to the logo. He'd said something that night at El Chico about joining a repeater society.

"Are you a ham radio guy?" I asked as we headed toward the door. I pointed to his jacket and tried to sound like I knew what I was talking about.

He may have actually blushed a little. "Yup. It's nerdy, but it's lots of fun."

"So I've heard. My neighbor's into that too."

"Yeah, there're lots of us out there. Over 700,000 in the country alone."

IT DOESN'T HAVE TO BE THAT WAY

"Wow," I said, suddenly remembering that Flaherty had invited me to his ham radio pancake breakfast on Sunday. "Hey, you're not going to some pancake thing in Saugus this weekend, are you? 'Cause I might be going with my neighbor."

He squinted. "Oh, you mean that repeater society event? Um, *maybe*. I'm not sure. I've got a lot going on this Sunday, but it'd be cool to meet some of the people in the group."

The FSI building was on the other side of the street, and as we walked toward it, I wondered how a day could possibly be any stranger. But right then, Andy reached down and gently took my hand again. "Hey," he said as every cell in my body froze, "thanks for eating with me. Or talking, anyway."

"Oh, sure."

"No. It was really nice." Then he pulled me toward him and gave me a peck on the cheek. "Sorry," he said, his voice shaky as he dropped my hand and we both started walking toward the building again. "That was a little impulsive."

My guts turned to liquid and my skin felt like it'd been shot through with electricity. Could such a tiny kiss cause spontaneous combustion? "Don't be sorry," I said, sounding like I'd sucked on a helium balloon.

"Okay," said Andy. "Then I'm not."

I must've walked beside him as we crossed the parking lot because we reached the building together. But I can't remember taking all those steps. The next thing I recall is reaching for the door handle and hearing Andy's cellphone ring.

"Oh," he said, glancing at the screen. "I gotta take this."

I could barely even process his words. "Sure," I said. "See you around."

Andy put the phone to his ear and held the door for me as I floated inside. "Hey, I got your text, dude," he said to the person on the other end. "So what'd the cop say?"

On Wednesday, Brad spoke to each one of his sales and marketing employees individually. It went on for hours, and since my cube was near his office, I got a front row seat at one of the bleakest parades ever. All day, people stumbled past, sobbing.

When it was my turn, I did my best not to cry. Poor Brad looked like he was ready to pass out, and I didn't want to make things worse for him.

"Hey Molly," he said, giving me a bear hug. "Gosh, it's nice not having to explain to you why I made this decision. I feel like a broken record today. A bad broken record. And a selfish one. I sure hope I'm doing the right thing."

"You are. And you're not selfish either. You're doing this for your family. Don't worry. Everyone'll be fine."

"Thanks for the vote of confidence," he said, releasing me from the hug. "I appreciate it. But what about you? Any hits on the job market?"

"A couple," I said, too embarrassed to tell the truth. "But I don't wanna jinx anything, so no details, okay?"

He smiled with his tired, red-rimmed eyes. "Go get 'em girl. And use me as a reference anytime. I mean *any*time. You know I've got nothing but praise for you."

"Thanks, Brad. And thanks for all the help you've given me over the years." The tears welled in my eyes, and he hugged me again. I loved him so much. But even as I sobbed on his shoulder, I could feel the shift in our relationship. Things with Brad would never be the same again. FSI had been one of his top priorities for so many years, and whether I liked it or not, I was part of his FSI journey. A journey that would soon end for all of us.

On the other hand, Andy had kissed me. The timing of the kiss couldn't have been odder, or better. In a moment when I could've easily descended into a dark, swirling river of depression, the kiss provided a life preserver to cling to. A sturdy, reliable life preserver. And he'd asked me to go out sometime too. I didn't want to set myself up for disappointment—because the date might never happen—but its possibility kept me afloat.

Brad took my hands and held me at arms' length. "I'll miss you, Molly. Oh, and one more thing. I'm making an announcement this afternoon. Friday will be FSI's final day."

"*This* Friday? I thought we were staying open another week."

"Yeah. I've been thinking about that, and it doesn't really make sense. Sales and marketing would just spin their wheels, and engineering could use a break. And the pay period goes through next week, so if we shut down this Friday, everyone'll get a week of paid vacation. It's not much, but it's the least I can do."

"Oh Brad, that's so sweet. It's just... so sudden."

"I know," he said. "It is. But sometimes it's better to pull the bandage off really fast. And, of course, your last paycheck will reflect that bonus we discussed. That should help a bit too."

"Thanks," I said, shaking his hand. "You've been the best boss."

But as I headed to the bathroom to cry a little more, I made a vow to myself. For the first time in my life, I'd be free to do whatever I wanted for at least a little while. Yes, I'd have to get going on that resume and start my job hunt, but I'd also have time to do orientation and training at that women's shelter. It wasn't too late to be a good person. In fact, maybe the demise of FSI would trigger the start of a whole new Molly.

No one even pretended to work Thursday. Since the next day would be the company's last—and the few folks who'd been chosen to stick around had been notified—everyone else used their time at FSI to chat and discuss the future. Some workers scrolled through online career sites together, while others made phone calls or searched for associates on LinkedIn. Brad encouraged us all to do that stuff, and he walked around the office, being supportive and making suggestions. But even though people went through the motions of looking for new jobs, a strong sense of denial filled the air. I think a lot of workers still hoped Brad would change his mind at the last minute.

He didn't, of course. And on Friday, by the time I arrived at the office, some people had already packed up most of the items from their cubicles. Thursday's denial had been replaced by full-on sadness spiked with anxiety. Lots of employees wept and declared that no workplace could ever be as great as FSI. Meanwhile, the building maintenance team had distributed extra trashcans and recycling bins throughout the office, which made tossing out sentimental items like special marketing brochures and promotional gadgets from various campaigns a little easier. By lunchtime, I'd gotten rid of everything that wouldn't fit into the large tote bag I was using as a purse that day.

"So are people going to El Chico after work?" I asked Diana at lunch. She and I had chosen to eat in the caf that day, partly for sentimental reasons, but also because she was too busy with last-minute administrative stuff to leave the building. I hadn't breathed a word to her about Andy and me. It seemed especially cruel to throw that in her face at a time when she—like everyone else—was facing the reality of unemployment.

She pushed a lock of red hair out of her eyes and tilted her head to one side. "Yeah, Mol. And I feel bad saying this, but I don't think you should go. Shane's gonna be there."

Pain stabbed my already-bleeding heart. I had no intention of going anywhere Shane planned to be, but hearing Diana say that Shane Armstrong was more welcome at El Chico than me hurt.

"Well," I said with a sigh, "it's not fair. I've worked here so much longer than that prick. And I'm a much nicer person."

The expression on Diana's face turned from sorry to slightly indignant. "I know, Molly, but Shane's wife's leaving him. He's going through a *really* rough time and he needs to find a new job—like yesterday—if he wants joint custody of his kid. The guy's gotta do all the networking he can."

I considered that. "I see. But *I'm* not going through a rough time, right? I mean, it's so *easy* for me to leave my job in disgrace, with all my coworkers thinking I'm a home-wrecker because some shithead keeps spreading false rumors about me."

"Come on, Mol. You know what I mean."

"Yeah. You mean you guys would rather support an asshole who cheats on his wife and blames it on a woman, than support the woman who happens to be me." My voice was rising and I didn't care. I think I was channeling Kate back in high school or something. "And don't even get me started on the shit he's been spewing about Brad and me, 'cause that's just sick."

"Molly," said Diana, "cut the crap. Please. You're my friend. And I'm here for *you*. It's just tonight. Starting tomorrow, everything'll be different."

"Maybe. But you know what? It still sucks."

I heard footsteps behind me, then a man's voice. He spoke very quietly, but I knew exactly who it was. "Don't listen to her, Di. She's a little *whore*."

Blood rushed to my head, and I swear I heard Kate telling me to stay strong in her *Thelma and Louise* accent. It freaked me out a little, but I pushed my chair back and somehow managed to stand, turn, and confront the crimson face of Shane. "Really?" I said in a voice just above a whisper. "Is that what I am?"

His hands were clenched into fists, and I got the sense he was trying hard to keep from hitting me. "You know it."

The cafeteria was packed because it was the last day, and suddenly everyone fell silent. All eyes were on the two of us. I breathed in and out a few times, feeling oddly calm. "Fine," I said, unconsciously assuming a slight Southern accent. "I accept that label. *Whore*. But you know what? You're one too. You're just too much of a wimp to admit it. That's the part that really pisses me off."

"You fucking—"

I saw him raise his arm, but it didn't make contact with me because Brad and one of the engineers grabbed him by the shoulders.

"Don't you *ever* attempt to assault one of my employees," said Brad, as he and the other guy walked Shane out of the caf. "This may be your last day at FSI, but I'm pretty sure I can still fire you."

The clinking of dishes and silverware in the kitchen took on a surreal quality. It would've been cool if people had clapped or cheered, but they didn't. I grabbed my tote bag purse and stormed out of the building.

No one followed.

Chapter 25
Tomorrow's Gonna Be A Brighter Day

Molly
November 9, 2012

When I got home at around two that afternoon, I changed into sweats, made a cup of tea, and curled up on the couch with my laptop. I'd cried most of the way home on the bus, but my tears had been tears of relief. I had no idea if Brad could actually fire Shane after he'd already been laid off, but I didn't care. I was just proud that I'd stood up for myself in front of my coworkers. They could believe whatever they wanted, but I hadn't caved. I felt more energized than I had in months.

Opening the application for the women's shelter, I saw that I'd answered all the main questions. My responses were brief, but satisfactory. The next step was choosing a week to attend orientation. It was early November and I had absolutely nothing to do, so I clicked the button for the session starting the following week and hit *submit*.

Yes! After so many years of vowing to do something, I finally had. Now, all I could do was wait for a response. Since it was Friday evening, I figured I wouldn't hear back until Monday, but that was fine.

Out of habit, I switched on the TV and found an old sitcom that looked silly and vaguely familiar. In it, the main character—a beautiful, classy, woman named Sandy—is in trouble because all the neighbors think she's having an affair with the married man in the apartment next door. But she's actually just helping the guy find the perfect anniversary necklace for his wife. The story unfolds the way you'd expect. More and more "evidence" of the "affair" piles up, until even the guy's wife thinks Sandy and her husband are screwing. But then, of course, the jeweler forgets the necklace is a surprise for the wife and calls her, informing her it's ready to be picked up. In the final scene, everyone comes to an anniversary party and apologizes to Sandy, and the husband and wife kiss passionately. And Sandy, like the classy lady she is, sneaks out of the party as show's theme song begins to play.

"Someday," says Sandy to herself over the music, "someone's gonna love *me* that much."

"Me too," I said, turning off the set but not feeling so sure. My dry eyes ached, so I lay back on the couch, suddenly wiped out. It occurred to me that I'd left my cellphone in the tote bag in my bedroom, but I didn't care. I had no interest in talking to anyone, not even Diana. If *she* wanted to apologize, she'd have to do it another time.

The sky was dark when I awoke. Across the street, Flaherty's house sat in darkness too — although his little porch light glowed dimly — and his truck was gone from the driveway. I wondered briefly where he was.

But I was too hungry to care all that much. Blinking away sleep, I got up and retrieved my phone, planning to call the local sub shop. But the first thing I saw on the screen was a text message. From Andy. It'd come in over an hour earlier.

In Cambridge all day for a meeting. Any chance you can meet me at the Middle East?

I knew about the Middle East in Cambridge, although I'd never been there. It was a funky restaurant and nightclub where Kate used to go see bands in high school. As fast as I could, I texted back. *Sorry, just saw this. Are you still there? I'm in Arlington.* Feeling shaky, I sat down and rubbed my eyes.

Yeah, at the bar now, he wrote. *Come down when you can.*

I wished I had time to shower, but didn't want to push my luck. So I washed up, brushed my teeth, and applied fresh makeup. Then I dressed in a pair of faded bellbottoms and a white poet shirt. My hair looked frumpy because I'd slept on it, but I brushed it out and sprayed some hairspray through it to add a little body. Then I checked the bus schedule. I didn't go to Cambridge often, and was glad to see that the bus that went straight down Mass. Ave. to Central Square ran regularly.

But just before I closed my laptop, I noticed a new email from Refuge Shelter and couldn't resist opening it.

Dear Molly,
We truly appreciate your offer to volunteer at Refuge Shelter. Unfortunately, due to some unexpected staffing changes, we've

decided not to bring on any new volunteers for several months. We apologize for the inconvenience, and will be sure to contact you when we're up and running again at full speed.

On a more positive note, we're planning some building renovations in the spring, and will need many, many hands to achieve our goals. Can we count on you to be part of that project? If you're interested, simply reply to this email with the word "yes" and we'll keep your name on file.

Thanks again for reaching out. All of us at Refuge Shelter wish you and yours wonderful, peaceful holiday season.
Best regards,
Sue McNeil
Volunteer coordinator

Damn it! I mean, the part about helping out in the spring sounded good, but I wanted to volunteer with the women right away. Before I found a new job. *Shit.* I'd procrastinated and procrastinated, and now it was too late. Or maybe not. Maybe I could find another shelter that needed help sooner. But I'd have to deal with that later because Andy was waiting for me at the Middle East.

I quickly replied *yes* to the email and sent it. Then I grabbed my coat and purse and headed out. My stomach was in knots, but they were the good kind of knots.

He was sitting at the bar alone, reading the *Globe* despite the noise and commotion surrounding him. Almost every chair at every table was occupied, and all the barstools were taken except for the one next to Andy. When I got closer, I noticed his ham radio jacket lying across the empty stool.

"Hey!" he said, looking up and smiling. "I saved you a seat."

I couldn't help blushing. Until that moment, I guess I hadn't truly believed he'd be there. Not that I'd expected him to blatantly stand me up or anything, but things happen.

And yet, there he was, pulling out the barstool for me.

And there I was, sitting down. In a daze, I ordered a dark beer. I like dark beer, and besides, that's what Andy was drinking, so I didn't think much about it.

"Did you eat?" he asked.

"Um, a little." I'd actually eaten nothing—and had only managed a few bites of lunch because of the drama in the cafeteria—but I didn't want to make him feel guilty if he'd already had dinner.

"Oh good. Wanna order some falafel and baba ghanoush? I'm starving."

I wondered if he remembered I was vegetarian or if he was just in the mood for that stuff. Either way, I liked the idea. "Sure. This place is packed, huh?" Most of the people around us were young, casually dressed, and emoting high energy.

"Yeah, some big hip hop group's playing downstairs later on. Unfortunately, I got a call from my sister while I was waiting for you, and I'm gonna need to leave right after we eat." He grimaced. "Family shit, you know? Otherwise, I'd suggest we stay for the show."

I was disappointed to learn it'd be a short date, but maybe that was better. I definitely got the sense he was telling the truth and not just trying to blow me off. "Oh, that's fine. I'm not a huge hip hop fan anyway."

"Yeah, me either, but I really like seeing bands here. Sometimes I just drop in and check out whoever's playing. Almost anything's good when it's live."

What a cool guy. I hadn't seen much live music since college because Joe had been more into movies and TV. In all the years I'd dated him, we'd only gone out to see one band, and that was because his friend from work was the drummer.

Andy ordered the food from the bartender—an athletic, blond woman with large white teeth—then turned to me. "So how'd the last day in the office go?"

"Weren't you... oh right! You were at that meeting all day."

"Yeah. I can't say I was too bummed. I hate goodbyes."

I considered that. "Yeah. Me too, actually. But today was... interesting. I actually had a little showdown with Shane in the caf."

"Seriously? What happened?"

"Long story short, he called me a whore and I said we were both whores. So he got pissed and almost smacked me, but Brad and another guy hauled his ass outta there. It was weird. No one knew what to do. Everyone just stood there. I took off without saying goodbye to *anyone*."

"Wait. Wait. Did that dirtbag actually try to hit you?"

"I think so. It all happened really fast. But yeah, it seemed that way. Brad said something about *assault* when he grabbed him."

"Oh, wow. Now I wish I *had* been there today. Molly, you're a hero and those FSI idiots need to realize that."

I felt like I was falling in love with him, but that was crazy. I mean, I barely knew him.

The bartender brought my beer and I took a big gulp. "I still can't really process it all."

He smiled. "Yeah, but you called Shane a whore. That's epic."

"Thanks." I didn't know what else to say. "It felt satisfying, I guess. And you know, when I got home, I did something I've been meaning to do for a long time. So I guess it's been a good day." For some reason, I got dizzy for a second but it passed quickly.

The bartender checked on us and Andy ordered a glass of water. "I have to pace myself with beer or I get in trouble," he said. "Plus, I've got a long drive ahead of me tonight. So what's the thing you got done?"

"Huh?"

"The thing you just mentioned. When you got home today."

I gulped some more beer. "Oh! I finally filled out the paperwork to volunteer at a women's shelter in Jamaica Plain."

"Really?" He seemed far more interested than I would've expected. "That's awesome! What're you gonna do there?"

"Well, it's sorta complicated 'cause apparently they're not taking new volunteers at the moment, but they do need people to help with renovations in the spring, so I signed up for that." I shrugged as the dizzy feeling in my head returned. "It's a start anyway."

Andy nodded slowly. "Yeah. That's a good cause for sure."

"It is," I said. "It really is." I started to take another sip of beer, but my head full-on reeled and I knew I shouldn't drink any more until I'd eaten some food. I *really* didn't want to pass out there.

"So the last time we were together, you mentioned knowing someone who'd been badly abused," said Andy.

Wow. The guy had a good memory. "Yeah. A friend in high school got attacked by a guy and... in the end, it turned out really bad. Like, the worst." I didn't enjoy talking about Kate, but right then, I was more concerned about myself. My voice sounded distant and distorted, almost like it was echoing in my head instead of coming out my mouth. *Oh please. I cannot faint.*

"Oh, that's terrible," he said. "But I guess that means you and I have something else in common."

"Huh." My head spun again and I pressed on my temples.

"Molly? You okay?" He reached over and grabbed my elbow.

"Yeah. I think I just need some air."

Andy said something to the bartender and helped me off the stool. My legs were rubber. Another guy came over to help.

"My purse," I blurted, as the two men escorted me toward the door. "I need my coat and purse..."

"No worries," said Andy. "Emily'll keep an eye on 'em."

"Emily?"

"The bartender. She's a friend. C'mon. Let's get you outta here."

I didn't actually pass out. The chilly, almost-winter air cleared my head, and within a few minutes, I felt much better. Andy thanked the guy who'd helped him with me, and the guy headed back inside.

"How you doin'?" asked Andy, taking my hands in his and looking me in the eye.

"Okay," I said, shivering. "Cold." I laughed nervously. "I'm sorry about this. It happens sometimes if I don't eat enough. Especially when I'm stressed."

He nodded. "You scared me for a sec. I thought I was gonna have to call 911." Just then, his phone buzzed. He took it out of his pocket, looked at it, and said, "Ugh."

"Something wrong?" I asked.

"Not really. Just this family situation. Molly, I'm sorry, but I think I might have to take you home now. Apparently, the traffic heading north is brutal, and my brother and sister expect me in Maine tonight. Asap."

My chin started to quiver. All of a sudden, everything was going wrong, and I couldn't help wondering if it was because of my fainting thing. "Okay. I'm sorry about all... this."

His eyes widened and he looked like he might cry too. "Oh hey. No, Molly. This isn't your fault. It's all me. C'mere." He held out his arms and pulled me in close for a hug. Neither of us was wearing a coat, and I could feel the warmth of his skin through his white dress shirt.

I breathed in his laundry soap scent, trying to absorb as much of him as possible. All week long, I'd been secretly touching my cheek, trying to recreate the electricity from the little peck he'd given me on Monday. It was almost too much to imagine a real kiss from him.

"I really like you," he said, placing his hands on my shoulders and pushing me back gently so he could see my face. "I'm just having a bad week. I know everyone's dealing with the FSI shit, but I've got some other stuff too, and—"

"Hey, hon, you okay?" It was Emily the bartender, wearing a funky leather jacket over her jeans and sweater. She was shorter than she'd appeared behind the bar, and slimmer.

"Yeah," I said. "I just got lightheaded for a minute."

"Phew. I'm glad I caught you guys. I put some tinfoil over your food, and Zeb stuck it in the fridge for you. He came in early, so I punched out. I'm so psyched. Sarah and I finally get to hang out together on a Saturday night."

"That's great," said Andy. "I'm actually bringing Molly home now too, but I'll go grab that food from Zeb. Molly, you should take the hummus and falafel with you. I've got a four-hour drive ahead of me — probably six with traffic — and that stuff won't survive."

My natural instinct was to protest — even though I was really hungry — but Emily spoke before I could. "Yeah, good luck on the roads. People are saying traffic's a bitch everywhere."

I felt confused, sad, and guilty. "You know what?" I said, "I'll get myself home on the T. I feel fine now. I just need to grab my coat and purse."

Andy smiled. "You sure, Molly?"

I was. "Yeah. Definitely. And I want you to get on the road."

"Okay," he said. "But I owe you big time. I wouldn't normally do this, but... yeah. How 'bout you wait here a second with Em, and I'll go collect all our stuff?"

"Yeah, sure." It occurred to me as he hurried back inside the restaurant that he'd end up paying for the food, but I was okay with that. Hummus and falafel couldn't cost that much.

"Andy's a good guy," said Emily.

"Yeah. He is."

She looked up and down Mass. Ave. "You know, I probably shouldn't say this, but he was pretty excited about you coming here to meet him tonight. He seems to like you a lot."

My heart melted a little, but I just shrugged. "That's cool. I like him too."

"Oh good. He and I go way back. I actually dated his sister Lori when we were in college together. At Orono."

"Oh. But you're not together anymore?"

"Nah. After she lost her mom, Lori wasn't, you know, in the best place for a while. But I think they're all doing better now. I hope so, anyway."

Knowing nothing about that situation, I just nodded.

Emily looked over her shoulder. "Oh look, here comes Andy. I'm gonna run, okay? Great meeting you, Molly. I hope you come back some other night when we all have more time."

Chapter 26
Another Day, Another Town

Molly
Sunday, November 11, 2012

"Morning," Fred said as I climbed into his truck. I couldn't remember the last time I'd been out of the house so early on a Sunday. It wasn't even nine o'clock. "Make sure you buckle your seatbelt, okay?"

"Yeah, of course."

"Well, I know some ladies don't like to wrinkle their clothes, but I'm a safety-first kinda guy."

I smiled to myself when he said that, wondering if he was referring to any *specific* lady. Because two nights earlier—about ten minutes after I'd returned from my abbreviated date at the Middle East—his truck had stopped right in front of my house. Normally, I wouldn't have paid much attention, but how could I look away when the passenger door opened and Jeannette got out? Yes, *my* Jeannette. She'd been wearing a short, flowered skirt and cowboy boots. Then, before I could even process that, Fred was there with her on the sidewalk, in a blue blazer and nice jeans. A blue blazer! Mr. Flaherty owned a blazer!

Of course I'd been safely inside my apartment at the time, so I had the luxury of watching Fred hold out his hand to Jeannette. It may have been the sweetest thing I've ever seen. But apparently Jeannette had more than a handshake in mind, because she reached up and touched Fred's face. Her dainty, pale fingers and long, red nails looked strangely beautiful against his weather-beaten cheek, and I'd actually held my breath in anticipation of their kiss.

But no. Poor Fred flinched and took a quick step back as if he'd been stung by a bee. My window was closed, but I clearly heard Jeannette ask if he was okay. Then, both of them did some nodding and shrugging before Jeannette patted him on the shoulder and walked into the house alone.

The primary reason I'd decided to attend the ham radio breakfast with Fred was because of Andy. I knew it was a long shot, but since he was an engineer, I assumed he'd be working at FSI on Monday and would go right through Saugus on the drive from Maine back to Boston. Besides, I felt bad for Fred, and he *had* invited me to join him.

"You're up bright and early," I said. If he'd been my father or uncle, I would've told him he looked handsome, because he did. He was wearing a pale blue, button-down shirt under his navy-blue LL Bean jacket, and his silvery hair was damp and combed back from his freshly-shaven face. He even smelled better than usual. Despite the strong odor of WD-40 in the truck, I detected Old Spice cologne too.

"Oh, I never sleep in." He squinted into the sun and pulled out of the driveway. "If I'm up later than seven, the whole day gets away from me."

I considered that. "I hope I don't start sleeping 'til eleven on weekdays now that I'm unemployed. But it's tempting, because my house is super quiet in the morning. Jeannette works late upstairs, then sleeps late."

His jaw tensed at Jeannette's name, but he just glanced at his watch and said, "I'm gonna take Route 16 over to 93, then get on 28."

I hadn't been to Saugus since childhood, and since I didn't drive anyway, I had no idea how to get there. The only thing I remembered about the town was eating at the Hilltop Steak House with my parents and loving the life-sized, fiberglass cows on the restaurant's front lawn. "Do you ever use a GPS?" I asked.

"Are you kidding? I'm not so old I need a gadget to tell me how to get around my own state. I grew up here, you know."

I considered telling him that lots of people use GPS simply to avoid heavy traffic, but wasn't in the mood for another technology discussion with him. So I nodded and gazed around the clean, black leather interior of the truck.

A small, radio-thingy was mounted with a clamp beneath the normal car radio, and a few cables and wires appeared to be connected to it in some way, along with a microphone with a squiggly cord, which was also clamped to the dashboard. "Is that a ham radio?" I asked.

"Yup. My travel rig," he said with a proud smile.

"Huh. I guess that's why you've got that big antenna on the back?"

"That's right. Can't communicate without an antenna."

He didn't seem to be feeling particularly conversational, which suited me just fine. My mind was on Andy anyway. I'd even laid out my clothes the night before: a scoop-necked, black cashmere sweater, and my favorite dark skinny jeans. Pretending to have something in my eye, I checked the mirror on the sunshade and decided my face looked all right. "So how often do they run these breakfasts?"

"Oh, every month, pretty much. They do a nice job. The president of the society's a real character. Hans. A pharmacist. His wife's a good egg too. She comes from a bundle o' money, but you'd never know it. Nice lady. Very friendly."

"Huh. Maybe I'll get to meet her."

Fred looked confused for a minute, then, under his breath, he said, "Jeez. I'm trying to remember the last time I saw Hans and Gertie together. I think it's been over ten years since I've been at one of these breakfasts."

"Wow."

"Yeah. Time flies." He rubbed his eyes. "And Davey was so sick, you know? Dealing with him sorta... I don't know. It took the wind outta my sails."

"I get it." I didn't know what else to say.

"And you know," he continued—I definitely got the sense he was figuring things out as he spoke—"it doesn't help if you stay away for a while, because as you get older—like me—sometimes when you *do* go back, you get bad news. If you know what I mean."

"Yeah. That must suck."

He was starting to sound like my mother. Almost every time she and I talked, she'd mention one of her sick or dying friends. It made me uncomfortable, and usually, I'd make an excuse and say I needed to get off the phone. But there was no escaping Flaherty's truck.

"Yeah, Louie was the first one in our group to go. Great guy. Big, fat fellow with a red face. Always runnin' around, knew everyone's name. Always had a joke for ya. Everyone loved Louie. Then, one day, he eats a sandwich and drops dead of a heart attack. No one could believe it." He shook his head. "Biggest funeral I've ever seen. Half the hams in the state musta been there."

"Wow."

"Yeah. Losing Louie was..." his voice trailed off, "... it was bad. You know, we do a tribute at all the parties to remember the silent keys—the hams from the society who've died—and every time they read Louie's name, guys cry. Every time. Poor Louie. He was one of a kind."

I was afraid Flaherty might start crying right there in the truck, so I tried changing the subject a little. "That sounds... really stressful."

"Hmm. Yeah."

"And will they, um, do one of those... tributes at the breakfast today?"

Flaherty sniffled and cleared his throat. "Nah, they only do it at the dinners. Which is fine by me. It's not something I look forward to." For about twenty seconds, he said nothing. Then, to my dismay, he picked up where he'd left off. "Yeah. And then, believe it or not, about six months after old Louie left us, we lost another great ham. Sammy Stuart. *Brilliant* guy. People called him the brains o' the whole outfit."

"I'm sorry," I said.

"Cancer. Of the lungs. And Sammy hadn't smoked in twenty years. Poor guy caught a cold that wouldn't go away. Finally, his wife drags him to the doctor thinking it's pneumonia, and a month later he's dead. Couldn't do a thing for him."

I looked out at the bright autumn sky. "Cancer sucks," I said.

"Yeah. That's one way to put it."

Fred got quiet again after that. Every once in a while, the ham radio would blurt out someone's voice saying something, but all the transmissions were accompanied by lots of static, beeps, and distortion, and Flaherty didn't seem to be paying much attention. Finally, we turned into a parking lot and drove toward a long, flat, brick building with an American flag out front. As we got closer, I saw that it was an Elks Lodge.

"The Elks give us a good deal on the place," he said as if I'd asked. I noticed a few beads of sweat on his forehead as he cruised around, looking for a parking spot. "I'd rather not walk too far today. My bum leg's acting up a little." His voice trembled slightly.

"Fred, are you all right?" After all that talk about his friends dying, I couldn't help worrying a little.

He pulled into a spot a few rows from the door. "Oh yeah. It just feels strange, after being away so long. I hope they recognize me in there. And I hope *I* recognize a few people too."

"Oh, I'm sure it'll be fine." Of course, I had no idea, but what was I supposed to say? I scanned the parking lot for signs of Andy even though I didn't know what kind of car he drove. I thought maybe I'd see an FSI parking sticker on a window or something like that, but no. An old station wagon with two antennas on the roof pulled into a spot near Flaherty's, and a young, pudgy guy hopped out and headed straight into the building, whistling.

"You're right," said Fred. "Let's go." He looked down at his crotch—perhaps checking to make sure his fly was zipped—and stepped onto the pavement.

I hurried over to his side, thinking I should offer to take his elbow, but he straightened up and made it clear he didn't want any assistance. Still, I stayed close behind him as we made our way up the stone steps.

A gangly teenage boy was stationed at a card table inside the door with a metal cashbox and a sign that said *Suggested Donation $10*. It

IT DOESN'T HAVE TO BE THAT WAY

hadn't occurred to me that the breakfast would cost money, so I was glad I'd gone to the bank the previous day. But Flaherty whipped a twenty out of his wallet and handed it to the kid.

"No!" I said. "Let me get this."

Fred held up his hands. "Absolutely not. This is my treat."

"But—"

"Don't embarrass me," he said, and I could tell he wasn't kidding.

I closed my purse. "Thank you, Fred." I breathed in the scents of maple syrup and sausage. "It smells great in here." Even though I don't eat meat, I adore the smell of sausage and bacon cooking.

"Fred Flaherty?" shouted a large bald man from across the room.

My neighbor's face went blank for a second, then he broke out in a wide smile. "Hans Helmdorf? Hey! Great to see you, big guy!"

"How's life treatin' ya, buddy?" bellowed Hans, bounding across the floor—quite gracefully, actually—and grabbing Flaherty's hand. "You haven't changed a bit, you old dog."

For a second, Fred looked tongue-tied, but he pulled it together as he shook Hans's hand. "Hey, you know what they say. None of us are gettin' older, right? We just keep gettin' better."

I couldn't help wincing. If Hans was getting better, I couldn't imagine what he'd been like in the past, because he did *not* look healthy. His face had a purple tinge to it, and his eyes bulged. "So who's this, Freddy?" he asked, turning to me. "Your daughtah? I didn't know you had a daughtah."

"Oh no," said Fred. "This is my neighbor, Molly Dolan. Molly, this is my friend Hans. Hans is the heart and soul of the repeater society."

"Aah!" said Hans. "Don't say *heart*!" He laughed a loud, hearty laugh and patted his chest. "Doc tells me the tickah's in lousy shape."

"Oh no," said Fred, his tone suddenly concerned.

But Hans waved his hand dismissively. "Aah, whadda they know? My dad lived to be eighty-nine and he had a bad tickah too."

Fred still looked worried. "Molly, lemme tell you something. Back in the 70s, Hans bought the very first antenna for this repeater society. Then he hauled it up the biggest hill he could find and planted it in the ground. We wouldn't be here now if it wasn't for him."

I opened my mouth to say *wow* or something of that nature, but Hans cut me off.

"Aah, your boyfriend's a modest SOB, isn't he, Molly? See, he forgot to mention that he was right there beside me all the way. I never coulda dragged that goddamn thing up the hill without him."

My *boyfriend?* Did Hans really think I was dating a guy in his seventies? I glanced at Fred in amusement, but his face was bright red.

"Oh gosh, I... no. No! Molly's my *friend,* Hans. Just a friend. A neighbor. Look at me. I'm a geezer. And you're a dirty old man."

I coughed and rubbed my eyes, not sure what to do. I didn't want to make Fred any more uncomfortable, but also wondered if I should say something about him not being a geezer.

Luckily, Hans recognized his error right away. "Aah!" He slapped his leg with his fat hand. "Ha hah! Oh god, I'm sorry, honey. You poor kid. I shoulda known a pretty girl like you wouldn't mess with an ugly old bastard like Flaherty here." Then he slapped Fred on the shoulder and both men laughed awkwardly.

"He's not so old," I said.

Hans raised his eyebrows. "Oh yes he is. Don't be fooled by his charms, honey."

I wasn't sure how to respond to that.

"All right, Hans," said Fred. "Enough of this, okay? Molly and I came to eat."

Hans kept grinning, but Fred turned to me. "You hungry, kiddo?"

He'd never called me *kiddo* before, but I didn't mind. I could tell he was trying to get things under control. "Yeah. Definitely."

Looking at Hans, he asked, "Did ya leave us any pancakes, big guy?"

"Plenty," said Hans. "Or plenty for Molly anyway. I'm not sure about you." They both laughed again, and Hans said something about needing to run a quick errand.

"Okay, then. Great to see ya, pal." Fred waved and watched his friend amble away. "Come on, Molly."

Once again, I felt like I should say something but wasn't sure what. I mean, Hans seemed nice enough, but Fred struck me as so much gentler. So much *classier.* It was hard to imagine the two of them in their younger days, hanging out together and dragging an antenna up a hill. Maybe people really do change with age.

I followed Fred toward a buffet table at the back of the room, smiling a little on the inside. The whole girlfriend misunderstanding didn't bother me at all, but he clearly still felt uncomfortable. The majority of the people in the place were male, but I did notice a fair number of women mixed in and a couple of little kids running around too.

"Plain or blueberry?" said the guy serving pancakes, and I asked if I could have a couple of both.

"Absolutely." He had dark, neatly combed hair, and was wearing a white t-shirt with the same *ARRL* logo as the one on Andy's fleece. "You're my kinda girl. I love a lady with an appetite."

The woman dishing out bacon gave him a sideways glance. "You better quit flirtin' with all the girls, Sal, or I'll tell Loretta."

"Hey, Lor coulda been here, but she's down the mall, so I gotta have my fun too," said the guy with a wink. "I bet she comes home with another pair o' those expensive designer jeans."

I smiled and thanked the guy for the pancakes, feeling a little jealous of Loretta at the mall. She was lucky to have a cute husband like that. I might date Sal if given the chance.

"So where would you like to sit?" asked Fred.

"Oh, I don't care." As far as I could tell, Andy Stevers wasn't in the room. For a moment, I wished I'd stayed at home, asleep.

"How 'bout over there, then?" he said, pointing to a long table with two empty seats. There were probably only about a hundred people in the whole function hall, but the linoleum floor and suspended ceiling made the chatter seem extra loud. A few men and women were making their way from table to table, refilling coffee cups, while others wiped up and tossed used paper products into trashcans.

"Sure."

Flaherty strolled over to the table, and a delicate, white-haired woman looked up at him. "Okay if my friend and I sit here?" he asked, emphasizing the word *friend*.

"Fred!" said the woman. "Oh my goodness!"

He took a step back and assessed her. "Do I... oh for crying out loud! You're Chet Flynn's wife. Jingoes. I forget your first name, but I'd know that face anywhere."

A younger guy with red hair sitting next to the woman stopped cutting his sausage, jumped up, and extended a hand to Fred. "Mr. Flaherty! I'm Eddie Flynn, and my mom's Cathy. How're you?" His eyes were a little too close together, and his mouth was sort of goofy and rubbery.

Flaherty laid his plate on the table and shook hands with the man. I could tell he was trying to get his head around the situation. "Right. You're Chet's son. And of course your mom's Cathy. Last time I saw you, you were about fourteen years old. And now you're all grown up."

"Funny how that happens, huh?" said Eddie as we all settled down in chairs.

Fred kept grinning, but I sensed that something was troubling him. He looked around the table, then back at Eddie. "So how *are* you all?" He seemed too overwhelmed to introduce me, so I just smiled a friendly hello to Cathy and Eddie.

"Well, I'm not sure you know this, but my dad passed about two years ago," said Eddie.

Fred blinked an extra long blink and my gut sank. "I'm sorry," he said. "I didn't know. I try to keep up with the obits, but I miss a day every now and then. I hope he didn't suffer."

Eddie's rubbery mouth turned down at the ends and he shrugged. "He had colon cancer, so he was sick on and off for a few years. The end was pretty rough."

"Aw, jeez," Fred said. "Poor guy. That's a tough break."

"He fought a very brave battle," said Cathy, her voice breaking.

"I'll bet he did," said Flaherty, looking down at his pancakes. "Chet was a good man."

Eddie chuckled softly. "He was. And you know, he softened up in his later years. Although I gotta say, he could be a ballbuster when I was a kid."

For the briefest second, I saw my neighbor's eyes flash in what appeared to be agreement.

"Hey, watch your language, Eddie," said Cathy. Then she turned to Fred and said, "He always spoke *so* highly of you, Fred. I remember one day, right near the end, he was talking about old friends, and your name came up. He called you a *ham's ham*."

Fred blushed. "Well, that was awfully nice of him."

"Hi," I said, figuring I should say *something*. "I'm Molly Dolan, and I'm sorry for your loss." As I spoke, I looked back and forth between Eddie and Cathy, doing my best to make it clear that I was addressing them both.

"Oh yes. Yes. This is my friend Molly," Fred said.

Eddie grinned while Cathy seemed unsure about how to greet me.

"How could I resist pancakes with Mr. Flaherty?" I said, hoping my use of his formal name would help to dispel suspicions about us dating. The pancakes were actually delicious—the best I'd had in a long time—and the maple syrup was real too.

"Are you a ham, Molly?" asked Eddie.

I almost rolled my eyes, but caught myself just in time. "No. I wish."

"Me too. My dad was always trying to get me interested, but I could never learn that damn Morse code. He used to call me a hopeless case."

"Oh Eddie, he *never* said that," said Cathy. "He just didn't understand why you didn't take to it the way he did."

"Well you know, Eddie," said Fred, "you might be in luck now. Did you hear they did away with the Morse code requirement for hams in '07?"

Eddie turned to Fred and frowned. "You're joking, right?"

"Uh-uh. Dead serious."

"Huh. You'd think my dad mighta mentioned that to me. Seeing as he lived 'til June of 2010."

"Eddie! Your father was *terribly* sick in his later years," said Cathy. "He had a lot more on his mind than Morse code."

"True," said Eddie. "Still, I wish I'da known. It woulda been cool to get a ham license while Dad was still alive."

The look in Cathy's eyes conveyed deep disappointment in her son. "Well, it's never too late. Your father's radios are just gathering dust down there in that cellar."

Eddie shrugged. "Whatever."

Flaherty stopped chewing and cleared his throat. "Cathy, don't take this the wrong way, but I remember Chet having some pretty fancy equipment. Have you ever tried selling any of that stuff? I'm sure it's worth a few bucks."

"I've certainly thought about it," she said, glancing at Eddie as she spoke. "But Chet warned me about jerks who take advantage of ham widows. Financially, I mean. I have no idea what's junk and what's valuable. It all looks the same to me. But if you'd ever like to come by and give me some advice, you'd be most welcome. And of course, if there's anything you'd like, you could just take it and—"

"Oh god no." Fred shook his head emphatically. "Absolutely not. I've got more than enough equipment already. But I'd be happy to give you a hand."

"That'd be *wonderful*," said Cathy. "I could make you dinner too. I'm a pretty good cook, if I do say so myself." With her well-groomed white hair, Cathy didn't look anything like Edith Bunker from *All in the Family*, but her voice and attitude were similar, and I felt sorry for her. And yet, I also got the sense she was flirting with Fred, and I really wanted him to date Jeannette. Not that Fred's love life was any of my business, but the guy was definitely on some kind of streak. I mean, he'd lived for years with zero women in his life, and all of a sudden, at least two were interested in him.

He squirmed in his seat. "On the other hand," he said, after chewing and swallowing, "I wouldn't wanna interfere, Eddie, if you're even slightly interested in getting involved. And I'll be honest with you, ham radio's a lot easier without the Code requirement."

"Nah. Go for it," said Ed. "Really."

I thought about Fred's Morse code bond with his younger brother Davey, his Code Society t-shirt, and the pillow in his basement with the word "Pal" embroidered on it in Code. "But you're a huge Morse code fan, aren't you, Fred?"

Fred raised his eyebrows and looked a bit sad. "Sure. But like poor Chet, I'm old school. I'm afraid there's not a lotta use for Code these days, although it still saves lives sometimes. Every once in a while, you read about a boat in trouble out on the ocean. All the equipment's gone down, and the only way the ship can signal for help is with Code."

"But," said Cathy, "couldn't people just learn how to signal S.O.S.? They don't need the whole alphabet, do they?"

"I guess so." But Fred's reticence came through loud and clear. "It's just that the Code is... well, it's so *efficient*. It's also one of the few things left in this world that still works without any type of man-made power. Someone stranded on an island can signal a clear message in Code with nothing more than sunlight and something reflective. A shiny stone... a piece of glass..." His voice faded out and he bit his lip.

Cathy's eyes glistened. "Oh Fred, you remind me so much of my Chet."

I was starting to cut up another pancake when I saw Andy Stevers in baggy Levi's and his ARRL fleece walking toward us, smiling, a paper coffee cup in his hand. "Hello, Molly! Fancy seeing you here!"

"Hey, Andy," I said, doing my best to act casual. "Everyone, this is Andy from my ex-job. Andy, this is my neighbor Fred. And this is Cathy, and Cathy's son, Eddie. Fred's a ham, and Cathy's husband was too."

"Nice to meet you all," said Andy, flashing his long dimples. "I was driving down Route 1, so I figured I'd drop in for a quick coffee. I just joined the repeater society a couple months ago."

"We've been discussing Morse code," I said.

"Hmm," said Andy, looking around the table. "Well, for the record, I'm a Code aficionado. In my opinion, getting rid of that requirement was a straight-up crime."

Flaherty pushed his chair back, stood, and reached across the table to shake Andy's hand. "Nice to meet you, sir. I share your opinion."

Andy smiled at Fred the way he smiled at the software engineers at FSI: a nerd-to-nerd smile. "I wish I could stick around, but I've got stuff to do in the city. Molly, any chance you're up for getting together later on?"

"You mean tonight?" I asked.

"Yeah. But only if you're up to it. Have you recovered from Friday?"

Fred shot me a quizzical look. "I almost fainted in a restaurant," I said. "But tonight... hmm, yeah. Yeah, I'm around. After seven, anyway. Should I meet you someplace?"

Andy laid a hand on my shoulder and gave it a gentle squeeze. "How 'bout I come pick you up this time? You're in Arlington, right?"

"Yeah." My heart raced as I gave him my address and he typed it into his phone.

"It's pretty easy to find," said Fred. "I live right across the street. Which direction are you coming from?"

Andy frowned. "Not actually sure at the moment. I live in Winthrop, but I've got a lotta errands to run today and traffic's been ridiculous lately. I think people have started holiday shopping or something. Thank god for GPS. Molly, I'll be there as close to seven as possible, okay? Maybe we can get some dinner?"

"You kids and your GPS," said Fred. "You know that whole system could go down in a solar storm or a terrorist attack, right?"

"Absolutely," said Andy. "That's why I keep maps in my car. But GPS works great most of the time. Anyway, I gotta run. It was nice meeting you all."

I liked the way he spoke respectfully to Flaherty, even though I doubted he spent much time worrying about terrorist attacks and solar storms, whatever they were.

Fred shrugged. "Yeah, well, hang onto those maps. Cause it's only a matter of time before GPS goes down. Maybe not for long, but people who depend on it too heavily are gonna be lost."

"Literally, right?" said Andy with a wave and a smile. "See you in a while, Molly."

"He seems like a bright young man," said Fred as Andy hurried off toward the door.

"He is," I answered, doing my best to sound nonchalant while everything inside me screamed.

Chapter 27
Five Short Minutes

Molly
November 11, 2012
Arlington, MA, 6:30 PM

I'd washed my dark blue jeans, dried them, and pulled them back on. They were my favorites, and I'd spilled maple syrup on them at breakfast. No matter what sort of eating establishment Andy had in mind—a bar, a pub, or even a fancy restaurant—the jeans would work.

The problem was what to wear on top. I had an awesome, sexy black silk blouse I'd bought on sale at Marshall's about a year earlier, but when I tried it on, I immediately knew it wasn't right. It was chic and sophisticated, but what if Andy wanted to go someplace really casual? I'd feel like a fool. Reluctantly, then, I put on a newish, oatmeal-colored, cable-knit sweater that buttoned up the front. That way, if he wanted to go someplace nice, I could open an extra button and throw on some silver jewelry. But if we decided to go to a pub or something, I'd be all set.

My cellphone rang and I glanced down at it. I'm not sure who I was expecting—maybe Diana, maybe my mom—but when I saw the name on the caller ID, I almost dropped the phone.

It was Joe.

Joe! What the hell? In all the time we'd been together, I'd never *once* refused a call from him. Never. He'd called when I was at the dentist, the gynecologist, even a Broadway play with my mom, and I'd answered every single time. Of course, there'd also been plenty of nights when I waited hours for him to call and he blew me off. But *I'd* always been there for *Joe*.

As the phone went on ringing, though, I didn't pick up. Because I didn't care what Joe was up to or what he wanted. And I sure as hell didn't want to see him again.

But wait. What if he was sick? What if something had happened to his father? Shit, what if his father had died? That last one almost got me—I liked his dad a lot—but I didn't swipe the answer button to the right. After all, that's why I had voicemail.

Eventually, the ringing stopped, and I stared at the phone for a full five minutes. But Joe didn't leave a message. Oh well.

At 6:55, the doorbell rang. I screamed silently, turned off the TV, smoothed my sweater, ran my fingers over my face to make sure nothing was stuck to it, and tiptoed to the door.

And there he stood, in faded jeans and a blue plaid flannel shirt, a brown paper bag under his arm. In the clear moonlight, he looked like an angel with dimples. Or perhaps the ghost of James Dean.

"Hey there," I said, in my calmest voice. *Pretend it's Joe. Pretend it's Joe. Just for a few minutes, so you don't lose your shit.* It wasn't working, though. My stomach flipped like a sick dolphin. "Wanna... come in for a beer?"

"Sure." He actually seemed a little nervous too as he stepped inside. "I brought you some actually. Beers, I mean."

"Oh. Cool. Thanks."

He handed me the paper bag. "I saw these at the liquor store near my house and figured we could both use some good karma."

I didn't know what he meant until I looked inside and saw that the beer was called *Dogfish Head Namaste*. "Oh, cool," I said again, realizing I was repeating myself. My face heated up and my chest tightened.

Closing the door, I peered out the window in an attempt to catch my breath. For the second time that weekend, all the lights at Fred's house were off. But since his truck was in the driveway, I assumed he was down in the hamshack. Meanwhile, a blue Volkswagen Golf sat parked in front of my house. "Nice car," I said. "You get good mileage in that?" By that point, I felt like a complete moron. I mean, who asks their date about gas mileage?

But Andy answered quite earnestly. "Oh yeah. Definitely. It's one of the old diesels. I'm actually thinking of converting the engine so it can run on vegetable oil."

"Awesome," I said, wondering if he was joking. I knew nothing about cars. "So... would you... like a beer... now?"

"Sure. Yeah, that'd be great."

My stomach flipped again. "Okay," I said, trying to keep my voice steady. "I'll go grab some glasses. Have a seat."

Andy sat on the far-left side of the couch. "Thanks."

I'd dusted and vacuumed the apartment and rearranged the beige Ikea furniture around the coffee table in a way that I hoped looked inviting and comfortable. But now that he was on the couch, I wasn't sure if I should sit next to him or in one of the armchairs. I'd have to try to read his body language.

In the kitchen, I opened two bottles and put the rest of the six-pack in the fridge. Then I peeked into the living room. Oh lord, he was looking through my magazines. I wished I had more intellectual stuff, but rags like *People* and *InStyle* were my guilty pleasures. I poured beers into the only two tall glasses I owned, took a deep breath, and returned to the living room.

Andy was thumbing through an issue of *Vogue*. "Oh," I said, handing him his beer and laughing nervously, "I can't resist that trash when I'm waiting in line at the supermarket. But as you can see, I'm not exactly a style maven."

He smiled and shrugged, his plaid flannel shirt totally making him look like a rock star. "Yeah, fashion's not my thing either. So are you a Rihanna fan?" As he spoke, he closed the magazine and pointed to the singer who graced the cover in a strapless red dress.

I decided honesty was the best policy. "Um, well, she's gorgeous, but I'm not really into pop music. Are you?"

Andy's brooding eyes brooded more deeply. "Not so much. But I hate the way she was abused by her boyfriend. Men who hit women should be locked up forever."

"I agree," I said, gathering my courage and taking a seat beside him on the couch.

Andy used one of those perfume sample things from the magazine as a coaster and laid his beer on the coffee table while I took a swig of mine. "So the other night in the bar, you mentioned a friend who got attacked by a guy."

Oh gosh, why did he keep bringing that stuff up? Couldn't we just have a fun conversation and maybe fool around a bit? I sat up straighter and focused my eyes on the floor. Andy's gaze was hard to hold. "Yeah. Yeah, it totally sucked. She actually died eventually, but it was... a really complicated situation." I drank some more beer, thought about Kate, and felt a little nauseous.

Andy's eyes narrowed. "I'm sorry." He sipped his beer and rubbed his forehead. "I don't wanna sound like an asshole, but I know how you feel."

"Thanks." Then, trying to lighten the mood, I added, "Luckily, it happened a long time ago. I'm pretty much over it now."

Without so much as a blink, he said, "Sure. That's what we tell ourselves, right? But the people who die never get over it. Do they?"

My body burned with a weird combination of frustration, sadness, and lust. So many emotions flowed through me that I couldn't speak, so I just drank some more beer. "Nope," I finally answered. "They don't."

He looked at me with something like confusion in his eyes. Then he leaned his head back, stared at the ceiling, and breathed a few short breaths, like he was doing an exercise he'd learned in therapy or something. "Oh my god," he said, facing me again and forcing a smile. "I really do need to calm down. Are you hungry?"

Phew. His intensity was actually scaring me a little. "Yeah. Pretty hungry. How 'bout you?"

"Yeah. Yeah. What's a good place to eat around here?"

Joe had always chosen our restaurants. *Joe, who'd called earlier.* "Oh, I don't know. I like just about everything. Except, like, steak houses."

"Yeah, I figured that." He smiled again, picked up his beer, and took another sip. "Do you have any local favorites? I hardly ever come out this way."

I didn't. Most of Arlington's decent restaurants were a little on the fancy side, and Joe liked cheap. Cheap as in pizza, pasta, and subs at places that let you bring your own beer. "Um, not really. Maybe I should check my phone?" I felt like an idiot.

"Sure. Sure. I'll do that too."

We both got out our smartphones and started tapping. It was incredibly awkward, and nothing was jumping out at me. I felt like a tourist in my own town. "Hey, can I grab you another beverage?" I asked. He didn't look ready for another beer, but I was.

"No thanks. Get one for yourself, though. I'm driving, so one's good for me."

"Okay," I said. "But you know, if you wanna drink more, we can take the bus. The buses around here are pretty reliable, and they run late."

He smiled. "Good to know. But I'll drive tonight."

"Okay. I'll be right back." Dammit, why did everything feel so *off*? On the way to the kitchen, I slipped into the bathroom to pee and apply fresh lipstick, then grabbed two more beers from the fridge in case Andy changed his mind.

But when I returned to the living room, the bottle in front of him was as full as before, and he was still scrolling through his phone. He glanced at the two beers in my hand and winced. "I'm sorry for being Debbie Downer, Molly. I probably shoulda stayed in tonight, but I didn't wanna cancel on you again. My family's going through some bad shit right now. I'm trying not to let it get to me, but seeing Rihanna on your magazine hit a nerve."

"Oh, I'm sorry." *Whatever.*

"No! Don't be sorry. *I'm* sorry for... all of this. And I appreciate you for putting up with me when you've got more than enough of your own shit to deal with right now. My god, you don't even have a job."

"I'll be fine."

"You know what?" he said. "I believe that. Because you're a cool woman. But before we head out, would you mind if I just told you what's going on with my family? 'Cause I'd like to take you out for a nice meal, and if I don't get this shit off my chest, it'll just fester inside me all night."

"Oh. Of course. Tell me anything you want."

He sighed heavily. "Okay. So... okay. My mother was... well, she was actually murdered. By a dude. Like, attacked and murdered. About ten years ago. I'm sorry, but it's still hard for me to say those words."

I'd been prepared for something like divorce or cancer, but not murder. "Whoa. Whoa. I'm sorry. I... wasn't expecting... that. I mean... wow. Yeah."

"I know," he said. "It's a lot. And now the case is open again. And... yeah. It sucks."

I didn't know what else to say. "I can't even...."

He shook his head and held up his hands in surrender. "I know. No words, right? But you've been through it. So you get it."

"No. I mean, I lost a friend. You lost your mom. That's different. How old were you?"

"Seventeen."

"Oh god."

He sighed. "Yeah. My parents had separated, and my brother and I were living with Dad. My mom was... I don't know. She was... having *issues*, and she'd moved in with a friend. That's a whole long story, but it doesn't really matter now. Anyway, she'd gotten a new job in a store, and apparently a customer got pissed at her. Then, a few hours later, they found her in the back lot. Strangled."

IT DOESN'T HAVE TO BE THAT WAY

When he said *strangled*, a shiver ran up my spine. Andy's story sounded a little too similar to the one Fred had told me about his brother. But it couldn't be the same thing. That'd be way too much of a coincidence. "So the customer *killed* her?" I managed to say.

"Yeah. I mean, it's the only logical conclusion. She had no enemies, not even my dad. He loved her so much. He'd been begging her to come home. He wanted to work things out, you know?"

"Yeah. Oh my god. Your poor family."

"Tell me about it. And now you understand why I get so pissed off when I see a woman being treated badly. In any way. People don't realize how bad it can get."

I should've let it end there. He seemed finished with his story. But for some reason, I couldn't help asking one more question. "So who was this... customer?"

Andy's eyes darkened. "An asshole." He shook his head slowly, then seemed to gain energy. "This fucking *loser*. This screwed up *pig*, who'd practically *blinded* another woman twenty years earlier by punching her in the face. A total *fuckup*." As he spoke, his cheeks turned pink. He drank some beer and swished it around his mouth before swallowing, like he was trying to wash away the words.

"So is the guy in jail?" I asked. *Please say yes. Please say yes.*

"No. Because guess what? The police couldn't find any *physical* evidence. And now he's dead. *Dead*. Meaning he'll never be punished. He was never even officially *charged* with the crime because the security camera in the store didn't have sound. You could see that the guy was angry at my mom and that she was upset by whatever he said, but that's it. But the owner of the store and everyone who knew the guy said he was all fucked up. And he was huge too. Like, obese."

My body trembled. "And you're *sure* he was the killer?"

For the first time ever, I heard irritation in Andy's voice. "Yeah. I mean, it only makes sense. But without some kind of evidence, the case is dead in the water. My family hired a new lawyer, but who knows if he'll find anything. I'll tell you one thing, though. If there's a hell, I sure hope David Flaherty's burning in it right now."

"Flaherty," I whispered, my blood running cold.

"Uh huh."

Beer shot up my throat, and I tried to re-swallow it.

But Andy was on a roll. "In the meantime, I just hope like hell they find the yellow scarf Mom was wearing that day. The medical examiner's almost certain she was strangled with it, and DNA evidence is so much better these days."

My stomach lurched, but even though I jumped and ran for the bathroom, I didn't make it. Vomit burst from deep in my guts. It was mostly beer, combined with chunks of pancakes and fruit salad from the breakfast. It sprayed everywhere too: on the walls, on my fake Oriental rug, all over my favorite jeans, on the front of my oatmeal-colored sweater. Freaked out, embarrassed, and weak, I sank to the floor in tears.

"Molly!" Andy ran and knelt beside me. "Are you okay? Do you need... medical help?"

"Go away!" I sobbed, tears pouring down my cheeks. "Please. Just leave. Please."

But Andy rubbed my back, quite possibly the only part of me that wasn't spattered with vomit. "Molly, what's going on? Did you eat bad shellfish or something?"

I considered saying yes just to stop the truth. But I didn't have it in me to lie. Instead, I looked straight into those dark, brooding eyes. "David Flaherty," I said. "He was my neighbor's brother. My neighbor, Fred Flaherty. The Morse Code guy from the breakfast this morning. That's why you've gotta go. Now. This is way too fucked up."

Andy's face lost its gentle, caring look, and his brooding eyes bulged. He looked terrifying, but then a sound unlike anything I'd ever heard came out of him. It didn't sound human, but maybe like an animal that'd been shot or hit by a car.

Chapter 28
I'll Have To Say I Love You In A Song

Fred
Sunday, November 10, 2012
Arlington, MA 7:05 PM

Jeannette had invited him over for wine and chocolate cake, and how could he refuse an offer like that? It wasn't that he drank wine or even liked dessert very much. But Jeannette? Well, even though she was a little too forward, he couldn't deny that she excited him too.

Not to mention that he wanted to make up for Friday night. What a disaster that'd been. He'd taken her out for a nice dinner at an Italian place in Arlington center, and she'd been so easy to talk to. Even when she told him about her writing—her *erotic* writing—he hadn't been too embarrassed. But then, when they arrived home, she made a move on him and he'd reacted badly. It'd all happened too fast.

It wasn't even that he didn't want to kiss her. He just hadn't been ready. With Barb, he'd waited at least three dates before even trying to hold her hand.

But he felt terrible about hurting Jeannette's feelings, so he'd called her on Saturday and they'd both ended up laughing. That was a nice thing about Jeannette: she had a good sense of humor.

"Don't worry," she said, "I'll get you next time."

"We'll see," he answered, feeling antsy again.

"Here's an idea, how 'bout you come over for wine and cake Sunday night? I promise to keep my hands to myself. Unless we make a con*sensual* decision otherwise."

He knew that meant she wouldn't touch him without his consent. But the way she said the word *consensual!* Damn it, that lady had a dirty mind. And yet, there he was, walking across the street in the dark with a box of chocolates.

A blue Volkswagen was parked out front, probably owned by Molly's friend from the breakfast. *A nice kid, and a big step up from that last joker. And a ham too. Gee, it'd be nice if Molly could find a boyfriend who'd treat her right.*

The thought of Molly marrying a ham made him smile, but just then, Jeannette opened her door in a long, black, flowy outfit that looked like half pants and half a dress. Like something a witch would wear. A sexy witch. A *sensual* witch. With an apartment that smelled like perfume and cake.

"Hello," he said, trying not to blush but unable to keep his eyes off Jeannette's breasts, which were pale, freckled, and showing quite a bit of themselves thanks to her low neckline.

Barb never would've worn such a thing; in fact, she probably would've made a nasty comment if she saw a lady in an outfit like that. Her rule of thumb on bosoms had been simple: no parts of them should be exposed — except maybe a little on the beach — and ladies who didn't follow that rule were "looking for something."

But as Jeannette welcomed him into her home, she honored her hands-off promise and gave no indication that she was looking for anything other than a nice visit. She thanked him for the chocolates, then led him into her cozy living room and offered him a seat on a pink armchair. Then she grabbed a bottle of red wine and some glasses from the kitchen, and settled herself in a matching chair on the opposite side of the coffee table. For anyone else, that behavior might seem completely normal, but coming from Jeannette, it felt chilly.

"So how was your pancake breakfast this mornin'?" she asked, skillfully uncorking the bottle. Barb had enjoyed a glass of white wine on occasion, but couldn't operate a corkscrew to save her life.

"Oh, it was nice. I saw lots of old friends. And I think Molly had a little fun too. Some young fellow from her job was there. In fact, he's downstairs with her now. I guess they're goin' out to dinner."

Jeannette grinned. "Oh, I've heard about *him*. The hot guy, right? Looks like James Dean?"

"James...? Uh, I don't know about that. But he likes the Morse code, so he's okay in my book." He stood up and walked over to the window. "Hmm. His car's still here, but they oughta be leaving any minute now."

Twenty minutes later, he found himself pacing around Jeannette's living room, holding his glass of wine, but not drinking. He'd forgotten how much he disliked the taste of wine, especially red. The blue Volkswagen hadn't moved, and he couldn't help worrying a little. "Jeez," he finally said. "I thought that guy was taking Molly *out*. What the heck are they doing downstairs?"

"Oh Fred," said Jeannette as she spread chocolate frosting on the small cake she'd baked. "Stop fretting. They're probably having a drink. Or maybe they took the bus."

"I don't think so. This guy strikes me as a driver. And a smart guy too. I noticed that car of his runs on diesel fuel. Very efficient."

"Yum," said Jeannette. "And he's not Joe. Now *that* guy was a dud."

"Oh that clown?" He waved his had dismissively. "He was a jerk." He glanced out the window again. "But it's getting late. Molly and this guy need to leave before all the restaurants close."

Jeannette rolled her eyes. "For god's sake, Fred, they're kids. They eat late. Relax."

"Yeah, but...." He did want to relax and enjoy the evening. He'd showered before coming over and had put on his nicest blue button-down shirt that he'd bought in the 80s. Actually, Barb had picked it out because she said it made his eyes look extra blue. He caught a glimpse of his reflection in the window and couldn't help feeling proud of his trim physique. "I just hope Molly's all right down there. I don't think she knows this guy very well."

Jeannette rolled her eyes and laid the cake on the table. "Molly's fine, Fred. Last time I checked, she was an adult, and a sexually aware woman too. She can take care of herself."

"Jeez!" said Fred. "Don't say things like that. I've been around long enough to know how men can be."

Jeannette's face softened and she almost smiled. "I'll bet. But I get the sense this Andy's a good one. And you know what? Molly can make her own choices about what she wants to do with him. Even if that does mean havin' sex tonight. Remember bein' young and havin' all those hormones racin' around inside you?"

Maybe it was the candle burning on the table that caused his mind to drift back to the summer he'd turned sixteen. His family had gone to Hampton Beach for two weeks, and he'd met a girl his age named Trish.

Trish was different than any other girl he knew. She lived at the beach year-round, and spent most afternoons collecting sticks and driftwood. Then, at night, she'd build bonfires and ask anyone who happened to be at the beach to sit around them with her. Fred got in the habit of bringing Davey along to the fires because conversation with Trish was easier with his cute, four-year-old brother in tow.

But the night before he left to go home to Arlington, Trish told him she didn't feel like having a fire, and the two of them ended up sitting down by the water, talking about music. She'd just gotten interested in Elvis Presley, and although he liked Elvis too, he was even more excited about Little Richard and Chuck Berry. Meanwhile, the tide was coming in fast, and the frothy waves crashed over their bare legs.

"You wanna kiss?" asked Trish.

Fred was shocked—no girl had ever asked him that before—but of course he said yes, and boy, it was something. Trish's mouth tasted like red licorice, and he'd just begun to wonder if she might let him touch her chest when her mother's voice pierced the air like a seagull's cry.

"Pa-tri-cia! Time to come home!"

He'd looked into Trish's eyes and whispered, "Can you stay out just a little longer?" His skinny teenage body was practically screaming.

"Sorry," said Trish with a sigh. "I'll get grounded. But you'll be back next summer, right?"

"I hope so."

That didn't happen, though. The following year, his family went to Lake Winnipesaukee, and he never saw Trish again.

"When I was a kid," he told Jeannette, "I respected girls. I liked 'em, but I never took advantage of anyone."

"Sure. 'Cause you're a nice guy. And Molly's told me nothin' but nice things about Andy. So relax."

Fred shook his silver head and started pacing again. "Hey, I've got an idea."

"Really? Now that's more like it. And just so you know, I put clean sheets on the bed. But I've gotta keep things under control, 'cause believe it or not, I've got jury duty in the morning."

He couldn't tell if she was joking or not about the sheets, so he focused on the jury duty. "Oh boy. You know, I got on a trial once. It was very interesting. I'd do it again if I could."

"Yeah, I'm hopin' they put me on one. There's gotta be some good material for stories in that stuff, right? Maybe a novella called *The Hung Jury*? Whadaya think?"

"Oh brother, Jeannette. Do you ever stop? But seriously, would you go downstairs and check on those two? Maybe you could borrow some milk? Or a cup of sugar?"

Jeannette looked horrified. "You're asking me to go *spy* on two adults on a date? Fred, I'm surprised at you."

"No! Not spy. I just wanna make sure she's okay. I'd do it myself, but she doesn't know I'm up here. Besides, it makes sense that you'd need sugar because you're baking."

"No. I'm done baking, and I was hoping to share this cake with you and—"

"Me too, but Molly feels almost like a daughter to me these days."

Jeannette squinted in disbelief. "Fred, you're delusional. Her parents are alive and kicking. She doesn't need another father."

"I know. But those parents don't seem very *involved* with her."

"Mmm," said Jeannette, leaning back on the counter and sipping her wine. "Have you ever considered the possibility that she doesn't *want* them to be?"

"Sure! But I think she likes having *me* in her life."

Jeannette dipped her finger in the cake's frosting and licked it. "I get it, Freddy. You're saying she's *choosing* you as a kind of foster dad. Sort of like my smut-writing family."

"What?"

"The erotic writers I talk to almost every day on Facebook. We've got a private group. Meanwhile, I speak to my actual brother and sister only a few times a year. Tops."

He frowned. "I think that's different."

"Maybe. But maybe not. Writing erotica's a lonely business, and those of us who do it need supportive friends. People who understand. Like the way you and Molly support each other."

"I don't know—"

"Yes. That's what it's all about. My smut-writing family's been through a lot together—professional stuff, personal stuff, you name it. We don't always agree, but we're always there to listen. Right now, one of my friends in the group's having chemo for breast cancer, and we're all trying to keep her spirits up."

"Oh, that's terrible. I'm sorry."

"Thanks. But I have faith in her. She's one tough bitch. On the other hand... cancer. Cancer's a bitch too."

He thought about Billy. "Yup. I've got a buddy in Florida whose wife's got it bad. Leukemia. I haven't talked to him about it much lately, but I get the sense things aren't great. I think it's only a matter of time now."

Jeannette's eyes glistened with sympathy. "Poor thing. When *did* you last speak to your friend?"

"Well, I talk to him on the air almost every night, but we don't get into stuff like that. The frequencies are public, you know?"

Jeannette dabbed under her eye with the corner of a napkin. "Do you think it might be time for you to make a *phone* call? It's none of my business, but I'm thinking your friend might appreciate it."

Guilt stabbed at his chest. He knew he needed to call Billy, but was afraid of hearing really bad news. And then there was all the Davey stuff too. If he talked to Billy on the phone, he'd need to fill him in on that. And yet, life was short. "Yeah, you're right. It won't be fun, but you're right. I'll give him a jingle tomorrow."

Jeannette regarded him with her large brown eyes. "So what's the deal with this ham radio thing, anyway? It sounds sorta like Facebook or maybe Twitter, but with voices instead of text. Am I right? You meet strangers, you befriend 'em, you help 'em out?"

He felt the same type of horror he'd felt when Molly called his ham radio a CB, but he bit his tongue. "No. It may be the same *basic* concept, but it's much more technical. And Billy's no stranger. He used to live right here in Arlington. He's a great friend."

Jeannette nodded and sipped more wine. "Okay. But I still don't really get it."

"Well," said Fred, taking a deep breath, "on ham radio, we don't usually share recipes or discuss what we had for breakfast."

Jeannette clicked her tongue. "Oh. So that's what you think I talk about with my writer friends?"

"No. Of course, not. At least not all the time."

"Actually, not *ever*," said Jeannette. "First of all, I've got zero time for that shit, and secondly, I always eat the same thing for breakfast—a banana and a bran muffin—and no one cares."

"Hey, I didn't mean to—"

"I know," said Jeannette with a wink. "I know you didn't mean to be sexist or stereotypical. Even though you were."

He felt ashamed. "I'm sorry. It's just... well, that's my impression of Facebook."

Jeannette nodded. "And Facebook can be that way for some people. Which isn't a bad thing. A lot of people are into food, and good for them. If someone can bond with someone else over a lemon meringue pie recipe, more power to 'em, right? But people talk about more serious things too. I'll bet there are even groups of ham radio folks on there. Maybe someday, you'll check it out."

"I don't think—"

"Freddy, you and I are a lot more similar than you're willing to admit."

He took a small sip of wine and smiled. Never in a million years would he agree that ham radio was anything like Facebook, but maybe Jeannette was right about the other stuff. "Sure," he said, standing up and walking over to the window again. Seeing the Volkswagen still outside, he resumed his pacing but didn't say anything.

"Do you ever read books, Fred?"

He stopped in his tracks and looked straight at her. "Of course. Not the way I used to, but a few a year. Arlington's got a great library."

"Hm. So what kind of books do you like?"

Shrugging, he went back to pacing. He glanced at Jeannette's bookshelf and noticed that most of the visible jackets featured various shades of pink, purple, and red. Some of them had shiny writing on them, making them look like girly, giftwrapped presents. Clearing his throat, he said, "Books about real life, I guess. Real things. *Believable* things. Over the summer, I read Jimmy Carter's memoir. I think it was called *White House Diary*. It was fascinating."

"Mmm-mmm. Well I don't know what's in that man's diary, but I wouldn't kick *him* outta bed, if you know what I mean. That Jimmy Carter's still got it. I've always found him very sexy."

Here we go again. "C'mon, Jeannette. The man was the president of the United States."

"I know. And I'm not being disrespectful. I'm just tellin' the truth. I've lusted after him in my heart."

"Right." But he couldn't help smiling.

"So are you hungry?"

He was, actually. Eyeing the chocolate cake on the table, he said, "Yeah, sure. And I haven't had cake in a while."

Jeannette smiled like she was enjoying a private joke. "Well I can fix that. And let me pour you a little more wine too."

"Oh, sure. What the heck, right? You only go around once." He looked out the window again, then went back to the table, pulled out his chair, and sat down as Jeannette refilled his glass.

"Should we cut it or just dig in?" she asked.

"Dig in?"

"Yeah. It's a small cake, I've got two forks, and like you said, we only go around this way once."

He'd been thinking about kissing Jeannette good night, but wasn't ready to *dig in* to a cake with her. "Nah, that'd make a mess, and we'd end up wasting a lot."

She laughed a flirty laugh. "Whatever you say, Freddy." Then she picked up the knife and began to cut a slice. But just as she did, a terrible moan rose up through the floor. Both of them jumped.

"That doesn't sound like good sex," said Jeannette.

But he was already out of his chair and headed for the back stairway. When he reached the bottom, he didn't even bother knocking on Molly's door; the sounds coming from inside were too frightening. Bursting through—it wasn't locked—he barged into her kitchen, taking a second to make sure she had a hardwired phone on the wall for calling 9-1-1. She did.

A strong odor of vomit permeated the air, and when he reached the living room, he saw someone lying face down on the rug, making that caterwauling noise. But it wasn't Molly. It was the guy. And there was Molly—spattered with puke—kneeling over the man, apparently trying to comfort him.

"Calm down, Andy!" she kept crying. "Please. Calm down."

"Molly!" shouted Fred, running over to her. "What's wrong with *him*? Does he need an ambulance?"

"I'm not sure, but you need to leave. Now." Her eyes were wild. She looked terrified.

Assessing the vomit, Fred felt pretty certain it'd come from Molly, so why was the guy on the floor? "What the hell, Molly? What's going on?"

"Just leave. Please."

But he wasn't going anywhere. "Molly, I'm callin' an ambulance."

Jeannette darted in, shouting and still holding the cake knife. "Molly, are you all right? Did this prick hurt you?"

"No! Not at all! It's all my fault. I... I said stuff I shouldn't have. But Fred, I'm not kiddin'. You gotta go."

"I don't understand," he said. "I'm here to help."

Right then, Andy rolled over and sat up. Veins protruded from both sides of his forehead, but he stopped wailing and appeared to be pulling himself together. Then, like a wild beast, he jumped to his feet and drew back his arm.

The last thing Fred felt was a terrible pain in the middle of his face. Then everything went white.

Chapter 29
Age

Molly
November 10, 2010

"Call 911!" I screamed, but Jeannette was already running for the phone.

"Is he dead?" said Andy. With crazed eyes, he gazed down at the man he'd just knocked out.

I rested my head on Fred's chest and detected a faint heartbeat. "Not yet anyway." My body trembled as I squeezed the poor man's limp hand. "Hurry up, Jeannette! Tell 'em to move it! He needs help! Fast!"

Flashing lights appeared in the driveway about two minutes later, and after hearing the quickest possible description of what'd happened, the EMTs lifted Fred onto a stretcher and rushed him—still unconscious—to Mass General Hospital. Andy, meanwhile, slipped into a trancelike state and calmly allowed a police officer to handcuff him and drive him away in a cruiser.

Jeannette lost it then. She'd been almost unnaturally calm up until that point, but as more cops arrived to ask more questions, she burst into tears and started apologizing.

"Why are *you* sorry?" asked one of the cops. "I thought you were upstairs the whole time."

"Yes, I was. But if I hadn't invited Fred over for cake, this never would've happened. I'm at least partly responsible."

"Ma'am," said the cop, "sometimes people are just in the wrong place at the wrong time. And based on everything I've heard tonight, you did nothing wrong. Come on, why don't you have a seat on the couch?"

My body continued to shake and my clothes were covered in vomit, but I was worried about Jeannette. I'd never seen her so upset. "Jeannette, I've got some beers in the fridge. Want one?"

But she kept sobbing. "It's too much. And I have jury duty in the morning."

"Jury duty? Tomorrow? No way. Can you cancel?" Like me, Jeannette—who didn't own a car—got around on public transportation and in the occasional taxi. I wasn't sure what time jury duty started, but it was early.

A female police officer who'd been talking to us earlier tiptoed over and sat beside Jeannette on the couch. "Ma'am, what courthouse is it?"

"Woburn," she muttered into her hands. "The one on 128. I was planning to call a cab at seven, but what'll they do if I don't show up?"

"They can fine you," said the cop. "But I'm working in the morning. I'll give you a lift if you'd like."

Jeannette smiled through her tears. "Seriously? At seven a.m.?"

The cop patted Jeannette's hand. "Sure. But just tomorrow, okay? I can't be a chauffeur for jurors on a regular basis. I'll flash the lights outside in the morning."

"You're an angel," said Jeannette. "You know, I believe in angels in this world, and you're one."

The officer shook her head. "Not me," she said. "But go get some rest. You've experienced real trauma tonight, and the sun'll be up before you know it."

"Okay," said Jeannette. "Thanks again, angel." She seemed calmer and more like herself. "Hey Molly, I think I will grab one of your beers on my way out. If that's all right."

"Sure," I said. "I'd give you a hug, but..." I looked down at my clothes, indicating the vomit. "I've gotta get in the shower."

Jeannette smiled sadly, then started crying again. "Oh Molly, I'm so worried about Fred. I love that man, you know."

Under normal circumstances, I might've pointed out that love is a strong word, but that night, I knew what she meant. "Just get some sleep, 'Nett. Fred'll be okay." But of course, I had no idea.

I called MGH when I awoke, but since I wasn't family, the nurse could only say that Fred Flaherty was a patient there. I asked if I could speak with him, but she said no because he wasn't conscious. So that gave me a little more info.

Not knowing what else to do, I threw on some clothes and took the T into Boston, wondering how Jeannette's jury duty was going. I imagined her on some high-profile murder trial like Whitey Bulger's, wearing her leopard-print jumpsuit with the matching hat. But on such a gray November day, even that image couldn't make me smile.

At the hospital, the guy at the front desk sent me to the floor for patients with head trauma. All morning, I'd been buzzing around on the jittery type of adrenaline that follows a sleepless night, but after the head nurse on Fred's wing gave me his room number, I walked partway down the hall, then stopped and stared out a window. I'd traveled over an hour to be there, but suddenly, I was stricken with fear.

Behind me, heels clicked on the linoleum, and I turned to see two middle-aged women making their way toward the elevator. One sobbed while her companion held her hand and tried to steady her. "I'm with you all the way, Laurie," said the companion. "Come on, let's get you home." Laurie cried harder, but she leaned into the other woman and kept moving.

Lord, I hate hospitals. But I summoned my courage, found the door to Fred's room, and pushed it open. And there he was. Lying on the bed, motionless under the smooth, undisturbed covers. He was so still that I actually wondered for a second if he was dead. But as I approached, I saw his chest rise and fall, and his perma-tanned cheekbones revealed the slightest hint of pink. Someone had combed the silver hair off his face, giving him a noble appearance. I couldn't help wondering if he was dreaming about rescuing people in a hurricane or helping Cathy — the ham radio widow — sell her husband's old equipment. Or maybe he was dreaming about Jeannette.

I shuddered. *How can this be real?* Twelve hours earlier, my biggest concern had been whether or not Andy would kiss me. Now I was wondering if Fred would survive. And who *was* Andy anyway? A dude who'd sucker punch a man in his seventies, that's who.

Poor Fred. Regardless of what he'd done to protect his brother Davey, he was a decent human being. I knew that in my heart. Life was hard, but Fred did his best.

I watched his breathing and almost cried. He'd looked so nice in that dark blue shirt the night before, so handsome. All dressed up for his date. But where was that shirt now? Had the ambulance people cut it off on the way to the hospital?

I'd also been avoiding another really big question: How much of the tragedy was my fault? I mean, *I* was the idiot who'd told Andy that Fred was Davey's brother. Why had I done that? Why had I opened my fat mouth when I didn't even know the whole truth? Why hadn't I simply told Andy I'd eaten bad shellfish?

Please Fred, I thought. *Please sit up and start talking about the cracks in the sidewalk. I promise I'll call Town Hall today with a full report if you just open your eyes.*

"So, you're *not* his daughter?" The voice from the doorway startled me. Standing there was a slight, white-coated man with dark brown skin.

"No," I said, trying to regain some composure. "I'm his neighbor. My name's Molly Dolan. The head nurse gave me permission to visit."

"Yes," said the white-coated man. "I'm Dr. Maalouf from the neurology team, and of course you can visit." His dark eyes were sharp, his handshake warm. Under his arm was a small notebook—an actual wire-bound notebook—with a pen clipped to the cover. "It's kind of you to come see him. Are you and Mr. Flaherty very close?"

Close? "I dunno. I mean, sort of. He lives across the street from me."

The doctor raised his eyebrows. "I see." He sized me up, then pulled the curtain around Fred's bed—and us—for privacy. Fred did have a roommate, but he was either asleep or unconscious too. Nevertheless, the doctor lowered his voice. "Molly, as you may know, this is a complicated case for many reasons. Lucky for me, my only job is to worry about Mr. Flaherty's health. So, I'm hoping you can help with that."

I was pretty sure I couldn't. "Um, I'll try. But I don't know much about his health."

"That's fine. Let me explain. You see, we've contacted his primary care doctor, but he's been unable to provide us with names of any next of kin."

The words *next of kin* made my breath come faster. "You mean—"

"Relatives. Family of any type."

I did my best to stay calm. "I... I don't know any by name, but... Fred's gonna be okay, right? I mean, I don't think he got hit *that* hard."

Dr. Maalouf sighed. "Look, we're gonna have to make some important decisions very soon, and the laws around medical privacy are quite strict. That's why we're hoping to find a family member to speak with. A sibling? A cousin? Even a very good friend."

I looked at Fred's inert body. "I know he used to have a brother, but... he died a few months ago. And sometimes he talks about a friend named Billy in Florida, but I don't know his last name." Then I remembered he'd been married. "Oh, and he's... divorced. He's been divorced for years. I don't *think* he stays in touch with his ex, but I really don't know."

The doctor opened his notebook and scribbled a few phrases in it. "Hmm. Any children?"

"No. I don't think so."

"You don't *think* so? Ma'am, how well *do* you know Mr. Flaherty?"

I felt like crying again. In that moment, I realized how much of Fred's life remained a mystery to me, but how much I really cared. "Well, he's never *mentioned* any kids."

"But he talks to you *regularly*? The report I read said he was injured in your apartment."

"Yes. That's true. I was having an... issue with a friend, and Fred came over to... try and help. I wish he hadn't, though. I just can't believe it."

He nodded. "Yes, the report's a bit complicated. The police will need to... sort out some things. I'm sorry."

"Me too." A tear slid down my cheek and I wiped it away. "You know, he's a ham radio guy, and he has friends he talks to on... his radio. Like Billy in Florida. Billy's a ham too."

Dr. Maalouf smiled half a smile. "That's good information, but I'm guessing there's more than one ham radio operator in Florida named Billy. Do you happen to know anyone—perhaps other hams—who might help us locate this Billy?"

The only other hams I'd met—aside from Andy—were the people from the pancake breakfast, and I had no idea what their last names were either or how to contact them. "No," I said.

Dr. Maalouf winced. "All right. So, who's the woman who called 911? Apparently, she said something to one of the EMTs about drinking wine with Mr. Flaherty last night? And there *was* a small amount of alcohol in his blood when he was admitted."

"Oh, that's Jeannette. She lives upstairs, and yeah, Fred was with her last night too. It seems like maybe they're... dating a little these days."

"Off to a great start, huh?" said the doctor with a sarcastic laugh.

I sighed, and neither of us spoke for a moment.

"So, I hate to ask this question," he said hesitantly, "but are you and Mr. Flaherty involved in a romantic relationship as well?"

"No!" I practically shouted, then turned to make sure Fred was still unconscious. "No. We're friends. Good friends. That's it."

"I see. And his relationship with... Jeannette? It's a new thing?"

I wasn't sure where he was going with that line of questioning but figured I should be as honest as possible. "Yeah. Pretty new. I think they had their first real date on Friday."

The doctor wrote some other stuff in his notebook, then looked up at me. "Molly, it appears that *you* may know Mr. Flaherty better than any other person we'll be able to contact in a reasonable amount of time. In other words, *you* might be his temporary next of kin."

I could barely breathe. "Seriously?"

"*Temporary*," repeated the doctor. "Of course, this is far from an ideal situation. But it's my job to try and understand what Mr. Flaherty would want if he could speak. Does that make sense?"

"Yee... ah? But how, um... *dire* is his situation?"

He cleared his throat and rubbed his eyes. "Again, this'd be entirely confidential if Mr. Flaherty were conscious, but he's suffered a traumatic brain injury. He's got a clot on his brain that'll require surgery, or he won't survive."

"Oh my god. How did—"

"He hit his head on the floor. At least that's what I surmise, based on the MRI and the report from the police—which I believe you helped compose—and the EMT report. Now, if we operate, he's got a decent chance. The big question is whether or not he'd want that."

"You mean, as opposed to... just dying?"

"Exactly. Many older people sign Do Not Resuscitate orders because they choose not to deal with the recovery process. And I'll tell you right now, recovery from brain surgery isn't easy."

I looked at Fred again, and thought about the day he'd gone down to Rhode Island to assist the hurricane victims. "Doctor, I don't think Fred's ready to die. In his own little way, he seems to really enjoy life."

For the first time, the doctor smiled. "Funny, but his personal care physician said almost the exact same thing. He said he thinks Mr. Flaherty's got lot of good years left in him."

Tears began streaming down my face. "So, does that mean you'll do the surgery?"

"I think so. It sounds as though we should try. Unless, of course, someone comes forward with different information. He's got good insurance too. But I won't lie to you. Things could go either way. All we have right now are images of his brain. I won't know the extent of the damage until I get in there. And we'll need to wait a few more days—maybe even a week or more—before we can do that. Some of his blood nutrients are very low, so we're giving him intravenous supplements. He needs to be as strong as possible before I'm willing to attempt this."

I felt like a boulder had somehow gotten lodged in my stomach. Fred looked so peaceful. How could he be so badly injured? "He's a pretty strong guy," I said through my tears.

"That's good," said the doctor. "And I'm glad he's got you to care about him. Because if he survives this, he'll need a lot of help when he gets home."

"Mom?" I said into the phone receiver.

"Honey! It's so nice to hear your voice. Are you all right?"

I held the mug of coffee against my chest for warmth. "Yeah, I'm fine. I was just, um, wondering if I could come up and see you for a couple days. Like... maybe you could pick me up at the train station in Portsmouth tomorrow? Around noon?"

She was silent for a few seconds. It was November, and I still hadn't seen my parents since July. "Of course, honey," she finally said. "We'd love to have you. But what's going on? Did something happen with Joe?"

Oh lord, I'd never even told her about our breakup. "No. No, but... yeah. I'll fill you in on everything tomorrow, okay? It's all good. I was just hoping to hang out with you and Dad a little."

"Oh gosh, that'd be great, honey. But are you sure you're okay?"

"Yes, mom, I'm excellent. I promise. Can't a girl visit her parents without the Spanish Inquisition?" I knew I deserved the guilt, but that didn't make it any easier to accept.

Mom's voice got deeper, the way it does when she cries or has a bad cold. "Okay, baby. I'm sorry. I just worry about you. But I'll be at the train station tomorrow at noon." She sniffled. "Hey, and maybe you and me could go to lunch. If you're hungry, that is. My treat, of course. They've got some nice new restaurants in Portsmouth these days."

It occurred to me that Mom and I had never gone out to lunch together, just the two of us. Not that she'd never asked, but in the past, the logistics hadn't worked out. Or, more accurately, I'd always made things more complicated than they needed to be. Why was I such an idiot?

"That'd be awesome, Mom. And don't worry. I'll be hungry."

Doctor Maalouf called the following Monday night to let me know Fred's surgery had gone as well as could be expected, and that he'd most likely make a slow but steady recovery.

"Wow," I said. "Wow, that's awesome." My hands fluttered with relief. All day long, Jeannette had been calling to ask if I'd heard anything, and unintentionally making me more nervous. "So, do you think he'll be, like, the same as he was before?"

"Time will tell," said the doctor. "Brain injuries heal slowly, but I have every reason to be optimistic. He's in and out of consciousness, which is a good sign."

"Wow," I said for the third time. "That's just... incredible news. So... can I visit him tomorrow?"

"Oh yes. I'm sure he'd love to see you. I should tell you he mentioned someone named Jeannette in the recovery room. That's the woman he's been dating, correct?"

"Yes! She's dying to visit him."

I couldn't wait to tell Jeannette Fred had asked about her. She'd been freaking out since the accident but hadn't seen him because the court had put her on a one-week trial. Plus, he'd been unconscious.

The doctor chuckled. "Great. But just one more thing, Molly. Please don't discuss any details of the accident with him. He doesn't remember it—at least not now—and he's quite fragile. We're just telling him he fell and hit his head. And so far, he seems to accept that."

"Fell and hit his head," I repeated. "O... kay. But... he'll need to know the truth at some point, right?"

"Oh yes. Oh yes. But that's not your concern. We'll have a social worker talk to him when he's feeling better."

The curtain around the bed was drawn, so Jeannette and I tiptoed into the room. "Freddy?" she whispered.

She was super excited, but my stomach was all messed up. For one thing, I worried about how Fred would *look* after brain surgery. Then, there was the fact that Jeannette and I were visiting together, and according to her, he'd asked her to keep their relationship quiet, at least for a while. Not to mention that we weren't permitted to discuss what'd happened to him, and I was pretty sure Fred would ask.

"Who's that?" came Fred's whisper from the other side of the curtain.

Jeannette grabbed the fabric and flung it open. "Oh my god! You look amazing, sweetie!" She darted to his side and gave him a quick peck on the cheek. "Ha!" she said. "I knew I'd get to kiss you in bed if I waited long enough."

Fred was clearly still heavily medicated, because he didn't blush.

"Jeez," he said. "You got some energy there, lady." A huge white bandage was wrapped around his head, and he had IVs in both arms. But even though he looked exhausted, his eyes smiled.

I walked slowly over to him and patted his shoulder. "Hi, Fred."

"Hi, Molly. Wow. Two pretty ladies here to see me. But you shouldn't have come to this terrible place." His throat sounded sore, which made sense because he'd been intubated during surgery.

"Are you crazy?" said Jeannette. "We've been countin' down the days. We gotta make sure they're takin' care of you."

I wondered if I should leave the two of them alone for a few minutes. "Yeah. How're you feeling, Fred?" I asked.

"Like I just lost a fight," he whispered. "But don't worry. I'll get 'em back."

Jeannette shot me an anxious glance, and I knew we were both wondering the same thing: Was Fred starting to remember what'd caused his injury? But her words came out calm and lighthearted. "Hey, who d'ya think you are, anyway? Arnold Schwarzenegger? The *Terminator*? No fightin' for you, mister. Okay?"

"That's right," I said. "You gotta rest up and get better. Kitty misses you."

Fred's face clouded. "You know, I was just thinkin' about Kitty. He must be awful hungry. Molly, could go over there and give him some food and water? I've got a key hidden in the back yard."

I was glad I could give him a little good news. "Oh, don't worry about Kitty, Fred. He's doin' just fine. The police helped me get into your house last week, and we found a key hanging right in your kitchen. So, I've been going over there once a day, feeding him and scooping his litter box. But he *is* lonely. He can't wait to have you home."

Fred's eyes misted over. "Aw, Molly, you're a good egg. Thanks a million."

Seeing him so vulnerable upset me, but I forced myself to keep smiling. "In fact," I said, "I brought you something." As I spoke, I opened the shopping bag I'd been carrying, and pulled out the bright yellow pillow with the word *Pal* embroidered on it in Morse code. "I know you've got plenty of pillows here, but I thought this one might make the hospital feel a little more... homey."

"Aw, Molly," he half-whispered.

I forced myself not to choke up as I propped the pillow against his bedrail so he could see it better. "You're *our* pal, after all," I said.

"Well, I can't wait to go home. It's too noisy here."

"Soon enough," I said.

He breathed heavily for a few seconds. "But you know what's funny? I dunno what happened. They keep sayin' I had an accident. But I think someone hit me over the head."

Panic shot through my body. "Nah," I said. "The ambulance guys said you fell on the floor. Like maybe you fainted?" I hated lying but had no choice. His health was at stake.

He shut his eyes tightly for a second, then opened them. "But who *called* the ambulance? It doesn't add up."

"Oh Freddy. You poor guy," said Jeannette. "This'll get better, I promise."

Fred sighed. "I hope so. My brain feels all jumbled. D'ya think I had a stroke?"

"I don't think so," I said quickly. "I'm pretty sure the doctors would know if you did."

"Yeah," said Jeannette. "I think it was just a freak thing." But when her eyes met mine, I saw her fear. "So... Molly and I should probably get going. You seem tired."

"Oh no," said Fred, his eyes fluttering. "Stay."

"We'll be back soon," I said. "But I've actually gotta hit the grocery store now. I promised to bring a pie to my parents' house for Thanksgiving."

Flaherty glanced over at the clock on the wall, "Thanksgiving? When *is* Thanksgiving?"

"Thursday," I said, glad to be on safer ground. "Day after tomorrow. I'd invite you to eat with my family, but I think they're keeping you in the hospital a little longer." *Or maybe a lot longer.*

"Hmm. So I'll be eatin' hospital turkey this year?"

Rainclouds of tears gathered in my head and threatened like a fast-approaching storm. "Aw, I bet it won't be so bad. People say hospital food's gotten better these days." I was talking out of my ass, but what else could I do?

"Yeah. And I'm an old Army guy. Not too picky."

Jeannette looked like she might cry too. "Tell you what, Freddy. I'm eatin' with my sister's family, so I'll bring you a plate o' food on Friday. I'm sure the nurses here have a microwave to heat things up. And lemme tell you, my sister's cooking's to die for."

Fred's eyes flashed. "Oh, so now you wanna kill me?"

"No, honey!" said Jeannette. "That's just an expression. I mean good food. *Outstanding* food."

For the first time, Fred actually smiled. "I know. I was pullin' your leg."

"Phew!" said Jeannette, fanning her face. "You had me scared there. But you know what, Freddy? Now I know you're gonna be okay. 'Cause you still have your sense o' humor. So there."

"Well, if I had my druthers, I'd be on my way home." The sadness returned to his eyes.

"Soon enough, buddy," said Jeannette. Then she leaned over and kissed his cheek again. "I'll be thinkin' about you. A lot."

"Me too, Fred," I said, patting his shoulder. "Happy Thanksgiving, mister. I'll be up in North Hampton for a few days, but I'll come see you early next week."

"North Hampton? In New Hampshire?"

"Yeah. My mom and dad live there now."

His eyes lit up. "On the beach?"

"No, but close to it."

"You know," he said, shutting his eyes, "I met a pretty girl at that beach one time."

Jeannette looked over at me with a playful smirk. "And he claims he's not a ladies' man."

But Fred didn't answer. He just lay there perfectly still with his eyes closed. Fear gripped me for a second, but then he snored and I realized he'd dozed off.

"Poor guy," said Jeannette.

"Yeah." He looked so small under the covers. I adjusted the yellow pillow a bit, so he'd have a better view of it when he awoke. Then, an idea struck me. Fred's left hand lay beside him on the mattress, so I touched his palm gently with my index finger and—in Morse code—started tapping out the letters that spell *Pal*.

> P: *dot dash dash dot*
> A: *dot dash*

I didn't know if I was doing it correctly, but Flaherty claimed code was designed to be simple. Not to mention that his eleven-year-old brother used to tap messages into his palm back in the day.

"What're you doin'?" asked Jeannette.

"Nothin'," I answered.

> L: *dot dash dot dot*

"C'mon, let's go."
Fred kept snoring, but he smiled in his sleep.

Jeannette and I didn't talk much on the crowded bus back to Arlington Heights, but she stopped in for a quick a cup of tea with me when we got home. The air outside remained damp and chilly. Very New England November.

"I bet your friend Andy feels like shit right now," she said as we waited for the kettle to boil. "Wherever he is."

"Yeah, well he deserves to. I wanna puke every time I think about him."

"Hmm," said Jeannette, taking a seat at the table. "That's too bad. The guy's a little hottie."

"Jeannette! How can you *say* that after the way he hurt Fred? He's a monster."

She shrugged. "I doubt it. Remember, he's been through hell too. Losing your mom like that's gotta suck."

"So, you blindside a seventy-two-year-old man who had nothing to do with your mom's death? How does that even make sense?" The kettle whistled and I shut it off.

Jeannette shrugged. "Molly, I've been alive long enough to know that people don't always use logic when they're under pressure. I'm sure you're familiar with the term 'crimes of passion.'"

"Listen to the writer," I said, tossing tea bags into cups and dousing them with boiling water. "That stuff's great for romance novels, but not real life. Can I tell you something really upsetting?"

"Of course, sweetie. You know you can tell me anythin'."

I took a deep breath. "Okay, so ever since I was in high school, I've had one goal. *One.* To find a guy. A boyfriend who really loves me. Like *really* loves me. Maybe even enough to wanna get married someday. And here I am, twenty-five years old, and I've never even come close to that, unless you count Joe, and let's not even go there."

Jeannette opened her mouth to speak, but I held up my hand to stop her because I was pretty sure I knew what she was going to say.

"And no," I continued, "I don't think I'm gay. And yes, I know *you* love me. And my parents love me. And Fred cares about me a lot. But why am I such a loser with men? I mean, what am I doing wrong? Why do I keep picking the worst guys?"

"Can I talk now?" she asked, sounding slightly irritated.

"Yes. I'm sorry." I brought the cups of tea over to the table and sat with her.

"No need to be sorry. I get it. But Molly, you're still a kid. Believe it or not, you've got lots of time."

"Yeah, but—"

"I know. You're frustrated and upset. But you know what? Not everyone finds that *one* special soulmate. And that's okay too. Take me, for example. I'm almost seventy, and I don't have one. But I'm not unhappy. Not at all. I take one day at a time and have as much fun as I can. And I really enjoy my life."

I didn't know how to respond, because I knew she was right. But it wasn't what I wanted to hear. "Yeah," I finally said. "I guess I just need to chill, huh?"

Jeannette shrugged. "That'd be my advice, Molly. For what it's worth."

The Tuesday morning after Thanksgiving, a female police officer showed up at my door, and this time I wasn't surprised. I invited her in, and she told me Andy had been charged with assault and had pleaded *no contest* at his arraignment. His attorney had requested probation and community service for him—rather than jail time—and since Andy had no prior record, the judge had sentenced him to three years probation and three-hundred hours of community service.

I thanked the officer with a shrug. "I guess that sounds fair, right? I mean, I can't really imagine Andy in jail."

The cop nodded. "Yeah. In this case, I'd say our court system worked the way it's supposed to." She cleared her throat. "But I'm here today to talk about the murder of Maryellen Stevers. As you may know, Ms. Stevers's case was recently reopened. And we're really hoping to solve it, once and for all."

"Yeah. For sure."

"Which is why I'm hoping you'll tell me everything you know about the case. Anything you've heard—either from Mr. Stevers or Mr. Flaherty—could be helpful to us."

I couldn't imagine I had any information about the case that the police hadn't already thoroughly investigated, but I did my best. As I spoke, the officer typed my words into a laptop computer.

"Okay. Thank you," she said, barely looking up. "Now, I'm gonna ask you about a different case. Did you ever hear anything about an incident involving David Flaherty and a woman named Elizabeth Barton?"

Oh, wow. I felt terrible admitting that I knew Fred had lied to the police all those years ago, but again, I held nothing back. When I'd finished, I asked if Fred could be arrested for obstructing justice.

"Doubtful," she said, "given the statute of limitations on these things. And from what we can deduce, Mr. Flaherty has fully cooperated with us in the Stevers case. He really does seem to believe—with his entire heart—that his brother's innocent in that one."

"But no one else does, right?"

She winced. "Evidence'll be the key, Molly. There's not enough right now."

I wanted so badly for Fred to get a break. After Kate's death, I'd lived with survivor's guilt for so many years, and Fred wasn't a young man. "Mr. Flaherty's a good guy," I said. "He's made mistakes, but he does his best."

"Agreed," said the cop. "My dad's known him for years. They're in the same ham radio club thingy. Whatever it's called."

"The repeater society?"

"Yes. The repeater society. White-haired superheroes, right?" She smiled for a second, then her tone grew serious again. "And like I said, I feel pretty confident about him avoiding personal legal trouble." She paused and sighed. "On the other hand, I bet he won't be pleased when he gets the full scoop on what went down here in your apartment that night."

Chapter 30
I Got A Name

Fred
Winter, 2012-2013

It was — by a long shot — the worst winter of his life. He hated his on-again-off-again wooziness and utter lack of interest in food. After one or two bites of *anything*, nausea would completely overcome him, and he'd lost so much weight that he refused to step on the scale anymore. All he knew for sure was that none of his pants stayed up without a belt; so most days, he just wore pajamas. He also hated the Ace bandage he kept wrapped around his head almost constantly, but it really did help with the dizziness. And worst of all was his dependence on Molly and Jeannette for simple things like groceries.

Nights were no bargain either. He'd toss in bed for hours, unable to shut off his brain until three or four in the morning. *Why did I ever tell Molly about Davey?* He pondered that question every single night. *If I'd just kept my damn mouth shut, she wouldn't have known anything. And none of this would've happened.*

Then he'd go the other way. *For crying out loud, I deserve every bit of this. Because if I'd just told the police the truth about Davey and Elizabeth Barton back in '84, he woulda gone to jail then. And maybe gotten some good help. Or at least rehab. I was a fool, thinking I could help him. I thought I knew the answers. There I was — a reasonably sane guy — and I failed my sick brother. Miserably.*

Still other nights, he'd get so angry that he'd actually shout out loud, "No one even knows if Davey killed that Stevers lady! Whatever happened to *innocent until proven guilty?*"

It was torture, and his strength wasn't coming back the way the doctors had hoped, probably because he wasn't eating and sleeping enough. But then, why was he even alive? Every day, hundreds of healthy young people died violently, yet *he* continued to exist: a geezer with a bum leg. Despite the fact that his only responsibility in the world was to a cat, he'd survived a near-fatal head injury and brain surgery too. Why?

Near the end of January, Jeannette suggested that he might be suffering from depression, but he assured her he wasn't. "I'm just in a funk. I'll feel better when this damn dizziness goes away and I can take a shower without a nurse helping me. I need to get outta this house too."

"In due time. It's too cold and icy out there now," said Jeannette. "But maybe listenin' to so much Jim Croce music's makin' things worse. I mean, he's good but not very upbeat."

"What're you talkin' about? 'Leroy Brown's' upbeat. And what about 'Don't Mess Around with Jim?' And 'One Less Set of Footsteps?' That's got a great beat."

"Okay," said Jeannette, "but 'Leroy Brown's' about a bar fight, 'Mess Around with Jim's' about fighting too, and 'One Less Set of Footsteps' is about a couple callin' it quits. Am I right? Not so uplifting, in my book."

She didn't understand. "Well, his songs make *me* feel better, okay? And what about 'I've Got a Name?'" But he stopped there because he didn't want to admit that "I've Got a Name" was his favorite song. Jeannette didn't need to know that a crusty old fool like him still dreamed of a better future. And he definitely wasn't ready to tell her that he believed—like the guy in the song—that maybe he still had time to share that dream with someone special.

"I don't know that one," said Jeannette.

"All right, then. Don't criticize what you don't know."

The two of them argued like that a lot, but he enjoyed her company so much. Sometimes she'd come over on a weekend night with pizza or Chinese food, and they'd watch an old movie on TV. Sure, she could get under his skin, but she also made the house feel warmer.

And ever since his injury, she'd put the brakes on the romantic advances toward him. Which he appreciated. He simply wasn't in the mood. He felt weak and queasy a lot, and sometimes he smelled dirty too because the visiting nurse only came three times a week.

Finally, one frigid February morning when the snowbanks in front of his house were so high he couldn't see the road from his kitchen window, he dialed the number for the rectory down at St. Mike's and asked if one of the priests might have time to stop by for a cup of tea. With the exception of a few weddings and funerals, Fred hadn't set foot in a church for over forty years, but he'd been raised Catholic and that had to count for something. And since nothing was helping with the ache in his heart, religion couldn't possibly make things worse. Could it?

"Oh, excuse me! I think I've got the wrong address," said the priest, shivering on the doorstep in a thin overcoat. "I'm looking for Fiona Flaherty."

"Uh, come in Father. I'm *Fred* Flaherty. I called the rectory earlier, so I think I'm the guy you're lookin' for."

The priest, who was about the same age as Fred, sounded disappointed. "I see. Is Fiona your... sister?"

"No, it's just me, Father," he said, hanging onto the door handle for support. "I don't have a sister." He'd planned to remove the Ace bandage from his head before the priest's visit, but the dizziness had been pretty lousy that day, so he'd left the foolish thing on.

The priest squinted. "Ah. We've got a charming widow in the parish named Fiona Flaherty. I must've misread the note."

Fred felt bad about the confusion, even though it wasn't his fault. "Well, have you got time for a quick cup o' tea with *me*?"

"Yes. Yes, of course," said the priest. "This is my job." He extended his gloved hand. "I'm Father Joyce. Pleasure to meet you, Fred."

He felt sick to his stomach again. *Another bad idea. More crossed signals. This poor fellow'd been planning on a visit with a pretty little lady, and here he was with a smelly old guy with a bandage around his head.*

But once he and Father Joyce got settled in the kitchen with some tea and banana bread—Molly had brought another loaf over the previous day—he relaxed a little. The priest asked if he could smoke, and Fred was glad he still had an ashtray to offer him.

"I'm afraid I haven't been very faithful lately, Father. I don't pray much, and when I do, it's only here in the house."

The priest's eyes looked disturbingly blue compared to his nicotine-stained teeth. "It's never too late to come home, Fred. St. Mike's will always welcome you back."

Home, he thought. He'd never felt at home in church, especially as he'd grown older. In his opinion, the Catholics were all wrong about lots of things, especially that stuff about babies. He and Barb had desperately wanted a kid, but not everyone was in that position, and the Catholics had no business telling people what to do in that department.

But the thing that'd really turned him off on religion was something that'd happened to Davey about two months before his brother got into the trouble with Elizabeth Barton. Apparently, he'd stumbled into an evening Mass one very cold Saturday in Maine, and an usher had turned him away because he smelled like booze. Poor Davey, who'd already been heading down a bad road at that point. His words still haunted Fred. "I just wanted to get warm and think, and that jerk kicked me to the curb. I told him I was a Catholic, but he didn't give a shit."

That'd pretty much hammered the last nail into Fred's Catholicism coffin. And yet, it felt strangely comforting to sit in his kitchen with Father Joyce. The priest sure seemed familiar with topics like grief and guilt. And once Fred started telling him Davey's story, something drove him to push through to the bitter end. Which wasn't at all typical of him. He even broke down and sobbed twice, but he pulled himself together and got back to it. Getting it off his chest felt good. Besides, he didn't expect the priest to visit again.

As he listened, Father Joyce smoked at least four cigarettes and sipped his tea slowly. "I'll keep you in my prayers," he said when Fred finished talking. "I can tell you've been trying to do the right thing, and that's not always easy. Life isn't easy. And the longer you live, the better you understand that. But I'll tell you what gives me hope, Fred. I believe God sees the good in us all."

Fred started sobbing again. "That's another thing, Father. I'm not even sure what's good anymore. I'm so confused."

The priest lit another cigarette, took a puff, and rested it in the ashtray. "I understand. You know, believe it or not, I struggle with dilemmas of good and evil every day. Some people think being a priest makes you a saint or something, but it doesn't."

Fred frowned. With all the news about pedophile priests in recent years, he doubted anyone still considered priests saints. "I see," he said.

"But I *do* believe," continued the priest, "that there are ways to make up for the errors we've committed."

Fred's chest tightened. "Without going to church? 'Cause I don't see that in the cards for me."

The priest inhaled deeply on his Marlboro and held the smoke for a moment before letting it out and coughing. "Yes. Just don't tell the pastor I said so."

Oh boy. Now he's gonna hit me up for a big check. But he had no plans to fall for that one either. He was old enough to know you can't buy your way out of things, and he'd rather give his money to almost anyone but the Catholics. "I'm all ears, Father." A tear leaked out of his eye. "But I gotta tell you, I'm really struggling. Sometimes I feel like life's just a bunch of terrible things with a few good minutes in between."

The priest reached out and laid his smooth, dry hand on Fred's course one. "It can seem that way sometimes, Fred. But even though I don't know you well, I believe you'll eventually find peace. You'll need to do some soul searching though—and probably some penance—but you deserve peace. Think long and hard, and I'll bet the good Lord will send you some answers."

Fred wasn't sure he deserved anything good, but it was nice to hear the priest say he did. "Penance? Like going to Confession?"

"No. You've already said you're not keen on coming to church. I'm talking more about making up for what you've done. You can't right a wrong, but you can use your power as a human being to make something better."

Fred breathed in the tobacco smoke. Gosh, he still loved that smell, even though cigarettes caused cancer. "Well, I guess I got nothin' to lose from trying, Father."

The priest stumped out his cigarette, cleared his throat, and stood up. "Fred, I wish you all the best. But I should probably shuffle off to Buffalo, as they say. Thank you for the tea."

"Thank *you*, Father," said Flaherty, also standing. "I appreciate you coming by. Even though I'm not Fiona."

The priest blushed slightly, and Fred suppressed a smile. But as he led his visitor to the door, he stopped short and turned around. "Hey, I've got one last question."

The priest had been buttoning his coat in preparation for the cold, but his fingers froze as he looked into Flaherty's troubled face. "What's that, Fred?"

"Well, I'm wondering what'll happen to me when I die. My body, I mean. My poor mother—God rest her—would've wanted me to have a Catholic funeral. It's all the same to me, but I'd like to do that for her. If I can."

Father Joyce nodded. "I get that question a lot. Have you been baptized?"

"Oh yeah. I even went to Catholic school, at least most of the years. So did Davey, but he didn't want a funeral. Although now I wish I'd given him one anyway. My poor mother must be spinning in her grave."

The priest smiled weakly. "Try to work on that guilt, Fred. You're doing your best. But to answer your question, when the time comes, you can have your funeral at Saint Mike's. Just make sure someone knows your wishes. Someone you trust."

Flaherty let out a breath of relief and thanked the man again. *I'll tell Molly.*

The day after the priest's visit, Fred went down to the hamshack and fired up his radio for the first time since his accident. He hadn't had the energy to tell Billy what'd happened, and he hadn't thought about antennas or frequencies in months.

But he knew one thing: When the going gets tough, the tough get going. And the longer he waited, the harder it'd be. So, he picked up the microphone, and for the first time in his life, actually felt nervous about pressing the button. He held it in his shaky hand for a moment before doing what he'd done at least a thousand times before. "K1QEC, K1QEC, this is W1RAP. You around tonight, Bill?"

"Hey, where you been, W1RAP?" came the measured response. "This is K1QEC and it's a relief to hear your voice, Fred. You know, I've called your house a few times, but you haven't picked up."

Oh god. Why does Billy sound so sad? And why has he been calling? Has he been worried about me, or... did something bad happen? I'll never forgive myself if Sally....

"Yeah, I'm sorry, Bill. I had a little setback, but I'm doin' better now. How're things with you?"

He braced himself when Billy paused for a few seconds. "Uh, awright. The weather's been lousy, but I can't complain. One day at a time. You know how it goes. So, what's that you said about a setback?"

"Uh, I'd rather not talk about it on the air."

"Oh yeah?" said Billy with what sounded like a forced chuckle. "Funny you should say that. That's why I've been calling you on the landline. You know, when that thing rings, you're supposed to answer it."

I think I'd hear it in his voice if Sally had passed. "Yeah. Yeah. I know. It's just that they've got so many of those damn telemarketers out there. I finally shut the ringer off."

"Oh yeah? But what if I'd been Ed McMahon calling to say you won a million bucks. You'd be kicking yourself right now."

Fred couldn't help smiling. "You know, I don't think Ed's with us anymore, Billy. And I think you gotta *buy* lottery tickets if you wanna win."

"Yeah, well I wouldn't know. I don't play the lottery." Billy's voice grew more sober. "Listen, how 'bout I give you a call right now? You got that ringer on?"

A chill ran down Fred's spine. *Oh god. Oh please, Sally. Please be alive.*

Sally was, in fact, still breathing air, but Billy made it clear that wouldn't be for much longer. His daughter had already spoken with the local hospice, and the family was considering various options regarding Sally's end-of-life plans.

The words *end-of-life plans* made Fred want to cry, but Billy was being so brave on the phone. *Sally.* She was one of those girls you met and knew right away was a good egg. Not the prettiest girl, but smart and on the ball. And honest. There was no bullshitting with Sally. Back when Fred and Barb were together, he'd wondered if Billy was jealous of him—after all, Barb had been such a looker—but later on, he'd come to understand why Bill loved Sally so much.

"So... you gonna tell me about your setback?" asked Billy.

"Oh sure. It's not much, especially compared to what you're goin' through. I got a bump on the head is the short story. The long one is... well, it's on the long side. How 'bout I tell ya when I see ya? The good news is I'm healing up."

"Jeez, Freddy. Sounds like you've been through the wringer. What'd you take a toss or somethin'?"

He did his best to laugh. "Yeah, I guess you could say that, although I had a little assistance. If you catch my drift."

"What? Are you saying someone knocked you down? Like in a fight? At your age, Fred?"

"Not exactly a fight. Like I said, I'll have to tell you in person. But I don't know if I'll make it down to Florida when... you know, when the time comes for Sally. I'm still not up to snuff, as they say. The doc won't even let me drive yet, let alone fly."

Billy sighed. "Hey buddy, like I said, one day at a time. I'll call you when it happens, just so you know. And I'll understand if you can't come to the funeral. But maybe in the spring, we can get you down here for a visit. I think some Florida sunshine might be good for you. You ever try playing golf?"

Fred wiped a tear from the corner of his eye. "Golf? Are you kiddin'?"

"No. The daughter's dragged me out on the course a few times now, and it's not half bad. I'm lousy at it, but it's nice being out on the grass. And the people are friendly. Most of 'em, anyway. It's not the worst way to spend a morning."

"Golf, huh? Jeez. That's one game I've never considered. But hey, I'd give it a shot. This old dog might still have a new trick in him."

In mid-March, he asked Molly to help him write a letter to Elizabeth Barton. He wanted to apologize for not being honest with the police but wasn't sure where to begin.

"I think this is a really good idea," said Molly.

"Thanks. I hope so. At first, I was thinking I'd tell her about Davey's mental problems, and what a great guy he was before the War. But now I'm thinking Elizabeth might not want to hear that."

"Yeah," said Molly. "Maybe not now. Maybe you should just say you're sorry. Then, if you end up talking to her on the phone or something, you could tell her more about Davey."

"Yeah. I like that idea."

And so, they wrote the letter together. It was only a few lines long, but it felt good to seal the envelope and lick the stamp.

"Hey Molly," he said after she'd promised to drop it at the post office for him, "I think Jeannette and I might go to the library on Saturday, if you'd like to come with us."

"The Robbins library? Here in town?"

"Yeah. We're gonna take the bus and listen to some author read from her book. Not an erotic book, though. Apparently, it's about an American family living in one of the Middle Eastern countries."

"Hmm, that sounds interesting. But I'm probably gonna stay home on Saturday and do some more work on my resume. These temp jobs I've been getting are okay, but I'd like to be working someplace permanently by summer."

"Jeez, I wish I could help you there, Molly. Maybe I can find a book about resumes when I'm at the library?"

"Oh no, Fred, it's okay. I can find the stuff I need on... actually, scratch that. I'd love to read a book about resumes. What a great idea."

Chapter 31
Alabama Rain

Fred
March 28, 2013

As it had been for most of March, the weather on his birthday was bleak and overcast. The thermometer claimed it was forty degrees outside his kitchen window, but the wind whipping through the tree branches made it look far colder.

He couldn't remember—for the life of him—if he'd ever told Jeannette his actual birthdate, or if he'd just told her it was in early spring. *Early spring* was his standard answer to the birthday question, but his brain was still fuzzy from everything it'd endured over the winter. And Jeannette was far from a standard woman.

I guess it'd be nice if she knows and comes over for a little visit. Even if that means we end up going on Facebook again.

Yes, in a weak moment, Jeannette had convinced him to take a look at that crazy thing. And it wasn't as bad as he'd imagined. In fact, in some ways, it was interesting. Jeannette had typed *ham radio* into a little box at the top of her page, and a whole bunch of Facebook pages and groups for hams and amateur radio had popped up. Then he'd asked her to type in Hans Helmdorf's's name, and wouldn't you know it? A second later, the old bugger's big red face was grinning at him.

"You see?" said Jeannette. "Everyone's on Facebook."

"Not everyone," said Fred. "I'm not, and neither is Billy."

Sally had passed away quietly in late February, and Billy was having a rough time of it. His daughter lived close to him in Florida, so she and her family had been helping him with the cooking and cleaning, but he hadn't been on the air much. And every time Fred talked to him on the phone, the poor guy broke down in tears.

"As soon as the doc clears me to fly, I'm coming down there to visit," Fred promised. "I'm thinkin' that'll be any day now."

The phone rang and he turned to answer it. A few days earlier, he'd stopped wearing the Ace bandage on his head because his dizziness had really improved, and he'd even showered that morning—against doctor's orders—in honor of his birthday.

Maybe this is Jeannette calling now. Glimpsing his reflection in the glass of the microwave oven, he smiled and gave himself a thumbs up.

"Hello?"

"Hello? Mr. Flaherty?" It was a man's voice. *Darn.*

"Yes. This is Fred."

"Hello, Fred. It's Sargent Marchand, Maine State Police. Are you sitting down, sir?"

Maine State Police. Oh no. "Uh, hang on a minute." The last thing he wanted was to fall again, so he pulled out a kitchen chair, sat slowly, and rested his trembling hand on the table. "Yeah. What's up?" His breath got unsteady, and the dizziness returned in full force.

"Mr. Flaherty, we've made an important discovery. We've found Mrs. Stevers's scarf, the one used in her murder."

"Oh god."

"But here's some interesting news—it wasn't found in Maine. Believe it or not, it was in the home of an Alabama man who was arrested a little over a week ago for another murder. I can't share any other info at this time, but preliminary reports show no sign of your brother's DNA on it."

His head reeled so badly that he couldn't fully process the words. "Wait. Wait. Slow down, please. I've had a head injury. Are you saying... are you saying Davey didn't kill that woman?"

"I'm sorry about your injury, sir," said the cop, "and as I said, it's too early to know anything conclusive. But at the moment, yes, it looks like Mrs. Stevers was murdered by someone other than your brother."

His mouth hung open and tears poured down his face. "I... I don't know what to say."

"I understand, sir. But we thought you should know."

"Yes. Yes, thank you." Then, barely knowing what he was doing, he hung up the phone. *Davey. Davey. I love you, Davey.* He buried his face in his hands and cried harder than he'd ever cried before.

Chapter 32
Life and Times

Molly
April, 2013

I leaned back in the driver's seat, closed my eyes, and breathed deeply. My arms were shaking and Fred's face was pained. I could tell he was biting his tongue.

"We made it," I said.

"Yes. Yes we did. Thank God."

"I'm sorry. I didn't expect the Jamaicaway to be so fast and twisty." No way in hell was I *ever* driving on that road again. If there was no other route back to Arlington, we'd have to Uber it or something. Amateurs like me didn't belong on the Jamaicaway.

"It's okay, Molly. And you're shifting better now. Much better than last time. But I've gotta say, I can't wait to get back behind the wheel."

"Yeah. I'm looking forward to that too." I hated driving—even with an automatic transmission—and learning to drive stick terrified me. Especially with Fred as a teacher. Plus, he was the worst passenger in the universe. Jeannette refused to drive him anywhere at all because he constantly gave her crap for riding the clutch.

Of course, I understood his need to get places, especially medical appointments. What I didn't understand was why he wouldn't at least *try* taking those vans the MBTA provides for people with disabilities. But when Jeannette and I suggested them—very gently—he'd claimed the vans were only intended for people who'd *never* drive again. Whereas he was simply on the walking wounded list for a while.

"Make sure you leave it in gear so it doesn't roll down the hill," he said as I parked his truck in the driveway of the big yellow Victorian.

"Right. Thanks for reminding me." I didn't mention that I'd already planned on doing that.

February and March had dumped almost sixty inches of snow on the Boston area—sixty inches that I'd shoveled off my own steps and front path, and Fred's driveway too—but that day, the air felt springlike. Even the faint odor of garbage from a dumpster across the street didn't bother me. It felt good to smell life, even if it was trash.

I glanced over at the large house we were about to enter. It was prettier than I'd expected. Pink tulips sprouted in a stone planter on the doorstep, and a few robins pecked around on the front lawn.

"Let's go," said Fred.

"Okay." I watched him cover his mobile ham radio with the towel he'd brought along because he was worried about someone smashing the truck's window and stealing the thing. I was pretty sure ham radios weren't in high demand on the street, but it was nice seeing him acting more like the old Fred again. "Hey," I said, as he stepped gingerly out of the truck, "I'm glad we're doing this together."

"Me too," he said, rocking on the balls of his feet. I followed him up the driveway, carrying the paintbrushes and rollers we'd found in his basement. His walking wasn't perfect yet, but I knew he'd get irritated if I took his arm. The Ace bandage he'd worn on his head all winter was gone, and he was back to shaving regularly. In fact, he was even wearing some Old Spice that morning.

"Welcome," said the pale woman with Bettie Page bangs who answered the door. Her dark hair was pulled up in a ponytail, and she had a colorful sleeve of tattoos on one arm. "I take it you're here to paint?"

"Uh huh," I said, wishing I looked half as cool as her. "I'm Molly. I spoke to someone named Sue on the phone the other day. And this is my friend Fred."

The woman looked weary, but her smile was sincere. "Hi, Molly and Fred. I'm Sue, and thanks for coming. Come on in. We've got a good group working out back in the kitchen today..." As she spoke, she led us down a little hallway and pointed toward a sunny room where several people were prepping for painting. "And we've got one volunteer upstairs now getting started on the bedrooms. Do you guys have any preference as to where you'd like to be?"

A faint odor of cooked onions lingered in the air. "No," said Fred. "Put us wherever you'd like, Sue. I just can't go up ladders yet." He tapped his forehead. "Had a bad accident over the winter."

"Oh, I'm sorry to hear that," said Sue. "This winter was a killer, huh?"

Fred frowned. "Almost. But you know, in some ways, I feel like it gave me a second chance at life."

IT DOESN'T HAVE TO BE THAT WAY

Hearing him say that made me cringe a little. Ever since his ordeal, Fred had been sharing more personal information with strangers. And even though that was probably a good thing, it embarrassed me sometimes.

"Hmm," said Sue, surveying the people working in the kitchen. "I think these guys are good for now. How about we head up?" Fred and I both nodded. The wide, almost regal staircase made the house look like a mansion, and from one of the rooms upstairs, I could hear the Rolling Stones playing "Let it Loose."

"I guess my volunteer brought his music along," said Sue. "You'll like this guy, I think. He's pretty cool."

"That's good," I answered. "But where are the women who live here?"

"Oh, some of the ones with little kids to care for are staying at a hotel for the week so we can get this work done, and a couple are planning to come by later on to help with the painting."

"Cool," I said. "What a beautiful home."

"Yeah, I love it," said Sue. "It was donated by an amazing woman named Jane Tyler Coolidge. She passed away about ten years ago. I was lucky enough to meet her once."

"Interesting," said Flaherty as he started up the steps. "Hey, would you folks ever be interested in a house out in Arlington if someone donated it to you?"

I stopped and turned to him. "Fred, what are you *talking* about? You don't have a house to donate. You're gonna be living in that place for, like, thirty more years or something."

Fred rolled his eyes but kept his attention focused on Sue. "I hope so, but it doesn't hurt to ask. I learned this winter that you never know what's around the corner."

Sue didn't flinch. "I hear you. And to answer your question, our group's always interested in new locations. You'd be shocked at how many women come to us in crisis these days. Sometimes we have to put guests on couches or even in sleeping bags on the floor."

"That's terrible," said Fred.

"Yeah, but at least they're safe," said Sue. "I can put you in touch with the person who handles donations later on if you'd like—"

"Is that you, Sue?" called a guy from upstairs. The voice was familiar, but I didn't place it immediately.

"Yeah. I'm bringing you some helpers, Andy."

And there he was on the landing, a roll of masking tape in one hand. Andy Stevers.

"Oh, holy shit!" I whispered. Fred froze mid-staircase, and I grabbed his arm in case he got dizzy.

Andy's dark eyes zeroed on me for a few seconds, then he saw Fred, whose mouth was hanging open. Andy looked thinner than I recalled, and maybe a bit older, even though it'd only been six months since that awful night.

"Hi, Andy," I managed to say.

I'm not sure what I should've expected, but crying wasn't it. And yet, that's what Andy did. As he stepped aside to allow the three of us to continue up the stairs, he began to weep.

When we were all safe on the landing, he walked straight over to Fred and threw his arms around his neck. "I'm so sorry, sir," he sobbed into Fred's shoulder, and Fred held him tightly.

At that moment, I realized he would've made a good father.

"So... I take it you folks know each other?" said Sue.

"Um, yeah," I said.

Andy went on sobbing, but eventually, Fred pushed him back gently and looked into his face. "Don't feel bad, kid. Everyone makes mistakes."

"Yeah, but—"

"No buts. I've screwed up plenty o' times, and so did Davey. I'm glad he didn't... you know... hurt your mother, but that doesn't make him an angel. Everyone in this world's guilty of something."

Andy pulled himself together a bit and stared at Fred. I could tell he was trying to process everything, but it was a lot.

Meanwhile, Sue clearly didn't know what to do. "So... is everything okay? I mean, I don't mean to intrude, but if you guys need some time..."

Fred sniffled, patted Andy on the shoulders with both hands, and took a few steps back. Wiping his eyes, he said, "Well, I'm here to paint."

"Me too," I said weakly.

Andy took a paint rag out of his pocket, wiped his face, and turned to me. "Molly, I'm sorry. I was a complete ass."

"Are you kidding? I'm the one who told you..."

But Sue was watching closely, and I'd come to my senses just enough to realize it'd be a mistake to discuss Andy knocking Fred unconscious as we stood there in a shelter for battered women.

"You know what I mean. I'm sorry too."

He shook his head. "You've got nothing to be sorry for, Molly." Then he turned to Sue and said in a shaky voice. "Sue, I've got the back bedroom all taped up. Maybe Molly and Fred can give me a hand in there?"

Sue raised her thin, plucked eyebrows and shrugged. "Is that cool with you guys? I mean, are you all cool with each other?"

The three of us said *yes* in unison.

"Okay then," said Sue. "Let's do it."

"Wow," I said as we entered the large room. All four beds had been pushed into the middle and covered with tarps, along with the dressers and other furniture. As promised, Andy had painstakingly masked the edges of the ceiling and floorboards with blue tape, and around the windows and doors too. The floor was covered with newspaper, and a ladder leaned against one wall. Over in a corner sat several cans of paint, some trays, and a couple of stepstools. The Rolling Stones were still playing through a little speaker, but the song had switched from "Let it Loose" to "All Down the Line."

"*Exile on Main Street*?" I asked.

"You got it," said Andy. "My favorite Stones album by far."

"Mine too," I said.

Sue seemed happy to have the conversation back on familiar ground. "I've always been partial to *Some Girls*," she said.

"Another great one," said Andy. Then we all stood there, awkwardly silent for a second.

"This place looks ready to paint," I said.

"It sure does," said Sue. "Nice prep work, Andy. And I love the color we picked for this room. It's sort of a periwinkle blue. And you guys brought brushes and rollers, which is awesome. Wanna get started and I'll be back in a bit? I'm gonna check on the folks in the kitchen. Give a holler if you need me."

Left alone, the three of us assessed each other again while Mick Jagger sang about the good Lord shining a light on someone. "So... why're you here?" I asked Andy. "I mean, I'm glad you are, but... it's a surprise."

He took a deep breath. "Well, I got assigned a lot of community service hours, and the judge wanted me to work in places that, you know, deal with victims of violence. Which was good with me. I did a ton of this kinda stuff over the winter. But now that I've finished my hours, I've just been volunteering on weekend projects when I have time. Maybe it's selfish to say, but it makes me feel better about... everything."

I looked back and forth between Fred and Andy. "Well, I really am sorry for opening my big mouth that night. I mean, look at us. We're all here because I was an idiot."

"Molly!" said Andy. "Are you kidding? I've been working on my guilt in therapy for months, but if anyone's at fault here, it's me."

"Well, jingoes," said Fred. "This room isn't gonna get painted if we all just stand here apologizing."

For the first time, Andy cracked his sexy smile. "I'm with you there, Mr. Flaherty. How 'bout we each take a wall? Then the three of us can split the last one?"

"Good plan," said Fred. "But I can't get up on a ladder yet. Oh, and call me Fred. All right?"

"Okay, Fred," said Andy. "And no worries about the ladder. Just do what you can, and I'll cover the high parts. Oh, and do you guys have any musical requests? This record's almost done, so I should probably switch it up."

"Are you using an iPod?" asked Fred. Jeannette had given him an iPod for his birthday and was actually trying to convince him to buy a smartphone. I'd told her a bunch of times that she was nuts, but the woman was persistent.

"Yup," said Andy. "And I've got more music on it than you can imagine. Old stuff, new stuff. Name your poison. I'll bet I've got it."

Fred rocked on the balls of his feet, and I was pretty sure I knew what he was going to say. "Got any Croce?" he asked shyly.

Andy's face clouded for a second, then he smiled. "You mean *Jim* Croce?"

"Yeah. I know he's an oldie, but I figured it was worth a shot."

Andy nodded. "Well, you know what? I think you may be in luck. I'm pretty sure I've got his greatest hits album on here, if that's okay."

Flaherty beamed. "Can't do better than that. Hey, I'm gonna get goin' on that wall there." He picked up a roller, tray, and can of paint, and headed toward the back of the room.

Meanwhile, Andy was fumbling with his iPod. "I like the paint color too," I said, just to avoid another silence.

"If you like purple," he said with a wink. "It wouldn't be my choice." He paused for a second but didn't take his eyes off me. "Hey, Molly, maybe it's too soon to ask, but would you ever wanna try having dinner with me again?"

I opened my mouth, but no sound came out.

"I'm sorry," he said. "I didn't mean... I mean, I totally understand if you're not up for it. Ever."

I smiled, and the stress seemed to rise off my body like steam or something. "No, Andy, I'm up for it. As long as it's someplace cheap, 'cause I haven't found a job yet."

"Yes!" he said, raising his arm. "I mean about the dinner, not the job stuff. And don't worry. It'll be my treat. I could even cook for you if you'd like. I bought a crockpot the other day."

I blushed as Fred turned around and squinted. "A crockpot?" he said.

"Yup. I'm learning how to make soups and stews. I made a good vegetarian one the other night." He winked at me again. "You're welcome to come over too, Fred."

Fred grinned and returned to his painting. "I'll probably let you two have a night together this time."

"Yeah, maybe that's a good idea," said Andy, smiling as the piano introduction to "Bad, Bad Leroy Brown" began playing through his little speaker. "So, Molly," he said, "it's really nice to see you."

I felt like I might burst. "It's nice to see you too, Andy."

The End

(Please continue for the Book Club Guide.)

Book Club Guide

1. How would you describe Molly in the first few chapters of the novel? Do you think she causes her own problems, or do you see her as a victim?

2. How do you feel about the dismissive way Molly treats Fred at the beginning of the story? Can you relate, or do you think she's insensitive and/or cruel?

3. What's your impression of Fred when you first meet him, and does this impression change as the story progresses? Why or why not?

4. After Molly's encounter with Shane, her office associates begin to shun her, and she gets the distinct impression that they blame her — exclusively — for what happened. Does this strike you as realistic? Have you known women who've had similar experiences at work, in social circles, or elsewhere?

5. Following up on the previous question, have you witnessed changes in attitudes regarding women and relationships with coworkers since the advent of the #MeToo movement? Discuss.

6. Fred has made mistakes in life that have seriously impacted others. Do you think he deserves forgiveness at the end? Why or why not?

7. As Molly gets to know Andy, she learns that he can be quite charming, but also violent. Shane also uses charm to get what he wants, but is emotionally abusive when things don't go his way. Compare and contrast these two characters, who share some similar traits but are portrayed very differently in this novel.

8. How does the scene in which Molly meets up with her old flame, Ethan, make you feel? If you were her and ended up in a similar situation, would you have done the same thing she did? If so, why? If not, what would you have done differently?

9. Who is your favorite character in *It Doesn't Have To Be That Way* and what do you like about them? Your least favorite?

10. If you were writing the sequel to this story, would Fred and Jeannette be a couple in it? Why or why not? What about Molly and Andy?

Acknowledgements

The idea for *It Doesn't Have To Be That Way* started in a parking lot in 2014. I'd been experiencing writer's block and wondered if I had another novel in me. Every new story concept I considered seemed too far-fetched, boring, or predictable. Then I walked past a car in the lot with a large antenna on the roof and a license plate displaying a ham radio call sign. Ham radio plates in Massachusetts have a distinctive lightning bolt in the middle of the letters.

I was familiar with the ham lifestyle because my dad—who died suddenly in 2001 of a brain aneurysm—was a ham for most of his life, and our family rarely went anywhere without at least one antenna and various other ham equipment. So, the sight of that vehicle awakened something deeply sentimental in me, and when I got home, I jotted down some ideas for a friendship story about a woman in her twenties and a much older male ham whose character would be loosely based on my dad.

I'm happy to say that more than six years later—after countless edits and revisions—*It Doesn't Have To Be That Way* is complete. Dozens of people have been involved in the process, and although I could never adequately thank everyone for their time, suggestions, and persistence, I'll take my best shot.

First, I'd like to thank the magnificent **Jim Croce**, a brilliant, generous musician who provided much of the soundtrack for my childhood. The title of this book and all the chapter titles are also titles of Croce songs. Jim left this world far too soon, but his music is ageless and haunting, and if you're not familiar with his work, I recommend checking it out.

Thank you to the folks at **Evolved Publishing**—especially **Dave Lane**—for believing in this story enough to take a chance on it. And to **Jessica West**, a dream of an editor if ever there was one, and a wonderful, supportive friend as well. Rounding out this superstar team is **Kabir Shah**, the kindest, most perceptive and patient cover designer any author could hope to work with.

Speaking of stars, I count my lucky ones every day for the opportunity to work with a literary agent as wonderful and insightful as **April Eberhardt**. April is a true gift.

Thank you, **Justin Bogdanovitch, Terri Brosius, Karen Harris**, and **Sheila Moeschen** for reading, critiquing, and offering vital edits to early drafts of this story. You guided me through a fog of ideas and encouraged me to keep going.

Thank you also to the dedicated folks who took time to read through a pre-publication version of this book in the midst of a global pandemic, including **Julie Anderson, Jackie Cioffa, Heather Culford, Meg Hannon, Janice Hayes-Cha, Marilyn Horgan, Lauren Jordahl, Kim McIlvenna, Brett Milano, Cat Needham, Karen Rooney, Joanne Rowen, Barbara Vitelli** and **Jan Wissmar**.

Thank you, **Mom, Chris, Steve, Beth, Sandra, Chris S., Tim, Joanne, Jerry H., Marilyn, Kathy D**, and all my other amazing family members. I'm always grateful for your support and willingness to talk and listen.

Thank you, **Mike, Walter,** and **Maggie**. I'll love you unconditionally, forever.

Finally, thank you, **Jerry,** for teaching me—by example—about the power of forgiveness, that being imperfect is an essential part of humanity, and that people really can change. I'm not sure I ever told you how much I loved having you as a dad, but I hope you knew.

About the Author

I'm drawn to stories about women facing and overcoming challenges at various stages of life, so I love reading and writing women's fiction. Music, musicians, and music fans tend to find their way into my work too.

Other interests include feminism, body image issues, parenting, and current events. I blog about that stuff and more whenever I can. My essays have been featured on numerous sites and blogs, including Mutha Magazine, Feminine Collective, Huffington Post, and The Girlfriend.

A graduate of Providence College, I was raised in the Massachusetts Merrimack Valley, and live in the Boston area with my family and pets.

For more, please visit me online at:
Website: www.MaryRowen.com
Goodreads: Mary Rowen
Facebook: @MaryRowenAuthor
Twitter: @MaryJRowen
Pinterest: @MaryRowenAuthor

More from Evolved Publishing

We offer great books across multiple genres, featuring high-quality editing (which we believe is second-to-none) and fantastic covers.

As a hybrid small press, your support as loyal readers is so important to us, and we have strived, with tireless dedication and sheer determination, to deliver on the promise of our motto:
QUALITY IS PRIORITY #1!

Please check out all of our great books,
which you can find at this link:

www.EvolvedPub.com/Catalog

Thank you!

CPSIA information can be obtained
at www.ICGtesting.com
Printed in the USA
BVHW031405091220
595282BV00002B/13